Deadly Engagement

LUCINDA BRANT BOOKS

'Quizzing glass and quill, into my sedan chair and away —— the 1700s rock!'

Lucinda Brant is a *New York Times*, *USA Today*, and *Audible* best-selling author of award-winning Georgian historical romances and mysteries. Her books are renowned for wit, drama and a happily ever-after. She has a degree in history and political science from the Australian National University and a post-graduate degree in education from Bond University, where she was awarded the Frank Surman Medal.

Noble Satyr, Lucinda's first novel, was awarded the $10,000 Random House/Woman's Day Romantic Fiction Prize, and she has twice been a finalist for the Romance Writers' of Australia Romantic Book of the Year. All her novels have garnered multiple awards and become worldwide bestsellers.

Lucinda lives in the middle of a koala reserve, in a writing cave that is wall-to-wall books on all aspects of the Eighteenth Century, collected over 40 years—Heaven. She loves to hear from her readers (and she'll write back!).

lucindabrant@gmail.com | lucindabrant.com

A GEORGIAN HISTORICAL MYSTERY

ALEC HALSEY MYSTERIES BOOK ONE

Lucinda Brant

A Sprigleaf Book
Published by Sprigleaf Pty Ltd

Deadly Engagement: A Georgian Historical Mystery
Copyright © 2010, 2019 Lucinda Brant
Editing & proofing: Martha Stites & Rob Van De Laak
Cover art and photography: Larry Rostant
Design, and formatting: Sprigleaf
Cover model: Dan Cook
All rights reserved

Typeset in Adobe Garamond Pro.

Also in ebook, audiobook, and other languages.

ISBN 978-0-9872430-5-8

10 9 8 7 6 5 4 3 2 (i) I

for my parents

Grace & Eric

ONE

LONDON, SPRING 1763

Alec Halsey strode into the cool of the wide marble hall of St. Neots House, home of his godmother the Duchess of Romney-St. Neots, and hastily struggled out of greatcoat, leather riding gloves, sash and sword. He pressed these on an attending footman then went up the curved marble staircase two steps at a time. On the first landing he paused, as if remembering his manners, and leaned over the mahogany balustrade.

"Neave?" he called out to the butler, "Tell the Duchess I'll be with her shortly!"

"Her Grace has guests to nuncheon, sir!" Neave called up into the dome of the cavernous entrance foyer. "And Miss Emily is—" Alec Halsey's head of black curls disappeared from view, and the butler spun around, saw two footmen juggling the visitor's belongings between them and pointed a finger at the youngest, a freckle-faced youth with a mop of red hair. "Go after him! He's not to disturb Miss Emily. Your job on it, boy."

Alec was in the passageway that led to the rooms occupied by the Duchess's granddaughter when quick breathing at his back made him turn. A young footman came scrambling towards him much in the fashion of a puppy not grown into its long legs.

From behind a set of double doors came the sounds of female chatter and laughter.

"Sir? Please, sir. No!" the young footman pleaded, coming to a dead stop in front of the tall, loose-limbed gentleman. "You can't go in there! Mr. Neave will have m'job if you do!"

Alec paused, long fingers curled about the door handle, and stared down at the freckle-faced youth, who respectfully lowered his eyes and shuffled his feet. Something about the boy was oddly familiar and made him pause.

"What's your name?"

The footman gave a start. The pleasant drawling voice wasn't angry, just curious and it made him glance up warily to wonder what was the intent behind the gentleman's question. But there was no hint of insolence in the kind, friendly blue eyes that crinkled at the corners; no fancy airs and affected voice like so many of the visitors to St. Neots House. Even the clothes this gentleman wore were not out of the ordinary—no silver lacings, no frothy lace at his wrists, no diamond buckles in the tongues of his leather shoes—just good dark cloth, a plain linen cravat, and shoes without high heels. Perhaps he could reason with him and not have his ears boxed for doing his job. He swallowed hard and let his gaze wander to the door.

"Beggin' pardon, sir. Thomas Fisher was what I was christened, but most call me Tam, sir."

"Thomas Fisher," stated Alec, racking his brain for a memory; he made no immediate connection. He followed the boy's gaze to the double doors. "Well, Thomas Fisher: Tam, I'm going in there with or without your approval. Think me presentable enough to announce?"

Tam wondered if he was being roasted. There was a look in those blue eyes he could not make out. If Neave discovered him in conversation with a visitor, he'd be out on the streets again. And gentlemen callers, if they *were* gentlemen, did not enter a lady's private apartments; they certainly didn't canvass the opinions of footmen. He set his jaw hard and put just enough insolence into his voice to make the gentleman know his place.

"Presentable, sir?"

Alec lifted a hand. "I'm not fragile. Out with it. It's the hair, isn't it?" he said, gathering the shoulder length hair tidily at the nape and retying the ribbon that held it in place. "Not enough wax and no powder. Can't abide either."

In spite of himself, Tam grinned. "It's just as you say, sir. Your shoes will pass inspection. Females don't care a whisker for dust on y'shoes, yet they like a gentleman to be *neat*. Least that's what Jenny says. She can't abide an ill-fitting wig or one with not enough powder. Says it ain't right. But your hair—"

"—is my own. Yes. It's my one concession to vanity," said Alec with a wink, and slipped behind the door before the footman could stop him.

Tam cursed under his breath and dashed after him, saying as he crossed into the decidedly feminine sitting room, "Please, sir! Miss Emily is with her dressmaker. She ain't receiving visitors and I doubt—"

"Don't worry, Tam, I'll vouch for you with Neave."

"—she'll notice your boots or your hair on account of the celebrations."

This brought Alec Halsey up short and he turned and stared at him, puzzled. "Celebrations?"

Tam stepped up to him. "The engagement celebrations, sir. There's to be a weekend party here. Here at St. Neots House."

"Engagement celebrations? *Here?*"

Tam saw the gentleman's look of total confusion. It was clear these tidings were new to him. "Yes, sir. Haven't you been told, sir?"

"I returned yesterday from the Continent. I've been away eight months. An engagement celebration you say. Whose?"

"Miss Emily's, sir."

"No!"

"Yes, sir. Miss Emily is engaged to be married."

"*When?*"

"Pardon, sir?"

"When. *When* did this happen?"

"Jenny, she's Miss Emily's maid—"

"I know who Jenny is!"

Tam lowered his eyes. He'd never seen a face turn as white as a sheet. He'd heard the expression. The housekeeper used it quite a bit. He was witness to it now. Alec Halsey's angular face had not only drained of natural color, but under his linen cravat his throat had constricted. He suddenly looked ill. Tam wondered if he should fetch up a brandy.

Alec swallowed. "I didn't mean… It's just—"

"No need to explain, sir," Tam said quickly, averting his gaze and shuffling his feet, feeling the gentleman's embarrassment.

He wished he could help him in some way. He didn't care for Miss Emily's betrothed, despite Jenny's opinion that the Earl of Delvin was the handsomest nobleman in the kingdom. Lord Delvin certainly presented well, dressed in the latest fashionable powdered wig, tight-shouldered frock coat of elaborately embroidered silk, diamonds in his shoe-buckles, and yards of frothy lace gathered up at his wrists and throat, but there was something about the nobleman that would not wash. Tam wished he had tangible evidence for this feeling, particularly when Jenny continually sang the Earl's praises.

"Jenny told me, sir," he added glumly. "Miss Emily became engaged three days ago."

"*Three days…*"

Tam winced at the wretchedness in the deep voice. "I'm—I'm sorry, sir."

There was a long silence. It was broken by Jenny who rushed out of her mistress's bedchamber, saying something over her shoulder, and ran straight into Tam. She fell back a pace and put a hand to her hair.

"Tam? What are you doing—Oh!" She saw Alec and dropped a respectful curtsy. "Mr.—Mr. Halsey? Sir!" Her eyes went very round and she glanced at Tam, who kept his eyes lowered and his hands behind his back.

There was a rush of silk petticoats behind her, one or two voices raised in protest, and then Emily stood there in all her fair loveliness, straw-blonde curls caught up off her shoulders with a couple of long pins. She had on a new gown of patterned silk that was held together with tacking and needed alteration at the bodice, for it was cut far too low for the Duchess's liking.

Madame the French dressmaker was at her elbow, urging her to come back into the room so she could continue with her work. Catching sight of a gentleman she gave a French squeak of alarm. Jenny spun about to shield her mistress from prying eyes, but when Emily saw who it was, she forgot Madame's pins and threw herself at Alec's inanimate form.

"You're home at last! You've no idea how much we've missed you. Grandmamma said not a word. Did you two conspire to surprise me? How like you! Oh, it's *so* good to see you." She grabbed Alec's hand and dragged him into the bedchamber, oblivious to the fact his mood did not match her own. "Careful where you step. It's fitting day today. Jenny? Jenny! Forget the tea. Bring champagne. *Yes*. Champagne. We're going to celebrate Alec's return." She shooed Madame and her assistants away. "I'll get out of this wretched thing and then I can give you a proper welcome home. So, what do you think of this gown? Do you approve?"

"The bodice is indecent."

"So Grandmamma says. But it's the fashion." She disappeared behind an ornate screen set in one corner of the sunny room and Madame followed, clucking over her in broken English. "You'll be pleased with me. I've kept Phoenix well exercised," Emily called out from behind the screen. "To the detriment of *my* horses. I was out on him this morning. Remember that problem he was having with his left hock? Well, it's all better, so you needn't worry. I suppose you'll be taking him back to St. James's Place? There!"

When she reappeared, Alec was by the window looking out on the long sweep of east lawn and not seeing any of it. He wished himself anywhere but here. He felt suddenly weary. When she came over to him and playfully tugged his sleeve, he could not bring himself to look at her.

"I'm decently dressed," she said, sitting on the window seat beside where he stood. "All up to the neck and shoes on my feet, too!" When he made no response to her playful banter she added conversationally, "How was Paris? Did you bring me something wonderful? Something to wear? Or something for this room perhaps? And I must thank you for the fan you sent at Christmastime. It's beautiful. Grandmamma was quite envious."

Alec turned and looked about the untidy room, at the deep carpets covered in dressmaking patterns and fabrics, at the familiar pictures on the patterned-papered walls, but not at her. Everything was as he remembered it. He had often come up here. To have tea at the little table by the window. To hear the latest news of town and to tell her in return the happenings at the Continental Courts. The look on Tam's face! The boy had no idea, had he? He wondered if Jenny was at this moment giving him a good tongue-lashing.

Jenny came back into the room then, followed by Tam carrying a tray. He put it down on the small table by the arrangement of sofa, chaise longue and chairs, and glanced at Alec to find him staring at him in a vacant sort of way. Jenny saw it too, and with a quick word, Tam left them alone.

"I brought you a brandy, sir," Jenny said gently.

"No, Jenny. We are going to drink champagne. Aren't we, Alec?"

Alec took the brandy glass and drank without tasting.

Emily sipped her champagne thoughtfully. "Will they give you a post here now? You—You aren't going away again so soon, are you?"

"What's his name?"

Emily blinked at his bluntness. "I beg your pardon?"

"The name of your *betrothed*," he enunciated coldly. "What—is—his—name?"

There was a scratch on the outer door and Jenny was glad to go in answer to it, leaving Emily all alone and feeling for the first time in her life uneasy with her grandmother's godson. She did not understand his coldness. She thought her own happiness would be sufficient for him to be happy for her. How many times had he lectured her in the manner of an elder brother, on the importance of being guided by her elders, but not to be forced into a marriage she disliked. And she had done precisely that. Perhaps he needed reassurance? Fortified with a gulp of champagne, she bravely stared up at him and said,

"I want to marry Edward. When he sought my hand in marriage, Grandmamma let it be known that the decision was mine, that I did not have to accept him if I did not want to. But," she said in a clearer voice, her happiness giving her strength, "I do want to marry him. I want to marry him *very much.*"

"Edward? Edward…" Alec repeated quietly. "That isn't much to go on. Who is this fellow?"

"We had only met on a few occasions, and those at public gatherings, but I knew straight away that if he did ask me I would accept him," Emily continued, because Alec looked wholly unconvinced. "Grandmamma is very happy for me, especially so because I am to marry an earl." She looked down at the bubbles of champagne, adding nervously, "Not that that circumstance means much to you—"

"It doesn't. I don't care for title," he stated. "Edward, earl of *what?*"

"—but it matters to Grandmamma," Emily said firmly, finishing the sentence despite being close to tears. She wished Jenny would return. She didn't know for how much longer she could sit here with Alec looking for all the world as if her engagement were the worse news he had ever heard in his life. "Edward warned me you'd take it badly," she confessed naively. "But I assured him you would only want for my happiness. And you do want me to be happy, don't you, Alec?" she asked in a small voice. "Regardless of the ill feeling between the two of you, I hope you'll

see that he wants to make me happy. He is very solicitous and
caring and, oh—*everything* a girl could ask for in a husband. I
know you've been estranged since small boys. You could very well
be strangers, not brothers at all…"

He stopped listening the moment he realized she was engaged
to his elder brother. If he was shocked into senselessness to
discover she was engaged to be married, he was now beyond
rational thought knowing that the man who had robbed him of
her was his own brother; this not the first time his brother had
interfered in Alec's life.

Six years ago, Delvin had put a stop to Alec's engagement to
Selina Vesey. A second son with a thousand a year wasn't entitled
to marry an heiress, whatever his brilliant prospects in the Foreign
Department. When his elder brother, who was also head of the
family, publicly voiced his opposition to such an unequal match,
Alec's fate was sealed. Alec not only endured the humiliation of
having his suit rejected by Selina's father, but was forced to stand
by while the love of his life was married off to George Jamison-
Lewis, who had ten thousand a year, was grandson of a duke and
one of his brother's cronies.

Alec never expected to fully recover from his disappointment,
but time helped close the wound. And just when he had convinced
himself that in asking Emily to marry him he would finally be
moving his life forward, his brother's timely interference had
robbed him once more of personal happiness. What was he to do?

Before he knew what he was about, he found himself halfway
down the curved staircase, full of purpose—to do what, he had no
idea. He just knew he had to get out of St. Neots House, to escape
from a thousand memories locked within its walls, and to get away
from Emily. He had to find a place where he could think calmly
and rationally. Failing that, he would find a place where he need
not think at all…

A LADY IN BLACK MOURNING CREPE HAD JUST ASCENDED THE

staircase, and it was inevitable that they would collide; such was the width of her hooped petticoats and Alec's blind determination to quit St. Neots House. The lady's quick thinking saved her from taking a tumble. She grabbed the banister rail with a gloved hand, while the other clung to the gentleman's sleeve; a small party taking leave in the foyer below breathed a collective sigh of relief.

It was not until the woman's body fell hard against him and he instinctively caught her that Alec realized he had run full force into someone coming up the staircase. He held her hard against his chest, their hearts thudding as one as he waited for them both to be steady on their feet. In the brief moment she was in his arms he breathed in the pleasing flowery scent of her hair, and inexplicably felt a stab of nostalgia. He knew her identity at once. Instantly he released her with a curt apology for crushing the silk of her petticoats and would have passed her then, but she unintentionally moved in the same direction, and again they blocked each other's path. The woman's quiet apology finally lifted Alec's gaze to her face.

She was one step below him and had gathered up her billowing petticoats, positioning herself with her straight back up against the mahogany balustrade to let him pass. Yet, Alec remained as if fixed to the marble step. He stared at her as if at an apparition, for he had not been within ten feet of her in six years. He never dreamed of seeing her in mourning, though in the darkest days of his despair he had wished it upon her time and again. But not here, not now, not on this of all days. Large dark eyes full of sorrow stared up at him and he turned his head away, color flooding his close-shaven cheeks.

"Did Emily tell you her news, Mr. Halsey?" Selina Jamison-Lewis asked quietly, the blood drumming so loudly in her ears at this unexpected encounter that she couldn't keep the tremble out of her voice. "Her engagement, it—it came as a surprise to all of us."

Alec's blue eyes stared pointedly at her mourning gown before again meeting her eyes. "No doubt an ill-timed and disappointing announcement for you, Madam…?"

Selina's lips parted, but she did not trust herself to speak and so stood mute as he made her a short bow and went on his way, her blush as red as the hair of the young footman who rudely bumped her shoulder in his pursuit of Alec Halsey.

Alec ignored the knot of persons leave-taking by the door and pushed through the ministering footmen without a word or a look. When the butler stepped forward with his greatcoat, he demanded his sword and put out a hand for his gloves. Neave said something to him, but he wasn't listening. A bejeweled hand touched his arm. It was his godmother. But Alec angrily shrugged off the Duchess of Romney-St. Neots as he snatched his sash and sword from a footman, oversetting the Duchess, who stumbled backwards, to be caught at the elbow by her butler. Five footmen rushed to her aid. An old man with gray-grizzled hair stepped forward, but it was the Earl of Delvin who took matters into his own hands.

The Earl poked his brother in the kidney with the end of his Malacca cane.

"You're in a hurry, *Second*," Delvin drawled. "Can't go bargin' about other people's houses knocking 'em willy-nilly. It's not done. Not done at all. Dear Mrs. Jamison-Lewis could've broken her neck on the stairs just now, and you of all people certainly wouldn't want to see the beautiful young widow join her dearly departed so soon, would you? For a diplomatist, you certainly show a marked lack of man—"

It needed only that. Alec snatched at the cane and threw it away from him before pushing his brother up against the nearest wall, a hand about the layers of lace at his throat, long fingers pushing the Earl's chin up until he was forced to look Alec directly in the eye. No match for his younger brother's strength born of rage, Delvin offered little resistance.

"You cold-hearted blood sucker," Alec spat in his face. "I wish to God you were no brother of mine!"

The Earl attempted a moment of bravado. "You're a *fool*, Second," he hissed viciously. "Time you learned your place: No female wants second best."

"If they want you then they're not worth the having," Alec sneered, fingers convulsing about his brother's throat until the Earl spluttered for breath and clawed at his strong hand.

A cluster of open-mouthed footmen stared at the two gentlemen struggling by the open front door. As mesmerized as his fellows, the butler stood rooted to the spot until the Duchess demanded that someone do something to break up the fight. With an imperious snap of his fingers, Neave scattered the footmen. It was left to the grizzled-haired old man to step in and put a stop to the one-sided fight between his nephews.

"Alec! Stop!" growled Plantagenet Halsey. "Let him be!"

Delvin was released at once and fell to his silken knees, gasping great gulps of air into his deprived lungs. He quickly picked himself up and attempted to regain his arrogant bravado by brushing the sleeves of his velvet frock coat and straightening the lace at his wrists as if he had been touched by something unclean. Alec stared at him with contempt, hands balled into fists of frustrated rage. He saw the butler with eyes suitably lowered, and standing beside him the freckled-faced footman who had introduced himself as Tam. And when he glanced at his uncle, he saw so much unspoken sadness in the old blue eyes that Alec turned away from him with impatience. A glance up at the staircase and there was Selina still on the step where he had left her. God, what had he done to deserve her silent witness? His humiliation complete, Alec made the Duchess a curt bow and strode from the house.

TAM FOLLOWED ALEC TO TOWN. HE TOOK A HORSE FROM the stables while the stable hands were busy with the Earl of Delvin's carriage horses. No one thought to question him. He was astride the animal and at full gallop down the gravel drive before one of his fellow footmen came to fetch him to answer to Neave.

The ride was not easy, nor was it a simple matter of following as close as he dared without being seen. Alec never looked back. He rode his mount as if his life depended upon it, oblivious to the horse and rider that fell in behind him and stayed close all the way to Hyde Park corner.

Closer to town, the open fields and hamlets turned into the newer suburbs of the wealthy merchant princes and town residences of the aristocracy. Then the openness of the new squares narrowed to filthy streets, congested with the continuous rumble of carriages, single horsemen, and carts laden with merchandise for markets in the city. Town criers competed to be heard with the sellers of oranges and apples, flowers, household wares, and freshly-cooked oysters, all shouting out in their sing-song voices the excellent value and superior quality of their merchandise.

Once they hit the congestion of town traffic, Alec's pace slackened. Tam still needed to keep his wits so as not to lose sight of his man. He could easily disappear up a side street never to be seen again. Where would that leave Tam? As it was, he knew he could never return to St. Neots House. Neave would make certain of that. His future now lay in Alec Halsey's hands. And if he didn't keep close to him, find out where he lived, there would be no opportunity to plead his case.

London was not new to Tam. In fact, he found it strangely exhilarating to be once again amongst the noise and the dirt, but he was careful to keep an undistracted eye on the straight back of Alec Halsey, just up ahead of him, who now dismounted in the cobbled yard of *The Rose* in Drury Lane—an establishment frequented by prostitutes and low-life, wanting nothing better to do than brawl with one another.

When Alec stepped back onto the street, it was late afternoon, and he was not alone. Three rough-looking men were at his back. Dressed in ill-fitting, coarse-clothed frock coats and darned stockings splattered with town muck, they jostled one another as if sharing a private joke as they followed Alec on foot in the direction of the Covent Garden markets. Tam, who had been dozing in a filthy corner of the stable yard, trying for all the world to look as if he belonged there, scrambled up and went after them; the horse he had taken from the St. Neots' stables left in the care of a toothless ostler.

It was at Covent Garden that Tam lost sight of Alec and his companions. Leaving *The Rose*, he ran up the road until he was only a few yards behind his quarry. Alec seemed in no hurry. He sauntered along the footpath, hands thrust deep in the pockets of his riding frock, while his new-found friends continued on with their banal banter, any remark made to Alec met with monosyllabic responses. Tam had a difficult time hanging back and was glad when they came to the edge of the market square. Here there were vegetable and fruit sellers, flower stalls, wagons and carts jostling with one another for space, and everywhere the smell of the country mingled with the soot and grime of the city. The noise was deafening.

Tam dodged in and around laden wagons, tripped on a cobbled street uneven and slick with rotting vegetables, and picked himself up to find he was the center of attention for a number of young ragged scamps, laughing at his expense. He shooed them off, brushed himself down and momentarily forgot his purpose catching the smell of hot pies and sweet fruit. He was suddenly ravenous and remembered he had not eaten since before dawn, and then only a fist of bread and chunk of cheese. Food was out of the question. He had no money.

Yet, as he continued along the street thinking of his empty stomach, the markets now behind him, the thought of a hot pie became suddenly repellent. He had lost Alec Halsey in the crowd. He stopped in the middle of the footpath wondering what to do and was shoved this way and that by pedestrians going about their business. A tradesman pushing a cart shouted at him, but Tam neither saw nor heard the man. He turned and retraced his steps to the corner where he had taken the fall and started a search of the side streets and alleyways. He ran almost to the Strand, out of breath and an ache in his side. There was no sign of the man and his companions. Again he returned to the corner where he had fallen, and this time crouched on his haunches in the doorway of a disused warehouse that had its lower windows boarded up.

He tried not to panic. There was possibly only an hour before dusk. Already the light was dimming. Although he knew the area well he did not like the thought of spending the night without food and shelter. That Alec Halsey might have fallen afoul of the three men from *The Rose* did not bear thinking about. The gentleman wore a sword, and by the width of his shoulders and the muscle in his calves he looked well able to take care of himself in a mill. Still, three on one were not good odds in anyone's books. And as Tam stared vacantly at the row of buildings diagonally opposite, at the coming and going of carriages and sedan chairs and men on foot, he wondered how it was possible for four men to vanish so completely. He watched the activity in the street for a long time before realizing the answer stared him in the face. His quarry had gone into one of those buildings. One building stood out from all the others.

Its entrance was set back off the street under an elegant portico and could be easily overlooked by the busy pedestrian. Tam crossed the street to better view the entrance. A doorman was in attendance. It must be a private club of sorts because the gentlemen being admitted were not of the class or position to frequent the area for any other purpose. If Alec had disappeared behind those doors, perhaps to be rid of his companions, then Tam would possibly have a long wait ahead of him. He curled up in a doorway across the street, kept his eyes fixed on the club's entrance, and waited.

He was kicked awake by a night watchman carrying a lantern in one hand and a cudgel in the other, who demanded to know his business and was prepared to dispense his particular form of justice if Tam did not give a good account of himself. Tam explained he was waiting for a gentleman who was in the building across the street, and added for good measure that he had a most important message to give him. The doorman had refused him entry and told him to wait outside. At this the night watchman let out a great peal of laughter and nudged Tam with his cudgel, but did so in a friendly fashion.

"Yer young fool! A'course he ain't goin' to let in the likes of you! Not less you got six guineas." This made him laugh harder.

"I don't understand," said Tam politely, scrambling to his feet and adding 'sir' for good measure because he was wary of night watchmen's cudgels.

The man wiped dry his eyes with the back of a grimy hand and shook his head. He pointed his cudgel at the building, its entrance now illuminated with flambeaux. "That, my lad, is a brothel. A very 'igh class brothel it is, too. Called a fancy name: Turkish Bath. That's what."

"Turkish Bath," repeated Tam.

"That's right. Six guineas'll get yer supper, a bathe in them Turkish baths, and a 'igh class 'arlot," the night watchman said knowledgeably, although he had never been inside such an establishment and never would. "Now, m'lad, yer best be pushin' along. Can't stand out 'ere all night and I got me duties to do. Take yer message round his 'ouse and give it to the porter."

"I-I can't. I was told to deliver it here."

"How d'yer know 'e's still in there? You've been asleep."

Tam's shoulders slumped. The man peered keenly at him, holding high his lantern. The boy looked genuinely unhappy and he noticed he was wearing livery so his story was probably true. He pocketed the cudgel. "This message. It ain't from 'is missus, is it?"

Tam shook his head.

The night watchman rubbed his stubbled chin.

"What's 'e look like, this gentleman?"

Tam gave the man a description of Alec.

"Tall gent who wears his own 'air?" the night watchman repeated with surprise. "And yer say 'e's a gentleman? The 'air will give 'im away sure enough. Stay 'ere."

He crossed the street to be met at the front steps of the Turkish
Bath by one of the doormen. The doorman peered into the blackness across the street as the night watchman spoke to him. The
conversation lasted no more than a few minutes and back across
the cobbles the night watchman came, his long coat unbuttoned
and flapping at his sides. In the light of the lantern Tam saw that
he was grinning, though his toothless smile died seeing the
concern on Tam's young face.

"Closed-mouthed lot, them over there," he confided, jerking a
thumb over his shoulder. "Won't say yes and won't say no. But I
managed to get 'em to tell me a thing or two."

"He's gone?"

"No need to fret yerself, lad. 'E's there all right, 'cause a
gentleman fittin' your description entered the premises with three
havey-cavey lookin' coves 'e said were 'is particular friends.
A'course, it ain't an establishment for low-life, and so says the
doormen to your gentleman. But they soon changed their minds
when 'e threw down five-and-twenty pounds. Opened the door as
wide as yer pleased for him and his friends then, didn't they!" He
chuckled to himself. "And I'll tell yer some'in' else for naught, lad.
'is friends are 'aving a right time of it, eatin' 'til they're fit to burst,
splashin' away in them Turkish baths and enjoyin' the particular
attentions of the three prettiest whores this side of Paris!"

Tam felt his face grow hot and moved out of the light. "Thank
you for your help, sir."

The night watchman peered at him closely and had a twinge of
remorse recounting the carryings on in a brothel to a well-spoken
young lad who obviously came from one of the big houses in
Westminster. "You'd best get 'ome to yer bed. There's no point you
waitin', cause by what 'im over there tells me, your gentleman is
sittin' in a corner drinkin' 'is self into a right stupor. Not interested
in supper, or them baths and when a sweet-mouthed whore tried
to interest 'im, he fairly growled at her. Waste of good guineas if
yer ask me!"

"Thank you, sir. But I must wait. He—he'll need my help to get home, if he's as drunk as you say…"

The night watchman considered him with an open look. The boy stared back at him, though he shuffled nervously from foot to foot.

"'Ere," he said and offered Tam the apple from his coat pocket. "I'll be on me rounds then. Remember: Keep yer wits about yer. It ain't safe in these parts for a lad." And with that piece of advice he went on his way, cudgel in hand, lantern held up high.

TWO

ALEC SAT UP IN BED AND SWUNG HIS LEGS OVER THE SIDE OF the mattress, dragging the coverlet with him. Bent over, elbows on his knees and with his face in his hands, he felt weak and empty. His mouth was tinder dry. He wanted fresh air, but knew his legs would not carry him to the windows. Through his fingers he saw a porcelain bowl being thrust at him and he shook his head.

"Take it away. I don't need it," he said thickly. "Open the windows."

He felt the growth on his face and grimaced. He waited for the first blast of cold air before he attempted to sit up straight, his hand gripping the edge of the mattress for support. He pulled the tangle of hair out of his eyes and squinted into the early morning light that flooded the bedchamber.

The room was in total disarray. Clothes littered the floor. Newssheets, rolled parchments, and several books had fallen off a side table onto the carpet. A chair was overturned. There was an assortment of bottles and dishes on the bureau, all new to him. Amongst their number were a mortar and pestle, and jars of unidentifiable liquids. The room smelled of stale air and medicinals.

Mercifully, the chamber pot was empty. He remembered he

had thrown up into it once. Later, a basin was used for the same purpose. He was forced to drink lemon water, and then a glass of syrupy liquid was pressed to his lips. When he had drunk it all, he collapsed exhausted amongst the pillows and was allowed to sleep. The way he felt, he wasn't sure if he had slept for five hours or five days.

"John. Help me to stand," he muttered. Instead of his poker-faced valet, a freckle-faced youth who looked vaguely familiar came to his aid. He frowned. "Where's John?"

"You dismissed him, sir," Tam answered levelly, though his heart was knocking against his ribs.

"When?"

"Night before last, sir."

"Did I?"

"Yes, sir. I wouldn't fret over it. He was glad to be gone. Packed his bag and was off within the hour. Give me your arm, sir, and I'll help you up. He looked right grateful, too. You should've seen his face when you came home."

"I'm sure I did but I don't remember it particularly," Alec murmured.

"No, sir. I expect you don't. Sit down here and I'll see to your bath."

Tam sat Alec in a wing chair by the window, and without permission pulled down the sash. He then scurried away before he could be asked further questions and returned carrying one of Alec's brightly-colored silk banyans. He placed this about the man's shoulders and began tidying the room. He felt Alec staring at him and knew he was remembered.

"I'll have everything straightened out in a trice. I didn't do it before because I didn't want to disturb you. But you slept so long I was beginning to worry I'd given you too much medicinal—"

"What are you doing here, Tam?"

"Me, sir?"

"Don't be obtuse. I haven't the strength or inclination for banter."

Tam collected up the parchments and stacked these and the books and newssheets in a neat pile on the table before turning to face Alec.

"Sorry, sir. I guess I'm nervous. I don't want you to tell me to leave. I've left St. Neots House and I'm not going back!"

"Did something happen?"

"No, sir." Tam lowered his eyes. "That is, not to me…"

"I see," Alec finally answered. "What do you want?"

"To be your valet, sir," Tam said in a rush. "I have a letter of introduction. I'll do a good job. I'll work hard. You won't have to tell me twice. I'll be better than that surly creature you had before. I don't know where everything is yet, but it won't take me long to sort through—"

"Tam. Have you ever been a gentleman's valet?"

"No. But—"

"It's not just a matter of shining boots and tying up hair."

"I know that, sir. But—"

"I frequently travel abroad."

"I want to travel—to see other places!"

"I have two hounds. They travel with me. You'd be expected to care for them, too."

"I love animals; dogs especially. And they like me. Yours do. I had them sleep with me in the dressing room so they wouldn't disturb you. They didn't mind a bit. I know their names too. Cromwell and Marzipan—"

"Marzi*ran*," Alec corrected with a sigh. He heard water being poured into his hip bath. "John was the best valet I ever employed."

"But he didn't care for Cromwell and Marz—Marzi*ran*, did he, sir?" Tam asked eagerly, following Alec through to the dressing room. "*Did he*, sir?"

"No, he did not," said Alec, smiling at the imploring note in the boy's voice. "You will excuse me if I don't ask you to share my bath."

He was left to soap and soak in peace. The water was deliciously hot and mildly scented. An extra pail was at the side of the tub with several folded towels and a fresh banyan. He listened to Tam in the next room, pulling out drawers, scraping them closed, banging doors on the tallboy, and quietly cursing when an object crashed to the polished wooden floor. It was a far cry from the soft-footed John, who crept about at his tasks, never spoke out of turn, and was precise to a hair in his appearance. And a complete bore, thought Alec. Having Tam about would never be boring, possibly disconcerting at times, and definitely not tranquil, but never boring. Yet, he knew nothing about him, except he was a footman at St. Neots House who said he had a letter of introduction. For him? From whom, he wondered. He also wondered what his godmother would have to say about a runaway footman becoming his valet. But he did not want to think about his godmother, or St. Neots House, or Emily or…

He toweled himself dry and slipped on the banyan. He was drying his hair when Tam gingerly came into the room. Alec took a good look at him. He was dirty and crumpled from head to foot, and there were dark rings under his eyes. He looked as if he hadn't slept in days. Something would have to be done about his clothes.

"I've laid out just a shirt and breeches and stockings on account of I don't know what your preference is in a waistcoat and frock," said Tam cheerfully. "And I've had a fire made in both rooms. And Mr. Wantage came to see about breakfast, sir. And your—"

"Thank you, Tam. Before I dress I think I ought to shave, don't you? Then when I am presentable, you and I are going to have a talk."

"Yes, sir," Tam replied in a much subdued voice, and remained silent while his master shaved and was dressed.

His hair plaited and tied with a black silk ribbon, Alec had Tam sit in the window seat and turned his dressing table stool to face him. "Firstly, I must apologize for being such a handful. Believe me, you saw the worst side of m—"

"Sir, I—"

"Please. Let me finish. I have no idea how you came to my front door, but I am deeply grateful you did."

Tam looked to the floor. "If you don't mind me saying so, sir, it seemed to me you were a fair way to drinking yourself into oblivion."

"Yes. What was in that foul brew you forced down my throat?"

"A mixture of things," Tam answered evasively. "Just enough of this and that to make certain you threw up everything you'd drunk. And then I gave you a dose of laudanum to help you sleep. That's all."

"I see. When you put it like that, it wasn't much at all, was it?"

Tam couldn't help a smile.

"Where did you learn to mix 'this and—er—that'?" asked Alec.

Tam frowned. "I was an apothecary's apprentice before I became a footman at St. Neots House."

"For how long?"

"Going on for six years, sir." He looked pleadingly at Alec. "There was some trouble. Not with me. Mr. Dobbs, my master, he got into trouble with the law and we had to close up shop. I tell you, sir, Mr. Dobbs was a good master. He didn't do half the things they said he did!"

"You couldn't find employment with another apothecary?"

Tam shook his head. "No one would have me after Mr. Dobbs's name was blackened. That is, no honest man would. And I didn't want to work for the other kind."

"How did you come to be a footman at St. Neots House?"

"The letter of introduction, sir," Tam answered simply. "It's old and worn and written before my time with Mr. Dobbs, but Mrs. Hendy said if ever I got into any bother I was to use it. It's addressed to you, sir."

Alec blinked. "Why?"

Tam colored painfully. "Mrs. Hendy said if there ever was a gentleman who'd help me out of a scrape it was you, sir. So after what happened to Mr. Dobbs, I went to the direction written on the envelope, but that was your old lodgings. The landlord couldn't or wouldn't help me. Can't say I blame him, sir. I was in a right state. But one of the lodgers, who said he was a friend of yours, took pity on me and sent me to St. Neots House. The letter of introduction got me in the door. Shall I get the letter for you, sir?" he asked eagerly.

"In a moment. This—Mrs. Hendy… Should I know her?"

"She was sister to Mr. Dobbs's wife who died, sir. And she was housekeeper at Delvin when your father was earl. I was born on the estate—"

"At *Delvin*?" Alec interrupted, more confused than ever. He had spent so little time at the ancestral pile in Kent that he was surprised anyone there would know him, least of all care to write him a letter of introduction. "Mrs. Hendy should've directed the letter to my brother. He is the present earl." But as soon as he voiced this private thought he realized his mistake, for the boy's lip began to tremble and the light of expectation in the green eyes was instantly extinguished. Alec smiled reassuringly. "I only meant, as head of the family, Lord Delvin is the one usually applied to by family retainers."

Tam was not greatly appeased. "Beggin' your pardon, sir," he said sulkily, "but Mrs. Hendy don't put much faith in his lordship doing right by those under his care."

Alec raised his eyebrows at this but refrained from comment, saying as he turned back to face the orderly dressing table, "After breakfast, you'd best show me Mrs. Hendy's letter and we'll talk some more."

Tam beamed. "Thank you, sir. Shall I finish tidying then, sir?"

Alec frowned at his reflection and then looked beyond at Tam scrambling to gather up clothes from the floor. "Tam… I have a vague memory of being escorted home by the watch."

"Yes, sir," Tam answered cheerfully. "Two of 'em brought you home in a wagon."

"Was anyone with me?"

"Yes, sir. Those three—um—men from *The Rose*. But Mr. Halsey got rid of 'em quick."

"My uncle was *here*?"

Tam nodded as he straightened, arms full of laundry, and was about to add that the old man was still in residence when there was a sharp tap on the door and the said gentleman strode in without invitation. The old man had eyes only for his nephew.

"You're up, then," Plantagenet Halsey stated gruffly, though a weight seemed to lift from his thin shoulders. "'bout time. Wantage has breakfast on the table. You need to put somethin' back into that stomach of yours." He turned his attention to Tam and stared him up and down. "You're filthy. You want a bath. Good for the soul; good for the spirit."

"Uncle, this is Ta—"

"I know who he is. Found him curled up on your doorstep. Thomas and I have had a good long talk. Tells me he's from Delvin. Strange how life takes quirky turns. Knew some Fishers there when I was a lad growin' up on the estate. Blacksmiths. All red-haired like this lad. He also tells me he was apprenticed to an apothecary. Wouldn't have believed it except I saw him muckin' about with all sorts of potions and such. He's a good lad, but he's filthy."

Tam shuffled his feet and hid a smile at such praise behind the bundle of laundry. The smile spread into a look of amazement at Alec's next words. The butler had slid into the room and announced his presence with a slight clearing of the throat. He wasn't given the opportunity to speak.

"Wantage? Good. Have someone fetch my tailor and my boot-maker. Yes. Now. I want half a dozen shirts and the same of breeches for my valet. He can measure for two frocks." Alec looked at Tam thoughtfully. "I think one pair of jockeyboots and two pair of shoes will suffice for now. Until then, Tam, you'd best dig out something from my wardrobe to make do. That's after you've bathed. See to it, Wantage, will you."

· · ·

ALONE TOGETHER IN THE BREAKFAST ROOM UNCLE AND nephew were at pains to avoid the topic uppermost in their thoughts. Thus conversation was somewhat halting and strained, serving only to underline the uncle's deep concern and the nephew's great reluctance to talk about the events of the previous day. Plantagenet Halsey pretended to concentrate on his food while Alec flipped through a stack of correspondence Wantage had placed before him on a silver tray. He tossed aside a number of invitations and packets and paused over one or two accounts, giving them more attention than they deserved. His uncle watched him closely, knew the moment when he had come across one invitation in particular, and wasn't surprised when Alec took off his gold-rimmed spectacles and pushed aside his plate, though he had eaten only a roll and a mouthful of egg.

"You've not told me about Paris," said Plantagenet Halsey.

"Paris?" Alec shrugged. "There isn't much to add to the last letter I sent. Bedford did all he could to secure adequate terms for the peace. It's just a pity he wasn't permitted to get on with it unencumbered."

"You mean without the interference of Bute?"

"Precisely. If he hadn't been so keen to secure the peace at any cost just to serve his political ends, we might have ended up with considerably more than we did. Then again, we did gain our objectives in America and India, so I'm not repining."

Plantagenet Halsey merely nodded and absently stirred his coffee.

"What?" Alec smiled and cocked an eyebrow. "At the very least I expected a lecture on the belligerent attitude of Mr. Pitt—if not, for you to fully endorse Bute's eagerness to reach an agreement with the French. Simon told me you gave them a hell of a time in the House over the introduction of a cider tax."

"Aye, I did. Deserved it too. No Englishman is going to stand for it! They don't seem to realize that. Then again, they don't care to. Cider tax to pay for a war that gained us next to nothing. Pah! Pack of self-servers. Alec! We need to talk—"

"More coffee, Uncle?" Alec interrupted. "I thought we might go to the club after dinner. I'd go earlier but I have this mountain of correspondence to work through. And I suppose I should begin writing up my final report for the department. Not that that will take up too much of my time. Tauton never reads them. He gives all his reports to a junior clerk to pore over and file as he sees fit. The man is a waste of space. A prime example of why the present system of sinecures and patronage just doesn't work."

If he hoped to draw his uncle into a discussion on one of his pet hates Alec failed to do so because Plantagenet Halsey wasn't to be diverted. He was only half-listening, his pale eyes surveying his nephew with a look something akin to sadness. It was enough to make Alec turn away and look out the window.

"The Duchess of Romney-St. Neots was at Ranelagh Gardens the other night," said the old man in an uncharacteristically quiet voice. "Went there in the company of that prim and proper daughter of hers—forget her name—and that bore of a son-in-law. Poor woman must've had a dreadful time of it. They saw you there…"

"Made it to Ranelagh, did I? I've no recollection."

"Seems you were with a party of—er—highly spirited individuals."

"Whores and pickpockets," Alec said flatly. "There's no need to be coy."

"You made a bit of an exhibition of yourself givin' one of those whores a diamond bracelet."

"I hope she was pretty enough to deserve it. If she has any sense she'll sell the damned thing and retire on the proceeds!"

"Alec—"

"What does it matter? What does *any* of it matter now? So Olivia saw me making a fool of myself? Saw me in company with a pack of low-life. Rather an anticlimax, I should think, after the exhibition I made of myself at St. Neots House. She must be thanking the gods her granddaughter chose the other brother. A bonus he comes with an earldom."

"Alec—"

"She'd have avoided any outrage to her sensibilities by simply penning me a civil letter informing me of her granddaughter's forthcoming nuptials. In fact, there was no need to go to that much trouble. An invitation to the engagement celebrations posted to my Paris lodgings would've more than sufficed. If one is to drink oneself into oblivion, Paris is a preferable watering hole."

"I wish you'd stop feelin' so damned sorry for yourself," the old man exploded. "I thought you had more spirit than that. Of all the stupid, inconsiderate, wasteful things to try and do! You not only scared a few more gray hairs out onto that poor woman's head, but you had me sick with worry. And you almost did it too. By God, Alec, I didn't raise you to see you throw it all away on a girl who has no more sense than to fall for the likes of Delvin!"

"Obviously Emily is still too young to know her own mind," Alec stated quietly. "Delvin made it up for her, and Olivia stupidly permitted it because she thinks her granddaughter will be happy as Countess of Delvin. She won't be, will she?" He pretended an interest in his porcelain coffee mug. "Your letters made no mention of Jamison-Lewis's death…?"

The old man's eyebrows lifted slightly. "That's 'cause he's barely cold. Happened less than a month back. Accidentally shot himself in the head. Bloody fool."

Alec felt his uncle's questioning gaze upon him. "Forgive me. I've been an inconsiderate ass. I didn't think… I presumed… To come home and find Emily engaged to Delvin… It was a shock."

"Believe me, my boy, if I'd known, I'd have told you long ago. And you do Olivia St. Neots an injustice. She had no idea Delvin was seriously courting her granddaughter until he asked for her hand in marriage."

Alec smiled crookedly. "Then I wonder when and how he discovered I was courting her?"

The old man's eyebrows drew together over his long nose.

"You don't think it a possibility?" asked Alec with surprise.

"Possibility? A'course I do! He hasn't been particularly subtle in his methods in wantin' to cause you grief. He interfered in your courtship with Selina and tried to have you run out of the Foreign Department on a trumped-up charge, though we can't prove it, so he's more than capable of marrying Emily St. Neots out of spite. Makes it all the more palatable that she is a granddaughter of the Duchess of Romney-St. Neots, and worth thirty thousand pounds."

"Is she? With that figure on her head it amazes me Olivia hasn't had a house full of fortune-hunting suitors to contend with."

"Well—er—she told me in confidence."

Alec grinned. "Sharing confidences with a duchess won't help your republican cause, should it become public knowledge, Uncle. Olivia is about as steeped in aristocratic vanity and privilege as one can get."

"Don't be absurd," the old man said gruffly. "I've been civil to the woman, that's all. She called on you yesterday, so naturally I invited her to have afternoon tea."

"Naturally."

Plantagenet Halsey met his nephew's playful smirk with a characteristic stern expression. "Listen, my boy. The woman has been put through enough over the past week without the need to worry herself sick over the likes of you! Her granddaughter up and gets engaged to Delvin and in the next breath Delvin fights a duel—"

"Delvin?" Alec interrupted, greatly surprised. "In a *duel*?"

"Aye, and he managed to skewer his opponent."

Alec blinked at his uncle. "Good Lord! I can't imagine Delvin risking his own fine neck, least of all in a fight of honor. How utterly unlike him."

"Well, Delvin says the fight was forced on him," Plantagenet Halsey said without conviction. "He says his opponent called him out on account of also being in love with Emily St. Neots. Jealousy. Pah! Delvin can say what he likes, can't he, when there were no seconds, no witnesses, no attendin' physician and his opponent's dead. The newssheets have been full of nothin' else for a week and with Emily St. Neots squarely at the center of a duel between two noblemen, you can imagine how the Duchess is feelin' at present."

Alec's brow furrowed. "If the encounter is as you say, then it was hardly an affair of honor, was it?"

The old man put up his brows. "Just as you say, m'boy."

"Delvin's opponent?"

"Lord Belsay."

Alec half rose out of his chair. "Belsay? *Jack* Belsay?"

"That's right."

"Jack's *dead*?"

The old man nodded and watched his nephew go to the window. "Her Grace said you knew Belsay."

Alec leaned a shoulder against the wall and stared out at the lush sweep of the Green Park. "Quite well. Not of late. We were at Harrow together. When I went into the Foreign Department we lost contact. He did write occasionally, but he was a shockingly lax correspondent. He and Sel—Mrs. Jamison-Lewis are first cousins. Lord! I can't believe the poor fellow is dead."

The old man joined his nephew at the window. "Alec. Somethin' don't smell right about the whole business."

"I agree. The Jack I remember was never one to cast caution to the winds. He certainly wouldn't do anything so outrageous as fight a duel. Certainly not without the proper formalities. He was a stickler for that sort of thing. Besides, he was a very mellow soul. He carried a sword for protection but I can't imagine him using it. As for forcing a fight on Delvin over Emily...? Yes, Wantage?" Alec asked as the butler trod quietly into the room.

"Excuse me, sir. There is a lady to see you. She wouldn't give her name."

Alec's jaw set hard. "You must be mistaken."

"No, sir."

Uncle and nephew looked at one another. The butler saw it as a sign to continue.

"I showed her the salon, sir. She said it is most urgent."

Plantagenet Halsey patted his nephew's arm. "I've got some business of my own in the city; I'll meet you at the club after y'dinner. And mind you eat it!"

ALEC WAS STILL SMILING AT HIS UNCLE'S CONCERNED pronouncement that he eat his dinner—just as he was used to doing when Alec was a boy—when Wantage announced him to the visitor.

It was indeed a lady, not one but two, and both dressed in deep mourning. The sight of them brought Alec up short. Gloves covered their hands and black netting concealed their faces. Agitation and distress showed in the mannerisms of the shorter woman. She could not be still. She kept clenching and unclenching her fingers in the folds of her petticoats. It was not until the taller one touched her arm and said a quiet word that Alec was noticed standing alone by the door. The shorter lady then carefully lifted her veil. Her eyes brimmed with tears.

Alec had no idea who she was.

"I don't suppose you remember me, Mr. Halsey?" the lady said in a clipped voice.

Alec came away from the door, none the wiser. On closer inspection, the woman was much older than she first appeared. Possibly she was in her late fifties. Although she looked fragile, her voice was strong and held a note of bitterness. He glanced at her companion who had not yet lifted her veil, and before he could reply was interrupted.

"I know I should have sent my card, or at the very least asked you to call on me at Cavendish Square. But the less gossip there is, the better. That's why I came to you. Quite frankly, I can't bear another day in that house!" She shuddered. "Solicitous relatives can be so overbearing. Except for my dear niece," she said with a teary smile and touched the other lady's sleeve affectionately, "who has been such a-a *rock*."

"Won't you both sit down?" Alec asked. "Would you care for a dish of tea?"

"Tea?" she said in a broken voice. "No. Something stronger for both of us, if we may."

When Alec came back into the salon carrying a decanter and glasses fetched from the library across the passageway, he found his guests seated on the striped sofa central to the room. He went about the business of pouring out a generous drop of brandy for both ladies with deliberate slowness, because out of the corner of an eye he saw that the lady who had spoken to him was being comforted by her niece. He handed both a glass, checking himself for the briefest of moments when he realized the niece, now unveiled to reveal her pale oval face and mop of tight apricot-colored curls, was none other than Selina Jamison-Lewis. She looked up at him but he ignored her, saying to her aunt,

"Tell me how I may help you, my lady."

"I hope you may, my boy," was the fierce reply. "But where are my manners? I can tell you haven't the faintest idea who I am, or what we are doing dressed in this atrocious color. Mourning is such a dull affair."

"I must confess I didn't know you when I first came into the room," he said gently. "But Jack had a great look of you. I will miss him, though we were not close after school. More my fault than his. I seem to spend a great deal of my time traveling. A circumstance which doesn't do much for one's social life. I suppose being a diplomatist has its advantages. New faces and a chance to taste the local fare are but two, though such things tend to lose their appeal after the third posting."

He was prattling on in his calm measured voice because the Lady Margaret Belsay was once again sobbing into her handkerchief, and he thought it best to let her do so without interference. She seemed in need of a good cry, and perhaps, confined to her house and surrounded by a dozen cloying relatives, she hadn't the opportunity to indulge herself. He handed her his clean white handkerchief and watched as Selina put a comforting arm about her aunt. But when she again tried to engage his eye, he turned away to refill Lady Margaret's glass.

"Thank you," Lady Margaret said, after wiping her eyes and sitting up straight. "Thank you for not fawning over me and for giving me a good drink. My daughters are all fools. If I ask for brandy, they immediately think I've turned to drink. If I don't feel like coming down to dinner, they jump to the conclusion I am trying to starve myself." She heaved a shattering breath and blew her nose. "I just wish they would all go away and leave me to my grief!"

"They obviously care a great deal about you, though perhaps they are a little unthinking. Possibly a circumstance of their own grief?"

Lady Margaret glanced at him slyly. "You are good with words, Mr. Halsey. Though I don't think you insincere. That brother of yours is also very smooth-spoken. Yet, he is totally insincere in word and deed. I knew so from the first, but Jack—Jack was thoroughly taken in by him. I tried to warn him. What grown son heeds the warnings of a parent, especially his mother? To Jack, Delvin was as he appeared: Charming, friendly, a trusty Trojan. Every mamma with an eligible daughter wanted Delvin as a son-in-law. Jack was impressed by it all. He failed to see beneath the shining facade until it was too late."

"Jack had just as much to recommend him, my lady," Alec said with a smile. "I should think many mammas coveted Viscount Belsay for their daughters. And he was not unhandsome, and to my memory, there was considerable wit in his talk. Not a bore by any means. Far from it."

Lady Margaret reached out and squeezed his hand. "Thank you, my boy. It's true. Jack was all those things and more. He was —He was extremely shy in female company. It came as a surprise to me, too. The boy grew up with six sisters who adored him, and yet he became the most awkward creature when forced to make small talk with a female. So you see why Jack was taken with Delvin, the consummate philanderer. Oh, he gives the impression of being one, but one always doubts men who constantly flaunt their virility. Nonetheless, whatever Delvin's ability with females, he made an indelible mark on my son."

"I imagine then that Jack became Delvin's shadow at such functions where he found it necessary to engage in small talk with eligible girls?"

"Precisely!"

"Poor Jack. He must have dreaded coming-out parties."

Lady Margaret gave the crystal tumbler to her niece and smoothed out her petticoats, weighing her next words carefully and yet eager to confide. "The newssheets say my son fought a duel with Delvin over Emily St. Neots. The gossips have fueled this claim with whispered recollections of my son's and Delvin's pursuit of the girl. No one can deny my son was seen often in her company, but then so was Delvin. Society wants to believe a rivalry existed between them. It makes for a romantic tale. I shall let them continue to believe so for the time being."

Alec frowned. "You do not set much store in the validity of such a story, my lady?"

Lady Margaret gave a snort. "It's absolute rot! There's not an ounce of truth in it. It's absurd to think my son—a *Belsay*—would seriously consider marriage with the likes of Emily St. Neots. I'll lay odds he didn't even flirt with the girl. He was probably comfortable in her company because Delvin was pursuing her, and so spent a moment or two longer in conversation with her than was acceptable, thus giving the gossips something to grasp at. But marriage? Never! Jack would never have sullied the family name so. He was a Belsay first and foremost. He knew what was due his name. He wasn't about to ally himself with bastard blood."

"Aunt, please," Selina Jamison-Lewis said in a strident whisper. "You shouldn't say—"

Lady Margaret glared at her niece wondering why the young woman's face had fired up red at the mention of Emily St. Neots. "Don't be a goose, Selina! I can and I will speak about Emily St. Neots' unfortunate parentage. For anyone to suggest Jack would entertain the idea of marrying the base-born granddaughter of a duchess is absolute nonsense!"

"Aunt, I wasn't suggesting—"

"Leaving aside her unfortunate paternity for the moment," Alec said, cutting off Selina. "You do not think it at all likely Jack might have become infatuated with Miss St. Neots in the course of Delvin's courtship of her?" he asked quietly, dropping his gaze to the silver buckle of his right shoe before lifting it to look directly at Lady Margaret. "After all, you say Jack was shy in the company of females and yet he was comfortable in hers. And Miss St. Neots is not—er—unattractive."

"Where are your eyes, young man? Emily St. Neots is a beauty —gray-eyed and yellow-haired. She has her mother's delicate features and there is a certain bearing about her person, not unlike Olivia. But I know my son was not so infatuated, and not so insanely jealous of Delvin, as to want to fight a duel for her." She shuddered. "As for marriage? *Never.*"

"Yet," Alec said with a dry throat, "Delvin is about to wed her?"

"I know. It's a disgrace. That's Delvin's affair. It only goes to prove what a mercenary snake he really is. Although I don't approve of the girl, I am not insensitive to her plight. I am amazed Olivia permitted it." Lady Margaret shrugged. "No doubt she is more than happy to have Delvin. It will make her granddaughter a countess. It's vastly more than she can have hoped for when she foolishly decided to bring up the bastard offspring of her disgraced daughter's affair with a stable hand!"

Alec was puzzled. "My lady, many people consider my brother to be a gentleman of character and bearing. Nor have I heard he has done anything to give society a disgust of him. Is he not one of the favored sons?"

"Your constraint is to be commended, Mr. Halsey," said Lady Margaret with a sad smile. "But it does not excuse the deplorable neglect you suffered at the hands of your father and brother." She saw him glance at Selina and added, "Oh, you needn't worry that I have discussed your circumstances with anyone except your mother. She and I were close friends, and it was she who confided in me, just before her death…"

"You were more fortunate than I, madam," Alec said flatly, a heightened color to his cheeks, his tone indication enough he had no wish to discuss the Countess of Delvin. "You have not told me how I may help you."

"I am at a loss to understand how you can be so insensitive to your circumstances," Lady Margaret continued, not to be diverted. "It was never my intention to break a promise I made to your mother many years ago, but after what her *monster* of a son did to my poor boy, my conscience is clear. Are you not outraged by what was done to you?"

Alec put up a hand, then dropped it. It was a gesture of resignation.

"Lady Margaret, I don't pretend to understand my parents' actions. To try and do so would surely send me mad. Nor can I blame Delvin. No one would be the wiser except my mother decided she needed to clear her conscience before she died. Her confession answered a good many questions about my upbringing. It can only have made my brother miserable—"

"—and what he is today," Lady Margaret said with finality, finishing the sentence for him, and Alec made no protest with her presumption. She stood and Selina did likewise. She needed to walk. There was stiffness in her knees and they ached. "I came to ask a favor of you, Mr. Halsey," she continued in an unsteady voice. "I was your mother's closest friend, and you and Jack were close at Harrow. Now my son—my *only* son—is dead. I want you to find out why Delvin saw fit to murder my blameless boy."

Alec looked at her sharply.

"Don't look at me as if I'm having a mental collapse!" Lady Margaret scoffed. "My son's death has devastated me, but I'm not about to be committed to Bedlam. I am made of stronger stuff. And I intend to remain strong because I am determined to see that monster strung up at Tyburn for his foul act!"

"There is no love lost between my brother and me," Alec replied evenly. "To be quite frank, I despise him, but you are asking too much that I believe him capable of murder—the murder of one of his closest friends at that."

Lady Margaret made movements to leave. She stuffed Alec's crumpled handkerchief into her reticule and shook out her petticoats. "Think on it, Mr. Halsey. It isn't as far-fetched as you suppose. Come, Selina."

"If it is as you say, then what proof have you?" Alec asked gently. "That Jack did not survive his injuries is hardly cause to brand his opponent a murderer, my lady. Duels often result in death. If Jack had survived…"

"Delvin made certain my son would not live," Lady Margaret stated.

Alec's blue eyes widened in disbelief. "My lady, I don't see how—"

"Mr. Halsey, Jack's body was covered in multiple wounds," Selina interrupted, leaping to her aunt's defense. She'd had enough of sitting silently by while her grief-stricken aunt was treated with condescension; however much the Lady Margaret wished that she remain a silent partner to the interview. "It is the physician's opinion that these wounds were inflicted, not in the coolness of an orchestrated duel where one elegant thrust of a rapier brings an encounter to a close, honor satisfied, but in a frenzied attack guaranteed to ensure my cousin did not live through the encounter. I believe that gives my aunt the right to brand Delvin a murderer."

Alec finally met Selina's gaze. "And if I discover that in truth Jack was in love with Emily St. Neots?"

"We wouldn't have come here today if we thought there was a grain of truth in what the newssheets say!" Lady Margaret said with contempt. She let down her veil and Alec opened the door for both ladies to go out of the room before him. "Mr. Halsey, my son was murdered; Selina and I know this as truth. I want you to find out why. I want to be able to sleep at night knowing my son did not lose his life over the bastard offspring of a fallen duchess and a-a stable hand! Jack was a *nobleman*, Mr. Halsey, not an adventurer."

ALEC WAS LEFT ALONE WITH HIS THOUGHTS, WANTAGE showing the ladies to the front door. But it was not many moments before the butler returned to the salon with Selina Jamison-Lewis in tow. He waited to be noticed by his master, who continued to scowl at the carpet, arms folded across his chest and sitting on the edge of a sofa back. But as he appeared deep in thought, Wantage cleared his throat loudly and said, "Excuse me, sir, but Mrs. Jamison-Lewis has misplaced her reticule," and stepped aside to allow the lady access to the room.

Alec looked about sharply and immediately felt his face grow hot. He had been thinking over Lady Margaret's startling accusation of murder against his brother when uninvited thoughts of Selina had intruded into these musings: The blackness of mourning suited her. She appeared almost ethereal with her skin so blinding white against the depths of black crepe. But had her eyes always been so dark, or perhaps mourning black made them appear so? She attributed her unusually dark eyes to a Spanish ancestor, one Mauricio Del Medico, physician to Philippe of Spain, who had settled in England when his master married Queen Mary. Dark eyes that regarded him as if he had something to answer for, when it was she who had accepted an arranged marriage with Jamison-Lewis rather than defy her parents' wishes and run away with him to be married in Scotland. God, he wished he'd never bumped into her on the stair at St. Neots House! In fact, he wished he'd not gone there at all. He'd made a damned fool of himself. As for his drunken behavior afterwards, he wished he could remember the half of it...

"I would like a word in private, Mr. Halsey," Selina stated in her clear strong voice, regaining possession of her reticule, which she had conveniently stuffed behind a sofa cushion. She watched Alec nod to the butler, who reluctantly took himself off, and waited for the door to be closed on the lingering servant's back. She took a breath, slightly disconcerted by Alec's blank look. "I want to reassure you that my aunt's grief has not clouded her judgment. She has every right to think Jack was murdered, and that the duel had little to do with Emily St. Neots."

"Why do you think they fought a duel, Madam?"

"I?" asked Selina, slightly taken aback by his bluntness. She chose her words carefully. "It was not in Jack's nature to fight a friend, particularly not over a woman. If Emily was the cause of the duel, it was at Delvin's instigation. Although it is my belief Emily is being used as the excuse to cover a more sinister intent. As to that, I have not the slightest idea."

"I'm sorry about Jack. He was a good fellow."

Selina nodded, a curious lump in her throat. She wanted to cry; instead she kept tight rein on her emotions and said dully, "Yes. He is greatly missed."

"A double blow for you?"

Selina mentally winced. "Jack's death has given purpose to my mourning, Mr. Halsey," she stated flatly. "Please excuse me. My aunt must not be kept waiting."

"You think my brother capable of murder, Mrs. Jamison-Lewis?"

This time Selina visibly cringed. She hated the way he emphasized her married name with a sneer. It made her give an unguarded response. "Yes. Delvin is a thief, a liar, and a cheat, so why not a murderer?"

"Such harsh words, Madam. And for a gentleman who was great friends with your late husband."

"Then you must allow me to be the better judge of his character," she answered frankly and started for the door.

Alec put himself between her and the door. "Yet you have lent your support to this marriage between Delvin and Miss St. Neots?"

Anger fired Selina's dark eyes. "You presume too much, Mr.

Halsey. I did not visit St. Neots House that day to offer up my congratulations!"

"Then you will speak to her about Delvin?" he asked eagerly. "Try and dissuade her from the match?"

Selina shook her head, anger giving way to sadness. Here was proof that he did indeed love Emily St. Neots. At the mention of Emily his handsome angular face lost its harsh lines, his mouth softened, and a light came into his deep blue eyes, eyes that had once looked on her lovingly and now regarded her with little more than contempt. She had trained herself not to think of the past. Six years had come and gone; too long to sustain hope and long enough for him to fall in love with someone else. She should not have been at all surprised. Yet, the unexpected death of Jamison-Lewis had sparked a glimmer of hope, and her encounter with Alec on the stairs of St. Neots House had renewed a physical ache she had long suppressed. And now, looking up at him, his eyes full of expectation, even this small sliver of hope was silently extinguished. She felt foolish and utterly wretched.

"Please open the door, Mr. Halsey," she stated, eyes leveled at the engraved buttons of his flowered waistcoat.

"You must speak to her!"

"No. That is impossible," she answered, a gloved hand outstretched for the brass handle.

He caught at her hand and brought her closer to him, the crush of her many-layered petticoats the only barrier between them. "Why? Why is it not possible?" he demanded. "Miss St. Neots will listen to you."

"No. She will not listen to anyone," Selina answered flatly, although the nearness of him was fast suffocating her senses. "Please. Let me go."

"You want to see her married to a man you call a cheat and a liar, whom you and your aunt have accused of murder?" he demanded angrily, head bent over her, a curl of coal-black hair falling into his eyes, his mouth almost brushing her forehead. "You want her to wake up one morning to find herself married to such a man, all because you chose unwisely—"

"How dare you! How *dare* you feel sorry for yourself at *my* expense!" Selina enunciated through gritted teeth, and with a mighty shove threw him off so that he staggered backwards and she fell back up against the door, breathless and seething with anger. "Do you have concern for no one but yourself? If you tried that rough treatment on Emily to get her to change her mind, I wouldn't be at all surprised if she never wishes to set eyes on you again! Lord! You step back into her life after an absence of eight months and expect her to fall into your arms because you wish it?"

"So you're in favor of her marriage to Delvin?"

Selina sighed in exasperation. "What does my endorsement matter?" But when Alec held her gaze, mouth shut hard, she knew he would persist until he had an answer. "No, of course I'm not," she replied calmly. "He is everything I declared him to be and more. And—he is not in love with her; it could never be a happy union."

"Then she must be told. She must be made to see what sort of man she is about to marry!"

"No."

Alec was all haughty incredulity. "No, Madam?"

"Don't you understand? Emily does not see the true Delvin because he has not allowed her to see anything but a polished, mannered nobleman of wealth and family. That is the being Emily fell in love with." When Alec's brow creased, she smiled wanly. "Emily is in love with your brother. That is why I cannot say a word against him."

Alec was incredulous. "She is in love with him? *In love* with Delvin?" He wiped his mouth as if he had eaten something distasteful.

"To show your opposition to the match, for me to voice doubts about Delvin, will only strengthen her resolve to marry your brother."

Alec looked away to the draped window seat with its view of

the inner courtyard of St. James's Place, but not before Selina saw the abject hurt in his face. It made her feel hollow inside. After a moment he opened the door and spoke as if addressing a stranger, "Thank you for your advice, Madam. I appreciate that you offer it in the spirit of wanting what is best for Emily."

"Indeed, Mr. Halsey," Selina replied flatly, yet her dark eyes were wet and bright. "There is nothing more soul-destroying than having one's hopes and dreams shattered by the one you love."

THREE

WHEN THE PORTER CALLED WANTAGE FROM HIS PANTRY THE
butler was about to give the man a piece of his early-morning
mind until he saw who was standing in the hallway. The Duchess
of Romney-St. Neots dumped her cloak, bonnet and muff on a
sleepy footman, straightened her upswept, powdered hair before a
gilded looking glass, and demanded to see the master of the house.

Wantage was extremely apologetic. He was unable to oblige.
Mr. Halsey had left the house two hours earlier. He did not say
when he would return. Perhaps Her Grace would care to leave her
card and come back in the afternoon?

She did not care to do such a thing! She would wait. And if
there was any hot chocolate in the house Wantage could bring it to
her in the drawing room overlooking the park. And he could send
Mr. Halsey's valet to her.

The butler did not hesitate to do as he was told.

ALEC SPENT THE EARLY MORNING AT M'SIEUR POISSON'S
fencing academy; the renowned fencing master had rooms in
Curzon Street. M'sieur was interested to discover what his pupil
had learned at the celebrated *salle d'escrime* in Paris. Alec had gone

there several times in the company of the Duc de le Tournelle's youngest son, who had gained him entry for the favor of a word in the English Ambassador's ear.

The hour passed too quickly for both. Regretfully M'sieur could not allot Alec any more time that day. Soon the rooms would fill with young gentlemen who made a habit of frequenting Poisson's academy because it was the fashionable thing to do before going off to the club or the coffeehouse.

These sprigs of fashion had no intention of working up a sweat. They came fully coiffured and in their best silks to learn a few fancy steps, to perfect their deportment, and to impress one another with the latest technique of parry and thrust. Half-hearted fencers themselves, they were avid spectators of the serious fencer who went through his paces with M'sieur.

Poisson confided to Alec that it was truly a waste of a good fencing master's time to bother with these silly younger sons of English noblemen, but as he over-charged them and they were prepared to pay such an exorbitant fee he, Poisson, could not very well turn them away. No. He would fawn over them, lavish compliments upon them, and spend his time conducting lessons in placement, even though it gave him excruciating ennui.

Poisson helped shrug Alec into his frock coat, saying with a grin, "In Paris, you visited Mme Sophie, yes? Did I not say that in all of Paris she keeps the best cathouse? Me, I cannot speak of it personally, but the Chevalier d'Fragnoré, he did not brag, no?"

"He did not brag."

M'sieur clapped his hands, well satisfied. "Good! Fencing and women, they are the same, are they not? Both require technique and a certain—how you say?—finesse. Yes!" He kissed the tips of his fingers and bowed with an exaggerated flourish. "Good-day, M'sieur Halsey."

Alec returned the salutation, turned to leave, and was confronted with a group of chattering young men crowding in through the door that opened on to the stairwell. He stepped aside to let them pass. There were at least a dozen of them, all young

men of good family with too much time and money on their
hands than was good for them, and with pretensions to being *à la
mode*. They were twittering away, laughing to one another over
silly nothings; powdered, patched, and enveloped in a heady cloud
of perfume.

In the commotion of arrival, Alec slipped behind them and
out to the landing only to come face-to-face with two of their
number stopped on the top step. The narrowness of the stairwell
prevented him from passing without interrupting what seemed a
barely controlled argument. He coughed into his closed fist to
warn them of his presence, but they did not notice him.

"Now what are you going to do?" demanded the one facing
Alec, his padded shoulder up against the wall. His powdered
toupee rose a ridiculous eight inches above his forehead and
complemented the affected nasal voice.

"I've got to have time to think it out. God, James, I still can't
believe Belsay's *dead*. What am I going to do?"

Alec knew at once to whom this second voice belonged and
was surprised. It was Simon Tremarton, a colleague in the
Foreign Department. He had recently shared a posting in Paris
with Simon, and before that they had been at The Hague
together. Simon was to have had dinner with him before leaving
Paris, but had sent his apologies at the last moment, saying he
needed to return to London early on account of his mother's ill
health. Alec wondered what a man who needed to work for a
living, and who could ill-afford to waste time or his hard-earned
guineas, was doing in company with these sprigs of fashion who
had nothing better to do with their lives than waste time in friv-
olous pursuits.

"Get the cash from someone else," replied the one in the eight-
inch toupee.

"*Cash?*" Simon Tremarton's voice broke on the word.

"Old Reubens will be on to you in less than that," was the
nasal response with a snap of two fingers, "if he even suspects you
can't repay what you owe him. I'd lend you the blunt myself, but I

live on credit as it is; much Father knows about it! What about your sister?"

"Cindy?" There was a pathetic catch to Simon Tremarton's voice. "She don't give a tester about me. Never has."

"She must have jewels you can pawn."

"Paste."

"All of them?"

"*All of them.*"

The gentleman facing Alec grimaced. "Damn! I thought—"

"—she was swimming in lard? She was once. Has a taste for Basset. Plays deep. Anything Delvin gave her she had copied, then sold off to pay her debts. Dressmakers' bills mostly. Cindy loves to look the lady. *Whore.*"

"Listen, Simon. You're going to have to swallow your pride and go back to her. See if she won't speak to Delvin for you. He must be able to pull strings, as many as he pleases with the position he's in."

Simon shook his powdered head slowly. "How can you ask it of me after what he did to Belsay?"

"But he took your money. He promised—"

"Which brings us full circle." Simon sighed. "Don't worry. Everything is so upside down for me now. I don't want to think about Reubens or Cindy or anything. If the worst comes, I'll try for a posting to Constantinople."

"Simon?"

It was Alec. He had coughed twice more to no avail, so he backed up the stairs and came down again, as if he had not been privy to the conversation. He hid his surprise at seeing Simon in Curzon Street, and said conversationally, "I thought you'd had enough punishment at the *salle d'escrime* in Paris with Henri. I warn you: Poisson is a hard taskmaster." He nodded to the outrageously dressed gentleman beside Simon, who acknowledged him with a short bow.

Simon Tremarton stuttered to say something. His face was white as cold marble but his ears were as red as the heels of his companion's pointed shoes. "Hal—Halsey? Alec! Wh-What a-a surprise! I'm just back from seeing mother. My sister—Cynthia—Perhaps you know her? Lady Gervais? She was with me." He saw Alec glance at his friend. "Oh! Ah! Alec Halsey, James, Lord Farnham. Alec works—well is a diplomat—"

"The word *work* is fine, Simon," said Alec extending his hand to Lord Farnham. "Brother of Freddie's?"

"No. Second cousin, thank God," Lord Farnham drawled. "No offense if he's a friend."

"I don't know him well. He's more an acquaintance," Alec replied, ignoring the sarcasm and the fact Lord Farnham was looking him up and down through his quizzing glass as if trying to place his name and face in his mental social register. If he intended to disconcert the object of his social scrutiny he failed dismally. Alec stared blankly back at him.

"Halsey? Halsey. *Egad!* Not *Delvin's* brother?" Lord Farnham let drop the quizzing glass on its silken cord. "You and Delvin don't look much alike."

"Thank you."

"You're the black sheep," Lord Farnham continued, mental social register turning another cog. "Raised by an uncle or somebody. An annoying old badger who plays at being a rabble-rousing eccentric MP. Wants to abolish slavery and give the Irish Home Rule—that sort of ridiculous nonsense. Father is forever boring on at dinner parties that your uncle should be strung up at Tyburn for treason."

Alec grinned. "Yes, that's the one."

Lord Farnham screwed up his mouth in distaste. "Egad! No wonder Delvin don't mention you."

"James—" Simon Tremarton whispered in acute embarrassment, not a glance in Alec's direction.

"A pity," Alec replied evenly, "it would give him something to talk about other than himself."

Lord Farnham peered closely at Alec, then burst into laughter, as if he suddenly got the joke. He nudged Simon sharply. "Simon says you're too boringly honest to be of much interest, but I own to liking you, Halsey. You've got back and you're prettier than your brother. No wonder Delvin don't talk about you." He put up his quizzing glass and turned a magnified eye on Simon Tremarton. "I've a mind to make him a member of the Ganymede Club before you, Simon," he teased his cringing and red-faced friend. "Unlike you, Halsey can well afford the subscription, and his father was an earl."

"James! *Don't*," Simon whispered fiercely.

Lord Farnham shrugged and sighed. "No, you're right, Simon. It wouldn't do to corrupt the innocent. Pity." He smiled crookedly at Alec and inclined his powdered head. "No offense, Halsey." And with that he sidled past Alec to the top of the stairs, where he called out to Simon, "I shall time your *tête-à-tête*!" and disappeared from view.

Alone in the narrow stairwell, Simon Tremarton forced a laugh, although he couldn't bring himself to look at Alec. "Of course, you can't believe everything James says. He likes to upset people. He—he—Of all the damnedest coincidences finding you here!"

"It's all right, Simon. I don't give a fig for Farnham's opinion."

"You must be wondering what a government flunky is doing in company with the likes of Farnham and his noble ilk."

"That's none of my business, is it?"

"Trust you to be patronizing!" Tremarton sneered.

Alec bowed slightly and continued down the stairs. When he reached street level Simon came thudding after him and closed the street door on the traffic noise.

"Alec! Wait! I'm an ass! I know you're not the sort of fellow to pass judgment on another. Look. I'm—I'm in a bit of a fix. The duel Delvin fought with Jack Belsay, your brother says it's all Belsay's fault. Newssheets say the same. But that's nonsense. Delvin's lying!"

"Is that so? You're the third person in as many days to say so," Alec replied evenly. "Why did Delvin and Belsay cross swords?"

"I—I don't know that!" Simon Tremarton blustered, deflated that his dramatic pronouncement had fallen flat. But he shouldn't have been surprised. Alec Halsey was renowned in Foreign Department circles for playing his cards close to his chest. "Alec, listen: What I do know is that Belsay wasn't the least interested in a chit from the schoolroom." He glanced over his shoulder. "I—I know things—*certain particulars*—about Belsay that proves your brother is lying."

Alec put up his black brows. If Simon was trying to put him on edge, he was succeeding, but for the wrong reasons. "Such as?"

"I can't tell you here!"

"You know where I live," was Alec's flat response as he opened the door and stepped out on the street. He turned his back on the traffic of carriages and sedan chairs and faced Simon. "Whatever it is you do know, Simon, be assured: Delvin must also know it or he wouldn't be so confident in getting away with the lie."

Simon Tremarton's eyes widened, as if this thought had never occurred to him and, startled, he stumbled backwards, turned and fled up the narrow stairs. Alec walked home, pondering the connection between three men of very different temperament: The mild-mannered, diffident Viscount Belsay; the Earl of Delvin, who paraded society as the consummate rakish nobleman; and Simon Tremarton, a self-made functionary of poor family. He was still thinking about these three when he entered No. 1 St. James's Place and discovered his valet being interrogated by the Duchess of Romney-St. Neots.

WANTAGE SENT TAM TO THE DRAWING ROOM WITH A FLICK of a finger, giving him no indication of who wished to see him. The butler disliked upheaval in his household, and he disapproved of the freckle-faced youth. He knew he was a runaway from St. Neots. That much he had ferreted out from the housekeeper, who had it from an upstairs footman, who had overheard a little of the conversation between the master's uncle and the boy, that first night when he was discovered by the porter on the doorstep. The lad was too familiar with the master and with the household servants, those above and below him. He needed putting in his place; to have the fear of knowing his station in life put back into him. The master's previous valet had come with excellent references and had once been a valet to the Marquess of Dartmouth. There had been an air about him that bespoke the perfect gentleman's gentleman. Wantage had disliked him intensely but had respected his position. He had no such respect for Tam, whom he considered an interloper and lacking the necessary social skills and character to hold the exalted position of valet to the master of the house.

Sending the boy to the Duchess unawares would give him the jolt he needed, Wantage thought with relish. With a grin, he shut the drawing room door and tiptoed around to the servant door to put an ear to the panel.

THE DUCHESS OF ROMNEY-ST. NEOTS WAS THE LAST PERSON Tam expected to see in his new master's house. Her small stout figure in hooped petticoats of Chinoiserie silk was comfortably seated on a chaise longue, a knitted shawl about her bare shoulders and small feet in their damask covered shoes with high heels and diamond buckles up upon the upholstery. She was reading the morning newssheet and sipping bittersweet chocolate from a fine porcelain dish. Tam's heart gave an odd leap and he forgot to bow. He wanted to run but his instinct told him to hold fast. Maybe she wouldn't recognize him? After all, he had only been a lowly under-footman and was hardly ever in the presence of members of her family, least of all her tiny exalted personage. That and the fact he had only been in her employ for six months meant she was unlikely to remember his face, least of all his name.

She heard the door close but finished reading the paragraph. "Well, John, I have a few questions…" She looked up and was startled. "Where's John? Come closer."

Tam shuffled forward and made her his best bow. "I am Mr. Halsey's valet, Your-Your Grace."

"Rot! You're much too young. Did John send you with some lame excuse?"

"No, Your Grace."

She peered at him intently and then sat bolt upright. Her eyes went very round and Tam knew all at once that he was not as anonymous as he supposed. He had not reckoned on the Duchess's extraordinary memory for names and faces.

"What did you do with my granddaughter's horse?" she demanded. "Do you realize what trouble you've caused my household? What are you doing here? Do you suppose you can just run away from one house and go to another and no one will be the wiser? Well, boy, what do you have to say for yourself? Don't gape at me! I'm not senile. I know exactly who you are! At least, I thought I did. What name do you go by here? Speak up! Speak up!"

"It's Thomas Fisher, Your Grace. It's always been Thomas Fisher. That's my name. Most call me Tam. I didn't steal Miss Emily's horse. I didn't! Phoenix is Mr. Halsey's mount. Beggin' your pardon, Your Grace, but that's the truth. Ask Mr. Halsey. He'll tell you so himself."

"As Mr. Halsey isn't at home I can hardly do that, can I?" she snapped. "Do you know what happens to boys who steal? They're strung up! Neave sent the local militia after you, you stupid, stupid boy. They are still out looking for you."

"But I didn't steal the horse!" Tam declared, his lower lip trembling. "Phoenix is in his stable. Honest! Please, please, you've got to tell them—"

The Duchess drew herself up. "I don't have to do anything of the sort. You are rude and I won't be shouted at by a horse thief! What are you doing here?"

"I'm Mr. Halsey's valet. I am. Honest. John was dismissed, Your Grace. Ask Mr. Wantage. He knows. He'll tell you all about it."

"I don't want to talk to the butler, or any other servant in this house except Mr. Halsey's valet. Go and fetch him this instant!"

Tam was at a loss as to what to do. He moved from foot to foot. He dug his hands in his pockets only to instantly withdraw them again. He turned about and then turned back to face the Duchess, arms limp and the palms of his hands sweaty. All the while the Duchess stared at him, her hands clasped in her lap.

"Your Grace, I am Mr. Halsey's valet. These clothes I'm wearing. They're his—"

"Stole those too, did you?"

"No, Your Grace! He, Mr. Halsey loaned them to me while his tailor makes me up a proper suit of clothes. He wouldn't have sent for his tailor if I wasn't to be his valet, would he, Your Grace?"

The Duchess pretended to be unmoved and her sharp eyes did not waver from Tam's red face. "You'll have to do better than that," she said haughtily. "You ran off with a horse from my stables and now you say you are a valet? Incredible! Just because you're out of livery and have a decent cloth on your back means nothing. I still maintain you're a thief."

Tam's green eyes filled with tears and then he had a flash of inspiration. "Your Grace! When I arrived at St. Neots House I gave Mr. Neave a reference from Mrs. Hendy of Delvin Hall. He must have showed it to you and—"

"Don't be an oaf, boy!" she said with haughty contempt, putting up her chin and turning it away from him. "As if I bother myself with references given to my butler. Pshaw!"

The ruse worked. In a great rush of tearful words, Tam told her everything she wanted to know: From the moment he set eyes on Mr. Halsey in the hall of St. Neots House, of following him to London to *The Rose* tavern, on through to overhearing Mr. Halsey give his address to a chairman and being found on the doorstep of his house. He omitted nothing. In his desperation to convince the Duchess he was no liar, he told her without a second thought about the Turkish Bath and his conversation with the night watchman; about Mr. Halsey's drunken state when escorted home by the

watch; how Mr. Halsey continued to drink until Plantagenet
Halsey had the servants force the door of the bedchamber, and
there they had found him almost dead. The boy even went into
unnecessary detail about the extent of Mr. Halsey's illness, with no
thought for the Duchess's sensibilities. In his desperation to
convince her of his honesty, he failed to notice when she screwed
up her face at the mention of the chamber pot, or how from time-
to-time a small smile played on her mouth at the naïve sincerity in
his pleading voice.

He was about to give her further details to prove his identity,
offering to fetch the letter of introduction, when the door opened
and in walked the master of the house, preceded by Cromwell and
Marziran who trotted up to the Duchess to receive a pat.

"Olivia?" Alec said and brought himself up short. One look at
her face, which was remarkably transparent to her feelings just
then, and a glance at Tam, and he had the situation in one. He
called the greyhounds to heel. "Tam, take Cromwell and Marziran
for a run in the park, will you? Be back within the hour. I need to
dress for dinner."

Tam glanced at the Duchess to see her reaction but she had
gone to look out the window. He took a step toward Alec. "Sir—
about Phoenix—will you... Her Grace doesn't believe... The
watch won't come for me, will they, sir?"

"It's all right, Tam. You're safe here. Now, off you go."

Tam opened his mouth to say more, shut it, and with a bow,
obediently went out with the dogs prancing at his heels.

"Was it necessary to threaten the boy to get the whole sordid
story?"

"I justified my tactics by telling myself he is officially still in
my employ until I am told otherwise," she said glibly. "And I didn't
tell him an untruth. If you intend to keep him may I suggest a
lesson in discretion? I never managed to get a scrap out of that
poker-faced individual you had before."

"I'm glad to hear it."

"How was Paris?"

Alec's mouth gave a twitch. "Olivia, you didn't come all this way to ask me that."

The Duchess remained at the window. She watched Tam and the two dogs appear from around the side of the house and run out into the openness of the Green Park. "I wish you would allow me to have a word in one or two appropriate ears," she said with a sigh as she turned to look at her godson. "Why should someone like that fish-faced Haverfield be an envoy-extraordinary and you only a minister? Everybody knows he was given the Russian posting only because his cousin is a Privy Councilor. You have twice his brain and more social address. Why, I don't think the imbecile can speak French! And you, you can speak—what is it?— four or five foreign tongues."

"Five, if we're counting."

"*Five* foreign tongues! Which are going to waste if you can't get anything better than glorified messenger boy to that buffoon Bedford. You should have gone into the law or politics. Been an MP—"

"What? And be forced to sit in the House all day and listen to the ravings of Uncle Plant?" Alec said with a laugh. "No, I thank you."

"Don't be flippant! You know what I mean. The diplomatic service must be the most unfashionable, the most unprofitable vocation in the Kingdom. It's a totally thankless task. And while everyone is falling over backwards to get out and secure a good living at home, you willingly go off to some distant corner of the Continent to drink tea or coffee or whatever, with sultans and such!"

"And while I was drinking coffee with sultans—or more to the point, making my bow at Versailles—my brother had ample opportunity to win Emily? I'm sorry, Olivia. You didn't dissuade her from accepting his offer."

"No, I didn't. Why should I? I let her choose and she chose one of the most eligible noblemen in the kingdom," the Duchess said defensively. "You may think this the whim of an old lady, but I was deter-

mined not to repeat the mistake I made with her mother. I forced
Madeleine into a loveless marriage when the last thing she wanted to
be was Duchess of Beauly." She came away from the window and stood
opposite Alec, fluttering her fan. "Delvin is Emily's choice. So be it.
But if I'd had my way… What I wanted for her… I wanted you," she
confessed in a small voice, looking down at the ivory sticks of her fan.

Alec kissed her forehead. "Thank you, Olivia. You have helped
my self-esteem inch itself out of the slime, where it was firmly
thrown this morning by Mrs. Jamison-Lewis." He gave a huff of
embarrassed laughter. "My pride took a great hammering, but I
shall live. Bruised and battered I may be, but as much as I hate to
admit it, hers is the voice of reason: I must accept the fact Emily
chose someone other than my esteemed self!"

The Duchess was not convinced. "You accept the
engagement?"

"I must accept it, but I don't approve of it. And I take exception to the fact her betrothed is my brother. Delvin doesn't deserve
her."

"Yes. Of course you must," she muttered, not wanting to be
drawn into the conflict between the brothers. She would always
prefer her godson to his elder brother, but Delvin was engaged to
be married to her granddaughter and so she must be loyal, and
secretly thankful that, by making Emily his countess, the Earl was
helping to wipe away the stain of her illegitimacy. "I suppose you
now know all about this shocking business between Jack and
Delvin?" she asked.

"Yes. Uncle Plant told me. I still find it hard to imagine Jack
forcing a fight on anyone, least of all one of his best friends."

The Duchess sighed. "It is truly remarkable. Yet, Delvin is
adamant Jack forced the fight on him, all because Jack was in love
with Emily. I was never more surprised of anything in my life. Jack
was fond of Emily, but jealous of Delvin?"

"What does Emily say?"

"She won't talk about Jack. She can't speak his name without bursting into tears." The Duchess glanced at her godson. "Of course, your little visit hasn't helped her state of mind. Despite what you might think, she sets great store in your opinion."

Alec tugged the bell pull. "My dear Olivia, you're headed for disappointment if you came here in the hopes of persuading me to offer Emily my congratulations on her engagement." He ordered an ale from the footman who came in answer to his summons and tea for the Duchess, and while they waited for the footman's return he told her about Lady Margaret Belsay's visit with her niece in tow, adding, "The poor woman is naturally so grief-stricken her reasoning is highly emotive. It is one thing to accuse Delvin of lying about why he and Jack fought a duel, but to suggest Delvin murdered Jack…"

"Poor Meg. Her mind is quite deranged with grief," said the Duchess, thinking over all her godson had told her. "But what of Selina? Surely she does not see the matter in the same light as her aunt?"

Alec smiled to himself. *Thief, liar and a cheat, so why not a murderer?* Those were Selina's words. Yet Alec could not bring himself to repeat them to the Duchess. Lady Margaret's damning indictment was sufficient for now. He was saved by the entrance of a footman with the tea tray.

"What did Selina say about Jack?" persisted the Duchess, taking the dish of tea Alec offered her. "She and Jack were very close. His death has been a great blow to her."

"Under the circumstances, given she is newly widowed, I'm surprised to see her holding up so well. The death of Jamison-Lewis is more than enough grief for—"

The Duchess gave a snort of disbelief. "*Grief?* Selina *grieve* for J-L? Good gracious, no! No one would've blamed Selina had she dispensed with mourning altogether, such was the abuse she suffered at the hands of that monster; and I don't use that word lightly, my boy. What that poor girl had to endure…" She mentally shook herself and shivered, a glance at Alec who was staring at her in a penetrating way. "Oh, it is not my place to tell you the sordid details of her marriage!"

"I thought… In public there was never any hint of discord between them," Alec stated, the shocked surprise evident in his voice. "On the few occasions I happened upon them at a public function, I received the impression she was determined to show me just how happy she was in her marriage. And there was that incident at the Drury Lane Theatre when—" He frowned at the Duchess. "Are you certain?"

The Duchess wondered, not for the first time, at the complete ignorance of the male brain to the workings of the female mind. "Did it never occur to you, given the history between the two of you, that her behavior was a grand display for your benefit?" she asked patiently. "After all, she could not allow you to see just how miserable she was—that would be admitting defeat, and you know Selina, she is particularly stubborn." She put aside the tea dish, out of the corner of her eye observing Alec, whose frown had deepened, and shook out her petticoats as she stood. "I will let you mull over that revelation in private. And if you want to know anything about Jack, speak with Selina. I'm off to visit Meg. Perhaps I will learn something about Jack if she's in the mood for confidences. I'll tell you all about it tomorrow. You are coming to the celebrations, aren't you? And you *must* stay. I'll have your old rooms made up."

"I give you fair warning, Olivia. I can't promise I'll be on my best behavior."

"It would be a very dull affair if you were, my boy!"

Alec grinned and pinched her chin. "You wicked woman."

She looked up into his handsome angular face and voiced her thoughts.

"Emily and Selina are both fools," she murmured and quickly moved away, fiddling with the strings of her reticule. "Are you certain you don't want me to have a word in Grenville's ear?" she asked in a matter-of-fact voice. "His wife, a silly hen of a woman, is a Romney—distant, but a Romney nevertheless. I know he will do anything for me. If I let it be known you wish to be an Ambassador…?"

"Ambassador? No, Olivia, I thank you," he said, amused by her sincerity, and took the yellowed letter she had produced from her reticule and held out to him. "What's this?"

"It's Mrs. Hendy's letter of introduction for one Thomas Fisher. In his hurry to go after you, the foolish boy left it behind."

"Have you read it?"

The Duchess smiled mischievously. "Of course I've read it!"

"And…?"

The Duchess shrugged her shoulders. "It won't help you know anything more about the boy, if that's your meaning by smirking at me! He's from Delvin, to be sure, but he was sent away and apprenticed out when he was twelve. Mrs. Hendy wasn't too happy about that circumstance and she asks that should the boy need a protective arm, he apply to you. Nothing more. A mystery. You read it and see." She touched Alec's arm. "Are you quite sure you don't want me to speak to Grenville?"

"Quite sure," he assured her. "It's not that I don't aspire to such dizzying heights. However, I will get there under my own sail or not at all."

"You, too, are very stubborn!" she complained, going out of the room before him. "All the fault of that uncle of yours. He's filled your head with republican nonsense."

"Don't be too harsh on him. He is much maligned. And not the ogre you th—"

"I don't think him an ogre!" the Duchess retorted. "He's —He's—"

"—very civil over a dish of tea?" Alec suggested lightly, and at the base of the staircase kissed her outstretched hand. "Don't worry, Olivia, I won't tell a living soul you took tea with a devout republican—"

"I don't give a fig who knows about—"

"—because it wouldn't redound to his credit."

FOUR

A DINNER FOR FIFTY PEOPLE AT ST. NEOTS HOUSE MARKED the beginning of the weekend engagement celebrations. Emily stood at the oak-paneled double doors, flanked by her grandmother and the Earl of Delvin, and made her curtsy to each guest as they filed into the state dining room with its three heavy chandeliers and string orchestra playing from the gallery.

Between introductions, the Earl took the opportunity to congratulate his betrothed on a job well done, and was about to compliment her on her pretty gown of antique silk and seed pearls when her attention was diverted by a late arrival. Delvin looked up and saw his brother. The sight of him made the thought of the long meal unappetizing, yet he continued to smile, perhaps a little wider than before.

Alec slid into the anteroom just as the last of the guests turned to go into dinner. He was late. He intended it that way. He smoothed back a curl and joined his friend Sir Cosmo Mahon, a corpulent gentleman in his late twenties who had waved Alec over to his side. He immediately introduced Alec to a man of middle years with a fleshy florid face and a morose disposition, one Justice Lord Gervais. With them was Lord Andrew Macara, who, as the Duchess of Romney-St. Neots' son-in-law, needed no introduction. He greeted Alec with a firm hand and a barrage of questions concerning his posting to Paris.

Lord Andrew was still quizzing Alec, this time on the customs prevalent in a certain mid-eastern European kingdom he had read about somewhere in a memoir written by some chap whose name he'd forgotten, when they arrived at the head of the receiving line.

If there was any sign of awkwardness between Alec and Emily it was on her part. Her curtsy was slightly clumsy, and when she looked up with a shy smile, he was regarding her without smile or frown. She made an innocuous remark that later she couldn't recall and barely listened to his equally innocuous reply. He moved on and she was required to be pleasant to Lord Gervais, who was now bowing over her hand, thus did not hear or see what was said between the brothers, only sensing it was a very short exchange. Now Lady Gervais curtsied before her, dressed in a vibrant red taffeta gown and towering headdress with matching dyed feathers, who prattled out compliments which, even to Emily in her distracted happiness, sounded forced and backhanded.

After a long twenty-three course dinner, the ladies took coffee and tea in the Chinese drawing room, arranging themselves on the sofas and chairs set out at one end of the vast room, away from a late afternoon sun. The Duchess presided over this chatty gathering of fan-waving powdered ladies with a serene smile that hid a quick eye and an open ear, should the conversation not flow to her liking. Lady Charlotte Macara helped her mother distribute the dishes of tea. Handing Emily a dish, she chastised her: A girl marrying the most eligible bachelor in London should carry herself with more decorum and not laugh out loud like a hoyden.

Emily ignored her aunt because she was too happy to be bothered with her and had struck up a conversation with Lady Gervais, who was pouring forth into Emily's little ear all the latest gossip about several ladies in the room. By the time the gentlemen rejoined the ladies, Lady Gervais was telling Emily a particularly humorous anecdote involving Lady Charlotte Macara and a pile of horse manure she had failed to notice while promenading up The Mall. Their giggles could be heard on the other side of the room.

"A little beauty, isn't she?" said a voice at Alec's shoulder.

"Yes," he answered absently, attention focused on the strand of rubies and diamonds encircling Emily's white throat. He recognized the necklace. It had belonged to his mother. He remembered her wearing it toward the end of her life, when she had finally found the courage to acknowledge him.

"She was only sixteen years old when I married her," the voice said, and heaved a sigh.

"I beg your pardon," said Alec, turning to discover Lord Gervais with quizzing glass up to one watery and bloodshot eye. "Sixteen?"

The man directed Alec's attention back to Emily and Lady Gervais. "My wife," he said. "Cynthia. Married her on her sixteenth birthday. Straight out of the schoolroom. Friends on the Bench warned me against it. But I wouldn't hear a word against her. Still won't. Lovely little thing. Makes me happy to see her happy. Can't have children. Pity."

"Y-yes it must be," Alec murmured, and guided the man to the back of the room with the excuse of getting a dish of coffee. He had noticed how the judge had been throwing back the brandy like water, and it was obvious the man's drunken state had brought on a melancholy mood. "But if you are happy, surely—"

"Happy? *Happy?*" Lord Gervais choked on the word. "I wish I could make her happy. It's laughable watching her share confidences with that yella-haired chit. Poor little fool."

Alec was startled. "Your—um—wife?"

"No, man! The chit! Delvin's little bride. Has no idea, has she? I mean she wouldn't. Just out of the schoolroom herself. Bound to have her heart broken. Bound to. It's not as if he'll give up Cynthia for her. Why should he? My wife's an accomplished whore." He jabbed Alec in the chest with a thick finger. "Know that, man. Delvin's mistress. Now that's nothing to sneeze at, is it?"

Alec blinked. He didn't know what to say. It wasn't every day a

husband bragged about his wife being another man's mistress.
Lord Gervais was proud of the fact. That Delvin had the audacity
to invite his mistress and her husband to his engagement celebrations should not have surprised Alec, but it did.

"Not that the chit isn't a taking little thing," mused his lordship and belched, admiring Emily's low-cut gown through his
quizzing glass. "There's something very appealing about innocence.
Don't find innocence in my profession. All whores and pickpockets not fit for spit. But innocence…? Ah! What I wouldn't
give to have my wedding night over again…"

Alec was spared further revelations by a group of gentlemen
who hailed his lordship over to join them in a game of whist. He
watched the judge stumble off, and found Sir Cosmo Mahon at
his side.

"Gervais boring you with talk of his judicial duties?" he asked
with a shake of his powdered head. "Don't know why Ned invited
him. A hanging judge, and one of the best by all accounts. Not
one of us."

"He was telling me about his wife," said Alec, sipping his
coffee.

"Aha."

Alec smiled. "Reason enough for him to be invited this weekend, wouldn't you say, Cosmo?"

Sir Cosmo frowned and jerked his powdered head in Emily's
direction. "Hope she never finds out. Rather bad form of Ned to
invite the woman here. One only needs to look at her twice—"

"Twice?"

"All right! Just *look* at her!" grumbled Sir Cosmo. "Nothing
discreet about the woman. Not to my liking. Dare say not to
yours."

"Absolutely not," said Alec with a twinkle at his friend's
awkwardness.

"Where's that uncle of yours?" Sir Cosmo asked, changing the
subject.

"He'll be here tomorrow. For the ball. He went out of town

today for a meeting of the anti-slavery league. Don't worry, Cosmo. He'll be the life of the party, I promise you."

"I'm rather hoping he will," said Sir Cosmo, scanning the room with his quizzing glass. He coughed. "He has a tendre for Aunt Olivia, y'know."

"Yes. That's why he'll be here."

"Who?" asked Lady Sybilla in a breathless voice.

The youngest daughter of the Duchess of Romney-St. Neots and married to an Admiral of the Fleet, it was common knowledge that the Lady Sybilla secretly adored the Earl of Delvin's younger brother. Her harmless infatuation provided endless entertainment for everyone except Alec, who had a soft spot for the harmless beauty and hated to see her an object of ridicule.

"Oh dear! Am I interrupting?" she wondered, the fluttering of her gouache fan becoming agitated. "I didn't mean... I'm—I'm *so* glad to see you safe home, Mr. Halsey."

Sir Cosmo lifted his eyebrows, smiled, and sidled away, much to Alec's annoyance, though he was too polite to show it. He offered Lady Sybilla a seat on a newly-vacated sofa and entertained her with a detailed description of the latest fashions worn at the Palace of Versailles, while doing his best to ignore her somewhat vacant smile—that is, until Emily swept up to them, champagne glass in hand.

"Aunt Sybilla! You're being so unfair," Emily announced and hiccupped. "You've kept Alec all to yourself for a good twenty minutes when Lady Gervais particularly wants to be introduced." She looked at him archly. "She was so surprised to learn you're Edward's brother. Her eyes almost left their sockets. With your somber clothes and unpowdered hair, she thought you a member of the clergy." She chuckled into the champagne bubbles. "She thinks you're dreadfully handsome. Imagine!" She shrugged a bare shoulder. "I suppose you must be. Everyone knows Aunt Sybilla's in love with your beauty."

Lady Sybilla's fan stopped in mid-wave and her face flamed under the layer of lead cosmetics at Emily's brazen comment. She stumbled into an excuse to leave without looking at Alec, swept up her heavily-embroidered petticoats and scurried away to the opposite side of the room to find a safe haven with Selina Jamison-Lewis, who sat languidly fanning herself, straight back to a group of gossiping ladies. Angry with Emily's childish taunt—though he realized it sprang from too much champagne—Alec turned on a heel and deliberately left her alone in the middle of the room while he sought the fresh air and solace of the balcony.

Humiliated to be so summarily deserted, a hundred pairs of eyes looking on, Emily followed Alec out into the night without a thought to what her actions might present to others. Of course, everyone was watching the threesome, and more than a few eyebrows lifted when the bride-to-be swept out after the other brother—these same raised eyebrows turning to observe through quizzing glasses and from behind raised fans the reaction of the Earl of Delvin. But his lordship seemed oblivious to one and all, and stood talking with Lord Gervais and Lord Andrew Macara, a scented lace handkerchief poised in his right hand.

"How dare you so rudely dismiss me!" Emily demanded, confronting Alec on the balcony, face flushed with anger tinged with bemusement that he could treat her in such a cavalier fashion. "Can I help it if Aunt Sybilla has been besotted with you for years and years? Poor Uncle Charles must be secretly mortified. But as he is *always* at sea, he is saved from enduring the humiliation of his wife's unfaithfulness."

"If you care for your aunt and uncle, you won't repeat such utter tripe," Alec replied woodenly, looking out on a cloudless night sky studded with stars. "There is no harm in your aunt and she is devoted to the Admiral."

"It isn't tripe," Emily contradicted, wondering what had possessed her to embarrass her favorite aunt and tarnish an unsullied reputation. She hiccupped and stared down into the bubbles in her champagne glass. She'd had too much to drink, but she was beyond caring. She put the glass aside and leaned against the cold marble of the balustrade. "What I don't understand is why she remains infatuated with you, when you broke her heart that day she discovered you with Selina Jamison-Lewis in the wood."

Alec frowned self-consciously and turned to look at her. "The wood? What do you know of the wood?"

"So Jack was right!" she cooed with conspiratorial satisfaction, all anger extinguished with revelation. She sidled up to him, her tight sleeve with its tiered lace cascading from the elbow brushing against him. "Will you tell me what happened in the wood?"

"Good God, no!"

Emily pouted. "What does it matter now?" she said with a careless shrug of a bare shoulder. "It's such ancient history."

Alec moved a little away, to the end of the balcony. "Is Jack ancient history, Emily?"

Emily's teasing smile vanished and she suddenly felt heavy of mind and heart. "That's unfair! Everyone thinks it's a great lark that Jack and Edward fought a duel over me, but I think it's horrid! It's not my fault Jack's—Jack's—gone."

"No, it's not your fault," Alec agreed in something of his old manner and came back to her. He held her hand. "Why do you think Jack and Edward dueled?"

"I don't know! Truly, I don't! It gives me the headache to think about it! Grandmamma asked me the same question, and all I can say is I had no idea Jack was jealous of Edward. He wasn't. I mean, he never said so and he never acted as if he cared two straws for me above the ordinary."

Alec brushed a loose powdered curl from her flushed cheek. "So why would Edward tell the world that the duel with Jack was fought over you?"

Emily sniffed. "Perhaps... Perhaps that's what Jack wanted Edward to believe? Yes! As some sort of excuse so that Jack could lure Edward into a fight?" She looked up expectantly. "That's reasonable, isn't it?"

"Yes. But not likely. The Jack I knew was not the sort of fellow to start fights. In fact, he wasn't a very good swordsman. And Edward made sure Jack wouldn't survive his injuries... Why?"

Emily felt like bursting into tears. She pulled her hand from his and put it behind her back. "You think Edward meant to kill Jack? That's a terrible accusation to make against your own brother! Edward said you hated him for no good reason, but I never believed it until now!"

"That's nonsense, Emily."

"Is it?" she asked archly, though tears now streamed down her cheeks. "Why shouldn't you hate him? He's the earl and you're not!"

"Now you're being childish."

"I'm not a child! I've grown up, or haven't you noticed?"

He took a good look at her then in the flickering light of the flambeaux: The upswept mass of blonde hair was thickly powdered out of all recognition; the liberal use of cosmetics hid her delicate skin; and the cut of her many-petticoated gown made her look the pouting coquette. She was no longer the Emily he had hoped to marry. He took a step toward her, saw a movement in the shadows by the open French door, and checked. His bow was formal.

"May I offer my felicitations on your engagement. Now you must excuse me. I am wanted by Lady Gervais."

She watched open-mouthed as he returned to the drawing room, leaving her alone on the balcony feeling wretched. He had not apologized for his rudeness and nothing had been resolved between them. As for offering his felicitations, he had done so in a mechanical, non-convincing way. The duel and Jack Belsay's unfortunate death had failed to rock her belief that in marrying the Earl of Delvin she would be made happy. Yet, ever since Alec had stormed out of her rooms, a small lingering doubt had flamed within her and was kept alight by his silent disfavor. She wanted everyone to be happy at her good fortune. She wanted the engagement party to be perfect. Yet what she wanted more than anything else was Alec's approval for the match. A hand on her shoulder made her quickly dry her eyes and spin about with a brave smile.

"Alec?"

But it wasn't Alec, it was Lord Delvin and looking down at her with concerned inquiry. He gave her his handkerchief.

"My dear, are you perfectly well?" he asked. "You had the Duchess and me worried when you disappeared so suddenly and with no thought to our guests."

Emily tried hard to smile brightly. "I'm sorry, Edward," she apologized. "Too much champagne has addled my brain and given me the headache. I ought not to have run out on you like that, but Alec he—"

"There is no need for you to explain, my dear," the Earl said soothingly and kissed her hand. "Second is entirely to blame. No, don't shake your pretty head. You know I speak the truth." He smiled, a little wider than before as he led her to the French doors. "How can you, a delicately nurtured female, know Second's true nature? Your grandmother, a most superior female, as Second's godmother will not say a word against him, particularly to her innocent granddaughter. She would not want to alarm you unnec-essarily. And I have no doubts he has always play-acted the gentleman within her walls. But as your betrothed, it is now my duty to protect you." He lifted the string of diamonds and rubies about Emily's throat and smiled into her wide gray eyes. "You must trust me, and me alone, to know what is in your best inter-ests; are we not to be man and wife soon?" He let drop the heavy string of precious stones on a sigh and said, "It pains me to tell you this, and I do so in the strictest confidence, but Second is not the man you think him. There have been times when I have lied, yes, *lied*, to protect the good name of Halsey on account of, let me just say, his *conduct unbecoming*. I know I will find disfavor in your eyes, but I lied, and to the very man she was to marry, to save Second's skin when he denied seducing Mrs. Jamison-Lewis. It weighs heavily on my conscience but I could not stand by and allow her chances of a brilliant match be ruined by my brother's lust. After all, who can blame her, for she was just your tender age after all, and seduced with false promises."

"Oh, Edward! Then he *did* seduce her in the wood?"

"The wood?" said Delvin, momentarily surprised. He let his lip curl. "Indeed, the wood, and anywhere else he could lay his filthy hands upon her."

"Alec had no intention of marrying Mrs. Jamison-Lewis?"

The Earl gave a bark of harsh laughter. "My poor innocent! *Marriage*? When have my brother's intentions ever been honorable? He is a confirmed rake and a cad. Do you understand me, Emily dear?"

Emily nodded slowly, the implication behind the Earl's words so depressingly shocking that her head felt as if it was filled with lead. Silently, she permitted the Earl to lead her back within the warmth and blazing light of the noise-filled Chinese drawing room.

"Edward?" she managed to whisper, fingers convulsing tightly about his velvet sleeve. "Selina's marriage to George Jamison-Lewis might never have taken place but for your timely interference…"

He smiled at her choice of the word interference, yet his pale blue eyes were fixed unblinkingly on a couple at the far side of the room. Lady Gervais, her voluptuous figure pressed suggestively to his brother's side, was playfully chiding Alec under the chin with the closed sticks of her fan, while her brooding husband watched on, not five feet away.

"Interference?" he drawled with a curl of his lip. "Yes. I should think Second and Mrs. Jamison-Lewis are only too well aware of my *interference*."

WHEN ALEC FINALLY LEFT THE DRAWING ROOM AND WENT UP to his rooms, he found his valet engaged in using his apothecary skills. The long table by the window in the dressing room had been turned into a workbench. It was covered with various apparatus, an assortment of cuttings from the Duchess's herb garden, an apothecary's traveling case, and, at Tam's elbow, a leather-bound Pharmacopoeia; all purchased at Alec's expense.

Tam was so busy stirring liquid to the boil over a naked flame that he failed to notice his master, even when the latter coughed politely to be recognized.

"Have you been at this since I went down to dinner?" Alec asked conversationally.

"Sir? Sir! Yes. I mean, no! I unpacked the bags, polished your boots, and put away your clothes," Tam said, unfurling his shirt-sleeves. "And I made sure the lackeys brought up a hip bath and had a fire built in the bedroom on account of a chilly breeze—"

"I don't want to know what you've been doing with your time. This need to constantly justify yourself isn't necessary. What are you making there?" Alec peered over the boy's shoulder and tentatively took a sniff of the rising steam from the glass flask. "Smells sweet."

"It's nothing special, sir. Just *Melissa officinalis*. I've made a tea with the leaves and sweetened it to make it drinkable. Common Balm is what most people call it."

"What's it for?'

"Good for headaches, sir."

Alec surveyed the array of cuttings. "All this from Her Grace's gardens? I am impressed."

"Nearly as good as the Chelsea Physic Garden, and so I told Mr. Heath. You've just got to know what to look for and what to use. A root of a plant here, a leaf, sometimes only the stem is needed. And then it matters how you use it. Some plants require little more than to be ground up. Other roots and stems have to be boiled for their juice. It's not difficult if you know what you're about," said Tam diffidently. He wiped his hands and left the table. "I didn't mean to keep you waiting, sir. I'll have warm water fetched." He reached for the bell pull. "Is there anything else you want, sir?"

"No, nothing," said Alec, and handed Tam his frock coat. "Did you have much trouble with Neave and the other servants?"

Tam avoided his eye. "No, sir. That is, not once they knew I was your valet. Mr. Neave wanted to throw me out of the house. He called me a horse thief. Jenny and Mrs. Travers, she's the housekeeper, persuaded him I was telling the truth. Mr. Neave wasn't happy about it, but he didn't say anything else. Besides, he was too busy to be bothered with the likes of me on account of this weekend house party. Mrs. Travers was better about it."

"I'm sure your reappearance gave downstairs an afternoon's conversational gossip." Alec glanced at his valet in the reflection of the dressing table looking glass as he absently untied his stock. "You, of course, only heightened their curiosity by being terribly discreet?"

"Not a word out of me, sir," Tam said firmly. "Not even to Jenny."

"She—pleased to see you...?"

Tam pretended a moment's deafness and disappeared into the closet to fetch a silk banyan and a pair of Moroccan leather slippers. He waited by the dressing table holding these articles and watching Alec polishing his nails, interrupting him to say, "Sir? If you don't object, when I'm done here, I need to run an errand. The tea—it's for Jenny. She says Miss Emily has the headache. I won't take but fifteen minutes."

"Fifteen minutes. And Tam, don't make a nuisance of yourself."

"No, sir. Thank you, sir."

A scratch on the outer door had master and servant looking at one another in surprise. The scratch persisted. Tam went in answer to it while Alec threw the banyan over his open-necked shirt and slipped his stockinged feet into the soft mules.

Tam returned with wide eyes. "A lady to see you, sir."

No sooner had he spoken than Lady Gervais stood in the doorway, an ostrich plumed fan fluttering across her very revealing cleavage.

"Thank you, Tam," Alec said calmly and dismissed him with a look, saying to his visitor, whose gaze had wandered to the curious assortment on the table, "I think we will be more comfortable in the sitting room," and ignored the accusatory glance from his valet.

Tam stomped off to the closet. Covent Garden bathhouses were one thing, but this was St. Neots House, Miss Emily's home! He shouldn't have been surprised or angry with anything the aristocracy got up to, but he hardly expected his master to entertain married females of low repute (and Lady Gervais was that, dressed as she was, or more the point, undressed!) under the Duchess's roof. Perhaps she had come to talk? Tam gave a snort of contempt. In his anger he had forgotten the tea for Jenny. He returned to the dressing room, collected what he needed, turned to leave, then stopped and listened for voices. Not a sound.

ALEC WATCHED LADY GERVAIS WANDER ABOUT THE SITTING room. Everything in her manner was suggestive. She reeked of artifice, and yet there was something oddly naïve about her. He ignored the hint to sit beside her. Instead, he leaned in the windowsill. He smiled to himself when she pouted and pretended offense.

"I must confess, I didn't expect to see you so soon, my lady."

"It's Cindy. I told you to call me that. I said I would come, didn't I?" she said, still a little put out. "Frankly, I didn't think it would be tonight, but Edward isn't in his rooms and I'm not the least tired."

"Should I offer you a nightcap?"

"Should you?" She smiled from under her blackened lashes. "I know you think I've drunk enough already. You're trying to be nice and considerate. You are, aren't you?" she said with surprise, and giggled. "I never expected someone like you."

"Like me?"

"To be Edward's brother. I never knew he had one."

"I hope I'm not a disappointment."

"Lord! Do you always talk that way? It's most entertaining. Won't you sit by me? I don't like talking across a room. It's so formal."

"Perhaps under different circumstances, but no, not tonight. I am sorry."

"You think I'm not beautiful enough," she said sullenly. "That's a shame. I was hoping to spend the night with you."

"I'm flattered, naturally—"

"Don't imagine Edward would care in the least. My guess is he's gone off for the evening with that whore Selina Jamison-Lewis. Poor, sweet, innocent Emily, she really has no idea."

"No idea?"

Lady Gervais stopped fanning herself and glanced slyly at Alec. "That Selina is Edward's whore; they've been lovers for years. Oh, Selina pretends to dislike Edward. She'll tell anyone who'll listen that she simply loathes him, but Edward told me she only says so in public because she was afraid *he* would discover the truth."

"He?"

"George Jamison-Lewis, her husband. He used to beat her, y'know. Regularly, so Edward says." She shrugged. "Edward says that's no small wonder because she made no effort to please him. She brought it all on herself really."

"No female deserves such mistreatment."

"I suppose not," she answered on a sigh. Oblivious to his flat note of anger, she settled back on the soft cushions and kicked off her muddied silk shoes. "I may not love Gervais, but I am mindful that he is my husband and would never do anything to provoke him to strike me. Edward says I have the most perfect feet," she said with a saucy smile, pointing a small damp stockinged foot in Alec's direction. "What does his brother think?"

"Do you care what I think?"

"Oh, yes, because Simon values your opinion. Did I tell you Simon Tremarton is my brother? He may be the most twisted person I know, yet when he plays at being serious he means it. I have suspicions that my little brother prefers his own kind…" She shuddered dramatically. "I can't think of anything more repulsive!"

Alec smiled crookedly. "Come now. I'm sure you can."

Far from being offended, Lady Gervais giggled. "Oh! I would

enjoy entertaining you! Are you sure you won't change your mind?"

"Believe me, you are entertaining me," he responded dryly, watching her stretch suggestively along the sofa. He stared down at his Moroccan slippers. "At dinner you mentioned you'd visited Lady Margaret Belsay yesterday afternoon; that she told you a most interesting piece of gossip about her son."

"Not about her son. About you."

Alec was startled. "Me?"

She smiled sweetly. "I only said it was about Jack Belsay because you seemed so interested. And I couldn't very well tell you what she said over a dish of coffee with all those prying eyes upon us. Especially with Edward not an arm's length away and staring daggers at me for flirting with you. But I couldn't let him get away with ogling Selina's breasts throughout soup, even if they are bigger than mine." She laughed. "You should've seen the way he stomped out onto the balcony after you and little Emily! I'd no idea you'd been out there alone with his silly betrothed until he brought her back inside."

"You said you saw Jack the day before the duel…"

"Don't you want to know what Lady Margaret said about you? It's all over town."

"First tell me about Jack."

She sighed impatiently. "Very well. Only if you come over here." She smiled when he complied but made no effort to give him any room on the sofa. "I saw Jack Belsay in Hyde Park. He was with Selina; they're cousins, y'know. Then Simon came up—"

"Your brother?"

She nodded. "He didn't seem to know Selina because I remember watching Lord Belsay introduce them. I remember particularly, because I thought it odd that Simon should even know Jack Belsay. Simon knows Edward, y'know."

"In passing, or something more?"

Lady Gervais looked at him saucily. "Oh, I'm sure not in *that* way. Edward loathes *petit-mâtres*." She traced the intricate pattern on the sleeve of his dressing gown. "Don't trust Simon. He and Edward have known each other for years, since before you went to —to—The Hague? Simon is in Edward's pay. Edward asks and Simon tells."

Alec slowly let out a breath. "I see. Thank you for telling me. I don't know why you did, but I am grateful."

"Don't you? You see, I can't resist the promise in a man's muscular thighs," she confessed on a purr, a hand to the front of his open-necked shirt. "It was Simon who blurted it about town you were courting Emily. Strange, that you would be interested in her too... Edward's not in love with her. He doesn't have strong feelings for any female, except perhaps Selina..."

"Is that so? And you want to share my bed so you can throw it in his face in the morning? That's hardly a novel approach, is it, Cindy?"

She slid a hand inside his shirt and said at her most seductive, "That is a direct way of putting it. Perhaps that was my original thought... But once I set eyes on you... Well, I couldn't pass up the opportunity to share your bed."

He caught up her hand. "I'm flattered, naturally. But I want you to tell me what Lady Margaret told you."

Lady Gervais pouted. "We're wasting a perfectly lovely evening. I'd much rather—"

"Please," he asked, and kissed the inside of her wrist, the smell of strong perfume mingled with stale smoke, unpleasant and lingering.

"Very well," she sighed, snuggling into him. Her free hand found the buttons of his breeches. "Of course Lady Margaret is furious with Edward for killing her son. That's not surprising. But what I don't understand is why Jack and Edward fought a duel over Emily in the first place. I mean, she has nothing to recommend her but her youth!"

"Then why did they fight a duel? Over you perhaps?"

"Oh! You are sweet!" she gasped, looking up into his eyes. "I wish it had been over me. But it wasn't. I've no idea why they dueled. But you want to know about my interview with Lady Margaret…" She deftly undid two breeches buttons. "Are you really the eldest brother? It's amazing to me that you can be, after all how can one make a younger brother an elder brother, if you understand my meaning? Your mother must've planned such a deception, and with the blessing of the attending physician! And how could such a circumstance be kept from your father? And then there are the servants. And why would she want to make such a switch unless she had a very good reason to do so—"

Alec stayed her hand at the third button. "I wouldn't believe all Lady Margaret told you. She is distraught with grief, and all her anger is directed against Delvin."

"But she's telling everyone of her acquaintance. She says her tongue is now free to reveal the truth, that she has no qualms about breaking a promise to your mamma, after what Edward did to her son. She's very convincing."

"A word of advice. Don't repeat to Del—"

"But I have," she answered naïvely, wriggling her hand free to slide it up the taut muscles of his arm. "I had to. It's the most extraordinary piece of gossip I've heard in ten years!"

"And his reaction?"

"I thought he would laugh off such an absurd accusation. Well, it is absurd, isn't it? He didn't. He was very rude and that's why he's gone to Selina, to teach me a lesson. Well, as far as I'm concerned, he is welcome to her! She can't know half the tricks I do. He'll have a miserable evening."

Alec grinned and shook his head at her pettishness. "I'm sure Selina can't hold a candle to you on that front."

"She can't," said Lady Gervais proudly, unhooking the front of her low cut bodice. "No one can."

"Is that so?" he said. "Then Delvin would be a fool to give you up."

She smiled saucily, and in one deft movement straddled his lap, her petticoats bunched up over her knees and her breasts spilling out of the confinement of a tight bodice. She put a hand about his neck, clutching at the satin bow that held his long hair in place while the other guided his right hand to cup an ample breast through her thin chemise. She then kissed him full on the mouth, smiling to herself in triumph that she had at last captured his interest when his thumb began to rub rhythmically against her nipple. Yet, for all that, his response was less than enthusiastic, and at the sound of a knock on the outer door he turned his head away. She was all for ignoring it and had a hand again to the buttons of his breeches when he kissed her on the forehead and gently lifted her off and put her aside. There was another knock on the door, more persistent than the first and Alec adjusted his clothing and went in answer to it.

"Damn!" she blurted out angrily, sprawling out suggestively on the sofa. She made no effort to cover herself, hoping he would deal with the interruption and come back to finish what she had started.

Alec opened the door, a hand through his tousled hair, to find a footman moving from foot to foot. Without preamble, he told Alec he was wanted immediately in the rooms occupied by Mrs. Jamison-Lewis. Then, taking a glance over Alec's shoulder at the naked woman lying across the cushions on the sofa, the footman turned on a heel and hurried away, eyes wide and unblinking.

SELINA CAREFULLY EXTRACTED A LONG PEARL-HANDLED hairpin entangled in one of her tight curls and shook out her abundant waist-length hair. "No, Evans, I'll brush it tonight," she said and took the silver-backed brush from her somber-faced personal maid. "Open the window in the bedchamber, would you?"

Why had she given in to her Aunt Olivia's pleadings and agreed to stay the weekend? A weekend of celebrations wasn't exactly the sort of social outing permitted new widows. But the Duchess of Romney-St. Neots had argued that, as long as Selina did not dance at the Fireworks Ball, no one would raise an objection to her being a house guest. The only house guest dressed in black, thought Selina with a frown. How was she going to endure a whole year dressed in widow's weeds? But she knew the answer to that. She had arranged to spend the summer with her brother Talgarth. He lived in the remote Mendip Hills and was a painter, and he had hated George Jamison-Lewis almost as much as she had hated him. She would wear Indian muslin and bright taffeta and Talgarth would make her laugh again and no one would look twice at her there. Yet the prospect of visiting her brother had lost much of its appeal since Jack's death.

She wondered if Talgarth had received her letter about Jack. Poor Jack. She missed him dreadfully. He had been her rock. If not for Jack, she was certain she'd have ended up in Bedlam before now. For all Jack's sweet placidity, he had known exactly how to manage the ill-tempered and violent George Jamison-Lewis, to the amazement of J-L's servants. But Selina knew all about her cousin's relationship with her husband. Jack had told her, and right at the beginning of her marriage. She and Jack had danced about her boudoir the day J-L was found shot dead in the wood. They had been set free. Jack's freedom lasted less than a month.

She tossed the hairbrush on the dressing table and stared critically at her reflection. She looked tired and there was no glow to her cheeks. What was she to do with this thick tangle of apricot-colored curls? Emily's gold hair shone in the sun. God help the poor girl, marrying such a vile toad; at least this toad was not a woman-hater. The change that had come over Alec's features, from talking to Emily to glancing across the room at her. She could only suppose her mere presence was enough to make him feel uncomfortable. How dare he regard her with an unforgiving eye... She turned away from the looking glass.

"Evans? I asked you to open the windows. It's too hot in here!"

"You've been thinking again," her lady's maid said stridently. "It doesn't do for you to think."

"Thank you, Evans. I shall remember that next time I feel the inner cogs taking a turn. Did you put the accounts on the table by the window?" Selina asked, slipping a flowered night robe over her cotton chemise but not bothering to button it. She went through to the bedchamber and sat at the small desk under the window where two thick ledgers, a bundle of bills tied up with black ribbon, and a standish with fresh ink had been carefully arranged. "I'll need another candle."

"You need to sleep, not fill your head with numbers," Evans lectured, roughly plumping the pillows and turning down the coverlet. "You have a man of business to do such menial tasks. I don't know why you brought those books here when you're supposed to be resting."

Selina looked over her shoulder at the older woman and smiled. "I've always had a head for figure work. And I especially enjoy these figures because they are now mine. Well, almost, once I finalize J-L's outstanding debts. Then we can start afresh." She turned back to the desk and untied the black ribbon. "That candle, Evans. If you please. Then you may go to bed." She ignored her maid's muffled noise of infuriation and settled down to an hour pouring over the last of her late husband's outstanding debts.

The candle burned too quickly in the cool night air which blew in through the open window. It had almost guttered twice, leaving a pool of hot wax in the bowl of the holder before Selina realized Evans had not returned with the requested replacement candle. She knew the woman thought she was doing her a favor by making her stop her calculations, but Selina wasn't tired enough, she needed to be exhausted before she could go to bed and sleep without dreaming. She put the ledger aside, the ink notations made in the columns still drying, and was about to fetch a candle herself when she heard a soft tread behind her.

"Thank you, Evans. Late, but just in time."

The hand that squeezed her shoulder did not belong to Evans.

TAM TOOK THE MAIN STAIRCASE UP TO MISS EMILY'S ROOMS knowing he was unlikely to meet any guests at this hour. If he did, they would be types like Lady Gervais, who wouldn't care a fig what the lackeys thought of their nocturnal wanderings. There was the usual night footman at the end of the passageway leading to Miss Emily's apartments, and Tam nodded to him as he went past.

He knocked on the furthest door of the suite of rooms. It was the door to Jenny's small bedchamber. As personal maid to Miss Emily, she had the privilege of a door off the main corridor and wasn't confined to the servant stairs to run her errands. A chambermaid answered the knock and unceremoniously closed the door in Tam's face.

Tam knocked again, and when he was bluntly told Miss Jenny was not there and to go away, he waited a moment and then opened the door, startling the chambermaid who was using Jenny's small hand mirror and comb to busily fix her hair. Only one candle burned in Jenny's bedchamber, a room with simple furnishings, feminine wall hangings and a pretty coverlet on the narrow bed. The window was shut tight against the cold night air. Tam set the porcelain dish with its flat porcelain cover on the dressing table while the chambermaid stomped her foot and hurriedly extracted a leaf from her tangled hair.

"Here. What you got there?" she demanded

"Tea for Miss Emily. For her headache," said Tam. "Where's Miss Jenny?"

"'ow should I know?" the girl answered sullenly. "I've been down in the kitchens this past 'our seein' t'things and fixin' Miss Emily's milk."

Tam nodded at the door cut into the wallpaper of the far wall that gave access to Miss Emily's rooms. "Door locked?"

"Don't know. Not tried it." She frowned as Tam crossed the room. "Eh! What y'think y'doin? You can't come bargin' in 'ere! Jenny'll be as mad as a hedgehog if she catches a lackey in 'er rooms."

"I'm not a lackey. I'm Mr. Halsey's valet. Jenny asked me to bring her the tea." He put an ear to the wallpapered door. "Is Miss Emily in her rooms?"

"Don't know, do I. I ain't been 'ere. Like I told you. I'll have to fetch more," she grumbled, looking at the mug of milk on the dressing table. "Missy don't like cold milk."

Tam bit his lip. He didn't know why, but he felt uneasy. In all probability Jenny and Miss Emily were huddled together gossiping about the dinner party. Yet it was unusual to keep the chambermaid waiting, especially when she had been sent to fetch hot milk. Why hadn't Jenny let her in to deliver it nice and hot?

"I'm goin' back to the kitchens," the girl said with a long sigh. "You'd better leave. Y'can't wait 'ere alone."

Tam stayed by the door. "Did you try and open it?"

"Not my place."

"Why don't you try the handle and see if the door's locked?"

The chambermaid shook her head and picked up the mug of milk. "It's cold."

Tam gently pulled on the handle and the door silently opened inwards. It was the chambermaid who screeched and tried to pull Tam back into the room. He shrugged her off, told her to hold her tongue and stuck his head around the door. There was no light. Something was not right. Tam had a terrible feeling all was dreadfully wrong.

The servant door at the far end of the darkened room was illuminated by the full moon and swinging wide, forced open by the air rushing up the narrow winding stair. Downstairs someone must have left a door open. The curtains billowed, letting in a gust of cold night air and the eerie glow of the full moon, giving Tam a glimpse of an overturned chair. Just as quickly the curtains were sucked back against the window frame and the room was in complete darkness again. From somewhere deep within the room there was uncontrolled sobbing. Tam slowly moved into the blackness and stumbled over the uneven carpet. He picked himself up just as the curtains billowed again and a thousand tiny lights twinkled across the floor. He felt the crunch of glass under foot and realized just what the tiny lights were.

And then the chambermaid let out a piercing scream just as

Tam reached the four-poster bed and caught a glimpse of someone tangled in the tumble of bed clothes. He pushed the girl back into Jenny's bedchamber.

"Get help! *Run*. Go! *Now*," he shouted then dashed back to the bed where Miss Emily lay sobbing face down with her arms over her head.

Emily's gown had been ripped from her back.

FIVE

"*GYPSY*," HISSED A VOICE AT SELINA'S EAR, THE HAND LEAVING her shoulder to brush a soft curl from her neck.

For a split second Selina thought it was J-L, and braced herself for the inevitable violence that accompanied her husband's infrequent and uninvited visits to her bedchamber. But her husband was dead, and having survived his unspeakable behavior, she was determined that no one would frighten or abuse her ever again. So she slapped the hand away and pushed the chair back, hoping to off-balance the intruder. She turned and came face-to-face with the Earl of Delvin.

He retreated to the bed and poured wine into two glasses from a bottle he had brought with him.

"Join me in a toast, Gypsy?" he asked, with all the aplomb of an invited guest. He held out a wine glass. When Selina refused it he put aside the bottle and her glass and sipped at his wine with a smile. "Oh, do you think I mean to poison you?"

"No," Selina answered calmly. "That form of murder is too subtle for you. Green Park is more your style."

Delvin was genuinely amused and sat down on the edge of the bed. "Yes, it is, isn't it. Poison is a woman's way; cowardly and unpredictable." He glanced at the table under the window. "In your countinghouse, Gypsy?"

Although his smile remained fixed, Selina heard the edge to his voice and smiled crookedly. "Oh, I don't think I could count all of my inheritance in one lifetime, do you?"

"Black and blue, but a wealthy widow nonetheless. It's just as well for you the magistrate found in your favor."

"Meaning?"

"We all know George blew his brains out. It wasn't a shooting accident. Suicides forfeit their inheritance. He should have been buried at the crossroads where cowards belong."

"Oh? Were you in expectation of receiving a legacy? How disappointing for you," Selina said without sympathy.

"Odd that a man who loathed and despised females bequeathed his entire fortune to the one female he hated above all others."

"Perhaps J-L had a conscience after all?" she retorted.

Delvin snorted. "George? A conscience? That's rich! Come on, *Gypsy*. Tell me: How did you get him to sign that scrap of a will just before he put a shotgun in his mouth?"

"You forget. Jack and Andrews were the only ones to witness J-L's signature."

The Earl sneered. "I'm unlikely ever to forget your insipid cousin's influence over George, Gypsy." His gaze wandered to the desk again. "I don't suppose that fool Andrews has come across that IOU?"

"No. Andrews has been through J-L's documents—and so have I," said Selina, as she closed the ledgers from his prying eyes and stacked them neatly, an eye to the guttering candle, thankful the candles in the wall sconce by the door still burned brightly enough to cast light across this half of the bedchamber. She heard the Earl swear softly, and turned to face him with a smug smile. "I'm sure a man of your substantial means can live without a simple IOU, especially now you are to marry an heiress…?"

Delvin drained his glass and put it on the bedside table next to Selina's untouched wine. "A debt is a debt and I want it repaid."

"Certainly. You need only produce J-L's IOU."

"We have been through this before, *Gypsy*. George and I shook hands on it. He gave me his word. That was good enough for me."

"Well, it isn't good enough for me!"

Delvin smiled through his teeth. "I suggest we come to some arrangement or I may be forced to extract payment. I assure you, if it comes to that, it won't be pleasant."

Selina laughed in his face. "What could you possibly do to me that would be in any way more unpleasant than the six years I've just endured?" She went to shoulder past him. "Now, if you've done threatening me…"

But the Earl blocked her exit, an arm outstretched to the wall, a long tear in the lace ruffles of his right sleeve exposing fresh deep scratches across his wrist. "You were wasted on George," he murmured, fingering the small collar of her chemise as he looked through the thin cotton fabric. "Not a man who appreciated the female form. And that you have in abundance, Gypsy. Nice and full, aren't they?"

"Take your hand off my breast, *murderer*."

"Murderer?"

"Jack—"

"Jack? Insipid, *mousy* Jack?" Delvin replied incredulously, continuing to knead her breast through the chemise, blood from his wrist smearing on the white cotton. "He had only himself to blame."

Selina pushed his hand off. "Jack would never have forced a fight on you over Emily or anyone else. And you know why."

"Do I?" He laughed in his throat and playfully pinched her nipple.

"Emily—"

"—will do as a wife. But it's you I want. I'll wager George never touched these magnificent breasts. Wasted," he whispered in her ear as he pushed the flowered robe off her shoulders and let it fall to the carpet. "Rode himself to a sweat but never once brought you to satisfaction, did he, Gypsy?" He tugged violently at the collar of the chemise, putting a long rent in the fabric and exposing the rounded milky whiteness of her left breast. "Tsk tsk. Nasty," he said without sympathy, gaze flickering over the healing welt across her bosom. "George's last beating must've been monumental. Happened just before his accident, did it?"

"As if you care," Selina spat at him, struggling to break free. Yet a hard swallow belied the anger in her dark eyes. "Poxy Cindy out of action this week?"

Delvin laughed heartily. "God! Cindy can't compare to you, sweetheart. Let's forget George's IOU and go to bed."

Selina looked up into his pale blue eyes with loathing. "*Never.*"

"Oh? Come now, Gypsy. After six miserable years you must be aching for a good rut."

"Yes, a good one. But you couldn't go the distance!"

The Earl laughed harder, enjoying her verbal sparing nearly as much as he did caressing her bare flesh. And when he kissed the base of her throat, running a hand the length of her back to cradle the roundness of her bottom, Selina finally ceased struggling and seemed to yield into his embrace. He laughed softly in triumph and lifted her onto the table, fondling her as he pushed the chemise up over her knees. He stooped to kiss both her breasts as one hand tugged frantically at the buttons of his breeches. To his surprised delight, she moved to accommodate him, opening her knees and arching her back sufficiently for her chemise to slide completely off her arms and torso to bunch at her hips, leaving her almost completely naked, and arousing him beyond the point of no return.

It took all Selina's self control to mask feelings of repulsion and nausea at having Delvin's hands upon her, but she needed him distracted enough so that she could grope behind her for the guttering candle by the window, with its bowl of hot liquid wax. She arched her back so that her torn chemise fell off her arms, giving her the freedom of movement she needed to find the loop of the candlestick holder. Using one finger in the loop, she slid the shallow bowl of melted wax across the table. Once she was sure she had a firm hold on the base, she waited, enduring Delvin's hungry fondling as he let his breeches drop to his knees and tugged up his shirt out of the way. She carefully positioned the candlestick holder precisely where she wanted it in relation to his aroused body, and then, just as he exposed himself in all his glory, she dared to smile into his eyes and dashed the hot liquid across his hard bare flesh.

His reaction was immediate and all that she hoped for. He fell back in shock, both hands between his legs as the hot wax instantly seared his tender flesh, then solidified like a second skin. He swore and stumbled to the bed, looking for something to relieve an intense stinging. He found Selina's untouched glass of wine and splashed its contents over his tortured flesh, but the burn lingered and he tried desperately to scrape off the now cold wax with shaking fingers. Fascinated, Selina watched the Earl's feeble attempts to ease the pain, her sheer relief and his look of complete shock and horror that she had dared do this to him only serving to set her off into a fit of unrestrained giggling.

Evans swept in on this scene, Alec on her heels, saying over her shoulder she knew nothing about a servant being sent to fetch him here. She had been down at the kitchens getting her mistress a glass of hot chocolate to help her sleep. She had certainly not sent for him. And her mistress could not be disturbed now, not at this late hour, and certainly not by a gentleman caller. Mrs. Jamison-Lewis was a respectable widow who kept respectable hours...

And there was the Earl of Delvin by the bed, tucking his shirt into his damp, unbuttoned breeches. The respectable widow, her face flushed with laughter, was sitting upon the desk with her crumpled chemise bunched at the hips, beautiful naked breasts on display and long shapely legs bare and swinging freely. With her bouncy ringlets in wild disorder down her back, she looked every inch a woman well satisfied. Neither she nor the Earl was aware of an intrusion until the old woman gasped in outrage, and then both reacted in very different ways.

Evans hurriedly went forward, scooped up Selina's flowered silk robe off the floor and made a great fuss of putting it about her mistress's bare shoulders, all the while muttering to herself about the outrageous liberties men took on unsuspecting and defenseless females. Selina endured the fuss because she had suffered a great shock and was wondering how best to deal with a situation that required an explanation and yet was inexplicable.

Delvin fastened the four buttons of his oyster-colored silk breeches and made a display of adjusting himself, the burning sensation between his legs suppressed at sight of his brother.

"Sweetheart, I've warned you in the past about bolting the door," he said to Selina with good-humored annoyance, a swift telling glance at Alec.

Selina stared open-mouthed at the sheer audacity of his presumption and went over to him, shooing Evans aside. "You knew he'd come," she whispered in furious disbelief. "You planned this."

Delvin winked at her, his supercilious smile widening into a grin at Selina's hot flush of defeat. "You can't expect poor Evans to keep constant watch, now can you, darling?" he lectured with a shake of his powdered head and maneuvered himself to stand between Selina and his brother, as if to shield her from prying eyes. "For modesty's sake," he added gently, "may I suggest you button your robe…?"

"How—how *dare* you do this to me!" Selina said in a choked whisper, hands balled into fists of frustrated rage. She pushed past the Earl and found herself standing before Alec in all her glorious dishevelment. She did not know which way to turn and took a step backward, a hand clutching at the front of her nightgown to cover her nakedness.

But Alec could not bring himself to look her way again. He had nothing to say. Having taken less than three steps into her bedchamber, he turned on a heel and walked out. He was completely numb.

TWO FOOTMEN CARRYING LIGHTED TAPERS RUSHED THROUGH the door of Miss Emily's bedchamber with the chambermaid close behind them. They ran around at her direction, tripping over furniture and swearing loudly in their attempt to light all the wall sconces. But no sooner was the room ablaze with light than they brought themselves up short, staring speechless at the destruction that surrounded them; and then they turned to the four-poster bed.

The chambermaid let out a great wail and threw herself at the bed. Tam, who still sat on the bed with a comforting hand on Miss Emily's arm, stood up and went to speak, but the footmen had already made up their minds as to what had gone on in this room. Seeing Miss Emily sobbing amongst the covers, her gown all twisted and torn from her shoulders, and that upstart red-haired footman, who now called himself a valet, with a hand on her was enough to stir them into action.

Before Tam could speak, one of the footmen grabbed him by the front of his worsted wool waistcoat and flung him across the room so hard that he fell against the far wall, winded. For good measure, a boot was laid into his side, just in case he decided to get up and make a run for it.

But Tam wasn't going anywhere. He got to his knees, gasping for breath, hands hugging his aching ribs, and mutely watched the two thugs retreat to the foot of the bed. He wished he'd been knocked unconscious. He wanted to look away but couldn't. One of the footmen rolled over the limp body and put an ear to the slack mouth and a hand to the pale cheek. But these actions were a mere formality, for it was obvious that the girl was dead, despite there being no apparent injury or loss of blood. Yet Tam refused to see who it was. How his ribs ached. He was sure one of them was broken. He refused to see that the lifeless form with her head curiously twisted to one side and her black hair wild about her was Jenny. His Jenny. Jenny with eyes wide open, dark-circled and yet seeing nothing.

The two footmen turned and stared at him then and he knew in an instant that not only did they think him a rapist but now he stood accused of murder. He dropped his head between his knees, ears filled with Miss Emily's quiet, aching sobs and the chamber-maid's piercing, wild screams, and prayed hard that Alec Halsey could rescue him from this nightmare.

"ALEC?! THERE YOU ARE!"

It was Sir Cosmo, an elaborately embroidered silk banyan over his nightshirt and a turban with a silver tassel atop his shaved head. He had a hand to this twisted silk affectation to stop it sliding onto his nose, because he was walking so fast he was almost running; not an easy task in yellow kid mules on terrace tiles wet from a light cold rain. He was puffing as he came to stand beside his friend and wondered how long Alec had been out in the rain. His friend's black hair was visibly damp, as was his open-necked shirt and he leaned against the marble balustrade in his shirt-sleeves, staring out into the blackness.

"The whole house… Up looking for you," Sir Cosmo managed to pant out. "Aunt Olivia… Wants you… *Subito*."

When Alec finally turned his head, Sir Cosmo wondered if he was drunk, such was the glazed faraway look in his normally sharp blue eyes.

"Why didn't anyone tell me about Jamison-Lewis?" Alec demanded in a restricted voice, hard-gripping the balustrade in an attempt to stop the tremors that coursed through his body.

Sir Cosmo blinked. "What about him?"

"What about him? Damn you! That he was a-a *wife beater*."

"Not my business."

"Yet everyone knew?"

Sir Cosmo swallowed. "Everyone knew. Yes."

"How often did it happen?"

"Alec—"

"How often?"

"There's no point to this now."

"How often did he—did he lay a hand on her?"

"Alec! For God's sake, leave it be. The brute's dead."

"Indulge me."

It was Sir Cosmo's turn to stare out into the blackness. "Enough," he said quietly. "To be honest, I don't know."

"Didn't want to know…?"

Sir Cosmo dug his cold hands deep into the pockets of his embroidered banyan and said lamely, "What goes on between husband and wife is really none of anybody's business, is it?"

Alec looked up into the night sky. "Marriage gives legitimacy to such bestial behavior, does it, Cosmo? Because they were man and wife he could hit her at will and no one gave a damn? *Jesu…*"

"We did what we could, Jack more than most, but J-L was her husband. He had rights; he owned her and he could do to her what he liked! That's it, plain and simple." Sir Cosmo let out a sigh. "Thank God he's dead and it's over with, is what I say."

The rain started to fall again, this time in big heavy drops.

"Why? Because you need no longer feel any guilt?"

Sir Cosmo blinked at him. His friend's expression of self-righteous indignation twisted his mouth into an ugly sneer. "You've got a nerve," he growled. "You ruined Selina's virtue and then abandoned her to that fate. And for the six years of her marriage you kept your distance, not caring to know what became of her. And now she's free of that monster's brutality, you decide to castigate the rest of us for not taking a stand against him? Damn you, Alec. *Damn you* for your mistreatment of her. If anyone should feel guilt it's you."

When Alec arrived at Emily's rooms, the Duchess of Romney-St. Neots was sitting on Jenny's narrow bed with her granddaughter cradled in her arms. Emily was being rocked to and fro as one does to soothe a small child. The Duchess thrust out a hand to Alec and he took it in an instant, eyes begging the question.

"She's in shock," the Duchess said, with an effort to control the tremble in her voice. "She won't speak about it. I need you to go into her bedchamber and see what you can do. Your valet... He was—he was discovered alone with her."

"Olivia, what's happened here?"

She swallowed and looked away. "I don't rightly know. And I can't bring myself to think the unthinkable."

It was then that Alec really looked at Emily and was startled. She was still dressed in the gown she had worn at dinner, with the rubies about her throat, but the petticoats were crumpled and torn off her shoulders; her hair was a mess of tangled curls and dislodged powder. He must have stood there staring at her for an age because the Duchess lifted her head and said in a broken voice,

"For pity's sake, go and see what that boy has done in there!"

Enough candles blazed in the bedchamber to light a cathedral. The room was in disarray. Shards of broken glass from a curio cabinet littered the carpet. A chair was upturned. Ink from a fallen standish had splashed up the side of the bureau and ruined the pretty wallpaper by the window. And there was Tam, huddled by the window seat and guarded over by a liveried servant who had his heel dug into the boy's back to keep him still. One sharp word from Alec and the footman reluctantly removed his boot, but he continued to hover menacingly over the valet until Alec ordered him out of the room.

"But, sir, Mr. Neave said he was to be watched, in case he made a run for it!"

"Out."

The servant eyed the cowering boy with resentment. "But, sir, y'can see he's run amuck!"

Alec opened the door with a jerk and the servant shuffled out, adding sullenly that he had his orders and he would stay by the door until Mr. Neave told him otherwise. Alec shut the door in his face and was about to cross to Tam when the unbelievable caught his eye. Jenny lay on her back on the carpet at the foot of the four-poster bed, a long strand of black hair across her pale face and with eyes open and unblinking at the ornate plaster ceiling.

Alec glanced away then looked again, as if the action of closing his eyes would bring her back to life. He squatted to gently close her eyelids, and removed the strand of hair so her face seemed more at peace and somehow content. It was then he noticed the bruising about her throat and jaw. Yet there was no blood from a wound to indicate what had expelled life. It would take a physician to determine cause of death. That it was no accident seemed obvious enough, what with the room a shambles and Emily in such distress. But why murder a lady's maid? What had gone on in this room? Shock. Anger. Frustration. All made it impossible for Alec to think clearly and he dared not cloud his thoughts with possible scenarios. A physician needed to be fetched and Jenny's body moved to a more dignified setting. He would have to talk to Emily, as painful as that would be for her, and to the lackeys and the chambermaid, and most importantly, to his valet.

He suddenly felt the cold damp chill from standing out in the drizzle and stood up, rubbing his eyes. Every muscle ached. And when he was tired, he needed his gold-rimmed spectacles to see and thus ward off an inevitable headache from eye strain. He looked about for something to place over Jenny's body and decided on the coverlet. It was then that Tam sprang up from the floor and rushed forward and tried to tug the coverlet out of Alec's hands.

"Don't touch her! Leave her be! The physician, he'll know what to do for her! To wake her up! Leave her be. Please, sir!"

Alec continued to strip the bed. "I'm sorry, Tam. She needs to be covered so she can be moved."

"No one is movin' her! Not even you!"

"Let go of the coverlet. You're being unreasonable. There's nothing anyone can do for her here."

"We've got to wait for the physician. He'll know what to do."

"Yes, he will. But he can't examine the body here—"

"It's not a body! It's Jenny. Can't you see that? *Can't you?*"

"Yes, Tam, I can," Alec said gently, and with the coverlet free of Tam's grasp placed it over Jenny's lifeless form. "But she isn't going to wake up... I'm truly very sorry..."

Tam stared at the shapeless coverlet and then at Alec, his eyes blinded by tears. "S-sorry? You're *sorry?* Well it's too late for that! She's gone and there's nothin' anybody can do about it! What do you care? Miss Emily can get another maid. Three if she wants. What's the loss of a maid to the likes of—"

"I'll give you your grief, Tam, but I won't stand for your impertinence," Alec said sharply. "You're being selfish and unreasonable. You know very well what Jenny meant to Emily and to St. Neots House!"

The boy's bottom lip quivered. Tears slid down his hot cheeks. Alec took a step toward him but his look of concern and sorrow was too much for Tam. The boy turned away and threw himself on the window seat, hugging a pillow to his stomach and crying until his whole body was racked with great, dry, shuddering sobs. When he was quiet Alec sat down beside him.

"Tam, I need to know what happened in here. And you must tell me everything and it must be the truth."

"I didn't k-kill her. I didn't! You've got to believe me! I didn't do it!" Tam said in an agonized whisper and began to sob anew.

"I believe you. Perhaps a drink would settle your nerves?"

The boy nodded and sniffed.

Alec returned to Jenny's bedchamber. The Duchess's lady-in-waiting, Peeble, was there. She had brought a tray of drinks. He helped himself to a brandy and poured a mug of punch for his valet. He saw that Emily was taking her milk and signaled for Peeble. The maid came at once, face devoid of emotion.

"I need two strong and discreet footmen," he said in a low voice, "and a room in which to put Jenny until the physician arrives. And send someone to fetch my spectacles. There are several pairs in a drawer of my dressing table." He glanced at Emily. "Has she said anything?"

Peeble shook her head.

Alec nodded and returned to Tam. When the valet had drunk most of the punch Alec questioned him about what had gone on in Emily's bedchamber, but Tam knew little. He recounted everything that had happened from the time the chambermaid had opened the door to him, to finding Emily face down on her bed and the footmen bursting into the dark room and jumping to the wrong conclusions because he happened to be giving Miss Emily a comforting pat on the back. The chambermaid had only made the situation worse for him by screaming and carrying on and being too overcome to be of any help in verifying his story.

"Where is the chambermaid now, Tam?"

"I don't know, sir. She fainted when she saw Jenny's—when she saw Jenny and they carried her out. Sir," Tam said quietly and looked up at his master sheepishly, "you do believe me, don't you, sir?"

Alec smiled and squeezed the boy's shoulder. "Yes. You obviously disturbed whoever attacked her and frightened him off before any real harm could come to Miss Emily."

"But I didn't disturb anyone, sir," Tam stated. "He—well, Miss Emily…"

"Go on."

Tam looked into the empty cup. "Sir. The murdering dog had already gone. The servant door to the stairs was wide open and making a great racket banging against the wall, and Miss Emily was on the bed sobbing. I saw in the moonlight her clothes were torn and…" He looked up at Alec. "Don't you see, sir? Whatever happened to Miss Emily had already happened before I got to her."

Alec wiped his mouth. "*Mon Dieu.*"

"Do you think—I mean—Why did he kill Jenny?"

"I don't know, Tam."

"I know one thing!" Tam said fiercely. "I'd like to kill the poxy bastard!"

The appearance of two burly lackeys in the doorway gave him a start. He looked to his master, then at the coverlet spread out over Jenny on the carpet and turned away. He did not want to see them pick her up. He could not bear it if they fumbled or the coverlet slid off. "Sir. I-I need to wash up."

"Of course," said Alec. With an arm about Tam's shoulders, he led him into the next room, keeping his back to the two men who silently went about their business. "You can go to bed."

"No, sir. I couldn't sleep. I'd prefer to do something to help. Anything but sleep."

"There is one thing you can do. Amongst your potions and powders do you have an opiate, a mixture of some sort, for Emily? I want her to sleep uninterrupted tonight. No dreams. No nightmares. Do you understand me, Tam?"

The valet nodded eagerly. "I know just the mixture, sir. I'll be back as soon as I can."

A disruption in the corridor had the Duchess on her feet. Peeble was arguing in frantic whispers with someone in the shadows. It was Neave. When he saw his mistress, there was no further argument from his lips and he looked at her as if he expected a moment of her time. Peeble was all for shutting the door in his face.

"Neave," the Duchess stated, "there's been an accident. Yes, a tragic accident. Miss Emily's maid, Jenny—Jenny fell down the back steps and-and broke her neck. It's a horrid business, as you can imagine."

"An accident, Your Grace," the butler repeated. Whether he believed her or not she did not care, and he did not seem to mind as long as some explanation was offered him for all the late-night servant activity and below-stairs air of mystery. "If I can be of any assistance, Your Grace?"

"No. Yes. Yes, you can. But not now. It's all happened so—so—"

"—unexpectedly, Your Grace?"

"Of course it was unexpected!" she snapped. "What I do want is for you to make certain there is no undue gossip and speculation. And I don't mean just from my household."

"Not a word will be spoken out of turn, Your Grace," he said with a glare at Peeble's tight-lipped countenance.

"It's all these others we have in the house at the moment. I don't want them meddling and asking questions. I don't want my guests disturbed by an—an *incident* which concerns no one but us."

"I perfectly understand, Your Grace. May I express the household's deepest regrets at the loss of Miss Jenny. She was well-liked by all. It certainly is a tragedy, Your Grace."

"Thank you, Neave. And should you hear—while going about your duties, of course—hear anything of interest from either servant or guest, I would appreciate your confidence."

The butler nodded gravely though his eyes shone triumphantly at Peeble, who instantly turned away into the shadows. "I shall of course wait up for the physician. I presume Sir John…?"

"No. I didn't disturb Oliphant. The village doctor was called some time ago. God knows where the wretched man is!" She dismissed him with a view of her back and called for her maid. "Nothing to Charlotte or Sybilla. Not a word."

Peeble pursed her thin lips. "Of course not, Your Grace."

The Duchess eyed her suspiciously. "Don't cross me, Janet. I know what you're thinking, but I am perfectly capable of handling this without my daughters' interference. I have to be. Emily needs me—needs all of us—to be strong. So don't pamper her, not outwardly. Understand me?"

Peeble nodded, saying abruptly, "I shall see to Miss Emily's night things," and disappeared before her mistress caught sight of her wet eyes.

The Duchess returned to Jenny's room just as Alec closed the door to Emily's bedchamber. "You sent the boy off then?" she said disapprovingly.

"Yes, Olivia," Alec replied evenly, drawing her aside so that Emily would not overhear their conversation. "He's told me everything he knows, and despite what those two thuggish footmen think to the contrary, I'm convinced of his innocence. An hysterical chambermaid, too overwrought to explain the situation, caused those over-zealous idiots to jump to the wrong conclusion about Tam's presence in Emily's bedchamber. The intruder had already escaped via the servant's stair, and Jenny was dead before Tam even entered the room. I'm confident Emily will assure me this is so when she is capable and ready to talk to us."

The Duchess stared at Alec then nodded. "If you are satisfied, then so am I. He may be a little misguided and a possible horse thief, but I don't think the boy inherently evil. I would hate to think he had anything to do with this horrid business." When Alec slipped on a pair of gold-rimmed spectacles the Duchess blinked. "When did this affectation take root?"

"If it were only that," he answered with a tired laugh, looking down his bony nose and over the rims. "My dear Olivia, you'll be disappointed to know I am an imperfect Adonis; my eyesight is failing me. Reading the printed page unaided is a thing of the past. Hideous, aren't they?" He glanced at Emily who still sat on the bed, wrapped in a shawl and drinking hot chocolate, staring blankly before her. "Emily sleeping with you tonight?"

"With a monster in my own home?" The Duchess snorted. "In my bed!"

Emily looked up at Alec then and said, "Eyeglasses make you look bookish; like an Oxford don."

"So you think? I don't know whether to be flattered or deflated," he said calmly, though his heart gave an odd leap at Emily's sudden animation. "You said once they made me appear distinguished," he continued casually. "Do you remember Cosmo laughed at that? The impudence of the man when he sports two quizzing glasses about his neck!"

"He just wishes he had a reason to do so," said Emily, sitting up and brushing the hair out of her eyes. "He laughed more because you were most annoyed we caught you wearing them. You really did look fit to strangle him, to—to—" She swallowed convulsively, a shaking hand to her mouth. She put aside the empty chocolate mug. "I'm sorry. I'm such a coward. I—I—*Oh, Alec.*"

"Emily."

She flew off the bed and into his open arms to be gathered up in a protective embrace.

"I—I didn't know what to do," she said haltingly. "He-He put his mouth over mine when I screamed and then—and he-he *kissed* me! Ugh, it was *horrid*. I couldn't breath. And then he—he pushed down on me... He wanted me to lie still. He wanted—He ripped my gown. I should've fought harder. I should've found the strength to push him off—I'm such a-a coward."

Alec hugged her closer, stroking her tangle of powdered hair, feeling sick to the stomach by such revelations, yet remaining calm for her sake.

"You're safe now," he said gently. "Your grandmother and I will keep you safe. No one will harm you ever again. That I promise you." He glanced over her powdered head at the Duchess and wasn't at all surprised that Emily's halting confession had greatly affected her grandmother. The Duchess had a shaking hand to her mouth to stifle a cry of outrage and was doing her best to remain upright and stoic, but nothing could hide the desolation in her tired eyes. "Emily, do you think you could help your grandmother to her rooms? She's much too frail to be up at this—"

"I beg your pardon—" interrupted the Duchess, not quick on the uptake until Alec glared at her significantly and then at Emily, and she shut her mouth tight.

"It's been a very tiring and long day for her," he enunciated with a smile at the Duchess. "And you know how possessive Peeble is of your grandmother's health."

To the Duchess's great surprise, Emily nodded and came over to take her arm. "Come, Grandmamma. We don't want Peeble fussing at us, do we?"

"No… No, I couldn't bear that; not tonight," answered the Duchess, choking back tears. "My dear boy, will you—will you take care of-of everything?"

"Of course," he said quietly, herding them both to the door that led on to the passageway. "Tam has gone to fetch something to help you sleep; you are both to take whatever concoction he gives you without question. Understand?"

At that Emily turned in her grandmother's embrace to look at Alec. "Please thank him for me. I-I don't think I can—not yet. He–he found me and was very kind to stay with me until Grand-mamma came."

The Duchess and Alec exchanged a significant look, and Alec kissed Emily's hand. "Tam will turn pink with pleasure to hear you say so."

AT THE BREAKFAST TABLE THE NEXT MORNING ALL ANYONE could talk about was the accidental death of Emily's maid; how could the poor girl break her neck on a servant stair she must have run up and down a hundred times a day? And of all the nights to have taken a tumble! Of course it was to be expected the engagement celebrations would continue, but one wondered how the bride-to-be would bear up under the strain of losing her personal maid in such tragic circumstances.

Into these ramblings about unthinking servant behavior and preparations for the Fireworks Ball, Alec arrived, very late for breakfast and the last of the house guests to do so. The majority had already tossed aside their napkins, but still stood about discussing whether to ride out or spend the time before dinner in a game of cards in the Long Gallery. A footman set clean cutlery before the latecomer and poured him out a dish of coffee, but Alec barely noticed. Nor did he acknowledge the several people who lingered over their coffee dishes. His thoughts were preoccupied with the late-night visit of the village doctor.

Though not a great and knighted physician like Sir John

Oliphant, Henry Oakes was nevertheless nobody's fool, and Alec did not treat him as one.

Oakes gave it as his opinion that Jenny had suffered a heavy blow to the head that had been sufficient to kill her. He had discovered pinkish red fluid leaking from her ear that he suspected meant her brain had been injured, but there was no wound to be found, and her skull was not smashed in. Oakes was honest enough to admit that it was beyond him to know whether murder had been the intruder's intention. Perhaps the intruder had just wanted to shut the girl up and had been too heavy-handed with her; witness the bruising about her throat and jaw, as if a strong hand had grabbed and held her there before throwing her away like a rag doll, intentionally hitting her head up against the bed post, or carelessly in that direction so that the outcome was the same.

Oakes signed the death certificate, writing as cause of death a broken neck. He doubted the authorities in London would think it worth their while to make inquiries into the suspicious death of a lady's maid, so he wrote in the word 'accidental' for good measure; far better for the poor girl to be buried peacefully.

He didn't ask Alec for any explanations, but Alec told him all he knew without giving him an ounce of his own thoughts. The man simply nodded. He was all for leaving the matter in Alec's hands, or more specifically, in the hands of the Duchess of Romney-St. Neots. He wanted no part in an investigation for murder, intentional or otherwise, and opined that it was unlikely the villain would be caught, saying that in such domestic matters involving the nobility, the pack stuck together closer than a bee to pollen.

Alec was inclined to agree. Yet he wondered if the man would have been so complacent had the victim been one of the Duchess's guests rather than one of her servants. But Alec did not argue with him, although he knew his Uncle Plant would have taken the physician to task, whatever the hour or circumstance. He was just grateful for the man's time. And he was right. The authorities in

London would think it a waste of time to look into the suspicious circumstances surrounding the death of a lady's maid.

Alec covered a yawn, wishing he'd had a few more hours of sleep, and sipped at his coffee. He was so deep in thought that it was not until Lady Charlotte's nasal voice carried the length of the table that he realized he was not eating alone. He went to the sideboard hoping to fill his empty stomach with food, but the sight of Lord Andrew Macara dishing up a large helping of deviled kidneys and kippers ruined his appetite. He settled for hot rolls and more strong black coffee, unaware all eyes were focused in his direction.

"As I said to Sybilla earlier," Lady Charlotte intoned in a clear, loud voice, "Mamma has always spoiled that child. She did the same with Madeleine, and look where that got her."

"Florence, isn't it?" Macara asked innocently and was glared at by his wife.

"Venice. If you must know. Venice and an impoverished Italian count. Hardly a fitting end for the daughter of an English Duke, is it, Sybilla?"

"Hardly fitting at all," murmured Lady Sybilla.

"Impoverished, Italian, and dashingly handsome," added Selina Jamison-Lewis with a conspiratorial twinkle across the table at her friend. "Don't you agree, Sybilla?"

"Oh, yes," breathed Lady Sybilla and giggled into her napkin.

Lady Charlotte sat up very straight. "Nonsense! He's an Italian. Thank God Madeleine had the good sense not to give him children. No one was more appalled than I when she had the bad manners to give birth to Emily. Not that Emily isn't a darling girl. She is. But she lacks something. Call it breeding for want of a better word. Not that one can blame her. It's all Mamma's fault. But the fact the maid broke her silly neck hardly necessitates Emily spending the night with Mamma." She gave a forced brittle laugh bordering on the hysterical. "Next she will expect us all to go into mourning for the wretched maid!"

"Not all of us, but Emily certainly," Selina answered tersely.

"The poor girl has just lost someone very dear to her, and in tragic circumstances. She has every right to her grief."

"It is only the tragedy of your circumstances which makes you defend Emily's absurd behavior, Mrs. Jamison-Lewis," Lady Charlotte responded with acid sweetness.

Selina put her dish on its saucer. "You think I gain any pleasure from wearing these hypocritical garments?"

"Very fetching hypocritical garments," murmured Macara, with the eye of a jaded connoisseur. He admired Selina's dark velvet low-cut gown and the fichu of thin silver tissue pinned into place over her deep bosom with a pearl and diamond circle brooch. "Black suits you, madam."

"Thank you, sir," Selina said sweetly, and to annoy her admirer's fuming wife, leaned in to whisper loudly in his lordship's ear, "It's Prussian Blue, but that will be our little secret."

"Prussian Blue?" inquired Lady Sybilla with a sigh. "How lovely."

"What I think—" began Lady Charlotte and was rudely cut short.

"Pardon me, Madam, but what we think hardly matters," Alec stated as he poured himself out a dish of coffee. "Mrs. Jamison-Lewis is in the right: Emily has lost someone very dear to her. Such a tragedy requires tolerance and understanding from us all."

"Hear! Hear!" agreed Macara, little realizing he had just crossed over into the enemy's camp. A glare from his wife sent him back behind the pages of an outstretched newssheet.

"I'm not disputing the tragedy of it, Mr. Halsey," Lady Charlotte said freezingly. "But perhaps it is you who do not understand —unaccustomed as you are to polite society—that there are certain occasions, certain topics, that one does not bare to all the world. Of course, it is hardly your fault you were disowned by your own mother and brought up by a pagan uncle who holds to barbaric beliefs."

"Are you telling me, my lady," Alec said with extreme politeness, "that because St. Neots House is full of guests, Emily has no right to her grief?"

"Precisely. It is the height of bad manners for her to refuse to do her duty. She can leave her grieving for private moments."

At this Selina couldn't stifle a laugh of disbelief. "Isn't it also the height of bad manners and very un-Christian of us to be discussing this topic at all, and especially at the breakfast table?"

Lady Charlotte ignored her, adding one last barb. "Had I the governing of her, she would be at this table now. She has even refused the solicitations of her betrothed! It defies reasoning."

"My sympathy is with your children, madam," Selina said curtly, pushing back her chair, a liveried footman quick to catch it before it crashed to the parquetry.

"Wouldn't waste my sympathies there," was Lord Andrew Macara's opinion of his own children from behind the newssheet. "Hen-hearted, the lot of 'em."

Selina bestowed a smile upon his lordship as she shook out her petticoats. She needed fresh air, and Alec's presence at the table—that he deliberately avoided looking her way—was the last straw to an altogether tedious breakfast. Besides, the Duchess had requested she meet with her privately in the rose garden. She excused herself, saying to Macara as she swept to the French doors, "Don't forget our croquet match, my lord…"

"Wouldn't miss it for the world, Madam!" he replied with a tobacco-stained smile as he tossed aside the folded newssheet and stood. "Damn shame about the maid. Nice girl as I recall."

"But, Macara, you must see that Emily can't allow the death of a domestic to overshadow her engagement celebrations," Lady Charlotte explained coolly. "What would Lord Delvin think?"

"Think less of her for not having feelings, I'd say," was her husband's blunt opinion. He drew out an engraved gold slim-line box that contained his precious cheroots. "I just don't understand it. Girl lived here all her life. Was always running about the place."

"Most probably tripped over her petticoats," Lady Charlotte grumbled. "Ungrateful wench."

Macara suddenly addressed himself to Alec as he put an unlit cheroot to the corner of his mouth. "My man said it was your man who found the maid."

Alec returned his open look. "Yes."

"Bit of a shock for the lad," Macara persisted. "He's new, isn't he? Your valet. Was an under-footman here. Quite young."

Alec agreed but did not elaborate. He wondered if his lordship was trying to unsettle him or was merely airing his curiosity.

"My man said the rumor is Neave ain't telling the whole story. And a lackey who works in the kitchens told my man it was your man who found little Emily's maid with her neck broken.

"Tam found Jenny's body, yes."

"The boots says your man was too fond of little Emily's maid. My man—"

"Your man ever thought of becoming a Bow Street Runner, my lord?" Alec asked politely.

Macara gave a bark of laughter. "Fact is, his brother's one. Ha! I know it's a lot of dishwater, but I thought you'd want to know what's being bandied about below stairs."

"Thank you," Alec answered evenly and collected the coffee pot from the sideboard. "Anyone for another dish?"

Macara declined, finally giving in to his craving, and stepped onto the terrace to smoke his cheroot, leaving Alec alone with the two sisters. He brought the silver coffee pot over to Lady Sybilla, amused that when he picked up her dish, she managed a shy *thank you* but could not make eye contact. "Her petticoats were all torn and she had bruises, y'know."

"Good God, Sybilla! You saw the body?" Lady Charlotte was horrified.

Lady Sybilla blinked. "Body? Whose body? Emily's petticoats were torn. I saw them draped over a chair in Mamma's dressing room. Peeble gathered them up as if she didn't want me to see them. But I saw the bruises on her legs—"

"Bruises?" demanded Lady Charlotte, glancing at Alec to find him staring fixedly at her sister. "What are you blathering about,

Sybilla? It's the maid who broke her silly neck. Show some sense!"

"I know what I saw," Lady Sybilla said with a trembling lip. She looked across at Alec, this time bravely meeting his gaze. "I know it was the maid who broke her neck. Mamma told me. But Emily had the most shocking bruises on her legs. I saw them when Peeble was helping her to dress. I know what I saw. You believe me, don't you, Mr. Halsey?"

"Of course."

Lady Sybilla was unable to hold his gaze. "I only wish…We… Selina and I were only saying the other day how we wished Emily had chosen more wisely. To be sure Lord Delvin is an earl and he cuts a fine figure, but I—but we-we would've preferred *you* to have offered for her."

"Sybilla! You-you *simpleton*. How dare you express such an outrageous opinion!" demanded Lady Charlotte, who had shot to her feet so fast and in such anger that her chair fell to the floor with a clatter. "Preferred? *Preferred* a foreign office flunky to a peer of the realm? Emily has chosen very wisely, very wisely indeed. Delvin's an earl of unimpeachable character, while his younger brother has few prospects, no title and is a sad rake. You talk nonsense because you are so morosely infatuated with his libertine good looks that you would prostitute yourself to him at the expense of your family and your husband. What about the dear Admiral, Sybilla? Have you no thought for dearest Charles, who is somewhere far out to sea? Sybilla! Come back here! How dare you run off in that manner! *Sybilla*."

SIX

THE EARL OF DELVIN STEPPED OFF THE TERRACE VIA THE French doors leading into the breakfast room, Sir Cosmo in tow. He was not his courteous self and barely controlled his temper when a sobbing Lady Sybilla pushed past him without a word of apology. She was closely followed by Lady Charlotte, who parried with the Earl for the door until he stood still and she was able sweep past him, only for her to bump into Sir Cosmo, who offered profuse apologies but was ignored by both ladies.

Supremacy for the French doors offered Alec some light relief and he was able to collect himself enough to greet his brother coolly, although his face betrayed a heightened color.

"I want to know your movements of last evening," Delvin demanded of Alec without preamble.

"Just up? Or have you already breakfasted?" Alec replied jovially. "Good morning, Cosmo."

"I don't want any of your diplomat's tongue!" Delvin growled. "Just tell me what I want to know!"

Sir Cosmo looked uncomfortable. "Perhaps I should leave…?" he muttered lamely, not meeting Alec's eye and retreating a step.

Delvin caught at his silken sleeve, eyes never wavering from his brother's face. "No. I want you to hear what he has to say for himself. Well, *Second*?"

Alec raised his brows but remained mute.

"Tell me," Delvin said through gritted teeth. "Tell me where you were last night, damn you!"

"Naturally I am flattered by your curiosity," Alec drawled, "but my habits are none of your concern."

Delvin brought his fist down hard on the sideboard. Plates rattled. "Don't be insolent with me! I won't stand for it!"

Alec shrugged and turned a shoulder in dismissal.

The Earl's face went livid with rage. Whereas he had set out to intimidate his brother he found himself in a few short sentences losing control of a situation of his own making. He willed himself to be calm. It wouldn't do to appear out of control before he had even begun. He took out his snuffbox; the elaborate act of taking a pinch of snuff up one nostril helped calm him.

"Perhaps if I tell you I have just come from an interview with the Duchess, you may change your mind?" Delvin said smoothly. "She requested to see me as soon as possible this morning. I found her deeply upset and troubled." He glanced at Sir Cosmo. "It took me a considerable time to pacify her."

"I'm sure it did," Alec murmured.

"Is it to do with this maid business?" asked Sir Cosmo, pouring himself out a dish of coffee for want of something to do but look uncomfortable and out of place.

"That is only the half of it, my friend," said the Earl with gravity. "I don't suppose you've had a chance to speak with the Duchess?" When Sir Cosmo shook his head, Delvin nodded gravely and gripped Sir Cosmo's padded shoulder, causing Alec to roll his eyes at the performance. "I suspect she is still in great shock. Very difficult for her to speak about it... I'm in shock myself. Reason for my barging in here. But when you know what's happened I'm sure you will forgive my lack of manners." He took a turn about the long room, another pinch of snuff inhaled in a leisurely fashion. "I still can't believe it. It doesn't seem real or possible. When Her Grace was able to collect herself enough to tell me—which naturally she would confide in me as Emily's intended husband—I didn't believe it at first. I couldn't. I was stunned with disbelief. I was—"

"I'm sure there is a point to your performance?" interrupted Alec. "If you want a sympathetic audience I think you have it."

Delvin viewed him with distaste. "You have the coarse sensibilities of Uncle Plant."

"Thank you. He would be flattered to hear you say so. But you are keeping Cosmo in suspense."

"Your flippant manner in this disgusts me!"

"As your melodramatic performance does me."

"You think it nothing to be dramatic about, when a young girl is violated in her own home?" asked Delvin in a thin voice. "Or perhaps you have reason to pass this violation off as something all too commonplace? Perhaps you would prefer we ignore it as a trifle? No doubt you have your reasons. I'm sure you understand my meaning."

Alec stared at him, unblinking. "I beg you to elaborate. In fact, I am eager for you to do so."

The brothers faced one another, one tall, dark-haired and angular, the other of middling height, fleshy and very fair; a contrast in every way. Sir Cosmo's mind's eye saw the thick air of hatred that separated these two related strangers. He coughed self-consciously.

"Pardon me, but did I hear you right, Ned? A girl was violated? Emily's maid?"

"Not the maid," Delvin replied. "No. She was just part of a more sinister purpose…"

Sir Cosmo looked at one brother and then the other. "The girl broke her neck on the stairs, didn't she?" In the silence which followed he added, "Is that why the Duchess sent out the servant regiment for you last night, Alec?"

"Yes."

"Ah? Now that is a *most* interesting piece of information," drawled Delvin. "Did you know, Cosmo, that last night some scoundrel forced his way into Emily's bedchamber? A scoundrel staying under this roof forced himself into a young girl's bedchamber—My God, I can hardly bring myself to tell you." He put his hands to his face. "It is so shocking a circumstance. It is beyond belief that someone would dare to—to…" He looked up and turned away to collect himself, a hand to the sideboard to steady himself. "Excuse me. Cosmo, but I cannot speak of it without emotion…"

Alec stepped into the breech. His annoyance at his brother's performance made him sound cold and detached. "Emily was attacked last night. Some scoundrel tried to rape her."

Sir Cosmo felt as if he had been struck in the face. He stuttered for something to say. "The devil! What monster… Who… What-what happened, Ned? Alec?" He fumbled for his snuffbox. "Dear God, that poor sweet child… And the maid—*murdered?*"

"So it seems," Alec replied quietly. "My valet possibly disturbed the intruder before…" His voice trailed off and it was his turn to look awkward. Unconsciously he ran a hand through his hair, trying to find the words to continue. "I don't know much more than that. Emily was given an opiate to make certain she had a restful night's sleep, and I haven't had a chance to speak with Olivia or Emily this morning."

"Nor will you," snarled the Earl. "I forbid you to go near her!"

"Now, Ned," Sir Cosmo said soothingly, "I know you're rattled but you can't forbid—"

"I can and I will."

Alec smiled. "She's not your wife—yet."

Delvin's fists clenched. "You are devoid of all decency! You heard him, Cosmo! You shall bear witness."

"I'm sorry, Ned. Witness to what?"

"Witness to his depravity!" The Earl sneered. "I've no proof yet. But I'll get it! How convenient it was your valet who disturbed this scoundrel. How convenient he happened to be lurking about Emily's apartments at that precise moment. I know all about your valet. He was apprenticed to a convicted sodomite; a worthless piece of scum who traded in male favors. That's the sort of company you keep, isn't it, Second? You're depraved. You lust after Selina Jamison-Lewis and can't have her, just as you lust after my bride and she too is now out of your reach. How do you manage to slake your thirst, eh? Is your boy an adequate substitute? Does he give satisfaction? Well, *does he*?"

"Steady on, Ned! Steady on! You're distraught, naturally. Who wouldn't be? It's a shocking business, but to take it out on your brother. To accuse him of—of—Well, it's just not done! It's ludicrous besides."

"Ask him, then! Ask him if he doesn't want Emily for himself. Ask him if he doesn't think of bedding her. Ask him if he doesn't hate me because she preferred me to him. Ask him what he was doing last night when this monster forced himself on my future wife. Well, Second? Speak up! Don't just stand there putting on a brave face. Tell Cosmo your whereabouts. Tell him you don't care in the least that it will be your elder brother in her bed on her wedding night. Eh, Second? Tell him."

Alec stood rigid. How he wanted to strike his brother's sneering face, to give back measure for measure. Yet he did not want him to see how deeply his words had wounded him. Thus he set his jaw and silently counted to ten.

The Earl smiled at Sir Cosmo. "You see. He can't answer you."

Sir Cosmo ignored Delvin, saying to Alec quietly, "It's all right, Alec. Nothing—nobody—could ever make me believe—"

Alec cut him off. Far from appearing angry he looked concerned.

"Dear me, Edward, you really do fear me. Does my very existence prey on your conscience?" He shook his head, hands shoved deep in the pockets of his frock coat, broad shoulders slightly hunched over with embarrassment. "I love Emily," he said to Sir Cosmo quietly, "and there was a time when I did hope to marry her, but—"

Delvin gave a half-laugh of disbelief. "—now that you've ruined her you don't want her any more? You piece of *filth*."

"I certainly won't stand by and let you marry her," Alec enunciated bitterly.

"Gentlemen! Gentlemen! Please! Let's not—"

"You can't tell Cosmo where you were last night because it was you who forced yourself on—"

Sir Cosmo growled. "That's enough, Ned! I won't have you spouting balderdash about your brother! When you come to your senses you'll regret—"

"I regret *nothing*. Answer me, *Second*. Where were you last night?"

"Your purpose in this is so transparent it's laughable," Alec said dismissively.

"You raped Emily because you wanted your revenge on me!"

"Revenge? Don't be absurd," Alec said coldly. "Your hatred of me is making you appear ridiculous."

"Then tell us where you went after you so rudely barged in on me *in flagrante delicto*."

Sir Cosmo stared wide eyed at the brothers. "*In flagrante delicto?*" He gave Delvin a friendly nudge. "You sly dog, Ned."

Alec scoffed at his brother's small mindedness. "You think because I caught you out that I immediately went off to Emily's bedchamber to avenge myself? You're pathetic." Alec turned on a heel. "Cosmo, excuse me…"

Delvin grabbed his brother's arm. "Stay where you are! I haven't finished with you yet."

Alec stared at the Earl's hand. "How dare you," he drawled and shrugged him off, a nod to a hovering footman who came up to him then, and in a whispered aside informed him the Duchess awaited him in the rose garden.

Delvin, who had let go at the tone of command in his brother's voice, instantly regretted having done so. He was infuriated to think Alec had once again gained the upper hand. "Damn you!"

he thundered, following his brother across the room. "Stay where you are and answer me!"

Alec stared at his brother then, face white. "Where were you in the time between leaving the drawing room and arriving at Mrs. Jamison-Lewis's bedchamber? Oh, spare Cosmo your look of offended sensibility that I mention the lady by name. I'm sure your sordid little affair is well-known in your circle."

Sir Cosmo regarded the Earl anew, and the silly grin was replaced by a storm of mixed emotions. "Ned. Not Selina. Never Selina…"

"Believe what you like!" the Earl threw at him as he lunged for Alec, but he recoiled when his brother took a decided step toward him, remembering their one-sided encounter in the hallway. "You can't answer me because you're guilty! And don't think to use your valet as an alibi. He's in this with you! But I'll find out! If not from you then from him: He'll have a price. Don't turn your back on me, *damn you*. Where were you last night? Answer me!"

Alec looked over his shoulder as he quietly closed the door. "Entertaining your mistress."

THE ROSE GARDEN WAS THE OLDEST SECTION OF GARDENS AT St. Neots House. With a moss-covered stone wall on three sides and beds that had been laid out in Queen Mary's time, and little altered since, it was private and inaccessible. No coincidence then that at the gate two workmen were repairing flagstones. They tipped their hats to Alec and continued on with their work.

The air was heavy with scent and a light breeze came up off the Thames. Altogether an idyll he had no desire to disturb. He waited a little way off from the small group, in no hurry to interrupt the animated discussion on rose varieties. He needed those few moments to calm himself.

In the breakfast room he had come close to accusing his brother of exactly what he was being accused of himself. He had no proof, no reason to think he was the intruder and when he thought about it he knew it to be logically absurd. Delvin had everything in his favor as it was. To jeopardize it all in that way was indeed the act of a madman. For his brother to accuse him was no surprise. Even if Delvin did not really believe Alec to be the rapist, an opportunity to ridicule and belittle him, to cast suspicion in his direction, all to strengthen his own position with Emily and distance Alec from her and her family and friends, was an opportunity not to be passed up.

He hoped Delvin wasn't the intruder. He might be estranged from him, loathe and distrust him, but he did not want to think him capable of raping an innocent girl and killing her maid. Just as he did not want to believe his brother capable of luring a friend into a duel for the sole purpose of killing him. As for Delvin's affair with Selina, this cut him to the quick and more than he cared to acknowledge. Watching her now as she talked to Emily amongst the flowerbeds he felt a curious lump form at the back of his throat.

They were a contrast in every way: Emily dressed prettily in a simple muslin gown without hoops, her blonde curls as bright as the sun, she smiling at something Selina whispered in her ear—it was easy to think the events of the previous night just a hideous nightmare; and Selina, her mass of tight apricot curls framing a flawless complexion, the blue-black of her velvet gown with its many layered petticoats of silver tissue and gauze tippet of the same shimmering fabric, looked every bit the majestic self-assured widow of the world to Emily's sweet naiveté. And both women belonged to his brother…

The Duchess saw him first, and in a piece of deft maneuvering Alec found admirable, she directed the group's attention to a row of yellow rose bushes Heath had recently staked, so she could slip away and join him in a stroll down a path of tall pink and white climbing roses.

"I've asked Selina to have a talk with her," she told him. "I hope Emily will tell her something she wouldn't say to this old woman. You don't know how difficult it is trying to be normal.

Every time I look at her I want to burst into tears. I don't know any more this morning than I did last night when you left us. The opiate helped us sleep, thank God. That poor boy, when I think of what we accused him! And Delvin, he's half out of his mind with anger and worry. He didn't ask what we all must want to know and I can't bring myself to find out." She peeped up at Alec. "What if—what if that monster did indeed rape her and-and has impregnated her?" She covered her mouth to stifle a sob. "Forgive me. I am not behaving myself very well."

Alec kissed her hand and kept it in a comforting clasp. "There is nothing to forgive, Olivia. And we don't know exactly what happened last night. We must wait until Emily is strong enough to speak about it."

"Yes. Yes, of course. I am hoping Emily will confide in Selina. It was selfish of me to ask Selina, but she was the same age as Emily is now when she—when she was married off to J-L."

"Why should Emily confide in Mrs. Jamison-Lewis any more than she would you or one of her aunts?"

The Duchess was not deaf to the note of censure in his voice. She knelt to reposition a wooden stake that strained to remain upright under the weight of its heavy burden of roses, wondering how best to answer him without breaking Selina's confidence. Alec helped her up then patiently waited while she inspected another flowering bush. Then they strolled arm-in-arm down a cobbled path that lead to the riverbank.

"If Emily has indeed been raped, who better to confide in than someone who has some understanding of her pain and suffering," the Duchess finally said.

Alec couldn't help a huff of annoyance and his gaze wandered out across the free flowing river to the opposite bank with its cluster of weeping willows, overhanging branches drooping into the cold water. "Emily's situation is entirely different. She neither provoked or encouraged her attacker."

The Duchess turned to face him and wasn't surprised when he

could not meet her open look. "The worst sort of wife didn't deserve the treatment J-L meted out to that poor girl."

Alec continued to stare out over her head to the river, but his mind's eye could not erase the vivid picture of Selina's shapely figure naked to the waist, her long bare legs swinging freely and dark eyes alight with mischief.

"I don't pretend to know the first thing about the Jamison-Lewis marriage, but one wonders what demon prompted him to take a hand to her."

The Duchess gaped at him and sighed her impatience. "That was unjustified and unlike you! But I will forgive you your uncharitable thoughts because I understand what motivates your ridiculous logic better than you know. It must be easier to live with yourself if you apportion blame."

"I beg your pardon, Your Grace," Alec said with extreme but angry politeness. "But I have no wish to unsettle the dust on a most painful episode."

"Do you know," she continued, anger causing her to ignore his request, "it took Madeleine's disastrous marriage before I came to the realization that arranged marriages are all well and good for those civilized persons who abide by the conventions and act accordingly. But I am certainly not in favor of such unions when a young girl is forced to marry a man no decent parent would ever consider for their daughter, and one whom everyone knew to be a sadistic brute. In such barbaric unions, exercising one's conjugal rites is nothing less than rape! Your uncle wrote a pamphlet on the subject. He narrowly escaped an action for defamation."

"Defamation?"

"Yes. He had the bravery—some would say stupidity—to name Jamison-Lewis as the prime example for his argument. Of course, no one would back him—"

"You need not have told me that, Olivia. Uncle Plant—"

"No, not your uncle, my boy. J-L. Not one of his friends would support him and no lawyer would touch the case, so the matter was dropped. Of course, no one would say this publicly, but privately we were all pleased as punch J-L got his come-uppance." She stood before him and waited until he met her eye. "It is the strangest of coincidences, but it was less than a month after the publication of that pamphlet that J-L was found dead with a bullet through his brain."

THE EARL OF DELVIN TURNED HIS BACK ON THE UPPER STORY window.

"You see what I am up against, madam?"

Lady Charlotte stayed a little longer at the window, back very straight and hands clasped tightly in front of her. Delvin did not need to see her face to read the disapproval in her voice. "I have always found Mr. Halsey's personality most volatile. He is hardly fit company for a well-bred girl of impressionable years. Mamma, of course, never listens to my entreaties."

"I dearly wish she would, my lady. Your counsel is something I value greatly. You are a woman of sense and infinite wisdom. Macara and your children are fortunate beyond price."

Lady Charlotte permitted herself to smile slightly. Again her attention returned to the rose garden two floors below. Her mother and Alec Halsey were walking arm-in-arm down one of the many paths; the Duchess stopped to correct a leaning wooden stake and he helped her, then kissed her mother's hand and she touched his cheek, and they continued on with their walk and out of her line of sight.

"Impudence! Damn impudence!" she breathed, her bosom rising with indignation. She came away from the view, fingers tensely intertwined. "You're absolutely right about everything you've told me. I see it all now. You've opened my eyes to things—to things, unpleasant as they are, which must be faced."

"You are very noble."

"Nothing of the sort. It's a question of knowing how to conduct oneself; of knowing what is important in life. There are particular rules that must be followed if life is to be at all tolerable.

I have tried to instill these values in my children, so that when it comes time for them to enter society they will do so with a minimum of fuss and in unexceptional circumstances. Far be it for any person to cast a questioning eye on a daughter of mine." She seemed to collect herself and hastily smiled. "Not that Emily is in any way to blame. She is a lovely girl. She will make a fine Countess of Delvin with just a little prompting in the right direction. She is still young enough to be molded to your will. Once she is married and taken to your country seat, away from all influence, you will see just how compliant she can be. If you want my advice, get her pregnant as soon as possible. A child will give her mind and body occupation."

Delvin took snuff. "Ah, madam, if only I could be certain…" He shut his gold box with a snap. "Yet, now I am tortured by doubts. You, I know, understand how it is for a gentleman of birth and property. Think how it was for Macara. When he chose you over all others there was never any doubt in his mind as to your suitability to share his life and his—er—bed; to be mother to his children. To *his* children, my lady."

"The very idea is laughable."

"Then again, my lady, Macara is not cursed with having Alec Halsey for a brother, is he?"

Lady Charlotte sat down on a spindle-legged chair. "You believe it was he who forced himself on Emily?"

"Can you think of an alternative, madam? I have tried and failed."

"And the maid? Did she fall down the stairs?"

Lord Delvin made an expansive gesture. "So I am told by Her Grace."

Lady Charlotte shuddered. "Jenny's death was a shame. It would be unchristian of me not to say so. Perhaps now Mamma will employ a more suitable companion for Emily. Jenny was apt to daydream and she was not a good influence." She sighed. "I still can't believe the poor child was set upon. He is an animal. She was always very forward with him which may have led him to believe… I blame Mamma entirely for encouraging his visits," she said with a sigh, voicing her thoughts. "God knows why. Secretly I think she is infatuated with her godson; Mamma always had a soft spot for a handsome rake." She smiled thinly at the Earl. "Of course, Mamma supervised Emily's upbringing in the strictest manner. I beg you not to think her in her mother's image. Her mother, as you are aware, disgraced herself beyond forgiveness. Emily is the product of that disgrace. But she is not a distillation of it."

"I have every faith in Emily, otherwise I would not have chosen her to be my wife." He returned her thin smile. "My choice, you realize, has not been without its critics. I am well aware I am marrying far beneath me. But tell me what noble family can boast an unpolluted bloodline? I am not adverse to adding a little water to the wine, but I want that water without taint. It must be pure, unquestionably so. I want to be able to drink it with a free and easy mind. In short, madam: I don't want to discover it has been sullied with another man's spittle."

Lady Charlotte grimaced at his choice of analogy, but she agreed wholeheartedly with the sentiment. His bluntness could be forgiven. He was coarse because he was angry and he had every right to that anger. "My lord Delvin, I am all in sympathy with you, as you know. Yet, surely, when you spoke to Mamma this morning she intimated…?"

Delvin pretended not to understand. "Intimated, madam?"

"About Emily's well-being," she answered brusquely, annoyed with herself for not being able to speak frankly. "She spent the night with Mamma. After such a brutal attack I would assume Mamma asked her certain particulars regarding the incident."

"If she did, she did not confide them in me."

"I thought… Surely she gave you her assurance that Emily was —untouched?"

Delvin looked at the gold signet ring on his left hand. "She did not, madam."

"Why not?"

"How can I answer you?" he said with a sigh. "It leads one to speculate, does it not?"

"But you have a right to know!" said Lady Charlotte in exasperation. "Obviously she is not thinking clearly. She has a bad heart. She needs rest. This business has been most distressing for her. What with the silly maid breaking her neck and the attack on Emily. The strain on her must be intolerable."

"That is why I came to you, madam. My greatest wish is to leave Her Grace in peace. As you say, she is under a great deal of strain and I do not want to burden her further." He smiled self-consciously. "I am confident that if we put our heads together, a simple and relatively painless solution to my dilemma will present itself. Her Grace need never be bothered. As her eldest daughter, do you not possess a considerable influence in this household? I await your counsel, my lady." He went to the window and gazed out, back to Lady Charlotte.

Lady Charlotte's mind was decided before Delvin reached the window. There was no argument. The Earl was entitled to know the truth. Yet, what if Emily had been raped? Would he still want her, and what if he did not? What a disaster for her marriage prospects! Such an offer was unlikely to come her way again, given her bastard blood and the fact the Earl had called off the marriage. Questions would be asked, and almost certainly the truth would come out. And what a disaster for the St. Neots family! She doubted her mother could live through another such scandal. And she, Lady Charlotte, how could she ever hold up her head in society again? She couldn't bear it if all the old wounds were opened, as she knew they would be, Emily being the natural daughter of the infamous and exiled Duchess of Beauly.

Even if Emily had been raped, why hadn't her mother lied to the Earl? Why stay silent? She could think of only one explanation and it horrified her. Perhaps her mother did suspect Alec Halsey of assaulting her granddaughter but her infatuation meant she could not bring herself to voice her suspicions to his estranged elder brother? But to protect him at the expense of her granddaughter's future? Lady Charlotte was mortified. No wonder the Earl was beside himself with doubt. It angered her that her mother had put her in such an awkward position. It angered her even more that Emily had been born at all.

She stood and shook out her petticoats. The Earl faced her.

"When I learned of the maid's accident, I immediately sent for Sir John Oliphant," Lady Charlotte told him. "Perhaps you have heard of him? A well-respected and most excellent physician. I know Mamma would prefer there to be as little fuss as possible, but I cannot be easy in my mind about the state of Mamma's health until Sir John has examined her."

"My lady, you are a worthy daughter. I commend your caring nature."

"Thank you. Though I am only doing my duty," answered Lady Charlotte primly. "As Sir John is coming all this way to see Mamma I don't see why he cannot see Emily too. Once he is in possession of the facts of this most shocking incident, I know he will be only too willing to oblige. He is a discreet man and utterly devoted to his profession. He has attended on Her Majesty. So you may rest easy, my lord."

Delvin bowed over her hand. "I cannot thank you enough. I was at a loss, I must confess, but I should have known you, madam, with your superior understanding and moral perceptibility, would find the perfect solution. Sir John sounds an admirable choice. May I then leave this matter in your capable hands?"

He pocketed his snuffbox and waited for Lady Charlotte to leave the room ahead of him.

She hesitated.

He raised an eyebrow. "My lady, do you perceive a problem?"

"No. That is, may I be frank?"

Delvin inclined his powdered head.

"Whatever Sir John's findings, what is your intention, my lord?"

"My intention? To make Emily my wife." He frowned. "Madam, you did not think... You could not think..." He looked

shocked. "I assure you, Sir John's findings will not alter my desire
to ally myself with your family. But you are sensible enough to see
that if Sir John does discover in truth that my dearest Emily has
been violated, then the wedding will be postponed until such time
as it can be determined whether she has been impregnated. There
are methods—I'm certain Sir John will advise us—to deal with
such a hideous prospect. Did you think I meant to cry off, my
lady?"

"Certainly not!" she retorted. "You are too noble a gentleman
not to stand by your convictions. Emily could not ask for a better
mate. I only hope she has sense enough to realize it." She squeezed
his velvet sleeve as she went before him out into the passageway.
"This conversation remains between you and me. You have my
word. And please, do not worry yourself unnecessarily. I will see to
everything."

Delvin grinned at her straight back. "Thank you, my lady. I
knew I could rely on you to do what was right and proper."

SELINA AND EMILY WALKED IN SILENCE ALONG THE NARROW
footpath that followed the river downstream and connected the
old pier to the new, then wound its way back up to the house. At
the new pier, workmen were busy erecting fireworks set-pieces
which were to be secured in the punts bobbing up and down on
their moorings in the reeds, and later anchored offshore to be set
alight during the Fireworks Ball. This building activity had effec-
tively closed off the path to any guest wishing to take a stroll along
the riverbank and return to the house; thus the two women were
forced to turn back. But Selina stopped at the old wooden pier,
hoping the swan family were nesting in the reeds and wondering
how best to broach the subject of last night's assault with Emily.

"Shall we see if *M'sieur and Mme de Cygne* are in residence
today?" she asked Emily cheerfully, and held out her hand so they
could cross the weathered boards together.

"The swans? Yes, I'd like that. Do you know, that's what Alec calls them. *M'sieur and Mme de Cygne* he says in his most thickly-accented French, and he speaks to them in French also."

"Yes," Selina said with a smile. "I remember."

"I wish we'd brought them something to nibble."

Selina produced two breakfast rolls from her pocket. "One cannot visit the *de Cygnes* without bringing them an offering. That would be *non pardonné*."

They sat on the edge of the pier, reining in their billowing petticoats from the strong breeze that also stirred the overhanging willow branches. It chopped at the surface of the water, causing it to swirl about the tall reeds struggling to poke through the rotted boards, and slapped against the encrusted pylons sending up the occasional cold spray of mist.

"I've heard Alec say that too," Emily answered in a distracted way, eyes on a fast-moving skiff headed downstream, a small boy on board waving frantically to them and clapping when the salutation was returned. "Selina, I miss Jack," she stated abruptly. "I wish he were here now. I wish... I don't know what induced him to foolishly fight a duel with Edward. Edward says Jack was in love with me and was jealous of him, but I know that can't be true. I do love Edward for wanting to protect me from the truth, but I hate the thought of everyone thinking it is my fault they fought a duel at all! What must Lady Margaret think of me? How shall I ever face her and her daughters again? And you, what must you think of me? You and Jack were so close and—"

"Jack's death is not something for which you need feel responsible," Selina firmly assured her. "I know the duel was not fought over you. Jack was in love, but it wasn't with you."

Emily sat up, her gray eyes very round. "Oh! So you do know," she said with a sigh of relief. "I should have realized Jack would confide in you. He told me about his feelings only days before he —before he died. He was so happy." She saw surprise register on Selina's face. "He—he didn't tell me her name and I wasn't so forward as to ask it of him. I was just so pleased he had finally met the right girl."

They broke the bread into the crown of Emily's straw hat.

"If we both know Jack was in love with someone else, then do you not see that Delvin told you a falsehood about the reasons for the duel?" Selina said gently. "Don't you think it a possibility it may have been Delvin who forced the fight on Jack?"

Emily thought about this and frowned. "That's what Alec said too, but Edward would not lie to me. He loves me."

"Emily dear, Delvin did lie to you by suggesting it was Jack's jealousy of him which prompted him to draw his sword."

"Then Edward must have had good reason to lie," Emily replied defensively. "Perhaps he wanted to protect me from the truth? He's like that."

"Perhaps he did," Selina answered lightly, fingers playing in the breadcrumbs, but her attention focused on Emily. "Although, I had thought you more like me... You'd want to know the truth, regardless of how that might affect you. You would not want to be lied to. I have never wanted to be one of these females who is forever treated as a child, to be spoon-fed only the information others feel it is fit to receive. Sybilla is one such female."

"How can you say such a thing about Aunt Sybilla when she is your friend?"

"That does not make her any less my friend. Besides, she likes to be treated that way. The Admiral is the perfect husband for her. I envy her that. She and Charles have a happy marriage."

"Because you were married against your will, Mrs. Jamison-Lewis?"

Selina smiled. "Oh, do call me Selina. I despise my married name. Here come the *de Cygnes*," and she leaned forward to throw small morsels of bread into the river as two swans and their brood of chicks came gliding up to the pier. "I was forced to marry J-L, but that was not the worst of it. I was in love with someone else and my husband knew this, and although he did not love me and really did not even care for me, he was one of those men who has to have something because another man wants it." As she said this, she undid the clasp of the pearl and diamond brooch that pinned her fichu to the front of her low-cut bodice. "He could not abide the thought of my mental unfaithfulness, so he beat me. Not very often. Some would say I deserved the beatings because I was not a good wife to him." She carefully removed the length of gossamer material from her breasts. "You see, I refused to have him in my bed, Emily, but he insisted upon it, which was his right as my husband. Do you understand what I am telling you?"

Emily watched the breeze catch the end of the fichu and toss it up into the air, only for Selina to bring it to earth and tie it about her wrist. And then Emily saw the healing welts across Selina's breasts. The sight of such cruelty turned Emily white before her face flooded with color and she began to cry. Selina took her in a comforting embrace and held her and assured her it could never happen again. It wasn't many minutes before Emily was telling her everything about the night before.

And this was how Alec found them, half an hour later, still on the pier. Selina had her back to the warmth of the sun and was leaning against a pylon with Emily dozing in her arms. She stared out across the water, the weight of her curls, glinting red-gold in the full sun and caught up off her lovely neck with ribbons and pins. He was struck by the determined set to her lovely straight jaw and the smile in her dark eyes. It was as if she had decided something there and then that had made her feel at peace with herself. It brought a smile to his lips. He could have gone on admiring her in this way for a lot longer had she not sensed a presence and turned to find him staring at her. He immediately looked away, unable to hold those dark expressive eyes. She did not register surprise, but her whole being tensed causing Emily to stir, sit up, and apologize sleepily to Selina for falling asleep.

Alec had not come alone. Peeble patiently waited at the end of the pier.

"Your grandmother needs you up at the house," Alec told Emily, helping her to stand, not a glance in Selina's direction. "Guests have begun arriving for afternoon tea and she can't greet them without you. Will you be all right?" he asked gently, giving her a searching look. When she nodded he kissed her hand. "Good. Peeble has come to take you back." He scooped up her straw bonnet and escorted her down the pier, turning his back on Selina who was left to fend for herself. Once he had Emily securely across the rotted boards and on firm ground he gave her over to Peeble's care.

Emily looked past his shoulder at Selina standing alone on the pier, brushing her petticoats free of crumbs and creases. "Selina—"

"Mrs. Jamison-Lewis and I shall be along shortly," he answered her with a smile, and with a nod to Peeble he returned to the pier. He had crossed most of the sturdy boards when Selina came up to him from the opposite direction and would have passed him had he not blocked her way. "I want to talk to you," he stated, and when she stubbornly stood there added, "It's about Jack."

Selina walked back to the edge of the pier and threw the last of the bread into the water, for the swans had glided in again. Alec squatted on his haunches, and finding a piece of bread roll wedged in the boards, held this out to *Mme de Cygne*, coaxing her forward in softly spoken French. He finally stood up to stretch his legs and said in English, eyes still on the swan family,

"Uncle Plant is bringing Cromwell and Marziran out to St. Neots. They'll enjoy the run of the grounds after the congested streets of Paris."

"After Paris? Indeed they will. Especially in the wood to catch rabbits."

"Or to frighten Olivia's deer into the park?"

Selina smiled at a memory. "I'd forgotten about that. She wasn't too pleased when her precious herd trampled the herb beds. Mayhap they'll stick to ferreting out the rabbit warrens."

"Those two rogues? Did you really think so?"

Selina shook her head. "As I recall they were never content until they had run to ground the biggest and best of Her Grace's bucks. Is your uncle truly coming here? I thought he deliberately kept his distance from *this idle class of wasteful good-for-nothings who succeed at nothing but succeeding*," she quoted and smiled. "The

Duchess and Lady Charlotte were none too pleased with that speech Plantagenet Halsey made in the Commons about abolishing primogeniture. Lady Charlotte was practically frothing at the mouth! When is he due?"

"Today, and staying on for the Fireworks Ball. Olivia asked him particularly."

"Indeed! Why?"

"Oh, because they are fond of each other."

"No?! The Duchess and the republican?" Selina's eyes twinkled mischief. "How diverting! And I had every expectation of being bored beyond belief tonight. Observing those two will give me no end of entertainment."

"Yes, I thought you'd be pleased. You always did have a way of discovering interesting and often quite shocking tidbits about people who looked for all the world to be about as exciting as a shoehorn."

They both laughed and then immediately fell into an awkward silence until Alec said bluntly, "Olivia suggested you may know why Jack and Delvin crossed swords."

"I have no idea," was her wooden response. "I told you so at St. James's Place."

"You saw him the day before he died, in Hyde Park in company with a colleague of mine, Simon Tremarton."

"Yes, I did. But Jack didn't mention Delvin." She regarded him candidly. "Jack told me Simon Tremarton is in the Foreign Department. Do you know him well?"

"We have been at a few embassies together and had drinks at our club from time to time, that's all."

"I see. So you don't know him at all really."

"Not intimately, no," he answered, wondering why her eyes suddenly sparked and how she had managed to turn the conversation so that it was she who was asking the questions. "Did Jack give you any indication of how he felt about Emily's engagement?"

"No. He didn't know about the engagement when I met him in the Park," she answered patiently. "He'd just returned from ten days away at his shooting box in Yorkshire. No one seems to remember that fact. Emily and Delvin had only announced their engagement the day before, and it wasn't due to be gazetted until the following morning—the morning of the duel." She brushed a stray curl off her cheek. "Besides," she said quietly, "Jack was too happy to be much bothered with anyone else's news, good or otherwise."

Alec looked down at his feet to where tall reeds poked up through the rotted boards. "Jack wasn't interested in female company, was he, Selina?"

She hesitated; it was the use of her name. He had always made a point of calling her by her married name. It was this and not the question that made her slow to respond. When he prompted her, she said flippantly with a shrug of one shoulder, "Oh, he and I were always together."

"You forget: Jack and I were at school together."

"And that makes you an expert on Jack's feelings?"

He smiled, the corners of his blue eyes crinkling up. "No. Not on his feelings. He tried hard to mask his true inclinations, but I suspected he was not the least interested in the petticoat line."

Selina turned her face away. "Then you know very well he didn't give two straws for women."

"Yes."

Absently, she played with the embroidered end of the gossamer fichu which she had tied loosely over her bosom but not pinned back into place, looking at some distant point on the opposite river bank. "Forgive me. I'm being stupidly cautious and there's no need to be with you. Jack would never have married, not even to continue the line. Poor Aunt Meg, she was destined to live in hope for the rest of her life. So you see why the duel couldn't have been fought over Emily. That's just a convenient excuse Delvin concocted—one most people will readily believe because the truth about Jack wasn't widely known."

Alec followed her gaze out across the water. "Do you think the duel may have had something to do with Jack's preference?"

Selina shook her head. "I don't believe so. Delvin may privately despise such men, but he has never voiced his disgust. As for calling Jack out because of it... Why? And why now, when Delvin's known for years about Jack. There has to be some other reason why he murdered my cousin."

"Thief, liar, cheat, and murderer," Alec stated. "Is there anything left of which you wish to accuse my brother, Madam?"

His light-hearted remark hid an undercurrent of mixed emotions, but all Selina heard was his sneering disgust. So he took the scene last night at face value. Well, she couldn't blame him for that. Delvin's stage-management may have taken an unexpectedly painful turn, but he had no less achieved his desired object in unsettling his brother. She forced herself to look Alec in the face.

"I did not invite Delvin into my bedchamber last night, or on any other night—"

Alec cut her off, putting up a hand with a smile that was a little too broad. "My dear, you need not justify your behavior—"

"No, I need not," she answered curtly. "But you are very wide of the mark if you believe what you think you saw last night. I thought you knew me better. And if not me, then surely you know your brother well enough to realize he is capable of the grossest deceit. That said, I'm sure you did not detain me to talk of what must be of so little interest to you..."

Alec took a moment to reply, for he was regarding her with an expression Selina found hard to interpret. She was uncertain if what she had said had angered or confused him. He went to speak, changed his mind, and with lips pressed firmly together took a quick turn along the rotted planks of the pier. When he came back he said in a level voice, "Were you able to speak with Emily about what happened to her last night?"

"Yes. We may all rest easy," she said calmly. "From what she described, and indeed from what she did not say, she was not raped—"

"Thank God."

"—but I am convinced that was the intent. She was extremely

fortunate that someone or something disturbed her attacker, causing him to flee before he had a chance to truly hurt her."

"My valet, perhaps, when he entered the bedchamber? Although, he says Emily was alone in the room, save poor Jenny dead at the foot of the bed."

"From what I could glean from Emily's halting confidences, when she retired for the evening she and Jenny sat for awhile in Jenny's room. Emily complained of the headache and the last time she remembers speaking with Jenny was to ask for a headache powder before dozing on Jenny's bed. When she woke she was alone. She has a vague recollection that she was awoken by a loud thud. That's when she went through to her bedchamber. The room was in darkness, an unusual circumstance, and she was grabbed and—You know the rest…"

"Did she mention the chambermaid?"

"No. Obviously the little wretch was playing truant." Selina sighed. "Perhaps she saw something but is too frightened to speak for fear of losing her place, or worse, ending up like Jenny? Perhaps that's why Jenny was attacked? She saw the intruder lurking about the servant stairs or in the bedchamber? Oh! Emily did confide one piece of information which should help you narrow the field."

"Yes?" he asked expectantly.

"Her attacker wore a wig. In the struggle she dislodged it. He has a shaved head."

"Is that all?"

"Yes. You don't look particularly impressed. The poor girl is still in shock. And she doesn't want to go over and over that night ever again. I don't blame her. To glean that much information took all my persuasion."

"I'm not ungrateful," he apologized. "It's just that the attacker's preference for a wig is not much to go on. After all, every gentleman in London with pretensions to being a gentleman wears a wig." He shrugged. "I suppose it means we can discount most of the servants. Oh, and you can let me off the hook."

Selina flushed up angrily. "You?" she retorted. "How dare you think I'd ever suspect you! What a *detestable* thing to say!" She picked up her petticoats and stormed off up the pier toward the riverbank. "I thought you knew me better than that, but obviously you've made a point of forgetting! As for your outrageous suggestion that I encouraged such an odious toad as your brother—Oh, damn you!"

After a stunned moment, he followed her. "Be careful! Watch your step! Selina! Wait! The boards... They're unsafe! You'll twist an ankle!"

"No, don't touch me! I'll make my own way!" She kept walking, barely able to see through tears fueled by an angry rage that was wholly unexpected but not inexplicable. "I'm not afraid of Thames water!" she grumbled, and just as she had crossed the worst of the splintered and broken planks, a protruding rusty nail snagged her under-petticoats and she tripped and lost her balance. She gasped, anticipating the rush of cold water, the reeds razor sharp against her skin, when suddenly she was caught about the waist and lifted up into the air before even a shoe had a chance to break the surface of the water.

Alec swung her up over his shoulder in a manner she found both undignified and exhilarating and continued along the pier, despite her protests that he put her down instantly, until they had reached the riverbank and he had both feet on firm land. He then swung her down off his shoulder but did not let her go.

She collapsed against his chest laughing. "Brute! Oh, my head. You've made me dizzy!"

"It's your own fault," he said loftily, trying not to laugh and holding her close. "Be still a moment," he said softly, breathing in the lovely floral scent lingering in her disordered hair. "The sensation will soon pass."

She closed her eyes and felt better for it, content to be still in his arms and listen to the thud of his strong heart through the linen shirt and embroidered silk waistcoat. They stood there for many minutes until Alec shifted slightly, the sun hot on the back of his navy-blue frock coat.

"We should return to the house before we're missed," he said quietly, and picked up the gossamer fichu that had loosened from her shoulders and floated to his feet in the grass.

She put out a hand for it but he carefully folded the fabric and gently arranged it across her shoulders. She tilted her chin and kept her gaze on his strong handsome face with its aquiline nose, square chin, and eyes so deep blue that in daylight they looked as coal black as his head of unruly curls. He was smiling down at her as he tied the fichu over her bosom but his smile suddenly dropped into a frown, and he let go of the material as if it were poisonous to the touch and took a step backward. She wondered what had happened for so sudden a change to come over him, and then she knew. Without the fichu the welts on her white translucent skin were starkly evident. Unthinking of her to forget to pin the gossamer fabric firmly back into place. She quickly covered her breasts and secured the brooch in place. When she looked up he was deathly pale and shaking.

"What is it?" she asked in alarm and touched his sleeve.

He hung his head, a curl falling across his forehead, and looked away, knuckles white in clenched fists. "God help me, Selina," he murmured in a broken voice. "I didn't know... *I didn't know...*"

"Please. It's over. That's all that matters."

"I'm—I'm sorry," he whispered in a dry throat. "Dear God, I'm so sorry."

She made him look at her and smiled reassuringly up into his damp blue eyes, only to receive a severe shock. What she saw was so unexpected and so unwanted that she was instantly utterly miserable. "You pity me?" she said in a small voice filled with wonderment, a hand to her white throat. "You want to offer me sympathy? Damn you! *Damn you.* Ignore me, reject me, *hate* me; think of me what you will," she lashed out angrily, "but don't pity me!" and stormed off down the path towards the new pier, leaving him by the river, wanting to be as far away from him as possible.

He did not attempt to follow her. Instead he sank down into the long grass and lay there, staring up into a cloudless sky, marveling at the twists and turns one's life took. He too had received a shock just now: The realization that what had started out as a small nagging doubt begun on the stairs of St. Neots House when he and Selina had collided, had, in the space of a few quiet moments with her in his arms, grown into a clear-sighted conviction that he had been on the verge of making the greatest mistake of his life. The consequences did not bear thinking about. Now he had to make amends, to Emily, to Selina, and ultimately to himself.

SEVEN

SIR COSMO MET ALEC AS HE CAME WANDERING ACROSS THE
south lawn, frock coat slung over one shoulder and his shirtsleeves
rolled up to the elbows. Sir Cosmo carried a croquet mallet, but he
wasn't part of the game taking place on the lawn below the terrace.
He had excused himself the moment he saw Selina crossing the
lawn from the direction of the river in a whirlwind of petticoats
and determination. But she had fobbed him off with a lame excuse
of having a headache, and strode into the house, causing the
raising of several eyebrows which lounged on the terrace. Sir
Cosmo knew Selina had never suffered a headache in her life so he
wasn't surprised when the headache had a name. Alec came across
the lawn from precisely the same direction as Selina and only ten
minutes behind her.

Sir Cosmo had spent the morning since the incident in the
breakfast room trying to extract any gossip he could about the
happenings of the previous evening. No one seemed to know
anything except that Emily's maid had broken her neck. As for
Delvin's heated accusations thrown at his brother's head, Sir
Cosmo's brain was still reeling in shocked disbelief. His own
heated outburst at Alec, out in the rain on the terrace, made him
decidedly sheepish to be alone in his friend's company, and thus

when he approached him he felt rather awkward and school-
boyish.

"May we talk?" he asked, tossing the croquet mallet aside and
falling into step beside his friend.

"Come up to the house. I need a drink."

"How—how are the punts coming along?"

"There's a lot of sawing and hammering, if that means
progress."

"Aunt Olivia's spent a sunken treasure on the fireworks alone.
Bound to be a spectacle."

Alec went up the terrace steps ahead of him and was met by
Neave carrying a silver salver holding two glasses and a bottle of
burgundy. The butler hovered, a significant glance at Sir Cosmo.

"Excuse us a moment, Cosmo," said Alec, stepping aside with
the butler. "Was the chambermaid able to tell you anything?"

"I am sorry to say, sir, the girl remains stubbornly silent about
her comings and goings last night. She says one thing, but then if
you press her she changes her story. If you ask me, sir, I'd say she
was up to no good out in the shrubbery with one of the lads
instead of being about her duties."

"That explains her garbled explanations. Keep pressing her. See
if you can find out who shared the shrubbery with her. And what
of the footmen in that particular section of the house—what did
they have to say?"

"There were only two at that hour, sir. They are adamant they
saw no one out of the ordinary. That is, they saw only Miss Jenny
come and go along the main passageway."

"What about the servant stair? Where does it lead?"

"Up to Old Nurse's room. It's above Miss Emily's apartments,
sir. And down to the billiard room and a passageway that runs to
the kitchen."

"Billiard room? Rather odd, isn't it, for the billiard room to be
below Miss Emily's apartment?"

"That it is, sir. It's on account of the fire that happened while
you were abroad."

"Fire? In what was the billiard room before this one?"

"That's right, sir. Burnt the room clear out. Nothing but a shell. So Her Grace had what was the old music room fixed up as the billiard room for the gentlemen here for the weekend party."

"How was the fire started?"

The butler coughed. "No one knows, sir. But Her Grace is of the opinion that perhaps one of Lord Andrew's cheroots might've done the trick…"

Alec put up his brows but said nothing. He took the bottle and two glasses. "Did you ensure Miss Emily's bedchamber remained untouched?"

"Yes, sir. I posted a footman at the passageway to Miss Emily's rooms and had the servant door at the bottom of the stairs bolted and padlocked. No one's been in there since Dr. Oakes."

"Good. Any news from other quarters?"

"Not as yet, sir. One's own servants are much more —*malleable*."

"I imagine they must be. Thank you, Neave. If I'm wanted I'll be in the new billiard room. Bring me the key to the padlock. I may take a look in on Miss Emily's bedchamber, but that's for your ears only."

The butler bowed with satisfaction, gratified to be in Mr. Halsey's confidence.

The billiard room was deserted and in darkness, the heavy curtains drawn against the afternoon sun. Sir Cosmo flung open a window to remove the smell of stale wine and cheroots. Several cues were leaning carelessly against the table and on the window seat were two empty bottles of claret and three glasses holding varying amounts of unfinished wine; flung in a corner, a crumpled frock coat, obviously forgotten in the heat of drunken competition. Sir Cosmo shrugged his shoulders at the laxness of the Duchess's servants and positioned the three billiard balls on the green baize felt, eager to have a game.

Yet, when Alec immediately crossed to the servant door cut into the wallpapered paneling and disappeared, Sir Cosmo should've guessed a game of billiards was the last thing on his friend's mind. But Alec returned moments later, satisfied that the door to the servant stair leading to Emily's bedchamber had indeed been bolted and padlocked. He poured himself and Sir Cosmo a glass of burgundy from the bottle he'd taken from Neave, and handed a wine glass to his friend.

"Thanks. Could do with a good drop," said Sir Cosmo. "Not been feeling myself this morning. Can't hold a decent conversation. Played a foul game of croquet. I'm all jumps and sweat. Selina ignored me just now. Aunt Olivia is in hiding with Emily, keeping their own counsel. Damned annoying for the rest of us…" He watched Alec set the bottle of burgundy on the window seat and said abruptly, "Damn it, Alec! I'm Emily's closest cousin. I've a right to know what happened last night, if what Ned said in the breakfast room has a speck of truth to it!"

Briefly, Alec confided the events of the previous evening, adding, "I hope Neave can squeeze some information out of the servants, and my own efforts turn up something new, or I may be forced to ask Emily to give an account of last night, and I am loath to do that, particularly after Selina's talk with her didn't reveal all that much."

Sir Cosmo shook his powdered head. "What gets into a man to want to force himself on a young girl? It's barbaric! And killing the maid in the process defies my powers of reasoning. Ugly. Damned ugly!"

"Why kill a lady's maid?"

"She saw him. That's obvious. Had to shut her up quick before Emily or a servant heard her."

"Why didn't a servant hear her scream for help? There was a footman on duty in the corridor just outside the sitting room door."

Sir Cosmo put aside the wine glass and randomly selected a cue from the rack. "Mayhap she didn't get a chance to scream? Jumped on her quick. Mayhap the candles had guttered or he snuffed 'em? It was dark, wasn't it?"

"How would he find her in the dark? How did he get the opportunity to snuff out all the candles, lie in wait, and then pounce on Jenny? She wouldn't have gone two steps into a darkened room. She'd have called a footman for a taper."

Sir Cosmo looked glum. He placed his billiard ball in the middle of the balkline, lined up his cue, and with one eye closed took aim and made the break. "So the candles weren't snuffed. We're back to what I first said. She saw him and he shut her up quick."

"Or she saw him and knew him, and thus not fearing him did not cry out," Alec postulated. "Perhaps it was she who let him in?"

"What about the footmen? Why didn't they see him?"

It was Alec's turn to frown. He had taken his time to select a suitable cue and waited for Sir Cosmo to end his run of easy shots, wine glass in hand.

"As much as it gives me a feeling of utter disgust I think you're right," Sir Cosmo agreed, and failed to score so he stepped back for Alec to begin his run of play. "She knew him. Can't imagine Emily's maid being free and easy with access to her mistress's rooms. And you said she was found in the bedchamber. Not a place to invite strangers, is it?"

"Not a place to invite anyone."

"What about that footman on duty?"

"Neave said the two footmen at the end of the corridor were adamant they saw no one."

"Lying," Sir Cosmo said flatly. "Got to be. Wandered from their posts. Not likely to confess to Neave, are they?"

"Or the murderer used the servant stairs from start to finish. And how in the name of Zeus am I to discover the murderer's identity before the weekend is over?" Alec wondered aloud. "How do I go ferreting into people's lives, discovering the whereabouts of each and every male guest after they left the drawing room last night? And without offending the innocent, and more importantly, without causing Olivia and Emily discomfort and embarrassment?"

"I don't know," Sir Cosmo said lamely, watching Alec play a winning hazard. "I'd like to help. Mayhap I can ask a few discreet questions in a couple of ears? And of course you can eliminate some of us. I mean, it wasn't her uncle Macara, or you, or I. And it certainly wasn't old General Wallbright with his gout and cane to get about. Then there's the vicar and Ned. Wouldn't be Ned. He's engaged to Emily. Some of the fellows were too drunk after dinner to even join the ladies for coffee. Footmen had to carry them up to their respective rooms."

Alec looked up before making his next shot, unconvinced. "Who's to say one of those drunken gentlemen wasn't faking it? That's why I have Neave trying to learn what he can from the valets."

"Ha! They'll be as easy to extract information from as a good tooth from a young head!"

"Mm. There are those gentlemen I can obviously discount for one reason or another. That still leaves a handful unaccounted for, besides myself, you, and Delvin."

"You can't think…"

"I don't know what to think!" Alec snapped and mistimed his shot, thus leaving the way open for Sir Cosmo to clean up the game. "A day ago I wouldn't have thought it possible for a young girl to be near raped in her own home, her maid killed into the bargain. It's the stuff of Haymarket melodrama, yet it's happened under this very roof. Will the others discount us so easily when they learn that last night you were running about in your Chinese banyan looking for me, and there was I, alone on the terrace in the rain? Delvin has an alibi in Selina—"

"I'll not believe that! *Ever*. She loathes him."

"Why shouldn't I believe my own eyes? I walked in on them. Thinking about it I'm convinced that's exactly how Delvin planned it. He wanted me to see them together. He wanted to gloat in my face."

Sir Cosmo clenched his jaw. He hesitated taking his final shot and faced Alec. "I don't care what you say you saw, but it wasn't what you think you saw!" he said stubbornly "Ned's been acting like a lunatic lately. Of course he wanted you to see Selina and him together. He's lusted after her since I can remember. But that don't mean she wants anything to do with him!" He lined up his shot again, saying with a huff, "That show he put on at breakfast had me coming up for air. Never heard such rot. Can't blame the man for being crazy with anger, but to accuse you..."

"You shouldn't be surprised by Edward's behavior. You've always known how it is between us."

"But I never realized how much he hated you," Sir Cosmo answered. "You've not done him a harm. You've kept out of his way. And as for this engagement, you've been more than decent about it considering you'd set your cap at Emily... Hadn't you?"

"I was heading in that direction, yes."

Sir Cosmo made successive misses and stood back unconcerned by his bad play because his mind was elsewhere. "A lesser man would've come between them before now."

"Yes, a lesser man would have."

Sir Cosmo groped for a reply, at the very least an apology, but Alec's accompanying smile made him feel foolish to think his friend would take offense. "What the devil is Ned's problem?" he wondered aloud. "It's not as if he's got anything to be concerned about. He's engaged to Emily, you're not. She's in love with him, not you. He's the earl, you're the acknowledged second son."

Alec came away from the window and repositioned the three billiard balls on the green baize. "What do you mean *acknowledged second son?*"

Sir Cosmo put his chin in the folds of his stock. "I'm sure I need not repeat the whispers about your mother..."

"Please, I beg you to elaborate."

"Tell you a truth, dear fellow, it's quite laughable," Sir Cosmo said in an off-handed manner to hide his embarrassment. He avoided his friend's smoldering blue-eyed gaze by choosing another cue in readiness for a second game. "The whole episode is something out of the Middle Ages. No doubt you've had a chuckle over it."

"Over what?"

"Oh, do come about, Alec!" Sir Cosmo scoffed. "You know damned well what I'm talking about. You've always played too close for your own good. I'm a friend, a sympathetic ear, not judge, jury, and executioner."

Alec chalked the tip of his cue. "I have nothing to say about Lady Delvin."

"Perhaps you don't, but Jack's mamma has had plenty to say. Lady Margaret says she has a letter written in your mother's fist. Says it proves your birthright."

"You've seen this letter?"

"No. Thing of it is, Selina says her aunt has misplaced it."

Alec huffed in disbelief.

"But that don't mean it don't exist! Lady Margaret has the servants turning her townhouse upside down looking for it. And when it's found she's determined to see justice done!"

"Cosmo. Lady Margaret must have dozens of letters written to her by Lady Delvin. But I doubt very much that amongst their number there exists a letter of confession. Even if the sordid rumors about my mother's past are true, she would never write them down for posterity. To what purpose? Such a confession would certainly ruin my brother, and that could not be Lady Delvin's object. She always supported his claim to the Earl's title. Lady Margaret's motive is simplistic. She wants her revenge on my brother for killing her son; that is understandable. But blind grief has clouded her judgment and given way to wishful thinking."

"What if Lady Margaret produces a letter written by Lady Delvin that substantiates the rumor? Wouldn't you want to see justice done?"

"Justice has nothing to do with it, Cosmo." Alec stepped to the table to lead off the play, feelings of uneasiness making his tone harsh. "Tell me if you find plausible this well-worn fable: When Lady Delvin learned she was pregnant, she hid this fact from the world because she was unsure who had fathered her child, her husband or her lover—a lover she had taken while the Earl was north visiting his estates. She intended to give birth in the seclusion of the country estate in Kent. However, the Earl returned unexpectedly. News had reached him of his wife's adultery. He was not prepared to entertain the idea that in all probability he, and not the lover, had fathered the child before his departure. He was determined to be rid of his wife's bastard. No sooner was the boy born than he was sent north to closed-mouthed tenant farmers on a remote estate in Northumberland."

"But that can't be the end to the story," Sir Cosmo said quietly.

"The child remained with the tenant farmers for a twelve-month, when the Earl's brother discovered his whereabouts. The baby had not thrived, was puny and not expected to live. Yet the uncle would not give up on the boy. He returned him to his parents in Kent. By this time, Lady Delvin had given birth to a second son just months before and it was this second son whom the Earl had declared his first born."

"But the first son was born in wedlock and so, legally, was heir to the earldom," Sir Cosmo argued. "Whatever the Earl's suspicions about the boy's paternity. That is the law. Besides, what proof did he have that the first born was not his?"

"Yes, that is the law, Cosmo, but the damage had been done. Lady Delvin had been unfaithful. That's all the Earl required for him to reject her firstborn as his. The best the uncle could do for this outcast son was to ensure the boy was at least acknowledged by his parents. He threatened to expose the Earl's gross deception if he did not. The Earl agreed on condition that the Countess's second son be declared the firstborn and thus heir to the Earl's title and lands. This satisfied the Earl's brother who took the outcast son to live with him, the Earl refusing to have in his house a daily reminder of his wife's infidelity. Publicly it was said the boy was consumptive and carrying the danger of contagion could infect his brother. Because there was only eleven months between the boys and they had been born in the seclusion of the country, no one in society was the wiser."

Sir Cosmo stepped up to take his turn, devoid of all enthusiasm for a game he knew he could not win from here. "When did you discover the truth?"

Alec returned to the window seat and poured himself another glass of wine. "When I was fifteen years old, Uncle Plant explained that my father had disowned me because of my mother's unfaithfulness. I hardly cared. My parents had never made the effort to know me. My uncle was all the family I'd ever had and ever needed."

"And—and Ned?"

"The favored son? The Earl went to great pains to instill in him the pride and haughtiness of our class. My brother was brought up to believe he was the eldest son and that one day the earldom and all that he surveyed would be his. He had no reason to question or believe otherwise."

"And the Countess, did she make a confession before she died?"

"The old Earl died unrepentant and never acknowledged his firstborn. In his eyes he had only one son and that son would succeed to the title, which Edward did with our mother's blessing. Then, quite unexpectedly, Lady Delvin asked to see her estranged son. It was only at the prompting of Uncle Plant that I made the effort. After all, she was a stranger to me. By this time my mother was bedridden. Yet, I do not believe her mental faculties were at all diminished. She made a confession of sorts…"

Alec drained his glass. Sir Cosmo dared not line up his cue. He was all rapt attention.

"Even now, I still find it incredible that the Earl and Countess were able to carry off such a deception," Alec continued. "No one would've been the wiser, certainly not I, had not Lady Delvin felt the need to make amends before she died. Naturally, Edward felt betrayed. He thought she'd gone mad. He sent two doctors to certify her insane. I went to see her every week… But I was abroad when she died. I regret that. She had no one else. No one except Uncle Plant, and near the end even he was too distraught to ride into Kent."

"If what your mother confessed is indeed the truth then—then there has been a hideous miscarriage of justice! Ned's whole life has been a-a—lie."

Alec smiled. "My dear Cosmo, Lady Delvin was shrewd enough not to reveal the identity of my father. So I could very well be the product of my mother's adulterous affair. Thus, despite our birth order, Edward could be the rightful heir to his father's earldom, and I? My use of the name of Halsey may be a grand presumption."

Sir Cosmo let out an involuntary cough that raised Alec's eyebrows. "Well, that's a moot point, dear fellow, if," he explained awkwardly, "you are in fact your uncle's son...?"

Alec stared at his friend not at all surprised but made no comment. They were interrupted then by Neave who came into the billiard room on a discreet knock. He had the key to the padlock and this he gave to Alec.

"I'm going to take a look about Emily's bedchamber," Alec said to Sir Cosmo, opening the servant door. "Don't feel you need come up. I shouldn't be many minutes."

Sir Cosmo remained a moment longer, indecisive, watching Neave decant the left-over wine from three glasses into one of the discarded bottles. It was only when the butler had scooped up the forgotten frock coat and departed with this crumpled article over one arm while juggling two bottles and three empty wine glasses that Sir Cosmo came to a sense of his surroundings. He hurriedly set aside his cue and scrambled through the servant door, Neave hearing him shout for his friend to wait up as he closed the door, and making a mental note to take to task the lax servant who had failed to clean up the billiard room earlier that morning.

"What does it really matter if your uncle is your father?" Sir Cosmo argued, watching Alec remove the padlock and scrape back the bolt. "The Earl and your uncle are brothers, both Halseys. It's all the same blood if you think about it. Lady Margaret's been telling everyone you are the Earl's firstborn. She says your mother confessed the truth to her in that letter that's gone missing. Of course, even if she finds the letter it may not, in all likelihood, reveal the identity of your father."

Alec put on his gold-rimmed spectacles. "I would not put my money on it, Cosmo."

Sir Cosmo followed Alec into the servant stairwell one step at a time, as his friend occasionally stooped to peer at the worn unpolished steps.

"Still, without that letter Ned has free reign to continue spreading an even uglier rumor about your paternity. It's been doing the rounds since Lady Delvin's death. Of course, no one who knows you believes a word of Ned's incredible claim so that's why it's never truly seen the light of day. Most believe he's merely spouting drivel to have his revenge on your mother for making a confession at all." Sir Cosmo peered down at Alec who was on his haunches. "May I know what it is you're doing?"

"The intruder may have dropped something on these stairs, and as it is dark one must grope around a bit. So far all I've managed to do is stick my fingers with bits of broken glass! What drivel?"

"Ah! That. Ned says the real reason the Countess disowned you was because her adultery wasn't with your uncle but with his mulatto valet." When Alec righted himself but did not turn about Sir Cosmo added in a rush, "I know! I know! It's absurd. But if the babe she carried belonged to her husband's brother, why would she need to give you up? The Earl'd never know the difference. No one would. But if in truth she and the mulatto were lovers, then it's understandable she was half-crazy with worry. After all, there was every chance the babe would be colored. According to Ned, she tried all sorts of ways to quicken the babe before its time, but nothing worked and she was forced to carry the child to term in secrecy." Sir Cosmo pulled a face and followed Alec up the remaining stairs to Emily's bedchamber. "Of course, it's only reasonable she'd want to rid herself of such unnatural offspring. After all, it's against nature; white and colored breeding. It don't bear thinking about. Sorry I mentioned it. Ned's a lunatic for even suggesting it!"

Alec threw open the servant door and stepped into the semi-darkened bedchamber. He faced his friend who had entered the room with a sheepish grin. "Uncle Plant's major domo, Joseph, was a mulatto freed slave from Uncle's plantations in the West Indies," he stated calmly, his tone belying the suppressed anger in his angular face. "He left my uncle's employment around the time I went up to Oxford, married the daughter of a Scot's lawyer and moved to Edinburgh. He and my uncle are regular correspondents; Joseph's most recent letter carried the news of the birth of his second grandchild and the fact he has decided to retire as head of chambers. He is a decent man and it is ludicrous to think he and my mother had an affair!"

"Of course! Ludicrous!" Sir Cosmo said with an uncertain smile. "As if the Countess of Delvin and a mulatto were lovers!"

Alec drew back the curtains so the room was fully bathed in light.

"I can well imagine Delvin spreading such utter tripe, for it not only degrades Lady Delvin but Joseph Cale's good character. I don't pretend to understand my brother's perverted mind; what I do know is that he detests me all the more because I don't give a fig which one of us is the eldest son. I am content with my life as it is. He, however, could be living a lie and that gnaws away at him day and night. Thing is, Cosmo, I don't want to be Earl of Delvin or of anything else."

Sir Cosmo could only gaze at him in wonderment, his back to the room. The fact that they now stood in Emily's disordered bedchamber was momentarily forgotten. "You really don't, do you?" He shook his head. "But to a man of Ned's disposition, Lady Delvin's confession must burn him up. Miserable, I'd say. Got it all, yet what is it all worth if he doubts it is truly his? I feel for him. Don't know what I'd do myself if I thought I was living a lie. Thank God I'm an only son. Still, it would be interesting to find this missing letter; to see your mamma's confession written in ink."

"Cosmo," said Alec, stepping past his friend to move into the room, "you may not want to stay…"

Sir Cosmo turned about at that and his mouth dropped open. It felt as if his jaw had swung to the floor, so startled was he by the wanton chaos in this feminine bedchamber, now starkly evident in the cruel light of day. On an expletive, he crossed to the narrow ebony curio cabinet by the four-poster bed, glass crunching underfoot. "I gave Emily this curio for her fifteenth birthday. Look at it now!" he said with angry incredulity, turning about to stare at the glass littering the carpet. "How dare that brute smash it up!"

Alec crouched at the doors to the cabinet and gingerly touched a long sliver of glass. "The glass door has been smashed inwards." He peered at the carpet. By the leg of the cabinet he found a rounded thickened piece of glass. "Looks like a water tumbler must've fallen off the cabinet and was ground underfoot. And a heavy foot at that… Reason for the glass on the stairs just now." He stood up, a frown between his brows. "I'd say your curio cabinet was accidentally struck during a struggle…"

Both men looked fleetingly at the tumble of bedclothes.

Sir Cosmo replaced a porcelain figurine of a King Charles Spaniel in the damaged curio cabinet and tugged at the folds of his cravat as if for air. "Must you do that?" he pleaded as Alec lifted the mountain of down pillows away from the mahogany headboard.

"Yes. As I said, you needn't stay."

Sir Cosmo stuck out his bottom lip in embarrassment, turned his back on proceedings and stared out of the window, determined to give his mind another direction than dwelling on what had happened in this room the night before. Looking out on the view, he caught sight of a party of riders crossing the velvet lawns from the direction of the river to the stables; amongst their number were Lord and Lady Gervais, she flirting outrageously with Lord

Andrew Macara, while her hulk of a husband followed, hunched broodingly in the saddle.

The continued silence at his back had Sir Cosmo looking over his shoulder, and he was relieved to see that Alec had moved away from the bed and that the bedclothes and pillows had been neatly rearranged. Somehow this made it easier for him to leave the window and join his friend who was setting a chair to rights.

"Find anything of interest?" he asked lightly, though his voice broke in the middle.

Alec shook his head. "Unfortunately, no. I had hoped the bedclothes might reveal a scrap of lace or ribbon or an object fallen from the attacker's pockets, but—nothing. Damn it! It's as if the man came up here cunningly devoid of frippery."

"You mean the monster wasn't wearing lace at his wrists or a frock coat?" He gulped. "That's fiendishly premeditated, Alec."

Alec looked over the rims of his spectacles. "Or devilishly coincidental."

"Meaning?"

"Just now in the billiard room," explained Alec. "You didn't notice the empty bottles, the cues left lying about, the frock coat in the corner?"

"Of course. Neave just tidied the mess up and took the frock coat and bottles with him. Damn lax of the servants to leave—"

"Damn! No matter. I'm sure Neave will return the frock coat to its rightful owner."

"Alec? You don't think the owner of that frock coat was the one who—" Sir Cosmo gripped the poster as if for support. "And just moments before he'd been playing at billiards as we had, with his fellows, when he got the urge to—That's positively bestial!"

"Cosmo, take your fingers away from the post."

Sir Cosmo did as he was told, wholly mystified.

"Look here," Alec said, inspecting the post through his spectacles. He pointed to a splinter in the wood just under where Sir Cosmo's hand had gripped the post. He ran a long finger down the carving. "Do you see the hairs caught here? Long, black hairs. Emily has fair hair. How would hair get caught in such a place?"

Sir Cosmo screwed up his eyes. He didn't understand what he was looking at.

Alec looked over his gold rims. "These few hairs must belong to Jenny. If I'm not very much mistaken, this is where Jenny's head hit the poster. Whether it was intentional or not... Although... The bruising about her neck and jaw, like that of a handprint, to my mind, suggests she did not merely run into the poster but— Cosmo? Are you perfectly well?"

Sir Cosmo's face was ashen. He groped in a frock coat pocket for his lace-bordered handkerchief. It fell to his feet and as he scrambled to pick it up he felt himself heave. With a muffled apology through the handkerchief pressed to his mouth, he made a dash to the window.

"IT'S WRONG!" LADY SYBILLA COMPLAINED, WRINGING HER hands. She was hot and shaking. "I won't have any part of this! I won't, Charlotte! *I won't*!"

"Oh, be quiet! I'm not asking you to do anything. As if you could," her sister said contemptuously. She wandered about the bedchamber. "This room will do nicely."

"What?" Lady Sybilla's eyes widened as she followed her sister. She swallowed convulsively when Lady Charlotte stopped by the bed. "Not here! You can't have my room. There must be a dozen empty bedchambers. There's *your* room."

"Don't be a complete simpleton. Macara's room is next door. He could very easily barge in on us. He does that occasionally. And we can't use one of the spares because they're in dust sheets. What would Oliphant think if we showed him into a room shut up and musty and without benefit of your maid and—fresh flowers?" Lady Charlotte admired the large colorful bouquet and inhaled the heady scent. "What fool gave you these?"

"Emily."

"How utterly sweet of her," Lady Charlotte said with a twisted smile, and pulled a petal from a white rose. "She's always preferred you. That's because you over-indulge her, just like Mamma."

"You know that isn't true. It's just that she and I are closer in age. I was still in the schoolroom when she was born and you were just married to Macara, so you weren't around to—"

"Thank God I wasn't! I couldn't have stood to watch Mamma fawn over Madeleine's bastard brat." Lady Charlotte shuddered dramatically and almost at once collected herself. "Oliphant will need the services of your maid. You will of course oblige. We can't stay here. Well, you won't. You can wait in your sitting room. If he asks for me to remain, I will have to agree."

"You can't mean to go through with this! It's *monstrous*."

"Stop blubbering and use your handkerchief! Of course it's not monstrous, you stupid woman. It's in her best interests. It will stop any scandal-mongering before it begins. Do you want people to think she isn't a virgin on her wedding night? Do you want to be stared at every time you go to Almacks? To have the family name bandied about like a common thing? Show sense, Sybilla. It's not as if this sort of thing isn't done from time to time. I realize it is unpleasant to think we have to stoop to seeking Oliphant's services in this way, but I assured Lord Delvin the man is terribly discreet."

"Delvin? You consulted him?"

Lady Charlotte drew herself up. "Don't look at me like that! If you must know he consulted me. And very proper of him, too!"

Lady Sybilla gave an hysterical sob.

"Be of some use and call your maid. Get her to find some towels and hot water and clean cloth. I suppose Oliphant requires all those things." She tidied her hair in the looking glass that hung over the mantel. "And tell her to be quick about it!" she called out, even though Lady Sybilla had not moved. "He can't be too much longer. How many dishes of tea can the man drink with Mamma?"

A scratch on the door, and at Lady Charlotte's command a footman came in to announce Sir John Oliphant—a man of middle height and prone to fat, who wore a creaking corset and the latest style of wig *à la pigeon.* The richness of his frock coat and breeches proclaimed the courtier rather than a learned man of medicine.

His keen eyes sensed hostility in the Lady Sybilla, who greeted him with nothing more than a pinched-face look. He acknowledged her with a bow, then focused all his attentions on the elder sister to whom he had spoken at length upon arriving at St. Neots House.

"As you predicted, my lady, Her Grace was not at all pleased to see me. However, I did leave her in a better mood. She has a weak heart, as you know, and a disturbance of so shocking a nature as you described can only have caused her much strain. I am pleased to say that she is in excellent health and bearing up well."

"That is good news, Sir John. I am relieved to hear you say so. Again I thank you for taking the time to come and see Mamma."

Sir John smiled. "My lady, please, it was the merest trifle of inconvenience. And it is always a pleasure to share a dish of the Duchess's most excellent tea."

And half a dozen cream cakes too, thought Lady Charlotte. She said aloud, "You did not mention your visit to this room or why …?"

"Of course not, my lady," he reassured her. "I agree with you wholeheartedly in the matter. The less Her Grace is disturbed, the better for her health."

Lady Sybilla twisted her handkerchief in a tight ball. "Mamma will be far more disturbed to be left ignorant of your intentions!"

"Dear lady," began Sir John and was interrupted by Lady Charlotte who lifted her hand.

"Sybilla! Did I not ask you to give orders to your maid?"

"It's horrid! *Horrid,*" Lady Sybilla threw at them, and rushed from the room with her lace handkerchief pressed to her mouth.

"She's very highly strung. Has been since a child," Lady Charlotte said with a dismissive smile. "Won't you be seated, Sir John? Emily will be here at any moment. Ah! Here she is now. Emily, dear, this is Sir John Oliphant come to pay you a visit."

Emily had come in without knocking. When she saw Lady Charlotte her first reaction was to go quietly out again, but she was seen. She knew Sir John as he had attended on her grandmother for several years. And just now, when she had wanted to speak to the Duchess, she was told by Neave Sir John was taking tea with her. Seeing the physician in Lady Sybilla's rooms she immediately presumed her aunt to be unwell.

"Is Aunt Sybilla feeling poorly?"

"Where is your curtsy, child?" Lady Charlotte said lightly, propelling Emily by the shoulders to where Sir John stood by the window. "You must forgive her, Sir John. The events of the past day…"

Emily shot her an angry look of embarrassment, but dutifully curtsied and had her hand kissed. "I am pleased to make your acquaintance, sir," she said, and wiped her wet hand across the small of her back, for which gesture her aunt could have slapped her face.

"How old are you, child?" asked Sir John, lifting Emily's chin to look in her gray eyes.

"Eighteen. Why do you want to see me, Sir John? You came to see Grandmamma."

Sir John smiled. "I have seen Her Grace and she is very well considering the strain she has been under of late. And now I am here to see you, my dear."

"Did Grandmamma ask for you to see me?"

"Emily, darling, you should be grateful Sir John has found the time to call on you. He is a distinguished physician who is much sought after."

"You are too kind, my lady. Open your mouth, child, so that I may see your tongue."

"Emily, do as you're bid!" Lady Charlotte snapped, her control at an end.

"There—There is nothing the matter with my tongue," Emily stammered, taking a step back, panic welling up within her.

"Forgive her, Sir John. She has been under tremendous strain.

What with her engagement and preparations for the Fireworks Ball, not to mention last night..."

Emily blushed. "Don't remind me of-of *that*. It's something I wish to forget."

"So do we all," retorted Lady Charlotte. "But it is something that cannot be ignored. So, please do as you are asked. It will mean less fuss and be much easier for you!"

"What-What do you want of me?" Emily asked, looking from her aunt to Sir John and back again.

"To ask you a few questions, child," Sir John said soothingly and again turned Emily's chin toward him. He took out his gold pocket watch and with two fat fingers pressed to her neck, studied its oyster shell face. Emily suffered this ministration, but when the physician put his pocket watch away she stepped back from him. He gave a sigh and looked to Lady Charlotte. "You said something about a maid, my lady?" And to Emily, "My dear child, I am here to help you. You have suffered a brutal attack and thus need to be seen by a physician such as myself. Your aunt is only concerned for your wellbeing, as is your intended husband. I have met the Earl of Delvin and find him to be a young man of superior manners and address. You are very fortunate indeed to be so honored. Won't you sit here and we shall talk a moment? Just we two." He held out a chair and gave Lady Charlotte a knowing look that sent her in search of her sister.

Emily hesitated, then sat on the very edge of the chair. With her aunt gone she felt less settled, but was relieved to see the sitting room door had been left ajar. Sir John went back to stand by the window, the light behind him leaving his face in shadow.

"You know I am a physician, child. You know I attend on your grandmother. Amongst society I have many female patients. I have attended the Queen at one of her lying-ins. What I am trying to say is this: You needn't fear me, or be embarrassed, or uncomfortable in my presence. I am here to help you, and what is said between us goes no further. Do you understand?"

"I am perfectly well, Sir John. I just wish to forget about last night."

"That is understandable. But tell me: Do you have any bruising on your body?"

Emily blinked.

"Do you feel in any pain?"

"My foot. I hit my foot on the curio cabinet."

"Anywhere else? The tops of your legs, perhaps?"

"Tops of my legs? N-no."

"No pain between your thighs? No pain in your belly?"

"Belly? He—he pushed down on me and his weight was uncomfortable but it wasn't painful."

"Did he lift your petticoats?"

Emily's face burned brick red and she averted her eyes.

"Did you feel his hands—" continued Sir John.

"His hands?" Emily repeated, nonplussed.

"Did he put his hands up your petticoats?"

"Yes—No! He tried but I—"

"My child, do you know how it is when a husband lies with his wife?"

Emily blinked. Then she understood and blanched.

Sir John took out his snuffbox. "Answer the question, my dear."

Emily stood on shaking legs. "That has nothing to do—to do with last night!"

"My child, it has everything to do with it," Sir John said calmly. "Girls of your birth and breeding are raised very carefully. It is only proper and natural you are kept ignorant of—er—certain facts until you are married. You may have been raped and not know it. Believe me, it has happened before, and to girls younger than yourself."

"That did not happen to me, Sir John," Emily answered on the verge of tears. "I—I may be—be ignorant, but I am not-not *witless*. If you must know, I've seen a horse mount a mare and it wasn't like that!"

"Emily," gasped Lady Charlotte, catching the last of this halting speech as she swept back into the room, Lady Sybilla and her maid in tow.

Sir John's fat cheeks were a brilliant pink and he collected himself only by turning to the window.

"Emily! How dare you talk in such a common fashion! You will most certainly give Sir John the wrong impression. Forgive her, Sir John. She is naturally high-spirited and has been known on occasion to say things just to shock and embarrass. A lamentable trait I fear she acquired associating with Mamma's godson, a mere clerk in the Foreign Department whose habits are Continental in the worst way imaginable."

"I—I don't know anything about his conduct on the Continent but Alec has always been kind and gentle and like a brother to me. I don't—"

"Be quiet!" demanded Lady Charlotte, and squeezed Emily's wrist so hard she cried out. "You will do as you are told," she whispered fiercely. "You are making a fool, not only of yourself, but of *us*. I won't stand for it! How can you expect to act the part of a countess when you can't act like a well-bred young lady?"

"I want to speak with Grandmamma," Emily demanded, pulling free and rubbing her wrist. "I want to see Edward!"

Lady Sybilla made a noise between a sob and a laugh. Lady Charlotte glared at her, then at Emily.

"Listen to me, you little fool," Lady Charlotte hissed, regaining possession of Emily's reddened wrist. "Four hundred people are coming here tonight to celebrate your engagement with a magnificent Fireworks Ball. Everything is arranged. But if you don't allow Sir John to examine you, Lord Delvin may very well call the whole thing off! Do you understand me?"

Emily did not understand at all. "Call what off? The—*the ball*? But why? He can't think me so poorly—"

Sir John coughed politely. "My lady, perhaps the child needs more time to—"

"Nonsense. There isn't time! Besides, it's not her place to

decide," Lady Charlotte said haughtily. "She's distraught. She may even have a fever. The shock of last night has addled her brain. She isn't herself. Be patient with her and I know—"

"I want to see Grandmamma!" Emily demanded, breaking free and trying the bedchamber door and finding it locked. When she made for the sitting room Lady Charlotte barred her way. "You can't make me stay here! I want to see Edward! I want him to tell me this is what *he* wants."

Lady Charlotte slapped her face.

"Excuse us a moment, Sir John," she said politely, and while Emily was still in shock from the stinging blow to her cheek, dragged her into the sitting room. "How *dare* you humiliate me in this way, you little witch! Now be still and listen to me! Oh, do shut up, Sybilla! If you must cry, for God's sake do it elsewhere."

"I won't leave Emily," sobbed her sister. "I won't!"

"Please, Aunt Sybilla, don't cry," Emily pleaded. She tried to pull away from Lady Charlotte. "Let go of me! You can't make me!"

"If you don't go through with this, it will be the end of your hopes of being Countess of Delvin. He expects a virgin on his wedding night and a virgin you will be! That's why Sir John is here, you little fool. We can't afford another family scandal, but if you refuse to allow Sir John to examine you it can only mean one thing: You permitted a man into your bed last night."

Tears spilled onto Emily's flushed cheeks. "How can you accuse me of being so horridly wicked?"

"Because that's what others will think if you don't allow Sir John to examine you! That's what Lord Delvin will think!"

Emily attempted a moment of bravado. "Edward would never believe me capable of such wanton behavior! He loves me."

"Loves you?" Lady Charlotte said with an hysterical laugh. "With thirty thousand pounds on your head I imagine any man could love you."

"Thirty thousand pounds?"

"Your dowry, little idiot. Enough money to catch a respectable husband. Enough money to wipe away the stain of your birth."

"But Grandmamma permitted me to choose."

"With thirty thousand pounds Mamma wasn't about to let you marry anything less than a title," Lady Charlotte stated contemptuously. "Certainly not throw yourself away on Delvin's nobody of a brother."

"Alec? He's never once said he wanted to marry me."

Lady Charlotte laughed shrilly. "You little fool! *Marry you*? Of course he never meant to marry you. Men of his stamp don't marry. But seduce you, ruin you, oh yes, that I can well believe!"

Emily looked at the Lady Sybilla with wide curiosity. "Is Alec truly like that, Aunt Sybilla? *Is he*?"

Before Sybilla could reply her sister said harshly, "Alec Halsey ruined Selina Jamison-Lewis's chances of a happy marriage when he seduced her in the wood, and for all we know, it was he who forced himself on you last night!"

Lady Sybilla burst into tears. "Charlotte! How can you make such vile accusations about a man who—"

"Because Emily has a right to the truth about Alec Halsey, particularly when his own brother considers him a moral abomination." Lady Charlotte pulled Emily to her and whispered in her face. "Your marriage to the Earl of Delvin means a great deal to Mamma. It will right all your mother's wrongs. But if you want to break Mamma's heart, just as your mother did before you, then I am only too willing to send Sir John back to London." She pushed Emily off, an ugly twisted line to her white mouth. "It is your choice not to go through with the examination," she stated in a bloodless voice. "No one will blame Lord Delvin when he steps back from this engagement. But where will that leave you? No one wants tainted milk. No one will want you. Mamma's heart will break, but at least her eyes will be open to the horrible truth: That her beloved granddaughter is the image of her disgraced daughter. What a pity. And what a waste of Mamma's careful nurturing." She turned away in a swish of stiff silk petticoats. "Come, Sybilla. We must make our apologies to Sir John…"

Emily opened her mouth to speak but not a word issued forth. She felt suddenly hot and close and yet at the same time cold and light-headed. Her head throbbed at the temples. She pressed her palms to her cheeks and shut her eyes because the room had begun to spin about her. She wished she knew what she should do. She wished her grandmother was with her. She wished she were anywhere but here. Suddenly, she felt her knees buckle and everything went dark, as if she had closed her eyes, although she knew she was staring wide-eyed at her sobbing aunt. Then, all at once, she crumpled to the floor in a heap of billowing petticoats, her ears ringing with Lady Sybilla's screams.

WHEN EMILY OPENED HER EYES SHE WAS ON LADY SYBILLA'S bed. The pleated silk canopy above her began to spin again. She shut tight her eyes. She felt listless and miserable. She wanted nothing more than to curl up under the soft coverlet and hope the nightmare would pass. There were whispered voices on both sides of her. A cool hand touched her forehead, then her neck, and stayed there a moment longer than she considered necessary so she pushed it off. The scent of a familiar perfume made her nose twitch.

"Drink this, dearest," Lady Sybilla said soothingly, smoothing the damp blonde hair off the girl's forehead. To someone across the bed she said, "You can see she isn't well enough to—"

"Sir John has been more than patient."

"Charlotte! You can't still mean to go through with this! *Please*."

"Certainly. We must."

"Oh, no, Charlotte! *No*."

Emily clutched at Lady Sybilla's hand. "It's all right, Aunt Sybilla."

"You're not well, dearest. You can't know what they mean to do."

"Yes, I do know," Emily answered listlessly. "I've done nothing wrong. I'm not afraid."

"See, Sybilla. Emily is a sensible girl after all."

"Stay with me, Aunt Sybilla."

Lady Sybilla couldn't look at her. "Charlotte would be better than I."

"I won't have anyone but you."

"Do as she wants," commanded Lady Charlotte. She left the bed to consult with Sir John who was removing the lace bands at his wrists. "Thank you for being so patient. I hardly expected her to be this difficult."

"Do not upset yourself, my lady. She is not the most difficult female I have attended on. The child is young and spirited, and it is only natural for her to be a little frightened."

Lady Charlotte smiled thinly. "You are all kindness and understanding."

EIGHT

HALF AN HOUR LATER, LADY CHARLOTTE CAME SAILING down the main staircase in search of the Earl of Delvin and found herself caught up in an early arrival for the Fireworks Ball.

An old gentleman with grizzled hair, a servant at his back leading two greyhounds, was being greeted by the Duchess of Romney-St. Neots, while footmen carried portmanteaux into the wide marble foyer. A younger gentleman in a scarlet frock with silver lacings and carrying an amber-headed cane came in behind the bag-carrying footmen and waited to be noticed, looking nervously about and up at the gold leaf and painted blue domed ceiling.

Lady Charlotte was not pleased to have her mission interrupted and was about to return to the second landing when her mother saw her and beckoned her down to join the group.

Plantagenet Halsey introduced Simon Tremarton to the Duchess saying, "He doesn't have a gilt-edged card of invitation, but I knew you wouldn't take exception to an extra pair of feet on the dance floor. He is brother to Lady Gervais and acquainted with Alec through the Foreign Department."

"Your Grace," Simon muttered and bowed low. "It was not my wish to intrude on your hospitality."

"Not at all, Mr. Tremarton," the Duchess said kindly, extending her hand to the old man. She introduced Lady Charlotte and was secretly pleased to see her daughter thrown off-balance to have her hand bowed over by a man she considered fit only for Tyburn. It served her to rights; the Duchess was still furious with her for fetching Sir John Oliphant.

Lady Charlotte almost recoiled when introduced to Plantagenet Halsey. She forced herself to give him her hand. In her opinion this old man with his republican sentiments had no place in a nobleman's house; better to invite a highwayman to sit down to dinner. To Simon Tremarton she was no better with her civilities. Obviously he was a friend of this traitor or he wouldn't have shared his carriage. When the greyhounds began sniffing at her silk mules, it was too much for her to bear, and she hurriedly excused herself with a whispered apology and an agitated wave of her gouache fan.

Plantagenet Halsey laughed openly at the woman's hurried exit. He sent Tam off with the dogs to find his nephew and turned to the Duchess with a grin.

"So that's the one Alec says is crab-faced. Are all your daughters like that one, Your Grace?"

"Fortunately, no. Though Sybilla is a little dim-witted," said the Duchess with a roll of her eyes. She took the arm he offered her, and with Mr. Tremarton following up behind, they went through to the Long Gallery where most of the house guests had assembled for an afternoon of card-playing. "I'll have Neave fetch Alec. Would you care for refreshment?"

Plantagenet Halsey patted her hand. "Don't you worry yourself about us. Tremarton and I can wait for afternoon tea. Tell me how you are," he said gruffly, looking down at her with concern. "And don't give me any flam!"

Flustered by such rough speech, but just as pleased by it, the Duchess sat with him on a settee away from her guests, and Simon Tremarton politely excused himself and sauntered off to the card tables.

He soon saw his sister. Her whole concentration was on the cards in her hand. When she casually glanced up Simon winked at her. She almost leapt up. She knocked her fan to the floor. A gentleman standing nearby scooped it up and placed it on the table beside her reticule. Her thank you was perfunctory. Everyone was awaiting her bid. She discarded recklessly. Simon's smile widened and he walked away to join a knot of people lounging about on a collection of chairs central to the long room. Lord Gervais was one of their number, and although he was not fond of his wife's brother, he had the good manners to invite Simon to join them.

"Hunt, Tremarton?" asked Lord Andrew Macara. "Sit down! Sit down! No ceremony here, what!"

"Sorry to say, my lord, I don't have the time to indulge that passion," said Simon, perching on the edge of a chair. "I shoot occasionally."

"Ah," replied Macara and lapsed into silence.

"Tremarton is in the diplomatic service," Lord Gervais explained to Selina, who sat on his right, languidly fanning air across her bare shoulders. "Always on the Continent."

"Mr. Tremarton and I have been introduced," Selina answered, her dark eyes never wavering from Simon's face. She watched him color up and look away. "Foreign courts and foreign customs! All that intrigue. Perhaps I will take up travel…?"

"You'd hate it, Selina," Sir Cosmo said with a laugh. "Mayhap not Paris. But the travel. The endless roads!"

"You're right of course." She sighed dramatically and put a long white hand to her temple. "Travel gives one the headache. Coming out here was arduous enough. All ninety minutes of it." She and Sir Cosmo shared a private laugh. "In that, I am not unlike my cousin Jack. Jack so hated to travel. He was very much a London man. I wonder what induced him to go into Yorkshire…?"

"Grouse," stated Macara. "Had to be the grouse."

"Truly? At this time of year?" Selina said with exaggerated

surprise, putting Sir Cosmo on alert and again turning her large dark eyes on Simon. "And all along I had presumed it was to bag a bird of an altogether different feather. Perhaps, Mr. Tremarton, you can enlighten us. After all, you did accompany Jack into York-shire, did you not?"

Simon Tremarton blanched and mumbled a response to the effect that, yes, he did go into Yorkshire at Jack Belsay's invitation, Lord Andrew Macara intervening by saying, "That so, Tremarton? Shoot anything worth talking about?"

Simon opened his mouth, a swift glance at Selina and it was she who said to his lordship with a smile, "I have no idea as to Mr. Tremarton's accuracy of eye, but Jack was very well pleased with his considerable skill in handling his weapon. Grouse, I suspect, was of secondary importance."

Macara nodded. "Got to have good technique. Nothing worse than a man who can't hold his weapon and discharge it in the proper manner!"

Selina grinned behind her fan, but her eyes were so brimful of laughter that Sir Cosmo made a mental note to find out what had so amused her. But right now his attention was diverted, as was everyone's, by the elderly couple deep in conversation across the room.

"Who's that scruffy fellow in close conversation with Her Grace? Eh, Tremarton? Know him?" asked Lord Gervais, quizzing glass up to a watery eye.

"Mr. Plantagenet Halsey, my lord," answered his brother-in-law, feeling a huge relief that curiosity had been deflected from him.

Several quizzing glasses turned in the old man's direction. Lord Gervais snorted contempt. Sir Cosmo grinned. Macara looked none the wiser and asked Selina to elaborate.

"Mr. Halsey is an outspoken Member of Parliament, my lord."

"Outspoken, be damned! Begging your pardon, Madam," growled Lord Gervais, "but that buzzard is a traitor to King and country!"

"He has certain republican sentiments, that's true," Sir Cosmo added calmly.

"Republican? Pah!" said Lord Gervais. "The man's a lunatic! If he weren't in the Commons he'd have been thrown in the Tower by now."

"I'm so glad he decided to come out here," Selina Jamison-Lewis said with relish. "I was beginning to despair of a little excitement."

"What in the name of all that's sacred is he doing here?" Lord Gervais demanded.

"He's Delvin's uncle," Sir Cosmo said with a grin and winked at Selina.

"The man's a nuisance to society!" grumbled Lord Gervais, slightly mollified to learn the old man had good lineage. "He thinks we ought to give in to those American colonists' demands. Writes seditious pamphlets inciting the cattle to riot."

"But they can't even read," Selina pointed out.

"Can't imagine what they've got to talk about," said Macara. "The man would have us all beheaded if he could. Frightening. What!"

"Oh, I don't know if Mr. Halsey's beliefs run to the blood-thirsty, my lord," said Selina, a pointed stare at Lord Gervais. "But seated at his table, you certainly wouldn't outrank a dung-carter."

Lord Andrew Macara's eyes widened and he blustered. "*Dung-carter*? Well! Indeed!"

"The man's certifiable!" stated Lord Gervais, whose anger showed no signs of abating. "You a disciple of his, Tremarton?"

"Certainly not, my lord. I barely know him. His nephew, Mr. Alec Halsey and I are in the service together. My association with Mr. Halsey is, thankfully, limited."

Sir Cosmo shook his powdered head. "That's a shame, Tremarton. Plantagenet Halsey is worth an acquaintance. Underneath all that rhetoric is a good honest man."

Simon Tremarton colored painfully. "I wasn't suggesting—"

"I don't give a fig for his honesty," interrupted Lord Gervais.

"He's a nuisance to society and a hypocrite showing his face here! He should be evicted at once!"

"Steady on, Gervais," Lord Andrew Macara said darkly. "Invited by Her Grace. Can't throw him out. Bad form. Wouldn't be polite."

"But the man don't even believe in primogeniture and entail," Lord Gervais persisted. "Where would that leave the continuance of your bloodline and property, my lord, if it were not passed onto your eldest son and heir? Whoever heard of a second and third son receiving equal portions of their elder brother's inherited right? Eh? Madness!"

Lord Andrew Macara put up his quizzing glass to better view Plantagenet Halsey, a frown between his brows, the only sign of disapproval he would permit himself to display at the Duchess's choice of house guest. The lull in the conversation gave Simon Tremarton the opportunity to excuse himself. No sooner did he stand than he was pounced on by his sister. She made no apology for dragging him away to the relative privacy of an alcove by a French window.

"Pleased to see me, love?" Simon Tremarton quipped as he disentangled his sister's fingers from the lace at his wrist.

"I can't imagine you were sent an invitation," Cynthia Gervais whispered, annoyed. "Why are you here, Simon?"

"I came to see Alec Halsey. He's the brother of your—"

"I know perfectly well who he is!"

"Ah. So you've met the walking Greek statue. Get your claws into him yet, Cindy?"

"Why do you suppose I'd be interested in him?" she said with a pout, little nose in the air.

Simon Tremarton grinned and flicked her under the chin. "Rejected, eh? Poor Cindy. What a blow to your self-esteem. You probably threw yourself at him, too."

"You try and do better!" she taunted.

Simon gave a shiver of delight, and said with a lift of his

eyebrows, "Given half a chance, I'd love to find out if he's as virile as he looks."

"You're disgusting!"

Simon shrugged. "No more disgusting than you getting on your knees for the likes of Delvin." He glanced down the length of the long room. "Where is the lover earl?"

"He wandered off with Lady Charlotte—"

"Rival, love?"

"No! The woman's a prude." She stopped fluttering her fan and stared hard at her brother. "What do you want with him, Simon? You're scheming something. Tell me!"

"I've unfinished business with the Earl—"

"Edward won't give you money."

"I don't want a paltry thousand."

Cynthia Gervais gasped. "Simon?! You've managed to raise the money for Reubens?"

"No, I haven't managed to raise the money," he mimicked sarcastically. "How in the space of a few days do you think I could? But I will, and have guineas to spare. You'll see."

"H-how?"

Simon smiled. From his frock coat pocket he produced a worn yellowed envelope. "With this. Your lover earl will want to hand over much more than a paltry thousand pounds. And I intend to squeeze him as hard as I can. If he's stupid enough to fob me off, then his brother will be mightily interested to see what I've got, and pay for it, too."

"You're mad! You can't blackmail Edward, or his brother. You'll not only lose your post, but most likely end up stuck with a sword, same as Belsay."

"Ha! Jack was a naïve fool to think Delvin would fight fair. Now go back to your game of Basset. Your dull-witted husband is staring at us."

"What do I care about that? He's always staring at me."

"Still peering at you and the lover earl through keyholes?"

Cynthia Gervais glanced over her bare shoulder and met her

husband's unblinking gaze. Lord Andrew Macara was talking at him but he wasn't paying attention. She turned to her brother with a twinge of conscience.

"Don't do anything to upset him, Simon. You've already tried his patience over that ghastly Ganymede business. He managed to pull you out of that mess, but he takes his judicial duties seriously. If you think he'll step in and save your neck a second time, you're much mistaken"

Simon smiled and kissed her cheek, eyes on his brother-in-law. "Don't worry, love. It's not *my* neck that needs saving." And with a bow, he strolled off to try his luck at one of the card tables.

TAM FOUND ALEC IN THE LITTLE-USED COURTYARD OFF THE servant wing. He was stripped to his shirtsleeves and engaged in giving a lesson in the finer points of fencing to a lanky youth with a spotty face. Four little girls sat perched high up on the stone wall. Tam noted with a crooked smile that his master's frock coat was being used to keep the damp from their petticoats. A boy who resembled Alec's fencing partner leaned on the wall close by, as silent as his sisters and just as preoccupied.

It said much for his master's performance that Tam's presence went unnoticed for a full minute. And then it was Cromwell and Marziran who interrupted the lesson, tugging on their leads, eager to go to their master. Watching a fencing lesson could not compete with the attractions of two prancing greyhounds. The squeals of the youngest children brought the lesson to a close, and Alec obliged his spectators' demands and lifted the girls off the wall.

They were well-behaved enough not to rush at Tam, and when he gave the hounds some slack, the children coyly moved forward, hands outstretched to offer scratches, pats and strokes. The two boys deemed themselves above such juvenile entertainment and detained Alec with a hundred questions until a servant girl emerged from the kitchen, carrying a tray of refreshments which she placed atop a sundial. A footman brought Alec a tankard of ale, which was almost over-set by six eager children scampering across the cobble-stones to receive their tumbler of punch and slice of seedy cake.

"Come to rescue me, Tam?" Alec smiled, pulling affectionately at the ears of his dogs. "My uncle arrive safely?"

"Mr. Halsey is with Her Grace, sir. We brought a visitor with us."

"Yes?"

"A Mr. Simon Tremarton."

"Tremarton?" Alec waited for Tam to continue, but the boy was frowning and a little distracted and fiddled with the dogs' leads.

"Mr. Tremarton was at St. James's Place when I arrived," Tam explained. "He asked to see you, sir, and was a bit agitated when Mr. Wantage told him you'd be away for the weekend. That's when Mr. Halsey showed up with his bag and they got to talking. One thing led to another and he's here now."

"Then I'll find out what he wants soon enough."

"Sir—!" Tam began, and then stopped because the boy with the spotty face, his brother in tow, came up to be noticed.

"Oliver and I want to thank you again, sir," said the boy, and pulled his brother forward with him. "We're not proper swordsmen yet, but we'll be better in a few years. Then perhaps we can use real swords instead of these blunt rapiers, which is something I'd—well, Oliver and I—would like more than anything!"

Their eldest sister called to them. They were all wanted inside at once. Charles shuffled his feet and felt painfully embarrassed to be seen at the beck and call of a female in front of his hero.

"Oliver and I aren't usually thrown together with our sisters," he confided. "Our tutor, Mr. Brown, has taken ill with the influenza, so Mamma wouldn't have him. Though Papa said Mr. Brown has nothing more than a sniffle."

"Lewis and Cousin Harry can't come out today on account of a trick they played on Old Nurse," explained Oliver in support of his brother. "Mamma made them stay indoors and work on their Latin." He looked to his elder brother for support. "That's why we are forced to keep company with our sisters."

"How unfortunate for you," Alec sympathized. "But I'm sure you take very good care of your sisters, even if it is a sad trial on a man's time."

Charles nodded seriously. "That's true, sir. They are a trial." He pulled Oliver's coat tail. "Come on, Oliver. Mr. Halsey doesn't want to hear about Cousin Harry and Lewis. Just a silly boy's prank," he assured Alec. "They were playing at ghosts on the servant stairs last night, all to scare Old Nurse, and were caught out, not once but twice."

"By whom, Charles?" interrupted Alec, trying to sound disinterested.

The brothers exchanged a puzzled look, then Charles said, "Lewis said the first gentleman growled at them, which scattered their wits and sent them running all the way to the bottom of the stairs into the servant passage. That's where the second gentleman caught them. Mamma says Lewis and Cousin Harry must write a note of apology to Lord Delvin. Serves them to rights, I say. Anyway, we must be going, sir, before we're fetched. Thanks again, sir!" He made Alec a short formal bow and scampered off with Oliver at his heels.

Tam picked up Alec's crumpled and dirty frock coat, put it over his arm and waited to be noticed. It said much for his new-found self-control that he held his tongue and did not immediately resume the conversation he had started when interrupted by the two boys. But he was not about to come between devoted animals and their master, so he leaned against the low stone wall and watched Alec messing about with his dogs, who scampered about the courtyard free of their leads. Finally, Alec finished off his ale and, calling the greyhounds to heel, came across to Tam.

"Time to change for afternoon tea, Tam. One must always look one's sartorial best, be it for tea and cake or the Fireworks

Ball," he said, rolling down his shirtsleeves. "Did you bring back the silver-threaded waistcoat for tonight?"

"Yes, sir."

"And the letter to Yarrborough and Yarrborough—did you personally deliver it to their chambers?"

"Yes, sir. Sir—!"

"Was there any reply?"

"Mr. Yarrborough the Younger said he'd have something for you tomorrow afternoon if at all possible—Sir! I didn't finish telling you about Simon Tremarton."

Alec stopped. "So you didn't. What about him?"

"I've seen him before, sir." When this revelation produced nothing more than a blank look, Tam added in a rush, "I seen him at Mr. Dobbs', sir. I did! I was never more surprised when he showed up at your house. I don't think he recognized me, so you can rest easy, sir."

"And had Mr. Tremarton recognized you, would there be a need for me to be uneasy?"

"He—he didn't come into the shop for the usual reasons, sir," Tam answered slowly, not meeting his master's gaze.

Alec leaned against the low stone wall and crossed his arms. "You surprise me. Why did he visit Dobbs?"

Tam was silent a moment. He looked up at Alec's impassive face.

"I-I haven't exactly been truthful with you, sir."

"Haven't you?"

"You wouldn't have let me stay if I had!" Tam burst out. "And it's not as if I lied to you! I didn't. I was Mr. Dobbs' apprentice, and that's all I was! Not that you'll believe me."

"I thought you knew me better than that."

Tam hung his head. "Well, you wouldn't have believed me if I'd told you straight out when I asked to be your valet," he amended. "It's not as if I've done a wrong. I haven't. Still, you wouldn't have had me."

"Do you want to tell me what it was Dobbs was engaged in,

other than his apothecary business, or shall I make an educated guess?"

"I'll tell you. I had been meaning to. It was just... I was going to tell you."

"But Mr. Tremarton's appearance at St. James's Place prompted this sudden willingness," Alec stated. "If it makes the task easier, I'm not about to dismiss you for something Dobbs did, legal or otherwise. You say you were his apprentice and confined yourself to those duties. I take you at your word."

"Thank you, sir." Tam breathed easier. "I just hope you'll believe me about Mr. Dobbs, sir, because he was a good man. There ain't a grain of truth in what they said about him. It's all lies. *Lies and treachery.* He couldn't have done what they said he did. I tell you, sir, Mr. Dobbs was a good man. Kind, honest, and nothin' nobody says will have me believin' otherwise!"

"Perhaps if you were to tell me exactly what it was Dobbs was supposed to have done?" Alec prompted gently.

"Yes, sir. Sorry, sir. It just makes me as mad as anything to think a good and worthy man was convicted of something he didn't do!" He took a deep breath and began his story. "Mr. Dobbs had his premises just off the Fleet Street, and we did a brisk business at most times. He preferred to live in the back two rooms behind the preparation room. I had a cot under the work bench and had my meals at Mr. Dobbs' table whenever he was in the mood for company. Sometimes his temper was short, especially if he'd been out in the parish. He'd go with the vicar, Mr. Blackwell, to treat the poor and such. I guess that's why he didn't turn much of a profit. He didn't talk about that side of the business, or about his family. Except I knew Mrs. Hendy was his sister—"

"The housekeeper at Delvin?"

"Yes, sir. When her ladyship died, Mrs. Hendy sent me to be apprenticed to Mr. Dobbs."

"Do you know why?"

Tam shook his head. "All Mrs. Hendy would say was that I couldn't expect to live on the charity of his lordship, now his mother was gone. She said his lordship wouldn't take too kindly to having me under his roof."

"And Dobbs…?"

"Mr. Dobbs had his apothecary shop on the ground floor," explained Tam. "And he forbade me to trespass to the other three floors. He said if ever I did, then I'd be dismissed. On the first floor there was a gaming hell called the Jack of Hearts, and the other two floors were rented out to this club too. It was frequented by fashionable gentlemen, with lace at their wrists and expensive frocks, who came and went at all hours of the night. On some nights there was so much noise and carryings-on above our heads that we didn't get much sleep." He glanced at Alec, whose face betrayed no emotion, whatever his thoughts, then continued.

"One day, in walks Mr. Tremarton. I recognized him because once he'd come into the shop drunk, and demanded to see a lad named Phillip. Said he was his regular. When Mr. Dobbs told him he was in the wrong place, Mr. Tremarton got angry. It was only when a soft-spoken gentleman came in and coaxed Mr. Tremarton outdoors that we got rid of him. The soft-spoken gentleman returned a few minutes later. He apologized to Mr. Dobbs and as he left he threw a couple of guineas on the counter.

"When Mr. Tremarton came into the shop a second time he wasn't drunk, and he demanded to speak to Mr. Dobbs in private. But Mr. Dobbs tried to get rid of him quick, saying he didn't want his kind in his shop; that he ran a respectable business. But Mr. Tremarton wouldn't be persuaded and said if Mr. Dobbs wouldn't talk to him quiet-like, he'd get the law onto him! So Mr. Dobbs took him through to the preparation room. They were there for some time before the same soft-spoken gentleman friend of Mr. Tremarton's came in and fetched him."

"Would you recognize this soft-spoken gentleman if you saw him again, Tam?"

"I'm sure I would, sir, because he spoke to me directly. He asked me if I liked living in the city and if I missed the country air, and then he offered Mr. Dobbs his regrets for disturbing us. I opened the door for them to pass out, and I remember Mr. Tremarton saying to the soft-spoken gentleman in a gleeful voice that if he wasn't very much mistaken they'd found the golden fleece, and what did he, Jack, think about that?"

"Jack? Are you certain Tremarton addressed his friend as Jack?"

"Yes, sir," answered Tam, watching his master set to pacing in front of the wall, the greyhounds remaining obediently still, yet their eyes never leaving their master for a moment. "I remember it particularly because the gaming hell upstairs was called the Jack of Hearts and I thought the circumstance an odd coincidence, that's all." When Alec merely nodded, a frown between his dark brows, Tam licked his dry lips, adding quietly, "I don't know what Mr. Tremarton and Mr. Dobbs talked about, but after that, Mr. Dobbs said if ever I spoke to any gentleman stranger with fine lace at his wrists he'd beat me raw. Sir..."

In the silence of Tam's hesitation, Alec turned and looked at him with an understanding smile. "Whatever you tell me goes no further, Tam. And I've seen a reasonable slice of life not to be shocked by anything you may wish to confide."

Tam nodded and cast his gaze to the uneven flagstones. "Living in that part of the city one gets to know about—about *life*, sir. All sorts of life. Whores on every corner and in every second building a brothel or one of them with the fancy name, Turkish Baths. But I never expected—what I'm trying to say is—I know the gentlemen who visited the Jack of Hearts weren't there just for the gambling and the wine! But I had no idea that the brothel on the third floor was a male brothel. It's beyond anything, sir!

After a pause that seemed an age to Tam, Alec said, "How did Dobbs get caught?"

"Mr. Dobbs had nothing to do with it!" Tam said with a mutinous pout. "He kept his shop. That's all he did!"

"He obviously knew what was going on over his head."

"Yes, I guess he must've. But just because he knew about those carryings-on don't make him a party to it, sir."

"Why didn't he report what he knew to the authorities?"

"To what purpose, sir? What would the beadles have done?" Tam forced himself to look Alec in the eyes. "Plenty of gentlemen visit brothels and the law don't give a tester because they're getting their cut. They turn a blind eye, none the wiser but a whole lot richer for doing so!"

Alec held the boy's gaze. "That's very true, but the law finally turned its eyes on this male brothel. Why?"

Tam felt tears in his eyes and he again dropped his gaze to the stones under his boots. "I don't know. That is, the beadles kept their distance all right, for a time, and then one day without warning the militia turned up and cleared the place out. And not only the floors above us. They wrecked the shop too. They overturned tables and smashed bottles and—and... All those years of work! All Mr. Dobbs' apparatus..."

"What did you do?"

"Me? I hid up the chimney. I knew if they found me they'd think I was one of them upstairs. Mr. Dobbs never gave me away. He kept his tongue. Sir!" Tam said suddenly, "I know Mr. Dobbs had nothin' to do with the goings-on upstairs. How could they blame him for what those gentlemen got up to behind closed doors?"

"If what you say is true, then it seems your Mr. Dobbs was used as a scapegoat for the crimes of others," Alec said gently. "Perhaps if he'd come forward when he first realized what was going on he might have avoided prosecution? To stand back and let such perversities continue... He deserved to be punished for—"

"Well, they hanged him!" Tam burst out rudely, tears spilling down his burning cheeks. "They branded him a sodomite and a pimp and hanged him! No one came forward to defend him. Not one of those wretches he doctored for free with his medicines. Not Mr. Blackwell. Not Mrs. Hendy. Not me; *no one*. And I'll lay you any odds you care that not one of those gentlemen who amused themselves with those lads was touched by the law. Look at Mr. Tremarton. Here he is at St. Neots House enjoying Her Grace's hospitality! It ain't fair and it ain't right!"

Alec gave Tam his handkerchief. "No it isn't. Especially for those with no recourse to privilege and power. That's a fact of life and there is very little you or I can do about it. I'm not saying it's right. It's not. My uncle tries his best to voice his concerns in Parliament, yet his is a lone voice. Those gentlemen who paid for the sexual favors of those young boys deserve to be dispatched in the same manner as your Mr. Dobbs. In fact, they deserve worse. To be publicly flogged and put in the pillory for all to see. There is no greater punishment for a gentleman than to have his character and good name besmirched." He sighed. "Tam, I can't bring Dobbs back. I don't even know if I can believe out-of-hand what you've told me. I'm not saying that I don't credit your story. I do. Yet, there may be circumstances that you don't fully understand."

Tam blew his nose and sniffed. "Mr. Dobbs was an honest man!"

"So you have said. I will make a few inquiries of my own—"

"Can—Can you, sir?"

"I will do my best. Now, tell me: Are you in any danger from the law?"

"I don't know, sir. I don't think so. Nobody came looking for me. Nobody but Mrs. Hendy knows I was Mr. Dobbs' apprentice. Oh, except Mr. Tremarton and his friend. Do you think they—"

"No. The soft-spoken gentleman certainly won't bother you," Alec assured him.

Poor Jack can be of bother to no one now, he thought sadly as he joined the rest of the guests for afternoon tea in the opulent Oriental drawing room, where there was laughter and music and the clinking of fine porcelain. He went immediately to the tea trolley, as if a dish of coffee could somehow wash away the disgust and anger he felt knowing Dobbs the apothecary had gone to the gallows a scapegoat to atone for the sins of his betters. He saw Simon Tremarton standing by the pianoforte, where Lady Sybilla and Sir Cosmo were banging out a duet, and avoided his eye, seeking refuge at the back of the room, in no mood to make small talk. It was a simple matter to remain by the window unnoticed while dishes of tea and coffee and plates of sweetmeats and pastries were passed around. He even managed to avoid saying more than a polite word to his hostess, as much as she seemed to want him to remain at her side when she handed him his dish.

His uncle was chatting with one of the guests. His brother strutted about the room dressed in a magnificent saffron satin frock embroidered at cuffs and skirt with vines and fruit, and matching breeches with diamond knee buckles. He smiled benevolently on all who fell under his gaze; he even smiled on his brother. Alec had to turn his back lest anyone see the look on his face. He stared out the window at the forest below, stretching out like a dense green carpet hugging the river as it meandered east toward the city, and felt panniered petticoats brush his stockinged legs. He turned to discover Lady Gervais smiling up at him with a perfectly painted and patched face. There was a twinkle in her eye as she sipped her tea and watched him under her long, darkened lashes.

"You will save a dance for me tonight, won't you?" she asked sweetly, the slight tremble in her voice indicating that she feared his rejection.

Alec smiled down at her, but his response was not what she was expecting. "Did you go directly to Delvin's apartments after leaving the Chinese drawing room last night, my lady?"

She blinked. "Before I came to you? I told you: He wasn't in his rooms—"

"But you didn't go to his rooms, did you?" When she looked bewildered he added, "There was no need. You saw him somewhere else in the house first."

"And if I did?" she asked defensively.

"Where did you see him?"

She took a small step closer, to press herself against his leg, her voluminous petticoats making those in the room none the wiser. "Later, shall we finish what we started last night?"

His smile in response was almost enough to make her swoon.

"Had we started something, my lady? So where did you see my brother?"

She huffed. "I told you: He was with Selina Jamison-Lewis."

"Not when you saw him."

She pretended an interest in the sticks of her carved ivory fan. "If you must know, I caught him in the shrubbery with a plain-faced kitchen slut."

"Was this immediately after he left the Chinese drawing room?"

"Not straight away," she said sullenly. "He had to escort his little bride up to her rooms because the excitement had given her the headache." She flicked opened her fan with an agitated shake. "Edward was to meet me on the terrace, but when he didn't appear after some five *freezing* minutes, I went in search of him. I was never more mortified when I discovered him being pleasured by a servant. Imagine preferring a cheap slut to me?"

"How ill-mannered of him."

"That's when I came to you."

"To have your pride restored and to teach Delvin a lesson?" Alec bowed over her hand. "Forgive me for not being more sensitive to your needs, my lady."

This restored her mood and she giggled. "But how did you know?"

"You'd been out of doors. There was mud on your shoes and the stockings covering your lovely feet were damp," he said and watched her eyes widen. "Oh, and you may rest easy, my lady. Mrs. Jamison-Lewis and my brother are not lovers."

"I do have lovely feet, don't I?" she said with a self-satisfied sigh then, taking in the rest of what he had said, a spark came into her eyes. "Not lovers? Truly? But Edward said…"

She was either a first rate actress or amazingly dull-witted. Alec inclined to the latter belief. As vacant as she was beautiful. Just the sort of female to suit Delvin. So his brother was out in the shrubbery with a servant; he would hazard a guess that the girl was none other than the chambermaid sent to fetch Emily's milk. Tam had described her appearance as disheveled. No wonder she was closed-mouthed with Neave. A chambermaid was not likely to confess to entertaining one of the gentleman guests; that would bring instant dismissal.

But what of Delvin? According to Cindy Gervais, he had taken Emily up to her rooms, but he must have left her at the door. And according to the boys Charles and Oliver, Lewis and Cousin Harry had stumbled upon Delvin in the servant passage at the bottom of the stairs leading up to Emily's rooms. If he had been playing at billiards, then he could easily have heard the boys running about in the passage. But was he playing at billiards before or after his liaison with the chambermaid? And who was the unknown gentleman who had growled at the boys? Perhaps Delvin had bumped into the chambermaid in the passage? Had he been in the shrubbery when the attack took place? So why hadn't he said this and used the girl as an alibi? But how would that look for him, to admit to fornicating with a servant while his bride-to-be was being attacked in her own rooms?

Alec hoped Cosmo had some news for him. He at least had spent the day mingling with the guests, while Alec had played nursemaid to a gaggle of children. Not that he was complaining. He had enjoyed himself, and Charles and Oliver had unwittingly told him a piece of interesting information. Aware that Lady Gervais was still looking up at him expectantly, he said,

"If you have space on your list I will be honored to dance with you, my lady."

Satisfied, she smiled and would have spoken but for a diversion at the double doors. She swirled about to see the Lady Charlotte, and at her side Emily, dressed in a confection of floral gauze petticoats, a simple string of pearls about her throat. The girl looked neither right or left and went to the tea trolley under her aunt's escort. Lady Sybilla left the pianoforte and spoke a few hurried whispered words to her niece before she was put in her place by a sharp word from her elder sister. But when the Earl of Delvin joined them, the Lady Charlotte bestowed a warm smile upon him and gave Emily into his care before retiring to the tea trolley to assist her mother. Lady Sybilla lingered, and it did not go unnoticed by Alec that Emily tried to go to her, but the Earl led her away to join a group of his intimates sitting adjacent to the pianoforte.

"I hope the ball is more lively than this lot," said Plantagenet Halsey, taking the place of Lady Gervais at Alec's side. He followed his nephew's gaze. "She's the spit of her mother, m'boy."

"I beg your pardon, Uncle? Olivia give you quarters to your liking?"

"Yes. Emily St. Neots is the image of her mamma."

"Is she?"

"The Duchess of Beauly was a beautiful woman. Turned heads wherever she went. Still does, if my Italian correspondent is to be believed."

"Indeed? If I'm posted into Italy should I present myself?"

"Do. Whatever the woman's failings, don't let anyone convince you she was solely to blame for that humiliating divorce. Beauly was a cad and a womanizer. And she was in love with a man other than her husband." He looked uncomfortable. "Don't believe in forced marriages. Females sold off like pieces of furniture. Pah!"

"I should like to read your latest pamphlet.... On conjugal rights...?"

Plantagenet Halsey grunted and put his dish on the window ledge. "Nothin' in it that you haven't heard me preach before."

"Olivia tells me you narrowly missed being sued for defamation over that particular publication."

The old man's bushy brows went up. "Blames me for that scoundrel's death, does she?"

"She sounded most grateful to you for having the audacity to name the fellow."

"She may be grateful, but I'll tell you who ain't, and that's the widow. Still, you can't blame her for that I suppose. I did expose her marriage to the world."

"'Tis a pity you didn't see the necessity in telling me before you told the world."

Plantagenet Halsey eyed his nephew curiously. "She was miserable enough. Having you lurking in the shadows would only have made matters worse for her. Better for you to stay right out of it. Her husband was a possessive lunatic."

Alec leaned in to his uncle and spoke while looking out across the room at Emily sitting mutely beside Delvin, who was chattering away to Sir Cosmo and an unknown woman in outrageous plumage. "Better that she be beaten than tell me so that I could put a stop to it?"

"Better to have you both alive!"

"Uncle?! He'd not have bested me in a duel!"

The old man looked at him squarely. "No. But he'd have killed her rather than let you near her."

Alec looked away, a tightness in his throat behind the expertly tied linen stock. "Then if you knew about the beatings, I'm surprised you didn't write that pamphlet years ago."

"My boy, it wasn't my pamphlet that caused him to blow his brains out," Plantagenet Halsey responded sympathetically. "Her Grace and the rest of her ilk may think that; let 'em. Right up to the day they found Jamison-Lewis dead in the wood he had every intention of pursuing me in the courts. His lawyer made that plain and simple. So you'll have to go elsewhere to find the reason for his death."

"Perhaps his death was an accident?" When his uncle snorted his skepticism, Alec added, "Then why did he shoot himself?"

Plantagenet Halsey shrugged. "Now that's somethin' you'll have to ask his widow. And here comes the virago now."

Alec was surprised by his uncle's expression of admiration as he watched Selina Jamison-Lewis sweep across the room in a very fetching gown of oyster gray silk with petticoats of silver tissue, fluttering a large gouache painted fan of stiffened silk with a heavy silver tassel. She acknowledged Alec with a brief nod, not meeting his eye, and playfully extended her hand to his uncle.

"I'm so glad you've come, sir. It has put your other nephew out of all countenance and stirred the toothless lions from their slumber!" she said with a smile, and laughed when he bowed over her hand with a flourish. "My boredom is at an end, and for that I am prepared to forgive you your impertinent writings."

Far from taking offense the old man chuckled and squeezed her hand. "Thank you, my dear. Allow me one last impertinence by tellin' you you look very well indeed as a widow!" He glanced significantly at Alec, "Ain't that so, my boy?"

But Alec wasn't attending. He was now wholly preoccupied with Emily and his brother, and without excusing himself crossed the room to Emily's side and said without preamble, "Are you quite well, my dear?"

She did not look up. "Yes, Mr. Halsey. Perfectly well. Thank you."

"Perhaps a walk about the terrace would restore your color?"

"No. No, thank you."

"Emily—"

At that Lord Delvin cut short his sentence to the lady on his left, stood and faced his brother. Laughter, music, and the chatter of voices persisted all around them, but more than a few powdered heads turned in their direction. The Earl opened his gold and enameled snuffbox and took a pinch. When he had finished he said with a drawl,

"I can't—really I can't allow you to take Emily away from me, Second. She belongs to me. Don't you, Emily dearest?"

"Let her tell me that herself," Alec enunciated.

But Emily, who had also risen, stared through him, her face like carved stone.

"Gentlemen, please," Lady Charlotte whispered stridently. "Mr. Halsey, you will please leave Emily to the care of her betrothed!"

The Earl offered Emily his arm. "Remember Oliphant's advice, my dear. You must have no more upsets."

Alec frowned. "Oliphant? The physician?"

"So this is Miss Emily," interrupted Plantagenet Halsey, and stepped between the brothers to take Emily's hand and bow over it. "You must excuse me if I introduce myself, but my nephews are

sadly lackin' in manners. And you'll forgive an old man's forward-
ness if you're anythin' like your dear grandmamma." While he
spoke, he wrapped Emily's arm about his own and patted her hand
comfortingly. "Need a breath of fresh air, m'self. Care to take a
walk? Mrs. Jamison-Lewis has kindly offered to show me the
terrace. I ain't been out that way yet. We'll leave this lot to their tea
and manners."

The Earl took a step forward, then retreated when his uncle
snarled at him, and said with forced cheerfulness,

"A capital idea, Uncle!" Then turned on a heel, and strolled off
to join a group of gentlemen gathered round the fireplace.

"I'll accompany you, Mr. Halsey," stated Lady Charlotte,
shaking out her petticoats.

"You'll stay where you are, madam, if you don't want me to
make a public exhibition of your meddlin'," retorted Plantagenet
Halsey. He nodded to Selina and she went with him and Emily
out of the drawing room.

Alec was left standing in the middle of the room with an
empty coffee dish until Sir Cosmo took him by the elbow and led
him to a far corner by a draped window.

"A word of advice," Sir Cosmo said under his breath as he
surveyed the room through his quizzing glass. "Keep your uncle
away from William Gervais. The man is foaming at the mouth to
come to cuffs with him. Hates your uncle's politics. Who doesn't?
But that's no reason to want to lock him up! And Gervais will if he
can find an excuse. Sits on the bench at Westminster Hall."

"Looks more pig farmer than judge."

"Doesn't he, what!" Sir Cosmo answered with a snort. "But
our William Gervais adores a good hanging. Sends all the poor
sods who come before him to the gallows—"

"Is that so? Is he the judge the newssheets dubbed Lord
Gallows?"

"The very same. Always hangs his man—woman or child for
that matter, does our William Gervais. And—er—somethin' else,"

Sir Cosmo stumbled on, slightly embarrassed. "Best stay away from his wife."

Alec grinned. "My dear Cosmo, if only she would stay away from me!"

Sir Cosmo gave a bark of laughter and nudged his friend. "Who wouldn't prefer a stallion to an ass, eh?"

"The wonder of it is, Cosmo," said Alec, gaze on the gentleman in question, who was devouring a cream pastry as he chatted to a distracted Lady Sybilla and a thin woman of advanced years. "If the man is as you say, then why does he permit himself to be cuckolded by Delvin?"

"That's simple," Sir Cosmo said matter-of-factly. "The man's dazzled by us; the nobility that is. A title is everything to a self-made man like that. He's only a life peer—for services to the law, you understand. He has to be eaten up with frustrated jealousy because his bird-witted wife shares her couch with Delvin. But Delvin is an earl. What can Gervais do? An earl has favored him by bedding his wife. Thus, the golden rays of the nobility shine down upon him, too."

"Good Lord! Is that what he thinks?"

"Fascinating, ain't it? I thought all that sort of rot died out in the Middle Ages. Ah, I think Mr. Tremarton wants a word."

"Alec, may I speak with you?" asked Simon Tremarton, who had been hovering close by and took Sir Cosmo's step away as a signal for him to interrupt.

"Not here," Alec answered curtly.

"It's rather urgent," stammered Simon, taken aback by the cold reception.

Alec showed him the way out of the room, taking his leave of the Duchess with a slight nod, and when he reached his sitting room flung wide the door.

"So what is it you want of me, Simon?"

NINE

CROMWELL AND MARZIRAN GAVE A LAZY YAWN AND LOOKED up from the Turkey rug in front of the fireplace as their master entered the sitting room. They were unsure of the visitor and would have gone to sniff at his shoes had Alec not called them to heel beside his wing chair. He offered Simon the chair opposite, but the man could not sit still, and after pacing the floor sat on the chair's arm biting a fingernail.

Simon wondered the best approach, his task made all the more difficult when Alec offered him nothing more than a blank face and cross-legged expectant silence.

"I'm not surprised you're annoyed," Simon said with a self-conscious laugh. "You've every right. I didn't keep our dinner appointment in Paris, and I didn't show for the departmental briefing. And then when you kindly invited me to your house, I was impolite enough not to turn up. I can only say I've not been myself lately, what with Mother's illness—"

"Your mother has been dead these past five years."

"So you know that?" Simon was only mildly surprised. "I suppose Cindy told you. Did she tell you I went into Yorkshire?"

"No. I worked that out for myself."

"Mother's illness is better than the truth, isn't it?"

"The truth, whatever that may be, is always preferable. If you were ashamed of your connection with Jack Belsay it's a wonder you accepted his invitation."

"Tell the department I was off to Belsay's shooting box? Do you think they'd have given me the time?"

"You needn't have lied about it to me. I'd not have said a word to the department. As for suspecting anything else, who in London, apart from his most intimate friends, knew Jack to be homosexual?" Alec's eyebrows rose when Simon winced at the word. "Jack was far more comfortable with his sexuality than you ever were. Isn't that so, Simon?"

"You can sneer! Comfortable? Ha! All right for the likes of Belsay to be comfortable about his preference for men! He had title and wealth and wanted for nothing. As for you, you could leave the service tomorrow and it wouldn't hurt your pocket or your prospects! You needn't be an ambassador's lackey if you don't choose. It's a wonder you bother. I wouldn't if I were in your position."

"I choose to because I want to be of use, and I enjoy the work."

"That's just it, you can choose! It's different for me. I must work or I starve," Simon said sullenly. "I must do—do things I don't enjoy to get ahead. It's all part of the game. You can play or not. More often you don't. And with your noble connections, you needn't lift a finger. You're one of them. They'll look out for you, give you an embassy of your own one day. Tomorrow, if you whispered in the right ear tonight!"

"I'll grant that the system of sinecures and patronage reeks of corruption, Simon, but it can be overcome, used to advantage, if you are prepared to work hard and play the game, but not lose sight of your principles. Look at Sir Harold Hegarty. He was the son of an illiterate wainwright."

Simon gave a snort of contempt. "The man's five-and-fifty. I can't wait that long. Others aren't obliged to. I'll do whatever it takes to get ahead, but working long hours and sweating over someone else's portfolio because they're off toad-eating with their good and titled friends isn't for me! I can't afford to be as noble as you."

"And was loving Jack part of the game, Simon? Something you *had to do* but did not enjoy?"

"Love?" Simon gave a huff and stared into the fire in the grate. "If I said no, you wouldn't believe me. If yes, you'd despise me all the more." He took out his silver snuffbox and tapped the lid before offering it to Alec, who declined. "I forgot," he said with a twisted smile. "You don't *dip*. Is there a vice that you do indulge?"

Alec's mouth twitched, but he gave no reply.

Simon took snuff and watched Alec tend the fire, prodding the flames to new life with a brass poker.

"I need a thousand pounds by Monday afternoon," he stated bluntly. "I borrowed from a moneylender named Reubens. Delvin said for eight hundred pounds he could get me a sinecure in the department. It came to nothing. He got me noticed, but that was all. Belsay was going to give me the money, but he stupidly got himself killed, leaving me in this fix."

Alec returned the poker to its elaborate stand. "You didn't give two straws for Jack, did you, Simon? You were only interested in what you could get out of him. You were using him."

Awkward embarrassment made Simon grin. "Jack Belsay was a fool. Romantics are. But he wasn't fool enough to think I'd be his lover without pecuniary reward. That he fell in love with me was his problem, not mine. And if Delvin hadn't run him through I'd be wealthy now. Jack would've done anything to keep me."

"Then he was indeed a fool. A man in love can be forgiven much, whereas you—you—"

"Is that how you justified your behavior towards that redhead downstairs?" Simon jeered. Yet, the look on Alec's face made him move away from the fireplace. "Jack told me you deflowered his cousin on her wedding day. Is that the particular vice of the department's Greek statue, deflowering virgin brides—"

Within the blink of an eye Simon Tremarton found himself

thrust against a wall, his neck cloth twisted so excruciatingly tight that nothing else mattered but to breathe. His arms hung helpless at his sides and he had the distinct feeling his feet were off the ground. All he could do was gasp and splutter and stare pop-eyed into a face full of utter contempt and rage.

"You dare. You *dare* sneer at *me*? You disgusting little catamite!" Alec seethed. He dropped Simon with a contemptuous push. "No, Cromwell! Marziran! He isn't fit to maul." He turned away and leaned outstretched arms on the mantel, head bowed. "A word of advice, Tremarton, though God knows why I offer it! Flee to the Continent. It's your only hope of avoiding Newgate." He glanced over his shoulder. The man was still recovering his breath. "With your predilections, I'd go as far as Persia. Anywhere else and you'll be strung up!"

Simon rearranged his neckcloth. "Your advice is noted. However, I prefer to try my luck with your brother. He'll give me much more than a thousand when I'm through with him."

"Don't be an ass! Delvin won't give you a tester. He ran Jack through, so what's to stop him murdering a contemptible worm such as yourself?"

"You think Jack was blackmailing Delvin and that's what got him killed?" Simon was incredulous. "Belsay couldn't threaten a gnat!"

"Then why did they cross swords? Perhaps I was wrong in choice of sibling. Perhaps they fought a duel over you?"

This made Simon laugh heartily. "Me? Much you know about your brother! He loathes our kind with a passion bordering on lunacy. He hated Belsay more than most."

"It wouldn't have anything to do with Jack's visits to a particular club above an apothecary's shop?"

Simon's brow puckered for a moment then he smiled. "You'd be surprised how many fine, upstanding gentlemen of good birth and character indulge in all sorts of deviant behavior. The Ganymede Club was just one such club catering to every taste and perversion, and populated with the likes of your drawing room crowd downstairs." He took another pinch of snuff, a sidelong glance at Alec. "Your new valet tell you what happened?"

"That the gaming hell and club were raided, and the apothecary Dobbs strung up for sodomy, a crime for which, his apprentice is convinced, he was wrongly convicted."

Simon Tremarton shrugged his indifference. "Someone had to fall and, luckily for the rest of us, Dobbs was at hand."

"You've no remorse—"

"*Remorse?*"

"—an innocent man was hanged for a crime he did not commit?"

Simon pulled a face full of disgust. "For God's sake, Halsey, the man was one rung above a muckraker. Better he than one of us."

Alec wrenched open the door onto the passageway. "You're despicable and conscienceless. Get out before I wring your neck!"

But Simon Tremarton was infuriatingly calm and hovered in the middle of the Turkey rug. He produced a yellowed envelope from an inner pocket of his frock coat and held this up. "For three thousand pounds you can have this letter. It proves your brother murdered Jack Belsay, and why."

"I'll not pay you a penny for it. Get out."

"No matter," said Simon with a sigh and pocketed the envelope. "I'll squeeze five thousand out of our dear earl. He can't afford not to agree to my terms." And with a flourish, he bowed. "If you're not careful I shall ask you for the first minuet!" he called out from the passageway. "*Au revoir, mon beau.*"

ALEC SLAMMED THE DOOR SO HARD IT SHOOK ON ITS HINGES. He paced the room, a hand to his hair, hoping the anger would burn itself out before he did damage to an inanimate object, and very possibly his hand. Out of the corner of his eye he caught movement, and looked round with a jerk to find Sir Cosmo lounging sheepishly in the doorway that connected sitting room to dressing room.

"I see your valet has a turn for chemistry," he said conversationally. "Heard the commotion out in the corridor and thought you might need a hand. Wandered in and found the lad hunched over all sorts of scientific apparatus. He was telling me about his apprenticeship as an apothecary. Interesting lad. Good of you to let him continue to mess about."

"Yes, and having an apothecary's apprentice as a valet is rather odd, I know. But there you have it. Frankly, Cosmo, it's a long and complicated story for which I don't have the patience or the time to apprise you."

"Want a drink? The lad fetched up a bottle of burgundy."

"Thank you," said Alec, and followed Cosmo through to the dressing room, the greyhounds prancing along behind. He took the glass Cosmo poured out for him and after a sip, said in a much calmer tone, "Did you have any success with the guests?"

Sir Cosmo glanced knowingly at Tam, who had scrambled to his feet.

Quick to understand, Alec sent Tam to take the dogs for a run saying, "I won't need you for another half hour."

Sir Cosmo waited to hear the outer door close. "You showed more patience than I with that weasel Tremarton."

"I wanted to throttle him! Hear the whole?"

"For the most part. The lad must have, too, though he kept on with his experimentation, as if deaf to it all. Do you give much credence to Tremarton's drivel?"

Alec sipped his wine thoughtfully. "That Delvin murdered Jack? Undoubtedly. The whole scene at Green Park points to it: The absence of seconds, of any of the formalities of dueling. Jack wasn't jealous of Delvin. He wasn't even interested in females. He was having an affair with Simon Tremarton."

Sir Cosmo shook his head. "Defies reasoning!" But his surprise sounded rehearsed.

Alec frowned.

"You've known all along about Jack's inclinations."

"Er, well, yes," confessed Sir Cosmo guiltily and added hurriedly when Alec's frown deepened, "Not that Jack told me. I dare say the majority didn't look beyond what they saw. Of course a few of us had our suspicions about J-L, though it's not something you want to ask a man or want to know about a man, and he had married Selina, so that somehow put it to rest. But when Selina confided in me about her marriage, it was a horrible shock, and then when she mentioned Jack's part in it all, and I thought about it a bit I could see how it was and then, well, there you are!"

"I beg your pardon, but I'm not understanding you," Alec said politely. "What did you know about Jamison-Lewis, and what has he to do with Jack and his preference?"

This time Sir Cosmo was surprised and he blinked.

"Ah! Well. I'm for it now..." he said more to himself and took snuff. He slipped the enameled box back into his frock coat pocket and wondered how best to explain himself. He coughed. "I presumed you knew. But as you had no idea about the—the beatings I can see now that you'd have absolutely no idea about the rest of the sordid business. Perhaps it would be best if I didn't say more. My tongue's running on and Selina might not want me to—"

"For God's sake, Cosmo!" Alec said with annoyed exasperation. "Tell me and be done with it. Now I know how that monster treated her, surely it can't be worse than that?"

"Jack was J-L's catamite," Sir Cosmo said bluntly, the color ripening in his face. "Had been for years. Nothing changed after J-L's marriage. Selina was there to provide an heir. George looked on her as nothing more than a brood mare and used her accordingly."

Alec sat down heavily. He felt as if the breath had been knocked out of him.

"What I don't understand is where this unsavory worm Tremarton comes in on the act," Sir Cosmo continued, oblivious to the impact of his words. He could very well have been talking to

Alec through a thick fog. "Jack must've kept the affair with Tremarton a well-guarded secret. Everyone knew what a jealous possessive monster J-L was with Selina, so imagine his feelings if he'd found out Jack was cheating on him!" Sir Cosmo rubbed his stubbled chin. "Come to think on it, Alec, Jack was much more comfortable with his inclination than J-L ever was. Went to a lot of trouble to be the man's man, did J-L. Think that's why he finally married. Ned knew about J-L, but he never openly showed his disgust for the man. I think your brother was a little afraid of him."

"I don't doubt it. And Delvin has the knack of preying on those weaker than himself," Alec said quietly, mind still reeling with new knowledge. "I can well imagine Delvin teasing Jack about his relationship with J-L out of earshot of the monster himself. And Jack was not the type to run with tales. He'd have dealt with the matter in his own quiet way."

"Fighting a duel in the Green Park is hardly that!"

"But threatening Delvin with something devastating to my brother's security is."

Sir Cosmo snapped his fingers. "Lady Margaret's letter! Jack threatened Ned with the letter your mother wrote to Lady Margaret. It has to be that. That's the trump Tremarton's got in his possession. I'll lay you odds it is! Did he show you paper?'

"A worn envelope. Personally, I believe Tremarton is playing an elaborate game of bluff. For all we know, half of London is now aware of the fable put about by Lady Margaret. Tremarton could've picked up on this, heard it from Jack perhaps, and merely skewed it to suit his own purposes. He's obviously desperate enough to do something half-brained. We have no way of knowing short of getting our hands on that envelope."

"Then we must get our hands on that envelope," Sir Cosmo repeated with relish, yet he deflated immediately when his friend did not show the same enthusiasm. He peered keenly at Alec and wondered if he had suddenly taken ill. Then it came to him in a flash, all the pieces slotted into place, and he blurted out, "Alec, my dear fellow, I'm sorry. It was wrong of me to tell you about J-L. I wish you'd found out from anyone but me…"

"Better from you than any other," Alec stated quietly with heightened color, and drank down the final mouthful of wine. He rallied himself enough to say abruptly, "Did you learn anything today which may help our inquiries?"

Sir Cosmo made himself comfortable in a wing chair opposite Alec's dressing table stool.

"Yes! That's why I'm here," he said, leaning forward with eyes bright. "I had my man do a bit of ferreting below stairs. He enjoys it. If I'm not careful he'll run off and join Macara's man's brother at Bow Street. Of course, they're all jumpy down there. All fearing for their places. Neave has put the hard word on 'em, but no one is saying mouse! He did, however, fall into conversation with Ned's valet, a greasy, nose-in-the-air fellow, who is prepared to swear on hot coals his master was in his rooms all evening."

Alec looked skeptical. "The word of Delvin's valet, Cosmo?"

"I know! I know! I don't set much store on his story either. And he had the boldness to tell me that his master was entertaining two of the maids—"

"*Two* maids?" Alec's shoulders shook. "Oh dear, the story gets better and better! I suppose his valet had an eye to the keyhole for this orgy? Look, Cosmo, Cynthia Gervais came to my room last night, after she'd discovered Delvin wasn't in his rooms."

"Ned's valet probably lied to her. Covering up for him."

"Undoubtedly. And Cindy Gervais tells me she discovered Delvin in the shrubbery with a kitchen slut. I think it was Emily's chambermaid."

"So there *is* a maid involved!" Sir Cosmo said with satisfaction.

"But that doesn't explain his whereabouts after he'd finished with the maid and before he went to Selina's rooms."

"Surely he didn't lift the maid's petticoats, then go off and try and rape Emily and then be caught *in flagrante delicto* with Selina? He'd need an ivory horn!"

Alec laughed. "Or he'd like us to believe he has one!"

Sir Cosmo tucked in his chin and brooded. "And I don't care what you saw with your own two eyes! It don't wash that Selina and Ned were—"

"Yes. I know that now and I apologize for jumping to conclusions. But that's exactly what Delvin wanted me to think."

"Why?"

Alec shrugged, looked uncomfortable and avoided answering the question. "I don't want to believe Delvin capable of rape or of murdering a lady's maid, because he is my brother. But I do have suspicions about him, Cosmo. The fact his valet is putting about a tale that he was in his rooms with two maids shows to what lengths he has gone to cover his tracks. As for being in the shrubbery with the chambermaid and Cynthia Gervais catching them out…? Think about it a moment. The chambermaid isn't going to come forward and tell us the intimate details of that encounter. Instant dismissal and no reference. Delvin can say what he damn well likes about the servants, and whether it be true or false, not one of them is about to deny the word of a nobleman. Therefore we have no way of knowing for how many minutes Delvin was out there amongst the foliage. It's too smooth, Cosmo. And just the sort of thing Delvin would use as an alibi. That his mistress caught him there may also be an elaborate ploy on his behalf."

"How do you reckon that?"

"It was the same ploy that ensured I caught him in Selina's rooms. And what you see, as you rightly pointed out to me, doesn't necessarily equate with what is actually going on."

"Blasted mess of a business!" Sir Cosmo grumbled. "I've spent all day with an ear to the ground and that was the best I could offer you. I'm not much help. Sorry."

"You're the only help I have," Alec replied with a smile. "Nothing of interest from Olivia's guests?"

"From what I can gather, all of 'em are pretty much accounted for after they retired for the evening. All except the ones we mentioned earlier. Macara was up late wandering the terrace smoking his infernal cheroots. Seems he doesn't sleep well; back injury. If Cynthia Gervais was with you, that's you covered," he said, tripping over his tongue at Alec's grin. "No pun intended! Which leaves Gervais. And what Neave tells me, our boorish judge was left prostrate beside the sideboard. Two footmen came to carry him up to bed when the port was locked up, but he'd gone. Then there's myself. Ah, yes, well, I'm afraid I was rather boring and slept alone, so remain the only celibate one amongst you!"

Alec chuckled. "Make that two of us, Cosmo. Oh, don't look so amazed. I'm no saint when it comes to beautiful women, but I draw the line at bedding another man's mistress, my brother's into the bargain!"

"Oh, there is one other thing," added Sir Cosmo. "That frock coat left in the billiard room. It belongs to Ned. His man snapped it up the moment Neave took it into the servants' hall. So that's not much use to us then, is it?"

"Isn't it? His valet claims Edward was entertaining two maids in his room; his mistress says she saw him out in the shrubbery with a maid; I discovered him annoying Selina; and his frock coat is found in the billiard room, suggesting he spent time playing a game of billiards at some point in the evening. That Sybilla's boy and his cousin were caught out in the servant passage outside the billiard room by Delvin seems to bear that out. All this happened around the time Emily was being attacked? Incredible!"

"You'd think there was more than one Ned running about the place!"

Alec smiled crookedly. "Yes. I imagine that's precisely what someone would like us to believe."

PLANTAGENET HALSEY CAME THROUGH TO HIS NEPHEW'S dressing room and stood watching Tam put the finishing touches to his master's toilette. Alec was being helped into a black velvet frock coat, the great upturned cuffs heavily embroidered with silver thread and the short skirts stiffened with whalebone. He wore fine white lace ruffles at both wrists, diamond-encrusted buckles in the leather tongues of highly-polished shoes, and a large, white satin bow at his nape. Another bow secured the end of a thick black plait that fell between his shoulder blades. To complete this ball dress, at his throat Alec wore a large diamond-headed pin in the folds of his intricately-tied lace cravat.

Tam stepped back to view the whole, and was just as pleased as the old man to see his master looking so splendidly handsome. Alec caught them both grinning and was instantly self-conscious.

"I do look a peacock, don't I? Or should I say magpie? I haven't worn Court dress since Versailles and I can tell you, Uncle, give me an old brown riding frock any day! This rig-out is damnably close."

"You ought to be pleased you cut such a fine figure without the need for buckram. Damned uncomfortable, buckram, and liable to shift when you least expect it," said Plantagenet Halsey, adjusting his own linen cravat in the long looking glass by the dressing table. He saw his nephew looking him up and down with a smile and frowned. "What do you find to smirk at, eh?"

"Oh, I was thinking what a fine figure you cut for a man who cannot abide frippery," Alec said lightly. "Olivia will be *most* impressed with her republican guest."

"Now, you stop that!" the old man said gruffly, turning to Tam who was still in the room. "Haven't you chores to do?"

"Come through to the sitting room," suggested Alec, ushering his uncle from the dressing room as he picked up a lace handkerchief from the clutter on the dressing table. "Don't be too hard on the lad. He's been through more than you know. Which reminds me, I'll ask it of you now because there'll not be another chance tonight. Tomorrow afternoon I'm expecting a visit from a Mr. Yarrborough, Junior or Senior. I'm not sure which—"

"The lawyers?"

"That's right. I've asked them to find out some information about a hanging that occurred some six or seven months ago. If for any reason I'm not about, I've instructed them to give you the information, so keep an eye open for their arrival. I don't want anyone else speaking with them."

"A'course, my boy. Who was hanged?"

"Dobbs, Tam's master."

The old man was incredulous. "For what? Dispensin' without a prescription?"

"For sodomy."

Plantagenet Halsey was too stunned to even swear.

"Above the apothecary's shop there was a gaming hell and a brothel: Apparently young male prostitutes for the well-heeled. But before you ask me, no, Tam was not involved. He tells me he was Dobbs' apprentice and nothing more and I believe him."

"Is the boy somehow mixed up with the law?"

"Not that he is aware." Alec flicked a speck of dust from his velvet sleeve. "Tam is adamant his master was innocent. He says Dobbs knew very well what was going on, but preferred to turn his back than to report it to the authorities."

"Then he's no better. I ain't sayin' he deserved to be hanged as a sodomite but—"

"I know. His complacency begs the question why he permitted such an outrage under his own roof. I intend to find out why, and who ran this so-called Ganymede Club, if in truth Dobbs was used as a scapegoat, and by whom. I'm hoping Yarrborough can help uncover the truth."

Plantagenet Halsey sucked in air through his clenched teeth. "Alec, if Dobbs was a scapegoat, if this Ganymede Club was frequented by men of fortune and rank, Yarrborough will be met with deaf ears wherever he asks a question."

"I don't disagree with you but there are truths which can't be covered up. Who was the trial judge who sentenced Dobbs? Who gave evidence against the man? Who owned the building that housed the apothecary and the businesses on the upper floors? That information should be relatively easy to come by." Alec glanced at his uncle. "Uncle, is there anything you know about the lad that you would like to tell me?"

"About Thomas Fisher?" The old man was puzzled.

"Tremarton knows he's from Delvin; that he was apprenticed out around the time of Lady Delvin's death."

"Does he? That don't say a whole lot. But for what it's worth, the first time I set eyes on the boy I knew there was something familiar about him. So I wasn't surprised to learn his aunt was housekeeper at Delvin and that his mother was that woman's younger sister, Iris Fisher. Both were carrot-topped like Tam. All the Fishers are. I don't recall ever seeing the boy when I visited Delvin. But he would've been kept below stairs. He's from the wrong side of the blanket. Iris Fisher was never married."

"Pretty, was she?"

Plantagenet Halsey's gray eyes surveyed his nephew blandly. "Very, by all accounts. Died in childbirth."

Alec smiled grimly. "Interesting you should know so much about the Fishers of Delvin."

"Not as interestin' as may be, my boy. Your mother didn't have much to occupy her time while she was bedridden, except in reminiscing. Naturally household gossip loomed large in her memories."

"Unlike her son," Alec muttered, one last glance in the looking glass.

"Alec, there's something I need to tell you before you join the festivities," said his uncle. "Emily St. Neots is determined to marry Delvin. She wants to be Countess of Delvin. She told me as much."

"Yes. I know."

Plantagenet Halsey was unsure how to interpret this short response and said diffidently, "There is the pull of a coronet. Helen —your mother... If I'd been earl and Roderick my second, well, things would've turned out differently."

"How differently?" Alec asked his uncle's reflection. "Would she have remained faithful to you, had your child, and not given it up as she did me? You'd have married such a shallow creature, knowing it was your coronet which had persuaded her?"

The old man looked down at his knotted hands. "You don't know the half of it, my boy—why she made the choices she did. And I—I loved her in spite of everything."

Alec adjusted a fold in his cravat. "She didn't deserve your devotion," he said brutally. "She gave you nothing in return."

"She gave me you," was his uncle's quiet reply before he turned away to fiddle unnecessarily with the large leather tongue of his left shoe.

Alec smiled lovingly at the stooped back. "For that I will be eternally grateful to her."

"Damme! I talked to the chit at length, and all I got was an earful of her damned wedding plans!" Plantagenet Halsey blustered to cover an embarrassing pause. "She spoke as if her whole dependence and delight were invested in this marriage, as if it's going to right the wrongs of her mother. If I didn't know better I'd say that child is as shallow-brained as they come!"

"Right the wrongs of her mother…" Alec repeated softly. "So that's Lady Charlotte's trump…"

"You wouldn't find two females more opposite than those two who took a turn about the terrace with me," continued his uncle in the same blustering tone. "One has yet to form any opinions of her own, and the other is too opinionated for her own good. And that titian-haired Amazon's got a quick tongue and a ready sense of the ridiculous. Marvelous she was able to pull through such a disastrous marriage virtually unscathed—"

"Uncle, I—"

"Which brings me to what I want to say to you. Delvin's interference aside, you should've fought harder to win that one! She's a hornet and she'll give you back measure for measure, but she won't stand for any nonsense and if you want my opinion she—"

"—was the one who rejected my suit," Alec explained calmly, a rueful smile when his uncle blinked. "I begged her to run away with me. I was ready to defy her parents, Delvin, you. I was all for Gretna, but she wouldn't have it. Her parents had accepted an offer from Jamison-Lewis, who had a fortune and was nephew to a

Duke. I, on the other hand, had, at that time, no fortune and a brother who let it be publicly known he would not support my marriage with a considerable heiress. All that in the balance and Selina's tender years were enough to make her shy off the idea of eloping with a nobody. Remember, she was the age Emily is now." He gave a self-deprecating laugh, pulling at his close upturned velvet cuffs. "You think I'd have learnt my lesson. Instead I set my cap at a girl who looks upon me with brotherly affection!" He shrugged. "Like Emily, obviously Selina's feelings weren't fixed. And she didn't have the strength of character to turn her back on her family's choice of husband and put our happiness above theirs."

Under hooded pale eyes, Plantagenet Halsey regarded his nephew dispassionately.

"You wrong her. What she did, lettin' you go like that, sacrificin' what was her only chance at happiness to marry a man she didn't give a fig for, so you wouldn't be ruined, that's true strength of character. Who's to say you'd have made it to Gretna? Eloping with an heiress would've ended your career; no more embassies, no preferment. Her parents, Jamison-Lewis and his cronies, not to mention your brother, all would've seen to it that you were politically and socially ruined. Did that never occur to you, my boy?"

It hadn't and Alec now knew what Cosmo meant by those words flung at him in the rain. It was a revelation. He wondered if there were another man alive who could claim such self-centeredness. He was to have his answer later that evening when, in the ballroom, he came face-to-face with his brother. He was startled out of this private reverie by a slap to his broad back.

"I'm feeling merry to the point of dissipation this evenin', my boy," his uncle said in a light tone, a twinkle in his eye. He flicked his nephew's black plait playfully. "Let's see if you and I can't turn a few pretty heads tonight, eh?"

"Well, at least one," murmured his nephew.

TEN

St. Neots House was thrown open for the Fireworks Ball. At the head of the main stairs stood Neave with a small battalion of yellow-coated footmen, straight-backed and chins up, to take gold-edged cards of invitation and announce each guest to the assembled company. Ladies in wide-hooped petticoats of shimmering silks, with their gentlemen in periwig and gold braid, strolled from one cavernous room to the next. Large plumed fans fluttered invitingly across rounded alabaster bosoms and quizzing glasses swung casually on silken cords, ever ready to be plastered up to a roving eye.

There were two orchestras. One in the ballroom, another in the drawing room, where guests sampled oysters and drank punch, and made such a din with their high-pitched laughter that the music was all but drowned out. Champagne flowed liberally into chilled crystal glasses. All was twinkling light, dazzling color, and clouds of heady scents.

The Fireworks Ball had been the talk of many a drawing room soirée and was predicted to be the event of the season. There was not a noble in London who did not think it a high honor to receive an invitation from the Duchess of Romney-St. Neots. The guest list included no fewer than five Ambassadors, four foreign princes and their retinues, and members from the English Royal house. All the governing families of the kingdom had sent representatives. So it was with no small feeling of trepidation that Emily approached her first grand occasion, the center of attention and the reason her grandmother had spared no expense to celebrate her engagement.

She presented a vision of youthful loveliness in a gown of silk gauze the shade of pearl, her blonde curls delicately powdered and upswept, and a smile that was as white as it was dazzling. She made small talk with every person presented to her, but the instant they moved on she forgot all about them, and could not even remember what they had talked about. She danced without thinking, yet she danced faultlessly, with a grace natural to her. The Earl danced the first minuet with her, then quite properly escorted her back to her chair, only for the Prince of Baden to return her to the dance floor. He said she danced like an angel. She smiled at the compliment and made more small talk, and when the minuet had come to an end, the Earl and a group of his friends whisked her away to the refreshment room, all praising her success with the Prince.

From a vantage point in the corner of the Saloon which was being used as the refreshment room, Sir Cosmo watched his cousin through his quizzing glass, surrounded by this loud, chattering cluster of fawning beaux. He was pleased she was smiling and more herself after her wooden appearance at afternoon tea. He swept the crowd with his eyeglass, and was about to return to the ballroom when he remembered he was not likely to find Selina in there; widows were not permitted to dance. He wondered if she intended putting in an appearance at all, then saw her framed in an archway, looking about as if she had just arrived. The sight of her made him draw in a quick breath. She so reminded him of a portrait he had once seen of the doomed Queen Mary of Scots, for she was dressed all in black velvet. The low-cut gown was seeded with pearls, as were her slippers. She carried a fan of stiffened lace on a cord of black silk with a knotted tassel. She wore no jewelry, but needed none with a skin so translucent and her flaming curls unpowdered and upswept off her long neck.

She responded to Cosmo's wave with a smile and would have gone to him, but he was at her side in an instant, having hurriedly grabbed two glasses of champagne on his way through the moving sea of silks and perfume. They clinked glasses and drank up.

Selina looked her friend up and down, from powdered wig with enormous scarlet bow to the festoons of scarlet ribbons at the knees of his silken breeches. He wore three gold seals and two quizzing glasses dangled about his neck. She chuckled into her champagne glass, the bubbles tickling her nose.

"I wish I could dance tonight, and with you looking like a macaw! You do put the Prince of Baden to shame in those festive silks, Cosmo."

He smiled uncertainly, unsure if she was flattering him or giving him a roasting. "Ah, and I had thought to play Bothwell to your Mary, my dear," he muttered.

"Oh! Do I look as if I'm for the block?" she answered with a laugh and shrugged a bare shoulder. "Better a doomed queen than the only spider in the sugar bowl!" She absently handed Sir Cosmo her empty glass, dark eyes scanning the chattering multitude, unaware of Sir Cosmo's scrutiny.

"You merely have to ask me, my dear, and I shall tell you where he can be found," he said lightly, eyeglass plastered to one bright eye.

"That champagne was rather good," she murmured, a sly glance at her friend.

"Yes. It must be the reason you have a delicious blush to your perfect complexion," he quipped, and received with a chuckle the good-natured rap over the knuckles with her fan. "Ah! Here comes your Bothwell now!"

Selina was about to tell him what she thought of his presumption when she was rudely bumped and forced to seek the protection of Sir Cosmo's robust person against what appeared to be an invasion by the French.

Two mincing French lackeys attached to the Ambassador's retinue went before the group of foreign dignitaries making their way toward the refreshment tables as if they were the forward raiding party of an invading army. The French Ambassador and his little group of fawning perfumed fops stopped close to Sir Cosmo and Selina to be catered to by three hovering waiters. All were speaking in such rapid French, full of subtle nuances and inflections, that no Englishman save the most ardently trained linguist could understand the run of conversation. A bawdy joke was being related, a long and involved tale, but it held its listeners enthralled. The French Ambassador interjected part way through with a bawdy recollection of his own, which won for him a hearty laugh from his companions. It was evident the French Ambassador was enjoying himself hugely, and at the tale's end burst into applause and high-pitched laughter, dabbing his shining eyes with a scrap of lace he used as a handkerchief.

The Marquise, his wife, found him then. But she did not want her husband. No, Madame la Marquise wanted the attentions of her husband's friend who had told the bawdy joke. She tapped his black velvet arm with the sticks of her gold and ivory fan and chided him playfully. The French Ambassador smiled on both, and with a quick whispered word in his friend's ear, he took himself off with his entourage to the card room, leaving Madame his wife to drink champagne with his good friend.

The French Ambassador had left his wife to flirt, and flirt outrageously, with Alec Halsey, who was the teller of the bawdy joke, and in such idiosyncratic French that anyone not knowing him would have taken him for a native Frenchman. He smiled and chatted with Madame la Marquise as if she were a dear friend.

"Startled me the first time I heard him rattling away in Frenchy," admitted Sir Cosmo. "Spent a fortnight with him in Paris. He was so comfortable in that tongue that I almost wondered if he'd forgotten he was an Englishman! Did y'know he can speak five tongues just as fluently?"

"Yes, the wretched man," agreed Selina and was determined to look anywhere else rather than bear witness to Alec's flirtation with Madame la Marquise.

Seeing him dressed in such rich magnificence as black velvet and lace always unsettled her. She had seen him at numerous functions, always at a distance, one of a number of Foreign Department functionaries assigned to look after foreign nobles, yet it was Alec who was constantly surrounded by a clutch of foreign beauties. Selina had managed on those occasions to turn away, yet she could not stop her thoughts wandering in his direction, as they did again tonight. While she was married, she was thankful that he had spent most of his time on the Continent. She supposed his fluency in five foreign languages was matched only by the frequency with which he bedded its female native speakers. She knew he had gained the reputation of a rake while abroad, but distance and her unavailability had made it easier to accept his numerous liaisons; they were, after all, not lasting and he had not fallen in love with any of them. But his feelings for Emily were different. He had wanted to marry her. And the way he looked at her...

She mentally castigated herself and was all for quitting the refreshment room to look in on the dancers when Sir Cosmo tugged on the lace at her elbow, saying in a loud whisper so as to be heard, "Something's afoot! The happy bridegroom has been ensnared."

The invading army of French diplomats had moved on, taking with them a cloud of perfume and a babble of high pitched chatter, but halted almost immediately because Madame la Marquise had found the object of her interest. The Earl of Delvin was being congratulated by a Prince of the Blood who had been introduced by the Duchess of Romney-St. Neots. Madame patiently waited her turn and soon the Prince of the Blood stepped back and, with a bow to Madame la Marquise, sauntered away with the Duchess on his arm, his entourage in tow.

Delvin was all smiles with the French Ambassador's wife, but when he saw who was her interpreter, his smile became fixed and not once did he glance his brother's way. He attempted to answer the Marquise in her own tongue, but she waved her hands in an agitated manner and said something in Alec's inclined ear. He then addressed the Earl's stony profile on her behalf.

"Mme la Marquise would prefer you returned your answers in English, my lord," Alec reported. "She has a great desire to practice her understanding of the English language. If you wish it I am happy to act as your interpreter—"

"I don't need your sniveling help," the Earl said in an undervoice, a dazzling smile through clenched teeth and a second deep bow to Madame.

Alec shrugged and spoke at length to Mme la Marquise before addressing his brother. "Madame would like to know when is the wedding."

"As soon as possible."

"Mme wishes to know of Lord Delvin if he intends to take his bride to Paris for the honeymoon. She says Paris it is a favorite destination with newlyweds, and with our two countries now at peace she is sure the commerce in this trade will only increase."

"No. Not Paris," Delvin replied with the widest of smiles at Madame. "I have every intention of taking my young bride to my seat in the country—"

"What?" Alec interrupted in an undertone, looking out at the crowd as if distracted, but with his attention very much trained on his brother. "You can't seriously mean to take Emily to that pile of tumbled stone." He scoffed. "Some honeymoon!"

"Stick to your job as Frenchman's lackey, *Second*," Delvin growled.

The Marquise spoke to Alec and he said, "Madame says that is a great shame you do not choose to go to Paris. She says Paris you should reconsider. Mme la Marquise is certain the English countryside is very pleasant, but it is not Paris. Paris, Madame says, is the only city for lovers."

The Earl inhaled a pinch of snuff. "For lovers, certainly, but not the place to take one's wife, surely?"

This intended quip fell sadly flat, Madame requesting Alec to retranslate the Earl's sentence and then looking at him in bewildered offense. Delvin did not like to be so scrutinized and by a Papist foreigner, and he made good his excuses. He bowed but found himself ignored, Madame and her retinue chattering amongst themselves and finally deciding to join the Marquis in the card room. There was more conversation between Madame and Alec, and then she left him with a little titter of laughter and a sparkle in her eyes as he kissed his fingertips to her in acknowledgment of her compliment.

The Earl gave his brother's straight back a nudge.

"You didn't translate the whole of what that Frenchwoman said to you, Second," he said viciously, seething that he should feel so out of his depth and that his brother should be considered by the French as worthy of acknowledgment. "And don't bamboozle me with any of your sweet-tongued lies!"

Alec glanced over a shoulder, a last bow to Madame. "Madame la Marquise said to wish you great happiness."

"She babbled more than that to you!"

Alec pulled a face. "I was merely sparing your feelings," he drawled. "But if you insist—"

"I do!"

Alec sighed his boredom and brushed an imaginary speck of dust from his velvet sleeve. "Madame is of the opinion that perhaps an Englishman must needs be surrounded by cows, sheep and pigs of the country if he is to discover what it is he must do with his appendage while on his honeymoon."

"How dare—"

"I wouldn't keep the Duchess of Beauly waiting," Alec interrupted, and grinned at his brother's flushed face.

He had the satisfaction of watching him stomp off in a temper, and with a wink at Sir Cosmo, crossed to Emily's side. She was on the arm of the young Duke of Beauly, her mother's only son and thus her half-brother. He had taken it upon himself, despite his mother's disgrace and Emily's bastardry, to acknowledge his sister now that she was to be made a countess. His presence at the Fireworks Ball meant a great deal to Emily, and despite her ordeal of the afternoon, her spirits had taken a decided turn for the better. That was until Alec bowed over her hand.

Beauly and Alec exchanged a word and then Alec said to Emily, who had colored up and become flustered, "May I claim the dance after Beauly's?"

Although he had spoken in a gentle tone she recoiled from him and clung to the Duke's satin sleeve, saying to the floor, "No! I can't. I'm sorry. I have no spaces."

"Surely you have left one space in your little book where I may place my name?"

She shook her powdered curls and said in a quick voice, "Your Grace, please, we must get on or we shall miss the dance and then my list will be quite out."

The Duke looked helpless to intervene and was somewhat relieved when Cynthia Gervais pounced on Alec, declaring his name to be next in her list of dance partners. She took possession of his velvet-clad arm and led him away to the Ballroom, the Duke of Beauly and his half-sister not very far behind them.

Cynthia Gervais spent her entire dance with Alec hinting broadly that she needed fresh air and that a walk about the lighted gardens would be just the thing. But her partner did not take the hint, and Lady Gervais was forced to offer him an open invitation to join her in the moonlight. But he apologized with his most generous smile, which caused the lady to sigh at such a wasted opportunity. Her hold on him was only relinquished when her lover came straight up to them and reclaimed what he considered his property to return her to the dance floor with as much self-control as he could muster, the mistress having the disloyal temerity to look over her shoulder with disappointment at Alec's departing broad back.

Alec went in search of his next partner, a cursory glance over at the row of opened French doors that led out onto the wide balcony, where stood amongst the crowd Sir Cosmo and Selina.

While dancing, he kept an eye on their whereabouts, and was pleased to see that Selina watched him even though she pretended her interest lay elsewhere.

Next the Lady Sybilla stood up with him, and for two country dances. He insisted, if only to make certain Cynthia Gervais did not come in search of him again and to annoy Lady Charlotte. Lady Sybilla did not look at all herself, and he soon found out why when he offered to fetch her a lemonade and to sit with her while she drank it. He had an ulterior motive to this solicitude, and that was to question Emily's aunt about the information he had gathered from his mock sword fight with the children in the servant's courtyard.

"I haven't enjoyed dancing so much since Charles and I went to the Wentworth Masquerade," Lady Sybilla said, a little breathless. "That was just before his last posting out to sea."

"You must get out more often. Take a house for the season, instead of spending all your time in Berkshire," said Alec. "Besides it would be good for Harry."

"Oh yes! I should like that. Harry would particularly like to be nearer his cousins, but—but the last thing I want to do is be obligated to spend time with Charlotte. She is quite suffocating. I know that is an uncharitable thing to say about one's own sister—"

"—but very true. I don't blame you. The thought of being suffocated by Charlotte quite unnerves one."

Lady Sybilla giggled.

Alec kissed her hand. "That's better. I don't like to see Emily's favorite aunt unhappy. You've been so all afternoon."

"Please. Please, don't ask me why. I can't tell you! I want to, but I—If you only knew. Charlotte will be so angry with me!"

"My lady, don't distress yourself. I'm not about to ask you any awkward questions," Alec assured her. He took her fan and fluttered it for her. "Charlotte's idea to fetch Sir John?"

"Y-yes."

"And you've been sadly tried by the prank those boys attempted to pull off last night?"

"Oh, that!" she said with a sigh of relief. "Lewis and Harry were so willful. I don't know what got into their heads to want to prowl about in the middle of the night! I suspect Harry was put up to it by Lewis. Charlotte's boys are all unmanageable and she is quite blind to their faults." When Alec smiled sympathetically Lady Sybilla rattled on. "It's just as well Old Nurse is deaf. Running up and down stairs wailing like ghosts is beyond anything!"

"I gather that they had a fright themselves when Delvin caught them at it?"

Lady Sybilla was puzzled. "Delvin? Oh no, that would have been bad enough, but having Lord Gervais take them by the scruff of the neck was positively mortifying."

"*Gervais?*"

Lady Sybilla blinked at the surprise in Alec's voice. "Yes. He and Delvin were playing at billiards when they were disturbed by noises in the servant passage. Lord Gervais said he suspected it was a couple of the servants playing a prank and so went to take a look. The boys practically ran into him in the passage."

"He spoke to you?"

"Y-yes. He came to my rooms. He was exceedingly angry. He huffed and puffed about for a good five minutes before he got to the point; as if in his anger he'd run all the way! I really think he expected me to punish Lewis and Harry there and then. Of course, I was very upset that Harry should get himself mixed up with Lewis, but I don't know what Lord Gervais expected me to do about it at that hour."

Alec impatiently waved away a waiter hovering with a tray of drinks. "At what hour did Lord Gervais disturb you?"

Lady Sybilla watched the waiter move on and mentally sighed. "Hour? Oh, I don't know the precise hour, but I was in my dressing gown having my hair brushed, so it was late."

"Do you think his lordship had been drinking excessively?"

At this question Lady Sybilla blushed rosily and was flustered into saying hurriedly, "Mr. Halsey, what sort of female do you take me for? I didn't get close enough to smell spirits on his breath!"

"Of course you wouldn't," he agreed soothingly. "But perhaps you noticed if he was wearing his frock coat?"

Lady Sybilla blinked at such an odd question. "Frock coat? You misunderstand me. I didn't see him at all. I was in my dressing gown," she told him, fluttering her fan in agitation. "I spoke to him from behind the dressing screen. It's what Charles would expect me to do."

Alec smiled reassuringly at her as he stood. "Of course. It was ill-mannered of him to have bothered you with something so trivial at such a late hour. He should've taken the boys directly to the nursery and spoken to you about the incident in the morning."

"Oh, Harry and Lewis weren't with him. He was alone."

THE CONSUMMATE GENTLEMAN, SIR COSMO REFRAINED FROM adding his name to any lady's list to remain at Selina's side, because she was prohibited from dancing. They strolled along the fringes of those who lingered at the edge of the dance floor, to observe the dances and to pass comment on dance and costume. More than once Selina's gaze stole out to the changing formations to catch sight of Alec. He was hard to miss, dressed in black velvet and his hair unpowdered, just as she was sure she too must be obvious in her widow's weeds. Thus she made a point not to glance his way for very long in case he caught her doing so. Though why he would even be on the look out for her was so conceited a thought on her part that it made her angry, as did the way that Gervais creature pressed herself against Alec's arm. Her only satisfaction was that the Earl of Delvin was also witness to his mistress's flirtation and his anger so far got the better of him that he waylaid the couple, his fixed smile at odds with the blazing anger in his set features.

When Alec next partnered Lady Sybilla, it was noted by many a swelling matronly bosom that he had the effrontery to dance consecutive dances with a married lady. Selina overheard a spiteful remark pass between two dowagers with plain-faced but eligible daughters, and smiled to herself. Alec Halsey might not be a member of the inner circle, was a younger son and considered a sad rake, but these facts could not outweigh his wealth and lineage; his dashing good looks were but icing on the cake. Let them try, she said to herself, annoyed that it had never occurred to her before his interest in Emily that he was remotely interested in the married state. At least she had the satisfaction of knowing he had asked her first... What a hollow victory!

"Talk about being out maneuvered by the French," Sir Cosmo commented with the ghost of a laugh, recalling Madame la Marquise's parting remarks in the refreshment room. "If Ned only knew the half of it! But it's as well for Ned's self-esteem that Alec did not translate the whole of that pretty speech."

"Yes. Madame's parting shot was only partially directed at my Lord Delvin and that uncomplimentary," said Selina, gaze on the dancers. "She left her sweet compliments for her interpreter. Something about Alec and the last time he was in Paris...? If I'm not mistaken in the translation, Madame was of the opinion that it did not require a barn full of hay for her to know a prize bull when she saw one."

Sir Cosmo, who was perusing the dancers through his quizzing glass, turned a magnified eye on Selina and choked. "Y-yes. Q-Quite sh-shocking of her to say s-so in m-mixed company!"

"Yes, very shocking." Her brow furrowed. "I wonder if the observation was made from personal experience or by common report...?"

Sir Cosmo deigned to ignore her question. "I must say how very impressed I am with your understanding of the idioms of the French language, Selina."

"As am I," said a low voice at her ear. "Come out onto the balcony. I need to talk to you."

It was Alec, and he gave Sir Cosmo to understand by one look

that he wished to be alone with Selina. Sir Cosmo did the noble
thing and departed to poke his head into the card room.

SERIOUS GAMESTERS OCCUPIED THE SEVERAL TABLES SET OUT
for the purpose of gambling. All were oblivious to the spectators
and other entertainments on offer and cared for nothing except
the cards in their hand. The French Ambassador with his
entourage lounged on sofas by the open windows, and a few dowagers were playing at piquet for small change, their interest in the
ballroom at an end with the close of the minuets. Country dances
did not amuse them, and more than one of them was shocked into
speechlessness at the sight of the Duchess of Romney-St. Neots on
the arm of that barbarian who would let the mob rule if he were
Prime Minister, and she as pink-cheeked as any girl in the midst of
a flirtation. It was outrageous! Spying Sir Cosmo, these deep-
bosomed matrons called him over. He was sure to know the latest
gossip—the boy always did.

Sir Cosmo waved his quizzing glass in acknowledgment of
these powdered and plumed old ladies and meant to cross straight
to their table, but his interest was diverted by two gentlemen
standing by the marble fireplace. So he lingered.

It was the Earl of Delvin and Simon Tremarton. To the casual
observer there was nothing in their behavior to invite comment.
Both men were smiling and seemingly at their ease. Sir Cosmo,
too, may not have given them more than a minute of his time had
he not witnessed the slim sheaf of parchment that Simon
Tremarton half-pulled from his pocket then slid back for safekeeping, patting the outside of his frock coat in a comforting manner.
Sir Cosmo's eyebrows shot up. He glanced at the Earl. The man
was still smiling, possibly broader than before.

Under cover of four gentlemen strolling toward one of the
tables, they in deep conversation about a prime filly to be entered
in the next meeting at Newmarket, Sir Cosmo moved closer in the
hopes of eavesdropping. He was too late. Tremarton had made his

departing bow and wandered off. Lord Delvin took snuff and turned to the looking glass above the mantel to adjust the folds of lace at his throat. Sir Cosmo had to content himself with what he'd seen and report it to Alec as soon as it was convenient to do so. Just now five dowagers awaited him, and he knew his friend had left the social whirl of the country dances to be private with Selina. Ah, what it was to be a popular young man with the ladies, albeit singularly deaf and wrinkled old dears. And while his ear was being filled with the latest on-dits culled from the refreshment room, his mind wandered, and he wondered with a deep mental sigh what was being discussed under the stars of a moonlit night...

THE BALCONY WAS DESERTED, BUT ON THE WIDE STEPS THAT gave access to the velvet front lawns there lounged a group of young gentlemen in padded frock coats and tight fitting satin breeches, smoking cheroots and drinking wine from tumblers. Two couples seeking fresh air after the perfumed claustrophobia of the ballroom followed Alec and Selina outside, and so Alec guided Selina past the group of merry-Andrews to the far corner where the ballroom's French windows, shut tight on the night air, flooded the balcony with light from within and gave an uninterrupted view of the dancers. The light did not reach as far as the balustrade and here Alec took up position, half in shadow.

"I apologize for taking you away from the entertainment, but this can't wait until morning."

"If it's about Emily's awkward behavior this afternoon I may be able to help you," she answered levelly, grateful to have the light at her back and still feeling uncomfortable with him after her emotional outburst at the jetty. When he waited for her to continue, she glanced down at her hands. "Charlotte had Sir John Oliphant examine Emily. On the surface that wasn't such a silly thing after what happened last night. But Charlotte being Char-lotte, her concern wasn't for Emily's welfare; she wanted Oliphant to certify Emily a virgin." She winced when Alec swore. "Delvin put Charlotte up to it. Which leads me to wonder if I was wrong to suspect him of the attempted rape, for why else would he want such confirmation?"

"Perhaps that's what he wants us to presume? Very cunning to deflect suspicion away from himself by seeking Oliphant's assurances that his bride remains untouched. No one is then likely to cast suspicion his way, if he makes out he is also an injured party."

"If you are prepared to suspect your brother of attempted rape, then you must be prepared to suspect him of murder; and I just don't mean of Jack's murder, but of that poor maid's..." When Alec nodded in his abstraction she smiled wryly. "Why this sudden change of opinion, Mr. Halsey?"

Alec looked at her then. "What was Delvin doing in your rooms?"

Selina stared back at him and said calmly, "Over the years, your brother has made an annoying habit of trying to coerce me to commit adultery. Naturally, he chose his moments well, when J-L was not about. *Coward.* I can only presume that his vanity permitted him to think it was the threat of J-L's violence that stopped me from falling into his arms. I guess he presumed that with widowhood I'd have an immediate change of heart. Thus he came to my rooms. For such gross presumption I intended to punish him." She swallowed and averted her face, her lovely profile silhouetted against the window of the chandeliers' bright lights. "Just because my husband... Just because J-L took liberties with my person didn't mean I had to take such treatment from any other man. And certainly not from one I've always despised and mistrusted. And when I think of his perverse pleasure in presenting himself to you as my—that he and I—that we were *lovers.* Ugh! I wish that wax had been acid!"

"I'm ashamed to admit it but for a moment he had me convinced," Alec confessed quietly, watching her pace in the light from the ballroom. He managed a lop-sided smile. "I only hope you can forgive me."

"What else were you to think, given the sight that met your eyes?"

"That is very magnanimous of you. I hardly deserve—"

"It was stupid of me to let him believe I was not averse to his embraces. I should've thrown him out at once! But I was determined to teach him a lesson."

"And did you?"

Her black eyes suddenly sparkled mischief. She stopped her pacing and faced him, a hand up to her mouth to stop a sudden involuntary giggle. "I threw hot wax on him at the *vital* moment."

Alec's shoulders shook with laughter. "How marvelous! Trust you to met out fit punishment, my clever girl!"

Selina smiled. "For one frightened moment I wondered if I could do it. Oh, and then when I did—to see the look of outrage on Delvin's face—Oh, it was worth it! I wish… I wish now I'd had the strength of character to do the same to J-L."

A cheer went up amongst the satin-clad young men on the stairs. One of their number had managed to down half a bottle of red in one gulp. A passing couple skipped deftly out of the way as another of these merry-Andrews plunged into the shrubbery to relieve his stomach of its contents. Alec crossed to Selina's side in the subsiding din. He wanted to take hold of her hands but instead thrust them into his frock coat pockets, one hand hard-gripping his gold-rimmed spectacles.

"Strength of character you have in abundance," he said gently. "Self-preservation too. Jamison-Lewis was possessed of many demons, wasn't he, Selina? He never came to terms with his homosexuality."

Selina gave a start, and after one swift look up into those deep blue eyes she looked away and nodded. "No. He would never admit to it. Not even to me, who knew all about his relationship with Jack. Jack, like me, was abused by J-L, but in a different way. J-L wasn't physically abusive toward Jack. He loved Jack as much as it was possible for him to love anyone, but he could not be faithful to him, and that's what Jack wanted." She swallowed, embarrassed to be discussing matters that were so out of the realms of an ordinary person's experience that it gave the whole a dream-like quality. But it hadn't been a dream; it had been a nightmare. "When Jack met Simon Tremarton and fell in love, that's when matters took a turn for the worse for Jack. He told J-L—"

"When did he tell him?"

Selina thought about this. "It was before Jack took Simon to his shooting box."

"Around the time of J-L's final beating?" he gently prompted.

"Yes. Jack was so happy. He told me that it was because of Simon he'd finally found the courage to tell J-L he wanted an end to their relationship."

Selina stared through the long windows of the ballroom and watched the dancers turn and go down the line in pairs.

"J-L blamed me for Jack's desertion. You see, it was I who pushed Jack to break off with J-L. There was no legally binding document holding them together." Unconsciously she took the handkerchief Alec offered her and wiped dry her eyes. "Jack came down to Jamison Park for the weekend, to say his farewells and that he would see me in London the following week. That night, Jack and J-L argued in the library. I knew it was about Simon. J-L was trying to convince Jack not to go away. Later Jack came to my rooms and we discussed it all, and he told me he intended to leave before dawn, so as to avoid another flare-up. Then J-L came to my bedchamber and he told Jack to get out. It was almost four in the morning; he hadn't been near me in six months—" She faltered and then resumed. "Jack refused to leave, so J-L dragged me into the closet and bolted the door. When—When he'd finished with me he let Jack in. He knew the effect that would have on Jack but he showed no remorse; he had no conscience, so how could he? Of course J-L blamed Jack for what he'd done to me." She broke off again and swallowed. "Poor Jack! The look on his face; I'll never forget it."

"Can you tell me what happened next?" he asked, taking hold of her hands, his gaze never leaving her face.

"Later that morning, or was it early afternoon? Jack came to my rooms with a breakfast tray. I was surprised to see him because he was supposed to have gone, and that's when he told me there had been an accident; that J-L was dead."

"Was it an accident?"

Selina withdrew her hands from his and wandered away from the bright light of the windows to stand in the shadows by the balustrade. Alec followed her, an eye to the young men on the stairs, who had risen as one to saunter back within doors at an announcement made by an officious footman that the fireworks were about to commence.

"When Jack told me the news, there was a decided gleam in his eye," she answered slowly. "And for one heart-stopping moment I had the oddest feeling that J-L's death was not an accident. But then the moment passed and I didn't care one way or the other. What mattered was the beast was dead, and Jack and I had been set free. That's all we cared about."

"But you don't think he shot himself, do you, Selina?"

"It hardly matters now!" she flung at him angrily. "I want Jack's memory to be left in peace. God knows when he was alive he never had a moment's peace. I was married to J-L for six years, but Jack—Jack suffered him for three times as many years! Please, just please let us not talk of it any more! I want to think about the future. I don't want to relive the past. Can't you understand that?"

"Yes. Of course," he said soothingly, and took her in his arms to rest his chin lightly on the top of her soft curls. "We shall speak of it no more. Let's preserve Jack's memory as he would wish it. He deserves to be left alone."

But what Alec was thinking made his heart race. If sweet placid Jack had shot J-L in cold blood, then perhaps Jack had forced the fight on Delvin? And if that were true, then were his suspicions about his own brother unfounded? Then what the deuce had their duel been about?

He felt Selina stir in his arms and lift her head off his chest where she had rested her cheek. He smiled down reassuringly into her upturned, flushed face with its lovely trembling mouth and dark questioning eyes, and had an overwhelming desire to want to protect her from the ills of the world. They stood so still, locked in the moment, neither one wanting to make a false move, yet each waiting for the other to take the first step.

It was Selina who moved time on, cross with herself for foolishly thinking he meant to kiss her, when it was obvious he regarded her as a brother does a sister, not as a lover does the object of his love and desire.

The ballroom was now quiet and emptied of guests. The dancers had crossed to the terrace with its view of the gardens that led down to the Thames, where bobbed punts stocked with fireworks waiting to be set alight. Distant rumblings like thunder came from that side of the house, then seconds later flashes of bright light, like lightning, illuminated the stars above. The fireworks had commenced. The eerie silence of the balcony was enough for Selina to realize they were now quite alone, and she pulled out of his comforting embrace.

"Please, Mr. Halsey," she said, flustered. "I would be most grateful if you'd stop regarding me as a lost puppy in need of a home! I am quite capable of taking care of myself and have done so now for—"

Alec blinked at her and flushed up. He was too angry to be distracted by the bang of the doors or notice the laughing couple who ran out onto the balcony, mistaking it for the terrace, then just as quickly disappearing again in a swish of silk petticoats and perfume.

"Dear God, Selina, you are the most infuriating woman of my acquaintance! Mr. Halsey indeed! What a ridiculous thing to call me given the history between us."

"It is precisely because of that history that you take great delight in throwing my married name in my face at every opportunity!" she answered bitterly, gathering up the folds of her velvet gown in readiness to excuse herself. "The fireworks have started and we shall be missed. Her Grace will be expecting us to—"

"Olivia can damn well wait as long as I have!" he growled, a hand about her upper arm. "Do you think I derive any pleasure from addressing you by that offensive name? How you wrong me! Every time I uttered it I wanted to make you a widow there and then!"

"Did you indeed?" she answered archly, her anger now as all consuming as his and making her throw caution to the four winds. "And by such declaration am I to take it that whenever you pleasured one of your countless lovers you fancied yourself taking *me* to Heaven and back? Ha! You never gave me a thought!"

"You are sadly mistaken in my character, Madam," he enunciated in a low voice, and before she had time to turn away, pulled her into a suffocating embrace and savagely pressed his mouth to hers, murmuring as he kissed her a second time in a wholly different manner, "Damn you for forcing me to act no better than he…"

ELEVEN

THE DUCHESS OF ROMNEY-ST. NEOTS STOOD ON THE
terrace surrounded by her family, the happy couple beside her and
the noisy, laughing crowd at her back. Neave had sent a footman
down to the riverbank where workmen waited to light the fireworks, and all eyes looked expectantly to the night sky in the
direction of the Thames.

Sir Cosmo was the last to join the perfumed multitudes, and
he stood at the back of the crowds pressing forward in awe of the
skyrocket spectacular, head craning to catch sight of Alec and
Selina. But after five minutes of standing on tip-toe he gave up the
attempt and opted for the open space of the gardens, where many
of the guests had taken up position on the steps and along the
paths bordering the formal flower beds to escape the crushing
confinement of the terrace. More than once he passed a shrub in
shadow, to hear giggles and moans and the sounds of love-making.
He thought he saw Macara dart behind a bush in pursuit of a lady
with her petticoats pulled up to her knees. He was not surprised
then when there came the high-pitched squeal of capture. He
rolled his eyes at such crude behavior and continued on his way.

Before he had strolled much further another round of
skyrockets burst forth into the night sky in quick and deafening

succession and sent a shower of diamond stars across the blackness; the sparkles of light illuminating the whole gardens for an instant, then falling in a dim cascade into the Thames. Then yellow stars, and orange, then white again, and finally an explosion of such magnificence that it seemed the sun had come out, and with such an accompanying rumble of thunder that many thought it about to rain.

It was a magical sight and one Sir Cosmo gaped up at in awe with the rest of the four hundred chins pointing skywards. A lull in the spectacle brought his head down to the mouth-gaping sight of Lady Gervais being pawed by Lord Andrew Macara. Under the red light of a Chinese lantern the man was kissing and fondling the woman's exposed breasts as if he had paid for the privilege; and she was calmly patting her hair into place as if she were standing alone in the privacy of her own dressing room! Finally she pushed him away, kissed his open mouth, and they parted company on the walk; she to trip down toward the ivy-covered rotunda, and he to trudge up the path toward the house, adjusting his clothes as he did so. He passed close by Sir Cosmo, but if he noticed him, he gave no indication and went up to the terrace, only remembering at the last moment to adjust his wig.

The fireworks finale saw the wooden structures erected on the punts set alight, and they flamed into outlines of swans and bears and a Chinese pagoda. Small rockets shot out from these flaming structures just as they burned themselves out, and there was a final, brilliant illumination of the night sky to the accompaniment of the oohs and aahs of the appreciative spectators. Then the crowd dispersed, to go indoors, or to take a last stroll in the grounds before calling for their carriages to return to town. And soon the Duchess and Emily were swamped by well-wishers full of verbose compliments and overflowing with praise for an evening's entertainment not equaled that season. The Duchess looked about her for the Earl and wondered why he had slipped away from Emily's side at the height of the night sky spectacle. He had missed the best of the skyrockets.

Sir Cosmo thought he had seen it all until he happened to venture further into the gardens, then he wished he had kept his attention skywards.

ALEC AND SELINA CAME TO A SENSE OF THEIR SURROUNDINGS with the final cheer from the spectators on the terrace. They fell apart and stood facing one another on the deserted balcony, a little disoriented yet acutely aware that there was no going back from what had just occurred between them. They had missed the entire skyrocket spectacular played out above their heads; neither cared.

Without a word, Selina put up a shaking hand to her disordered curls and Alec picked up her fan from the tiles where she had dropped it, and stood holding it. He did not look at her but at the fan with its sticks of carved ivory and heavy silver tassel, and tried to gather his thoughts, wanting to explain his disordered emotions to her, yet fearful that any words spoken at that particular moment would hardly match the depth of his feelings. He was saved a stumbling speech when Selina gave a start and he turned to find Emily coming towards them, face flushed and looking very agitated. When she saw Alec she burst into tears.

AFTER SAYING HER FAREWELLS TO THE DUKE AND DUCHESS of Beauly, Emily excused herself from her grandmother's side and went in search of the Earl of Delvin. She, like her grandmother, had not been so preoccupied with the fireworks that she did not notice her betrothed had vanished half way through the spectacle. It spoiled her enjoyment of what should have been the finale of a wonderful evening, and when he did not reappear to say farewell to their guests Emily became worried that something untoward had happened to him. Saying nothing to the Duchess she went quickly back into the house and began her search of the public rooms. She had crossed to the middle of the deserted ballroom where only the musicians remained, packing away their instruments and talking amongst themselves, when she was distracted by a couple who entered the ballroom in the midst of an argument. So consumed with rage were they that they failed to notice they were not alone. Their shouts bounced off the four walls.

The woman screeched when the man tried to take hold of her again. She retreated further into the room. He followed, hand outstretched. Emily couldn't believe it—it was Lord and Lady Gervais.

"I didn't know it was Delvin!" he shouted. "Cindy! Cindy. I didn't *know*. I thought it was Macara. I saw you with Macara!"

"So you think!" she threw at him. "You drunken fool. You great baboon. It wasn't Macara in the rotunda, was it? It was Edward. Edward you disturbed. Lord! I wish I'd seen his face when you stormed through the bushes like an idiot, demanding to know what he was about!" She laughed shrilly. "But as I was on my knees with my mouth full, I was denied the privilege!"

"Shut up, you foul-mouthed slut!"

"Oho! That's better!" she teased, jumping away from him and skipping up the room. "If I am a whore, whose fault is that, William? Not mine to be sure! And you know it. When was the last time you felt any natural stirrings between your legs? When?"

"Come here! *Come here*," he bellowed, lunged for her and missed. "I'll show you! I'll show you, you poxy slut!"

"Show me? Show me *what*? Hasn't it dropped off by now? I declare I haven't seen it this last decade. Perhaps you still take it out for special occasions? Such as a good hanging or when you spy on Edward's visits?"

"I don't spy! I never—"

"Oh, don't lie to me! I'm your wife, remember? The pretty innocent you deflowered, then failed to perform for thereafter. God! And for all those years I thought I was at fault! That's your real fetish, isn't it? You can't perform unless it's with a girl who hasn't a clue how disgustingly bad you are as a lover!"

Lord Gervais's face turned white. "Just because I won't share your disease-ridden couch! Come here, I said!" He made a final lunge and caught a handful of her petticoats. "I'll show you!"

"You couldn't even if you wanted to!" she taunted.

He grabbed her about the waist, pushed her against the wall, scattering several chairs, and drove a hand up her petticoats. She made no attempt to escape him now. She merely laughed and continued to taunt him. It only inflamed him all the more. She struggled, but it was only a pretense. He had her billowing petticoats bunched up over her knees, exposing her white thighs, and was fumbling with the flap of his breeches when Emily came to her senses and turned blindly for the balcony doors. But she could not help a last look and stood riveted, unable to take her eyes off the couple until there was a loud crash of a music stand hitting the floor. A few of the musicians still remained, and by their grins of appreciation they were enjoying what they considered the highlight of the evening. Emily glared at them, flushed up scarlet, and finally escaped into the fresh air to the sounds of Lord and Lady Gervais consummating their rage.

ALEC PUSHED THE FAN ON SELINA AND WENT TO MEET Emily. He took hold of her hands. They were unnaturally cold. "What is it? What's happened?"

Emily continued to sob as she groped for her lace handkerchief. She shook her powdered head when Alec asked her a second time to tell him what had upset her. He continued to hold her hands and this was a comfort to her and finally, with a great sniff, she said in a rush,

"Have you seen Edward? I can't find him anywhere. He's—he's not on the terrace. He was to farewell the guests and Grandmamma will be cross with him for not seeing the Beaulys off. And, oh, Alec! He didn't see out the skyrockets with me! I don't know where he is! I must find him! Please help me find him!"

"But surely Delvin's disappearance didn't bring this on?" he asked gently.

"Yes! Yes, it did!" she assured him. "I must find him you see. I must."

"He can't be far away," he said soothingly, taking her lace handkerchief and wiping her wet cheeks. "Why don't we go into the Saloon? I know there is to be a supper for the house guests. Perhaps he is in there now?"

This idea struck her and she nodded agreement and would have gone with him, but when Selina came out of the shadows she balked. Instantly, she felt an intruder. Selina's face and throat were flushed and a few tangled curls had come loose from their pearl-headed pins to tumble across her bosom. She did not look at Alec nor he at her, yet it was painfully obvious even to Emily in her distress that they were embarrassingly happy in their silence. It was all too much for her to bear. How could they be happy when she was utterly miserable? This night of all nights was to have been her happiest yet. She was engaged to the nobleman of her choice and everyone said it was going to be the match of the season! So why did she feel utterly wretched? Why had Edward deserted her? Had he really gone off with that painted and patched whore Cynthia Gervais? She couldn't be his mistress, could she...?

When Alec tried to take her hand again, Emily pulled away, and so quickly that she almost tripped over her petticoats. In her wretchedness she turned on Selina fiercely; the woman had no right to happiness when she was miserable.

"Aunt Charlotte blames Alec for what happened to you in the wood!" she blurted out. "But I think *you* encouraged him! You wanted him to seduce you! You lured him to the wood and you-you *bewitched* him. You're no better than that adulterous slut Cynthia Gervais—"

"Emily!" Alec interjected stridently and took a step toward her but Selina cut him off.

"What took place in the wood happened before my wedding, Emily," Selina said, as she slowly advanced on the girl. "But you are quite right. It was at my instigation. No one can blame Alec."

"Aunt Sybilla thinks she stopped you before it was too late, but she didn't did she? He took your vir—"

"This has gone far enough!" Alec growled.

"I want to know! I *must* know!" Emily cried out, looking to Selina.

"Yes. Sybilla was too late, thankfully," Selina told her calmly. "I was never more glad of anything in my life. Sybilla saw what she wanted to believe, but in fact Alec was helping me to dress not undress."

Emily stared openly at Alec and he turned away from her watery, unwavering gaze, a hand to his black hair in a gesture of embarrassment, and walked to the balustrade. But Selina smiled at the girl with understanding. The balcony was so quiet that the sounds of servant activity in the Saloon—of tables being laid with clean silver, china and glass—could be heard distinctly through one of the open French doors. Emily came up to Selina, as if the servants in that part of the house could overhear.

"Thank you," she said quietly. "I'm glad that Aunt Charlotte is wrong about Alec and that you had a moment's happiness together before your wretched marriage to that horrid man. You deserve to be happy. You deserve—Oh, Selina! I'm so mis-*miserable*," Emily sobbed and buried her fair hair in Selina's velvet bodice.

Into this scene walked Sir Cosmo, followed by Plantagenet Halsey. They came up the steps from the lawns, having walked the perimeter of the house from the terrace rather than cut through the public rooms and chance an encounter with a nosy servant or an inquisitive guest. Both were grim-faced, but Alec still breathed a sigh of relief at being thus fortuitously interrupted. He left Emily in Selina's capable hands and went to meet them halfway across the balcony. It was then that he saw the dark stains splashed across the front of Sir Cosmo's oyster silk waistcoat. The man was ashen-faced.

"What's happened?" he demanded, taking in Sir Cosmo's disheveled state; he was missing his frock coat and his shirtsleeves were pushed up over his elbows. Alec noted the grass stains on his silk breeches and the state of his hands. They were dirty. But it wasn't dirt, it was blood.

"Come round to the gardens, my boy," Plantagenet Halsey said quietly, a glance over at the two women, and led the way.

"Are you unwell, Cosmo?" Alec asked.

"Yes. Yes. Bit of a shock, that's all," said Sir Cosmo in a clipped voice.

"It's Tremarton," explained the old man. "Mahon found him. His feet were sticking out from under the shrubbery. Dragged there I wouldn't wonder. He wasn't quite dead then, was he, Mahon?"

"Not quite dead, sir. Still breathing, in fact. No hope for him though. Poor chap."

PLANTAGENET HALSEY LED HIS NEPHEW TO THE GARDENS below the terrace. He left the path and pushed through a hedgerow to a small clearing of grass that divided the flower beds. Two servants stood guard and another joined them carrying a folded coverlet under his arm. All three looked at one another as if this sort of thing was not new to them. Flambeaux had been rammed into the soft earth at either side of the clearing, casting an eerie glow on a grisly scene.

Simon Tremarton's lifeless body lay on its back, eyes closed, head propped up on Sir Cosmo's hastily folded frock coat and a little to one side. He was in such a seemingly relaxed pose that it was hard to believe the man was dead and not just sleeping off a heavy bout of drinking. Yet, on closer inspection, Alec realized his first impression was nothing more than a trick of the flickering light. There was a tenseness about the mouth. Blood and spittle oozed from between his lips. A trickle of the same slid down the left side of the chin. A hand clutched at the stomach, fingers contorted about wadding soaked with blood and pressed to a gaping hole in the man's left side. Blood drenched the shirt and breeches and had soaked the sodden grass.

Alec got up off one knee and looked away. Sir Cosmo lurched into the hedgerow for a second time, the great heaving shudders of his stomach punctuating the still night air.

"The shot went straight through him," Alec observed numbly for want of something to say.

"Yes," confirmed his uncle, taking him to the side of the clearing, away from the servants. "Hole as big as my fist. Ghastly business. The damn fool hadn't a chance. By the time he was found, it was all but over. I came along and found Mahon in a frenzy to get the fellow's neck cloth unraveled. Poor Mahon. If I hadn't shoved him aside and bitten his head off to pull himself together he might've turned into a case for Bedlam. Wouldn't believe the fellow had been shot until I showed him a hand covered in blood. That did the trick. Sent him heaving! I tried to staunch the flow but it was useless. It only caused him more pain, so I stopped. It was soon over."

"Damn!" muttered Alec. He let out a great breath. "No chance of there being a witness? That's asking too much. And the murderer wouldn't be that careless. Too dark and too much going on for anyone to take much notice of two gentlemen strolling out to take a breath of fresh air. Damn! Damn and blast!" He said to Sir Cosmo, who came over to them mopping his forehead, "I don't suppose you saw anyone?"

"Sorry. Came down this way looking for you and Selina. Met my fair share of debauchees dashin' in and out of the shrubbery, but that was all fun and games; nothing to take notice of. And then there were the fireworks to keep one entertained." He pocketed his handkerchief with a shaking hand. "Frankly, I had my head skywards for the most part."

"Like everyone else," the old man said with annoyance. "A perfect opportunity to shoot someone at point blank. Enough noise and carry-on for a damn volley of shots, if you ask me!"

"Shouldn't we do something with him?" suggested Sir Cosmo, handkerchief again at the ready. "Cover him up; take him away? What? What does one do with a freshly dead body?"

"I'll need to call Oakes out again," said Alec. "He was willing to write up a death certificate for poor Jenny without a question asked, but God knows what he'll make of this!"

"One of these men who feel beholden to his betters, eh?" growled Plantagenet Halsey. "Willin' to do anythin' for a lord if it means less fuss for them! Trencherfly!"

Alec directed the servants to wrap up the body as best they could and carry it into the cellars below the kitchen. Sir Cosmo took himself off for a walk while this gruesome task was completed.

"To give Oakes his due, Uncle, he wanted to see Jenny buried without a fuss. I doubt he'll be so complaisant this time, what with Jenny's death still unsolved. And now one of Olivia's guests has been shot dead. Besides, I'll be quite pleased if Oakes does cause an uproar."

"Get the magistracy involved?"

"Yes, I intend to."

"What good is a damn magistrate when there ain't no witnesses, no murder weapon, and nothin' to go on, eh?" the old man grumbled, following Alec through the gardens to the bench where Sir Cosmo sat with his powdered head in his hands. "And very likely there never will be."

Alec regarded his uncle solemnly. "This isn't as neat as a duel in Green Park."

The old man stared at him hard. "You'd best tell me about this fellow Tremarton. He told me he was a colleague of yours in the Foreign Department."

"He was. He was also a member of the Ganymede Club."

Plantagenet Halsey was surprised. "He mixed up with that lot?"

"Yes. And he and Jack Belsay were lovers."

"You know about this chap, Mahon?"

"Only what Alec has told me. And I—er—overheard a conversation between Alec and Tremarton which fairly made my blood boil." Sir Cosmo gave a shudder. "The man wasn't worth a man's spit!"

The old man slumped on to the bench beside him. "Damme! I wouldn't be at all surprised if he was shot for makin' up to some young buck who took his fancy. I'd have shot him myself."

Alec smiled crookedly. "You don't believe that's what happened, do you, Uncle?"

"Of course I don't. But there ain't anythin' to stop anyone else from sayin' so, is there? And there would be plenty of sympathy for the murderer too." He looked up at his nephew. "What's his involvement with Delvin?"

"He gave Delvin eight hundred pounds to buy him a sinecure. It came to nothing and he found himself in debt to a moneylender who wanted a thousand pounds repaid by Monday. Tremarton didn't have it." Alec put his hands in his pockets. "He tried to sell me a letter he said threatened Delvin's security. When I refused he was determined to blackmail Delvin into giving him five thousand pounds in exchange for the letter."

"Lady Margaret's letter!" interrupted Sir Cosmo, sitting up straight. He addressed himself to the old man. "It's my belief Jack had in his possession a letter written by the Countess of Delvin to Lady Margaret confessing the truth about the birth order of her two sons. That in fact Alec is the eldest and thus heir—"

"Rumor! Nothin' more!" interrupted Plantagenet Halsey, waving a hand in dismissal. "Don't believe a word of it! And I can't picture Helen writin' it down in some chatty epistle. Most unlike her."

"But, sir! Lady Margaret was a particular friend and correspondent of the Countess of Delvin and has been saying just that. She's told the town the tale in revenge for Jack's murder." He looked at Alec. "What do you think?"

Alec raised a shoulder. "You know what I think."

"But…" spluttered Sir Cosmo.

"As to Jack getting his hands on such a document," continued

Alec, "and to what purpose, who knows? As for Tremarton coming by the letter so opportunely, I am more than skeptical."

"Then why was he shot?" demanded Sir Cosmo. "If not for that letter, then why? He told you he'd squeeze the money out of Ned. And you prophesied Ned would kill him if he tried. And hasn't that just happened? Well, hasn't it?"

"With not a shred of evidence to prove it," said Plantagenet Halsey.

Sir Cosmo spread out his left hand and counted off on his fingers. "We have Tremarton's threat to Alec, which I overheard. Two: We have Lady Margaret spouting off all over town about her lost letter proving Alec's true birthright. Three: We have Tremarton's association with Ned, and four: Don't forget Jack and Ned's duel, which is somehow mixed up in this business. Then five: There's the fact I saw Ned and Tremarton in the card room tonight being as chummy as can be, *and* witnessed Tremarton pull an envelope from his pocket in a highly suspicious manner. That had to be the letter! And—"

"You've run out of fingers, Mahon," murmured the old man.

Sir Cosmo instantly deflated. "You don't see any connection? No reason on Ned's part to—"

"There's motive enough," said Alec. "Even if Tremarton was bluffing, Delvin needed to get his hands on that envelope."

"And that's why he ran Jack through and now he's murdered Tremarton," Sir Cosmo argued. "It's so damned obvious that he's the murderer!"

Plantagenet Halsey regarded him anew. "You've certainly changed your colors, Mahon. As I recall, you were all for excusing Delvin's escapade in Green Park as a duel."

"So I was!" Sir Cosmo said defensively. "That was before all this business. I was never more shocked when Ned accused Alec of forcing himself on Emily. And that's another mark against him. Well, Alec? You ain't convinced yet?"

"I want to be certain. I want… Never mind!" Alec said dismissively. "I've got to summon Oakes, and perhaps I can bring myself to look over Simon's body for the envelope." He turned on a heel. "Are you coming?"

The two men followed him up to the house, Sir Cosmo falling behind to say in an undertone to Plantagenet Halsey, "You know him better than anyone, sir. Why his reluctance in this?"

The old man took time to answer. He was staring at some point in the middle of his nephew's wide shoulders, a crease between his bushy brows. "Despisin' Delvin is one thing. Thinkin' him a cold, bloodless killer is an altogether different matter. They're brothers. There's a bond there that can't be broken. It's damn hard on him, Mahon. Damned hard."

As Alec predicted, Henry Oakes was in no mood to sign death certificates, or do much else except rant and rave about his professional standing in the community and the impositions of the situation at hand. He took one look at the body under the sheet and refused to proceed further. He wanted a magistrate and he wanted one immediately. Alec was prepared to talk the matter over with him. Plantagenet Halsey was not possessed of such patience.

"We aren't askin' you to do anythin' outside the realm of your callin', man!" he snapped. "You were fetched to view the body and give your opinion as to the cause of death. Ain't nothin' simpler! Eh? Or ain't you fit to pass an opinion? Been hittin' the bottle?"

Henry Oakes stuck out his double chin. "Certainly not! I resent the accusation! And as I haven't the pleasure of your name, or know your involvement in this matter, I kindly ask that you keep your opinions to yourself."

"So that's the way you see it. The name's Halsey, P. MP. And if I had my way, tooth doctors like y'self wouldn't get a goat to examine, least of all a dead man!"

The physician stammered uncontrollably, his chins bouncing up and down, so that he resembled to Sir Cosmo's tired eye a startled turkey. As they were all standing about a cold, damp cellar, the first of many cellars housing bottles and bottles of wine, preserves, and cold meats, the thought was not so absurd to Sir Cosmo's present state of mind. He sneezed and shifted from foot to foot. He did not like being shut up in a damp place in the middle of the night with a room full of swinging carcasses, and a dead body laid out on a table in its center.

"Uncle, be good enough to find Neave," ordered Alec. "It's a winter's day in here and we could all do with something hot to drink. What think you, Cosmo? Oakes?" Both nodded eagerly, teeth chattering, relief showing in Sir Cosmo's face when Alec added, "If we can get through the formalities of an examination, Oakes, we can then go upstairs to discuss the matter in more comfortable surroundings."

Oakes demurred. Plantagenet Halsey opened his mouth but promptly shut it at a glance from his nephew. He went off to find Neave, knowing the task to be an easy one. The butler had a knack for being just where one wanted him.

"I'll conduct an examination if you give me your word you'll fetch a magistrate."

"It's as good as done," Alec assured him. "The deceased man's brother-in-law is a judge and a guest in this house. I took the liberty of speaking to him while we were waiting your arrival. He is at this moment consoling his wife. As you can imagine Lady Gervais has taken the news extremely badly. Simon Tremarton was her only brother. Naturally Lord Gervais is willing to do all he can."

"Aye, he'll do," Oakes muttered sullenly, though it was plain from the look on his face that he was more than satisfied. What better balm to the man's lacerated self-esteem than to have a titled judge awaiting his pleasure. "Her ladyship in need of a sedative, sir?"

"Thank you. It has already been attended to. My valet is also an apothecary and was good enough to prescribe an opiate for her ladyship. Yes," Alec said when the physician jumped at this, "I am well aware it is much frowned upon by the Royal Academy for apothecaries to prescribe, but I am confident of your under-standing in this. The woman, to put it mildly, was hysterical."

Sir Cosmo excused himself from attending the examination. He joined Plantagenet Halsey in the small with-drawing room off the breakfast room. They sat in silence over brandy and coffee, the slightest creak of a door or a floorboard, the sound of distant footsteps, causing Sir Cosmo to jump, which irri-tated the old man's nerves. Neave and a bleary-eyed footman came and went, the two men did not ask what for, nor cared to know. Time seemed not to matter. Only the immediate minutes mattered and passed slowly. Alec and the physician were still occupied in the cellar.

Tam poked his head through the doorway and came in at Plantagenet Halsey's signal. "Does Mr. Halsey need anything, sir?"

"No, lad. If you're determined to wait up, have a seat. There's brandy and coffee or whatever on the sideboard. Help yourself."

"No, thank you, sir," Tam said stiffly, catching Sir Cosmo's look of surprise. He knew his place, even if his master's uncle did not.

"Don't be a martyr! Mahon here don't care, do you?"

"Of course not."

"Besides, you've earned it. Lady Gervais quieter now?"

"Yes, sir. I gave her a draught which should see her sleep well into the morning."

"Thank God for that! The last thing we need is an hysterical female screamin' the bats from the belfry."

Sir Cosmo shuddered at the idea and sipped at his brandy.

The door opened and Neave entered, followed by Lord Gervais attired in a magnificently-embroidered Chinese silk dressing gown. He wore a freshly powdered periwig on his bald pate and an expression of cool superiority on his florid face. Plantagenet Halsey rolled his eyes. The man was a bore and a fumbler at the social niceties, but give him his legal milieu and he exuded haughty authority. He could see the man was going to be a diffi-cult prig.

Lord Gervais cast a critical eye about the room and let it fall on Sir Cosmo. "Ah! Mahon! Good." He turned to the butler. "Inform Oakes I will see him now." He poured himself out a dish of coffee and slurped at it in an irritating manner. "Mahon! Tell me what you know about this unfortunate accident—"

"*Accident?*" blustered the old man.

"I don't recall having asked for your opinion, sir," Lord Gervais said coldly.

"I found the—the body," Sir Cosmo said dully. "Well, it wasn't a body then. The man was still alive—"

Lord Gervais pounced. "Alive? Are you certain?"

"Yes, I'm certain! He was breathing. And then Mr. Halsey came upon me and tried to help. Well, he did it all, to point out fact. I was in no fit state to be of much use."

"Don't be hard on yourself, Mahon," Plantagenet Halsey said gently.

"Will you allow Sir Cosmo to speak?" interjected Lord Gervais.

"Mr. Halsey did all he could to make Tremarton comfortable. That's all one could do. There was no hope of the man making a recovery. None at all."

"Are you saying that Halsey here interfered with my brother-in-law?"

"Interfered?" The old man was on his feet. "*In-ter-fered?*"

"Gervais! That's rich!" Sir Cosmo stated angrily. "If it hadn't been for Mr. Halsey's interference, as you call it, Tremarton would have spent his last moments in total agony. As it was, Mr. Halsey did everything in his power to ensure the man felt as little discom-fort as possible. You owe him your gratitude, not your censure!"

"As to that," said Lord Gervais with a quick smile, "you will allow me to decide. Tell me, Mahon, did my brother-in-law speak to you before he passed away?"

"No."

"Nothing? Not a word?"

"No! Look, Gervais, Tremarton was dying a horrible death," Sir Cosmo said in exasperation. "He was bleeding all over the place from a great gaping hole in his side. He wouldn't be in any mood to chat, now would he?"

Lord Gervais sniffed. "There is no need for sarcasm at such a grave time. I merely require of you to answer my questions." He seemed to see Tam for the first time and frowned. "What, pray tell, is this menial doing drinking a dish of coffee?"

"Lord! As if that has anythin' to do with the investigation!" the old man laughed. "Leave the lad be. He's worked hard for his refreshment."

"Indeed. Nevertheless, he can go and drink coffee in the servants' hall where he belongs. I don't want him here."

Tam's face flamed as red as his mop of hair. He put down the coffee dish and saucer and took a step toward the door when Plantagenet Halsey ordered him to stay where he was.

"When did God give you the right to ordain men beneath your touch? The lad has as much right to be in this room as any snot-nosed, toad-eatin' hangin' judge!"

"Are you defaming me, Halsey?"

"Gentlemen! Please!" Sir Cosmo demanded in a thin voice.

"It is men like you, Halsey, who would, if they could, tear our well-ordered society asunder."

"In the snap of two fingers if it would answer the purpose, and rid it of cold-blooded trencherflies such as yourself!"

"You, sir, are a menace to society and ought to be locked up! I've a mind—"

"Now don't puff up too much or you'll burst on your own self-consequence!"

Sir Cosmo thrust himself between them. "Gentlemen! For God's sake! Remember why we are here. This petty bickering—"

"*Bickering?*"

"*Petty?*"

Alec entered the room in time to witness the last of this scene, and had he not been tired he would have laughed out loud. Henry Oakes was behind him and immediately spotted the brandy. Neave came in after them and stood to one side of the refreshments, silent and poker-faced. Lord Gervais collected himself enough to be introduced to the physician, and asked him all sorts of stock questions under the mantle of his absolute authority as a judge. Sir Cosmo and Plantagenet Halsey retreated to their chairs, and if the old man was tempted to interject with a few caustic remarks he checked himself for the sake of his nephew, who was trying his hardest to have the physician and Lord Gervais come to the point so that everyone could retire for what was left of the early morning hours.

An hour later, Lord Gervais, having questioned everyone to his satisfaction and everyone else's frustration, announced gravely, "Gentlemen, I am forced to conclude that Simon Tremarton did not die by his own hand, but was cruelly and brutally murdered. It is given as Henry Oakes' opinion that the instrument of death was a pistol, fired at close range, once only, and that the bullet entered the stomach, rupturing internal organs and causing Tremarton to bleed to death. I accept his findings. Yet an absence of the murder weapon, and the difficult circumstances surrounding the scene of this heinous act—there being in progress a fireworks celebration, and at least four hundred or more guests in attendance; the gardens being insufficiently lit; and the absence of any witnesses, or if there being such persons, that they failed in their duty to come forward for whatever reason or reasons—I am unable to proceed in this matter until such time as further evidence is put before me and a person, or persons, comes forward with substantial information that can lead to an arrest."

"Bravo!" the old man declared. "The man's a marvel! It took him an hour to figure out what we did in five minutes! If it pleases your lordship I'm off to my bed before the lackeys start settin' the table for breakfast."

"Sir! I hold you in contempt!" announced Lord Gervais. "Stand where you are!"

Plantagenet Halsey waved a hand at him and left the room, saying a pointed good night to his nephew and Sir Cosmo. Tam quietly followed to ready his master's bedchamber. Lord Gervais was left to stare wild-eyed at Alec.

"I warn you, Halsey, your uncle has not heard the last of this!" he spluttered. "I hold him in contempt and I intend to prosecute him to the full extent of the law. He is nothing but a menace and has thwarted me at every turn!"

"Now, steady on, Gervais," interjected Sir Cosmo. "He's a bit rough around the edges, but he hasn't done you an ounce of harm. In fact, he put it rather well, if you ask me."

"Mahon! Are you, the son of a baron, the nephew to a ducal house, supporting the likes of that usurper? That *republican*—"

"Gervais, you cannot but forgive my uncle his outspokenness," Alec said with cold politeness. "As son of an earl, indeed uncle to another, not to mention his connection by birth to most of the governing families in the kingdom, my uncle is naturally used to speaking his mind and doing just as he pleases. Is that not the way with those of noble birth?"

"WELL! IF YOUR PUT-DOWN DIDN'T RUFFLE OLD GERVAIS'S feathers!" Sir Cosmo laughed, leaning on the landing rail just outside Alec's bedchamber. "Pity your uncle wasn't there to hear it."

"It was a despicable thing to throw at a man like Gervais, whose *raison d'être* is his slim connection to the nobility."

"Here! Before you go," Sir Cosmo whispered, looking about the darkened landing. "What happens now? Gervais can't leave it there, can he? A man's been murdered."

"There's nothing else he can do. Until someone comes forward and makes an accusation of murder against another, our judge can't proceed. He may get the Runners onto the matter, to have an ear to gossip and rumors, just in case there is something to be gleaned of relevance from the guests, although I doubt the Duchess would approve of her home being overrun."

"Devil! I can't say I'm sorry Tremarton's gone, but it ain't right his murderer gets off just like that! From what you say it seems unlikely we'll ever know who put that bullet in him. Well," Sir Cosmo corrected, "we know, but it ain't going to be public knowledge, is it?"

"Not unless one of us is prepared to bring an accusation before Lord Gervais. And from my understanding of the law, there's nothing to say an accusation can't be brought against a person for lack of evidence."

Sir Cosmo breathed deeply. "Thing is, how can we be absolutely certain?"

"Yes. How can we?" said Alec with a grim smile and turned the door handle.

"Wait! The envelope! You looked? Did you find it?"

"I searched his frock coat pockets and the pocket of his waistcoat."

"And?"

"There was an envelope—"

"There was? I thought—"

"—the murderer would have absconded with it? Had it contained anything of interest I dare say he would have."

"Must've been a damned bloody business."

"Excessively bloody, Cosmo. Good night."

"What if the murderer took whatever was in the envelope, replaced it in Tremarton's pocket to look as if he'd never touched it, shot him, and was off? Perhaps he shot him first, then took the letter from the envelope. Wait a minute! What if he—"

Alec laughed. "Good night, Cosmo," and slipped into his bedchamber, the smile wiped from his face the moment the door closed on his back.

Tam was using the warming pan to take the chill off his master's bed sheets when Alec strode through from the sitting room, struggling out of his black velvet frock coat. Tam said something, but such was Alec's preoccupation that he went through to the closet without a word or a look. He sat before the dressing table and absently removed the diamond-headed pin from the folds of fine white lace about his throat. From a pocket of his silver-threaded waistcoat he removed a creased and yellowed envelope he had found on Simon Tremarton's bloodied body.

He propped the envelope before the looking glass and stared at it, as if it were possible to read the contents without actually removing the folded parchment from its cover. Alec wasn't entirely sure he wanted to read what was written on that sheet of parchment. Opening the letter was likely to change his life forever, and he wasn't sure it would be for the better. The tall elegant handwriting on the envelope's face was not unknown to him. It belonged to his mother, Helen, Countess of Delvin. And the envelope was addressed to Lady Margaret Belsay, Cavendish Square, Westminster.

EVANS PLACED THE TRAY ON THE LITTLE TABLE BY THE fireplace and silently went about her duties in the bedchamber, an ear to the conversation in the sitting room where Selina and Emily sat close on the chaise longue, their feet to the warmth of the fire. The hot chocolate would also help warm them after the cold night air of the balcony, but Selina thought something stronger was in order after such an evening. Putting a finger to her lips so Emily would not speak, she removed a couple of tasseled cushions from one end of the chaise and found the monogrammed silver flask where she had hidden it earlier that afternoon. She added a generous nip of the flask's contents to each mug and gave one over to Emily.

"It will help us sleep," she assured her when Emily sniffed tentatively at the curls of steam. "Better than laudanum and no headache in the morning."

Emily smiled and drank up, and found that the additive to the chocolate gave it a smooth, velvety finish. "Why do you hide it?"

she asked, indicating the flask that Selina returned behind the cushions.

"Oh, I don't. But it would be no fun for Evans if I left it in full view. It gives her occupation. Better for her to save me from the evils of drink than let her mind run on to other things. She's a disciple of Methodism, y'know."

"Has she been with you a good many years?" Emily asked, preferring to talk about anything and anyone other than what was on her mind.

"Since I left the schoolroom," Selina answered lightly, yet her dark eyes watched Emily closely. "My parents thought very highly of her; little did they suspect Evans of a romantic disposition! She'd have been banished to the wilds of the Welsh border country from whence she came." She sipped at her hot chocolate and said with a smile, "Dear dour Evans was heartbroken when my parents arranged a perfectly respectable marriage for me."

"I'm not surprised. You allowed yourself to be married off to Jamison-Lewis when you were in love with Alec," Emily said fiercely, showing animation for the first time since she and Selina escaped up the back stairs to Selina's rooms rather than attend the supper in the Saloon. "I just don't understand it!"

"You know as I do that heiresses do not choose their husbands, my dear," Selina said matter-of-factly. She shrugged a shoulder, making light of it for Emily's benefit. "All my parents cared about was J-L's ancestry; that he was grandson of a duke and worth twelve thousand a year. You are lucky indeed that Olivia wants for your happiness above all other considerations."

"Yes. Yes she does, doesn't she?" Emily said in a small voice and felt the tears at the back of her eyes. "I want her to be happy for me."

"Then *you* must be happy," said Selina and touched Emily's cheek with the back of her hand. "Are you happy, Emily?"

Emily shook her head as she stared into the empty mug. "I thought I was. I know I was—yesterday. But today... I'm not so certain."

Selina put aside their mugs and curled up on the end of the chaise to face Emily, her black petticoats billowing around her like a cloud. "Then you must not marry until you are completely happy with your decision."

"Oh, but I can't postpone the wedding. Grandmamma and Edward, our friends, they all expect the wedding to be—"

"Nonsense! Olivia has given you the gift of choice and you must use it wisely. If you are unhappy, if you have a single doubt about marriage to Delvin, now is the time to exercise your gift. Your mother's marriage was a disaster; my marriage was a disaster. But it is a simple thing for us to blame parental ambition. You, however, can blame no one but yourself if you choose unwisely." Selina smiled reassuringly. "Olivia gave you a gift, but with it comes a huge responsibility."

Emily swallowed. She had never thought of her decision to marry the nobleman of her choice in this way before and it seemed to add weight to her already burdened shoulders. Yesterday she would not have given Selina's advice a second thought, but after finding herself an unwilling audience to the sordid scene played out between Lord and Lady Gervais, her faith in her betrothed had been shaken to its core. She stood and shook out her petticoats and stared into the burning logs in the grate.

"Aunt Charlotte says Grandmamma will be heartbroken if I don't marry Edward," she explained in a small voice. "Aunt Charlotte says marriage to Edward will right the wrongs of my mother."

Selina interrupted her with a huff of disbelief. "What rot! Charlotte's opinion of your mother is corrupted by her jealousy. Charlotte was passed over by Beauly in favor of your mother; not the done thing for a younger sister to wed before the eldest is safely married off. Macara finally offered for her because he was bought off by your grandparents and really didn't give a fig who fathered his legitimate children, provided the mother had a pedigree. That Charlotte has in abundance, and she gave him an heir." When Emily turned and regarded Selina with surprise, she added, "I'm sure Olivia will excuse me for telling you your uncle has another family. In fact he set up house with this common-law wife about twenty years ago, and she has given him eight brats. Everyone knows about this other family, but of course no one is going to mention it in polite circles. Can you wonder then at Charlotte's bitter disposition when she keeps up the façade of the contented married lady and castigates your mother's lifestyle, when it is Madeleine who is happier married to her Italian count? You will hurt Olivia far more by going through with this marriage if it is not what you truly want."

Emily sighed. Her head hurt, and she turned back to the flames frowning because she was determined to overcome the last hurdle of doubt. "Is that woman—Is Lady Gervais Edward's mistress?"

"I have heard it said so."

Emily nodded in a detached way, as if they were talking about someone unconnected to her and not her betrothed. "Thank you for telling me. I didn't know. I found out tonight. Plenty of noblemen have mistresses, and common-law wives it seems! But—"

"—it is an entirely different matter when it is the man you love who is lavishing his attentions on another?" Selina joined her in front of the fire and took hold of her hands. "Believe me, Emily, that is the hardest hurt of all to bear. To be so in love with someone that they merely have to look another's way for you to feel such a stab of pain that your heart aches…"

There came a knock on the outer door and Evans was heard speaking to someone before she came to the doorway. Selina nodded to her maid and said to Emily softly,

"Peeble is here for you. Talk to Olivia in the morning. I know you will find her remarkably responsive to your request for a postponement. Six months will go very quickly. Delvin will understand if he loves you…"

"And if he doesn't?"

Selina kissed her forehead and hugged her. "Oh, I am sure he loves you in his way, dearest Emily. But ask yourself this," she whispered in her ear, for Peeble had come to stand beside Evans in the doorway, "are you prepared to share him?"

"Poor lost lamb," Evans said with a heavy sigh when the door had shut on Peeble's back, yet subconsciously she was humming a tune and walking as if on air. "Forced to marry that philanderer I shouldn't wonder."

"No, you shouldn't wonder," said Selina, giving her a suspicious sidelong glance as she went through to the bedchamber. "It's behind the smaller of the three cushions," she called out. "And it needs refilling!"

She heard the maid grumble under her breath and smiled to herself as she began to undress behind the ornately carved dressing screen in the corner of the room. Evans soon joined her and by the look on her face she was going to be difficult about the flask, so Selina held her tongue until she was made ready for bed.

"I didn't dance, if you were wondering about that," she said, another glance at Evans who was folding Selina's stockings with a light touch and a small smile on her usually prim mouth. "But I didn't behave myself either."

This had the maid fast on her heels, face full of expectation as Selina crossed to the small table under the window.

"I know you are only thinking of my mental health, but it is no use hiding the account books from me," Selina admonished her gently. "I need to check an entry. It's been bothering me all evening. Evans?"

"I know. I saw," Evans confessed almost with a squeak of excitement. "We saw you together, through the window."

Selina brought her head up out of one of the drawers of the tallboy and frowned. "Saw us? Through the window? We? Dear me!" She turned away with a telltale blush. "Have—have you put the account books in one of the trunks?"

Evans regarded her with a silly sentimental smile. "Miss Peeble and I stole a look in at the ballroom from the gallery just as the final dance was coming to a close. We were on our way to the roof with the other upper servants to view the skyrockets. Such a spectacle! I've never seen the like before."

Selina closed the lid of the traveling trunk. "Was it a spectacle? I—I missed it I'm afraid. Do tell me where you've stashed the ledgers, Mary."

Evans looked across at Selina standing in her white chemise and bare feet with her hair down her back, and thought her so absurdly youthful that it brought a lump to her throat. She could barely keep herself from throwing her arms around the girl with joy; instead she sniffed and said stridently,

"If you know what's good for you, you won't let him go a second time!"

Selina suppressed a smile. "Your advice is noted, Evans. Now where did you put the ledgers?"

"Ledgers? They were on the table there when I left to view the skyrockets," said Evans, who went over to the table and put a hand on the spot where she had last seen the three account books, as if physical contact with the wooden surface would satisfy her that the books had indeed vanished. "I remember it precisely because I thought about putting them out of the way, but then Miss Peeble arrived."

Selina sat down heavily on the edge of the bed. "But how did he find the time to steal the ledgers if he was on the terrace with Emily and the hordes watching the fireworks…?" she wondered to herself and looked across at Evans. "You didn't embark on a cleaning crusade today and annoy the chambermaids to remake the bed, did you?"

Evans was affronted. "I beg your pardon, ma'am?"

Selina smiled and hopped off the bed so she could push aside the pillows that rested against the carved headboard.

"Then may I beg your pardon, Evans."

She tossed her long curls back over a shoulder, reached a hand down into the tight space between the mattress and the headboard, and with an effort extracted a thick parcel wrapped in a pillowcase. This she placed on the coverlet. From within the pillowcase she removed one of the three ledgers that had been left on the table.

"He thinks he's been very clever but thankfully I've outsmarted him," she said with a deep sigh of satisfaction. "Tomorrow I mean to prove it." She placed the ledger under the covers and climbed into the bed. "Evans, you may think what you like but *M'sieur Livre de Comptes* and I are spending the night together. And in the morning we will need an hour undisturbed. Good night."

Evans said nothing. Privately she was of the opinion that the sooner her dear girl remarried, the sooner her head could be cleared of this obsession for mathematical nonsense. She extinguished the candle and went out, making a mental note to refill the silver flask with lemon water.

TWELVE

"Mayhap I will take up your offer of a few weeks in the wilds of the Mendips," Sir Cosmo said gloomily upon entering Selina's small sitting room off the bedchamber.

He saw the tray of breakfast things and was about to make his way to the chaise longue by the fire, but Selina had disappeared into the bedchamber and called him to come through. He did so gingerly, aware that the ever-present Evans must be lurking about in a cupboard and it wouldn't do to be discovered in her mistress's bedchamber. Attending an open toilette with hovering maids and visitors while madam sat at her dressing table being coiffured was one thing, but to be alone in a lady's bedchamber with her clad only in chemise and dressing gown, and—he stifled a gasp—bare feet, was being a mite too familiar. Still, he obeyed and came to stand by Selina at the small table by the window.

"Gorges and waterfalls and limestone," he added and shuddered, still feeling seedy after the night before. "But thankfully there won't be any dead bodies to stumble upon…"

Selina had collected the ledger from the bed where she had left it under a pillow and opened it out on the small table by the window.

"Tremarton didn't manage to say anything to you, did he?" she asked casually, flicking through pages filled with rows and rows of figures entered in neat, heavy handwriting.

Sir Cosmo shook his head, peering over her shoulder. "Nothing. In shock I'd say. Hole in his side and bleeding all over the place."

She frowned thoughtfully. "Shame. Simon Tremarton was an opportunistic weasel but he didn't deserve a violent end." She pulled Sir Cosmo by his silk sleeve so that he stood beside her and pointed to a series of scrawled notations made in the left hand margin. "See these? They've been bothering me. For most of the payments the amounts vary, which you'd expect for items such as food, wax, coal and what-not, but two payments are constant in timing and amount. And what is even more puzzling is that all incoming monies are notated with the letters GC, and correspond to an identical amount taken from the estate ledger but not noted. I'm surprised Andrews never inquired; but perhaps he did and J-L fobbed him off...?

"The regular monthly outgoings are also notated, but one is more puzzling than the other. The first is marked LJG; the second is simply marked with the letter D. The first I have no idea to whom or what, but I can make a very good guess as to the second."

Sir Cosmo, who had no head for figures, had no idea what she was talking about. "Spoken to J-L's man of business about it?" he asked.

"Andrews?" Selina was scornful. "He had no idea this ledger existed. Seems J-L was withdrawing substantial sums of money from the estate and placing the lot into this account. Well, he was so wealthy he could afford to siphon off bags of money without it really impacting on our day-to-day lives, couldn't he? I guess that's why Andrews never made a fuss." Selina flicked through a few pages and stopped at a month at random. "See. The same occurs for March and for April and May. The money J-L was depositing into this account is clearly written, as are the usual expenses for food, coal and so on, but I have no idea why he felt he needed to channel it into this secret account. And who or what was getting the monthly wad of bills?"

"How did you come by this ledger if Andrews knew nothing about it?"

Selina closed the account book. "It was lying open on J-L's desk the morning he was found in the wood."

Sir Cosmo's mouth dropped into a frown. "Odd."

"Odd?"

"Odd that he should leave open on his desk a ledger he obviously kept secret from his man of business, and then go out to shoot. You think he would've secured it before heading off."

"He may have intended coming back to it. It wasn't Andrews' day. No one else was likely to enter the study. Maybe he went to the wood to clear his mind before returning to finish up the figure work?"

Sir Cosmo rubbed his clean-shaven chin. He wasn't convinced. "Clear his mind? He blew his head off, my dear girl. Why have the ledger open at all? More important to leave a note behind than try to balance the books before you're about to shoot yourself in the temple!"

"I wonder what the letters GC stand for?" Selina muttered, ignoring her friend's incredulity. "This ledger had nothing to do with his racing interests or his gambling or payment of IOUs made at his club. Andrews saw to those, and I checked the accounts. They are all correctly accounted for. But studying this ledger, one would almost presume J-L to be running a quite separate and secret establishment, as if he kept a mistress. But we know that not to be the case so—"

"There is the Ganymede Club," Sir Cosmo suggested lightly. "The initials fit." When Selina stared at him uncomprehendingly, he gulped. "Ah. Don't know about that then?"

He drew a deep breath. Why was it left to him to dredge up the muck? First Alec about J-L, and now Selina about her husband's sordid other life. He cursed his ability to get himself into such tight corners. Tucking his chin into the high collar of his striped silk banyan, he said in a clipped voice,

"Male brothel above an apothecary's shop in Fleet Street. Tremarton was an habitué; so, it seems, was Jack. Can't think why any self-respecting gentleman would be interested in young boys—"

"Young *boys*?" The word was wrenched from her.

Sir Cosmo put up his hands. "No! No! Not boys. No. Youths."

"Boys? Youths? Both are underage and ill-used by men of means and position. Wherein is the difference?" Selina answered in an anguished whisper. She leaned against the table and looked so white Sir Cosmo wondered if she were about to faint. Yet her voice did not waver as she held tight to the table, gaze fixed on her friend's face. "You knew about this male brothel, this Ganymede Club?"

"I've only just found out about the place, m'self," explained Sir Cosmo, following her into the sitting room. "Believe me, Selina. Had I known—"

"Had you known, what then, Cosmo?" Selina asked angrily, and tossed the ledger on the chaise and sat down heavily beside it. "You'd have ignored its very existence, as obviously everyone else did, just as a blind eye was turned to J-L's wife beating. As long as the Honorable George Jamison-Lewis played at being duke's grandson in public, frequented White's and Newmarket as good-fellow-well-met, presented his wife in drawing rooms and at balls with her bruising carefully concealed, what he did in private was best not thought about." She ran cold hands over her face, her throat so dry it hurt to swallow. "Did no one confront J-L about this Ganymede Club?"

Sir Cosmo hunched his padded shoulders and could not look at her.

"One must presume not. I had no idea of the club's existence until yesterday. And obviously those who did were clients. We are all guilty of hypocrisy, Selina. Some of us probably wouldn't have believed it of George had he proclaimed it to the world. Not the sort of thing one wants to believe of a man who belongs to your club." He sighed and shifted the ledger onto the table with the breakfast things so he could sit beside her. "Forgive me, my dear, for not rescuing you... For not being man enough to stand up to George... For—"

"For God's sake, Cosmo!" she demanded impatiently, to hide her embarrassment at his look of contrition. "There was nothing you could've done! You know as well as I that wife beating is a tolerated prerogative of a husband. Besides, George would've killed you. He was without conscience and for you to step in and do the manly thing would've served no purpose. I'd have lost one of my dearest friends! As it is we have lost Jack, and that's almost too much for both of us to bear. Here," she said, thrusting the chocolate pot at him, "be useful and pour us both a mug while I take another look at these ledger entries." She balanced the book on her knees. "If we assume you are right about the GC denoting the Ganymede Club, then it looks to me as if J-L was running the place as his own private male brothel. And quite an expensive establishment to run by the amounts deposited into this account. But what I don't understand is the notated outgoings..."

"Must have cost a bit to run such an establishment," Sir Cosmo suggested meekly as he handed her a full mug. And then he had a flash of brilliance and hurriedly gulped down a mouthful of warm chocolate. "And when you think about it, brothels can only keep their doors open through the unspoken cooperation of the local authorities: Paying off shopkeepers, the beadles and the parish magistrate. They'd all put their hands out for a share of the profits to keep their eyes and ears shut to the carryings-on of the nobility."

Selina was not at all surprised. Her eyes narrowed. "Then it is very likely that the letter D does stand for Delvin—"

"Delvin? *What*?" Sir Cosmo's mind boggled at the thought. "Egad, Selina! Delvin wouldn't go within ten feet of a male brothel!"

Selina looked smug. "He wouldn't need to. Not to collect

payment."

Sir Cosmo set down his chocolate mug with an unsteady hand. "You think Ned was blackmailing J-L?"

"He was most interested in J-L's account books when he forced his presence on me the other night. Couldn't keep his eyes off them. And now those three ledgers are missing."

"But to blackmail J-L?" Sir Cosmo shuddered. "It's not that I don't doubt Ned capable—after what he did to Jack and his appalling behavior toward Alec this weekend—it's just that to blackmail J-L... God, Ned must be mad!"

"There is a fine line between fearlessness and madness, Cosmo," Selina said with a smile. "Besides, J-L could afford the payment. The question is, why did Delvin need the money?"

"What about the other initials mentioned in the ledger? Perhaps this other unknown blackmailer is the one who stole the ledgers?"

Selina took a sip of the sweetened hot chocolate and pulled her silk dressing gown closer about her shoulders. "Then you must presume that we have *two* blackmailers here in this house."

"God. I never thought of that!"

"I stand corrected," Selina added. "*Three* blackmailers. Although, as the third is the recently deceased Mr. Tremarton, he hardly counts, does he? You seem certain Delvin shot Simon. Just as he coldly and callously murdered Jack, and all because Tremarton threatened to expose our dear Earl as a fraud with a letter that he did not have, and that does not actually exist. But that's not a very convincing argument is it, Cosmo?"

"It's as if you don't believe in the existence of Lady Margaret's letter," he replied, a little wounded by her skepticism. "I need not remind you, my dear, that you helped flame that rumor into a house fire."

"Willingly. But I don't have to believe such a letter exists to do so." She smiled mischievously. "I'll happily spread any scurrilous piece of gossip about Delvin, if it helps tarnish the gloss. The man is not worth his birthright."

"But that's just it!" Sir Cosmo argued, eyes brightening. "Ned isn't worthy of his birthright because it isn't his to claim. It's my belief Jack discovered the truth about Ned and Alec, and threatened Ned with exposure. Perhaps Jack was using the letter to counter Delvin's blackmail of J-L? Jack probably discussed the letter with Tremarton, or showed it to him. He may have given it to the man for safekeeping, and then when Jack died, Tremarton sought to use the letter for his own ends. He had nothing to lose."

"Except his life. Stupid man! Cosmo... Have you mentioned any of this to Alec?"

"Discussed it in depth," was Sir Cosmo's smug reply. "A'course Alec's not convinced his mamma would commit to paper something so damning of her character. But I'll tell you one thing, my dear girl, your Bothwell knows his brother for a fraud."

Sir Cosmo's earnestness did not lift Selina's frown.

"If that's so, then Plantagenet Halsey also knows it, and if he knows it, why hasn't he, the upholder of justice and truth in all manner of causes, seen fit to expose his nephew the Earl as a fraud? And don't tell me the uncle would keep his tongue between his teeth to avoid a family scandal; he's no hypocrite."

Sir Cosmo continued to look smug which only annoyed Selina.

"Ah, now here's where I amaze you, my dear," he said. "Plantagenet Halsey considers a man's achievements in life, what he has himself accomplished, of greater merit than, say, a mere earldom."

"Oh, I know that," Selina said dismissively. "But it doesn't explain the old man's unwillingness to right a wrong."

"Well, there is the fact Alec don't want to be an earl."

This had an immediate effect on Selina whose annoyance turned to anger.

"How like him to dismiss what is rightfully his because of some ridiculous prejudice instilled in him by that silly old fool!" She threw a cushion at Sir Cosmo who was grinning at her. "I don't see why you are being horridly gleeful, Cosmo!"

Sir Cosmo chuckled. "Our republican friend's worth rises and falls with the tide of your feelings, my dear."

"There is the possibility Plantagenet Halsey didn't champion Alec's cause because he knew all about the Countess of Delvin's adultery, and although Alec is legally the eldest son, he is not his father's son and thus not entitled to the earldom."

"Meaning?"

"That Alec may be his mother's firstborn, but that does not necessarily make him the earl's firstborn son. If that is the case, Plantagenet Halsey, in good conscience, could not support Alec's claim, when in truth Delvin is the earl's rightful heir, despite being the second son. Did you not think of that possibility, Cosmo?"

"No," Sir Cosmo answered glumly, and devoured a breakfast roll in two bites, adding in a forced, disinterested tone, "You mean to have him anyway, though, don't you?"

"Nothing has been resolved between us."

"I would've thought his declaration on the balcony resolution enough…?"

Selina turned her face to the window, but not before Sir Cosmo saw her ready blush. He sighed deeply.

"It wounds me, but I shall live, my dear. Though don't expect me to be at your wedding. I shall go into a decline and take the waters at Bath or some such watering hole for the ill and the mentally wounded."

She laughed but said perfectly seriously, "Well, we can take the waters together because I intend to remain a widow."

"I can well understand your prejudice against the married state, but we're talking about Alec. Marriage to him would be a wholly different proposition from that of your first."

"Yes. But for the first time in my life I have my freedom and I cannot contemplate giving it up so soon…"

Sir Cosmo screwed up his mouth and shook his head. "He'll not understand it, y'know. He may have the reputation in foreign court circles of being a bit of a rake, but once wedded he'll give and expect total devotion; that's his nature." He flicked her cheek. "Be careful, my dear. Alec won't settle for anything less. He has scruples—his uncle's upbringing, I'm afraid. And he won't take you as his mistress, if that's what you're thinking. You must play by his rules or you risk losing him… Perhaps this time forever."

"Here you are!" Lord Gervais bellowed at Plantagenet Halsey as he entered the breakfast room, the Earl of Delvin two steps behind him. "Be so good as to close the door, my lord," he said to the Earl and fixed an eye on Sir Cosmo. "You're here, too, are you, Mahon? Very well. For that I am glad. If this—*gentleman* is unwilling to cooperate perhaps you will!"

Lord Gervais's very manner instantly put Sir Cosmo off side. He frowned and looked to the Earl, who merely shrugged and took out his snuffbox.

"What do you mean by this intrusion, Gervais?" Sir Cosmo asked.

"You may very well ask!" said Lord Gervais puffing out his cheeks.

"He is askin'," the old man quipped, and speared the kipper on his plate.

"Uncle, you will not be so snide when you hear what Gervais has to say," the Earl said quietly.

Plantagenet Halsey ate the kipper. "No? Tell me. You've come to arrest me?"

Sir Cosmo reached out a hand to him. "Sir! Please do not even fun about such things."

"Where is your nephew, sir?" Lord Gervais demanded.

Plantagenet Halsey put down his knife and fork. "Standin' behind you."

Lord Gervais's face fired. Sir Cosmo let out an involuntary laugh. The Earl rolled his eyes.

"Where is Mr. Alec Halsey, if you please?" Lord Gervais said in a voice that was near to breaking.

"How should I know," the old man shrugged. "He don't make a habit of tellin' me his whereabouts. And that's as it should be."

"Sir, if you frustrate my efforts in this, I will have no choice but to arrest you for complicity! You will answer my question and answer it truthfully!"

"Will I?"

Delvin frowned. "I advise you to answer him, Uncle."

"And when did I ever take your advice?" Plantagenet Halsey snapped.

Lord Gervais puffed out his cheeks even further. "Sir—"

Sir Cosmo interrupted with a cough into his fist. "May I ask a question?"

All three gentlemen looked at him.

"Why do you wish to know Alec's whereabouts?"

"Because, Mahon," said Lord Gervais in a voice that could not hide its note of triumph, "he is wanted for the murder of Simon Tremarton!"

Lord Gervais's proclamation failed to produce the desired effect. No sooner had the words left his mouth than Plantagenet Halsey laughed in his face. A great bellyache of a laugh it was too, which only deepened the color in the judge's cheeks. When he had recovered from the initial shock of such an absurd accusation, Sir Cosmo also laughed. His effort was more of a titter, and he did nothing to stifle the absurd sound. Lord Gervais demanded calm. He demanded to be heard, but his audience, bar one, stared at him as if he had gone raving mad. He looked to the Earl for guidance. The Earl was no help to him. He had propped himself in the window and was gazing out on the terrace.

"I fail to see—" stuttered his lordship.

"—how you became a judge!" scoffed Plantagenet Halsey.

Sir Cosmo smiled at the old man and mouthed the word 'buffoon' as he took snuff.

"You may think of me what you will, sir," Lord Gervais said through thinning nostrils. "I have an accusation brought against Alec Halsey for the murder of Simon Tremarton, and I mean to see that he is brought to answer the charge."

"Ballocks! I don't know why I'm still here listenin' to this tripe!" the old man jeered. "Accusation by whom? Alec was nowhere near the gardens when it happened. He was with the rest of us on the terrace and surrounded by half-a-dozen bared breasts, I shouldn't wonder!"

Sir Cosmo's eyes went very wide and he slowly shook his head at the old man, who squinted at him.

Fortunately for them both, Lord Gervais had his back to Sir Cosmo as he said, "He may well have been, yet he must answer to the charge. That is the law, sir."

"Is it? Well, it's a damned stupid law! Accusin' Alec, indeed!" The old man fixed a blazing eye on the Earl. "What have you got to say to this, eh?"

The Earl turned his powdered head to look at him. "I? Nothing whatsoever. As Lord Gervais has told you, Second must answer to the charge. If he is innocent, then he merely has to say so. I'm sure there must be half-a-dozen—er—bare breasts who can vouch for his whereabouts. Mayhap even yourself and—Cosmo?" When his uncle looked instantly uncomfortable the Earl smiled slightly. "Can't, can you, Uncle? A pity. Such an outstanding member of the community as yourself would make an excellent witness for the defense."

Sir Cosmo blinked. "You can't be serious, Ned! You can't really think there is anything in this accusation?"

"I don't know what to think, Cosmo. Sad, isn't it?"

"But… But what earthly reason could Alec have for wanting to —" Sir Cosmo stopped himself and unconvincingly went into a coughing fit.

"Yes, Cosmo?" the Earl prompted silkily.

"Who brought this accusation?" demanded Plantagenet Halsey.

"You think it was I?" The Earl looked astonished. "Come, come, Uncle. The last thing I relish is a family scandal."

"Not unless it is of your own makin'!"

The Earl sneered. "How well you know me."

"Gentlemen! Gentlemen! If—you—please!" Lord Gervais

bellowed. "Now, Mr. Halsey, you will tell me your nephew's whereabouts."

"Rot in hell!" exploded the old man, and stormed out of the breakfast room, slamming the door.

In the silence that followed, Sir Cosmo snapped shut his snuff-box, slightly inclined his head to the Earl, and ignoring the judge, followed Plantagenet Halsey out of the room.

Lord Justice Gervais stared helplessly at the Earl.

"I warned you," Delvin said calmly.

Lord Gervais loosened his neck cloth with the crook of one finger. He had never been treated with such contempt. He was used to respect, respect for his calling if not for his person, and now anger burst through his embarrassment. "Your uncle is a menace to society! I've a mind to lock him up!"

The Earl sighed. "Incarcerating an old man don't solve the problem at hand."

"The accusation will stick. You'll see."

"Will it?" The Earl looked skeptical and leisurely dipped a finger into his snuffbox. "You should've arrested Second last night when you had the opportunity."

"Without the authority to back up the accusation? Do you take me for a fool, my lord? I must await the arrival of the Bow Street Runners."

Delvin snorted a goodly quantity of snuff. "But will they do what you want?"

"Aye. Men who owe their positions to me. There'll be no dissent."

The Earl beamed. "Splendid! You've done this sort of thing before I see."

Lord Gervais eyed him with resentment. "And you know it, my lord."

The Earl's smiled widened, but the glint in his pale blue eyes was icy. "I'm unlikely to forget a piece of cowardice that has considerably reduced my income."

"What would you've had me do when that gaming hell was

merely a cover for a more sinister intent?"

Delvin feigned surprise. "Really, Gervais, you had no idea that the rooms above the apothecary's shop housed a male brothel?"

"The two floors were leased as a gaming establishment. It was not until information was put before me by a member of the peerage who insisted upon action that I was fully apprised of the real situation."

"Liar," Delvin said very low. "For two years you turned a blind eye to the goings-on of a male brothel and were paid handsomely for such selective blindness. And I was proudly shown the ledger by our wealthy and very perverted mutual acquaintance that implicates both you and me."

Gervais looked uncomfortable. "You can't really have expected me, a respected judge, to ignore Lord Belsay's information? I'd have faced ruination; as would have you, my lord. Guilt by association. And you know it, for you fought a duel with his lordship over that very thing."

The Earl looked the pale-faced judge up and down with a sneer. "What would the grandson of a slaughterman know about dueling? Belsay wanted that brothel closed to teach his lover a lesson and because he was smitten with your mealy-mouthed brother-in-law. Do you think I'd have cared a tester had it become public knowledge that my mistress is the kneeling-whore wife of a corrupt judge, who puts his hand out for payment from the ill-gotten gains of a male brothel? *More fool you.*"

Lord Gervais strode forward, livid with rage. "Have a care, my lord, or I'll—"

"What?" taunted the Earl, and hopped down off the window sill with a jaunty step. He dusted powder from an embroidered upturned cuff. "I have that ledger now, and it's about time you began paying me for your judicial lapse. And I expect Second to be in custody by dinner time."

"Delvin!"

The Earl stopped in the doorway but said nothing.

"She—Cynthia may change her story once the laudanum—"

"She won't."

"It's been a great shock," continued the judge meekly, all the fight gone out of him. "He was worthless scum, but he was her brother."

"Reason enough to want to catch his murderer," replied the Earl, and left Lord Gervais standing alone in the middle of the room where he remained for several seconds, convincing himself that arresting Alec Halsey for murder would serve everyone's best interests.

Resolute, he stomped from the room, more than ever determined to carry out his plan of action, and in the corridor bumped into Emily St. Neots. In fact, she bumped into him. She had come in search of the Earl. In the confusion that followed she dropped her straw hat. Lord Gervais scooped it up.

"Thank you," she said a little breathlessly. "How careless of me! Have—have you seen Lord Delvin, sir?"

"He's in the gardens. You must be more careful, Miss Emily," he said dully, still holding her hat.

"Yes, I must," she answered, feeling a sudden rush of embarrassment remembering his behavior in the ballroom the night before. "How is—is Lady Gervais? I heard the dreadful news."

"She is resting. It was a great shock. A great shock for all of us."

"Yes—yes, it was," said Emily after a moment's hesitation because although she did not look up into his eyes she had the uncomfortable sensation of feeling his gaze upon her heaving breasts. "My hat, sir, if you please…"

At that he shoved the hat at her, and would have stepped past her, but as such things go, she stepped in the same direction and they collided once again. This time he made no attempt to get out of her way but stood close, so close she could smell him, his breath quick and hot on her burning cheek. Feeling trapped, terror seized her and she pushed past him, forcing him to the wall with hurried words of apology as she fled out into the gardens. It was an almost welcome relief to find the Earl alone.

. . .

"My dear! How lovely you look!" Delvin said cheerily, and went forward to kiss Emily's hand. "That gown. Indian muslin, isn't it? Very fetching!"

She kept her fingers firmly about the brim of her straw hat. "Thank you. I'm glad I find you alone, Edward."

His smile widened. "This is very flattering."

He offered her his arm. Instead she walked ahead of him to the far end of the garden where a knot of gardeners worked in the flower beds at the bottom of the terraced steps. She tied on her bonnet, taking longer than was necessary because she did not know how to begin this interview. She was spared the necessity.

"My dearest Emily," he said soothingly as he took her hand in his, "you are looking a little tired. Last night was a great success and yet you appear less than happy? Can it be that you are still haunted by that dreadful ordeal of the other evening? I would not have you so, my dearest. We must put that unpleasantness behind us and think of our future—together."

"Sir, it—it is our future together that I wish to discuss."

He beamed and kissed her hand. "That's better! And so we should discuss it. I am eager to. In fact, I am so eager that I have spoken to the Duchess this very morning and have persuaded her to bring the wedding forward."

Emily was startled. "Forward? But why?"

"Can't you guess?" he purred. "I want you for my own today, now, this instant. Do you not wish it also? Your blush is sufficient answer."

Emily withdrew her hand, and breathed deeply. She felt life was moving too fast all of a sudden. And the Earl's eagerness was not having the desired effect; in fact she felt as if she were no longer in control, when all along she had believed she was the one to make the decision to marry the Earl. She recalled what Selina had said to her about responsibility, and it almost overwhelmed her.

"My lord! Please. I realize the great honor you do me by wishing to marry me. I know I am the envy of many, but... But I have had time to think matters through and I wish I could marry you tomorrow with a clear conscience. I wish I could feel as confident as you do about our marriage. But after all that has happened, after thinking the matter through, I would like more time to consider. It is not that I do not wish to marry you, it's just that I feel that if we were to have a period apart to reflect—"

"Come, my dear," he interrupted with his most understanding smile. "It is not unnatural for you to feel apprehensive. I feel it myself. It is a large step that you and I take, but it is a step I wish to take with you, and you alone."

"I am flattered, Edward, truly I am, but I need time to—"

"Consider what a grand couple you and I will make once we are settled!" he said and drew her away from the prying eyes at the library windows. "You shall be denied nothing as Countess of Delvin. Society will take you under its wing!"

"Please, Edward! Please. I am only asking for six months..."

"No," he said, and with such finality that Emily's eyes flew up to his face, and in an instant she saw a coldness in those pale blue eyes that sent a shiver through her trembling body. "We will be married at the end of the month."

When she tried to draw away from him he would not let her go and anger got the better of him. "Second put you up to this, did he?"

Emily swallowed. "No! No! No one has said a word to me!"

The Earl fought hard to master his anger and forced himself to smile sadly. "My dear, do you think me without a brain? You are too sweet a child. You have been gently bred to do as you are told, what we think is best for you. These harsh words, these doubts, they are not in your nature. How may I set your mind at rest? Have I offended you in any way? My one desire is to make you my wife. I had thought it your only wish too."

Emily felt hot tears behind her eyes. "Edward. Edward—is Lady Gervais—is that creature your mistress?"

Delvin looked away from her and took out his snuffbox. "My dear, you cheapen yourself by asking such a base question. I shall not answer it."

"But I must know!" she demanded, wringing her hands. "She is your mistress, isn't she? I know because I overheard her and Lord Gervais in the ballroom—"

He put up his hand. "That is quite enough. I will not discuss that woman with you, now or ever."

"No? But you bed her nonetheless?"

"Listen to me!" he snapped, grabbing her hard by the shoulders and sticking his face in hers. "My one desire in life is to marry you. It is you I want as my countess. You are all the things a man can hope for in a wife: Beauty, obedience, youth. I will make you a good husband, but the rest of my life is none of your business; nor will you make it your business. I want you to give me sons. I want—"

Tears streamed down her face. "Please, my lord, you are hurting me."

The Earl stared at her blankly, then released her suddenly, realizing he was fast losing control over her. "The weekend has exhausted you. You are not yourself. Upon a week's reflection you will see that I am in the right. I will speak to Her Grace and—"

Emily shook her head. She pulled her shoulders back and adjusted her straw bonnet. "It is not you, my lord. It's just that I cannot marry a man who keeps such a woman as a mistress; who fornicates with her at his own engagement party! Is that not what occurred last night? Did you not go off with her into the gardens? Do you know how that makes me feel? To be consumed in such misery—"

"*Misery?*" The word was wrenched from him, and with that one word his cool and charming facade was shattered forever in her eyes. "What do you know of *misery?*" he spat out. "You dare to cast *me* aside, all because I am a man? You, the product of a debased liaison between a whore and a cowherd? You should've been well-satisfied had I made you my mistress! As it stands, I am considered a laughing stock by my fellows for wanting to ally myself with the likes of you! I shall not turn 'round now and allow you to make me a buffoon—the butt of every joke in town!"

Used to receiving only his courtesy, she was so startled by the sudden change in him that for a few moments she lost the ability to speak. Her cheeks burned red and she picked up her petticoats in readiness to flee inside to find her grandmother, when she caught sight of Sir Cosmo and Plantagenet Halsey coming across the gardens towards them.

"I—I am sorry, my lord, but it would be for the best if we—"

The Earl caught her arm before she could brush past him and pulled her close. "I'll strike a bargain with you," he hissed in her ear. "Marry me and I'll save Second from the hangman's noose."

Emily stared up at him wildly, unable to fathom this new frightening being who resembled the Earl of Delvin in form only.

"Hangman's noose?" she repeated in bewilderment and turned swiftly to face Plantagenet Halsey when he ordered his nephew to let her go. She was so relieved she fell into the old man's arms, sobbing.

Sir Cosmo put up his quizzing glass to better view the Earl, but it was Plantagenet Halsey who spoke.

"Your life's goin' from bad to worse," he said in a flat, unapologetic tone. "Nothin' more pathetic than a man who's unequal to his birthright."

And he walked into the house with a protective arm around Emily's shoulders, Sir Cosmo two steps behind, leaving the Earl abandoned on the terrace, red-faced and seething.

ALEC SAT IN HIS SHIRTSLEEVES ON A LARGE RAISED GNARLED root of an old oak, his long booted legs stretched out before him and his back up against the massive trunk. He had come to the grove with his two faithful hounds just as the sun and the servants were rising, and before Tam was awake and had a chance to ask where he was off to. He needed the quiet that only this idyllic spot in the home wood could provide. Last night he had been in two minds whether to read his mother's letter or burn it unopened. Yet, here in the grove with the sun filtering through the tree tops onto deep beds of ancient fallen leaves, moss-covered tree roots, and the small open space dotted with bluebells, he was confident that whatever secrets the Countess of Delvin had committed to paper, the past could not possibly unsettle his future.

He was wrong.

With his gold-rimmed spectacles perched on the end of his narrow nose, he opened the envelope, its seal broken long ago, and removed two pages. The paper was thin, yellowed at the edges and written on one side only. A glance at both and it was obvious that these sheets were the opening pages of two different letters. Both were written in the Countess of Delvin's feminine fist and both addressed to Lady Margaret Belsay. The top sheet was dated some six years earlier while the second sheet was more yellowed and much older, having been written almost sixteen years ago. Alec chose the older letter first and read:

Dearest Meg (it began)

*Today, I saw him! I was in my carriage in Oxford Street.
There was some sort of accident up ahead which forced me to
sit and wait for almost half an hour in the heat and noise.
Why I decided to come to town in the middle of August I shall
never know! Now I wish I never had, and yet part of me is
glad I did, because I saw him. Yes! I can hardly believe it
myself and I am sorry if I am keeping you in suspense, but I
do like to tease you, don't I?*

*I was staring blankly out of the window (I had stared blankly
at the upholstery ten minutes or more, wishing I were home
and cursing myself for my stupidity) watching the town go
about its business, when out from a booksellers stepped Plantagenet Halsey, a weight of books all tied up in brown paper and*

*cord tucked under his arm. No doubt a collection of treaso-
nous writings that he favors and I do not understand in the
least. We were so close that had I extended my parasol from the
window I could have touched him. I did not, of course, do so!
I was about to fall back against the seat so that he would not
see me, when out from behind him stepped a tall young man
with a mop of blue-black curls falling into his eyes.*

*I did not know him immediately, only that he was handsome
in an angular sort of way, with a long nose and a most
engaging smile, oh! and the bluest of blue eyes I have ever
known a gentleman to possess. In truth, Meg, an Adonis. I
know you will laugh at me and think me fallen in love with a
pretty face but it is the truth. You will laugh even louder
when I tell you that I stared at him quite brazenly, my nose
pressed up against the glass. You can imagine then how flustered I was when he stared straight at me. I know I blushed.
Me, an old woman put to the blush! And for one agonizing
moment I was transported back to when I was a bride and
passionately in love and an adulteress. Seeing this young man,
seeing how much he resembles his father… He took my breath
away.*

*I threw myself against the upholstery. I was shaking! Then, not
a moment later, I was at the window again to catch another
glimpse of my son, and he had gone. Gone! Gone off arm-in-
arm with Plantagenet Halsey up the street in the opposite
direction, so that I never did see his face again.*

*Meg, it was my son! My son Alec. My firstborn son whom I
was forced to give up at birth as penance for my adultery. I
shall never forget his face, the look of him, that smile. He has
my eyes, Meg! But, oh, he is his father's son. He haunts me.
Not only at night when I am in my bed alone, but during the
day when I am at my needlework, or in the garden, or talking*

*to Mrs. Pringly about how best to bottle my strawberry
preserves.*

*It is my wretched conscience. I can no longer live with myself,
with this secret I have kept so tightly bound about my heart
that it threatens to squeeze the life out of me. I must tell someone. I must tell you, though in the telling, I risk losing your
love and friendship. I pray for your understanding for it is the
truth, Meg, as God is my witness. I shall burn in Hell for
what I did, for what I permitted Delvin to do. I do not care
now. Somehow I must right this wrong. Somehow—*

Alec came up for air, his face lacking all natural color. He had
come to the end of the page and he quickly turned the sheet over
as if expecting there to be more, yet what he had just read was
more than enough to overwhelm him. Over the rims of his spectacles he saw the two greyhounds at the edge of the grove frolicking
in the undergrowth. They had found the burrow of some hapless
wood creature. Watching them, Alec unconsciously folded the
sheet and slipped it into an inner pocket of his waistcoat before
dropping his gaze to the second sheet.

Dearest Meg (it also began)

*My illness prevents me from writing much at all these days. I
do tire so easily and spend the greater part of my day chair-
bound and being fussed over by Martha. The pain in my
joints is considerable. Nothing gives relief.*

*The matter I spoke to you about on your last visit, do you
recall it? The time has come for me to confront my son. I don't
expect a warm response, perhaps no response at all. Yet, in
good conscience before I die I must persuade him to do what is
right and proper. After all we are talking about his own flesh
and blood whatever he may say to the contrary.*

*I had no option but to send the boy away, for who wants a
constant reminder of one's lack of moral fiber staring one in
the face day in and day out? I am no fit person to judge on
that score! I sent him to his uncle, and with enough money for
the boy to get an education so that he might make his own
way in the world. God knows he deserves better, the title, if it
were in my power to bestow! It matters not a jot to me that his
father is—*

Here the writing had come to the end of the page, but this
time Alec did not turn the sheet over. And for a long time he just
sat there with this page in his hands, staring out across the small
field of bluebells, wondering what he was going to do with his
mother's letters. He wondered what had happened to the subse-
quent pages and reasoned that they must have been withheld,
possibly secreted in a safe place, for all that was required to blackmail his brother were these pages, proof that there did indeed exist
damning letters written by their mother. He wondered too what
revelations were contained in the missing pages, if their mother
having mentioned her adultery so openly had mentioned his father
by name. But there was no doubt in his mind that Jack Belsay had
taken the letters from his mother, but whether he had then given
them to Simon Tremarton for safekeeping or Simon had stolen
them from Jack, he could only guess at.

Finally, after what seemed like an hour of sitting still, he
returned this page to the worn envelope, took off his spectacles
and put both in a pocket of his discarded frock coat. He still felt
dazed, so much so that the hard snap of a twig underfoot made
him look up with only mild interest to see who trespassed on his
solitude.

It was Selina. She came across the grove through the filtered
light, a hesitant smile on those beautifully curved lips he so wanted
to kiss again and again. He returned the smile, convinced he had
dozed off because the last time he and Selina had met in the grove
was, unbeknownst to him, the morning of her wedding day. Selina

was now a widow and wore mourning, not a velvet cloak of deepest purple, its hood pulled lightly over her abundance of apricot curls. She stopped a few feet away, gloved hands clasped in front of her holding a riding crop, and frowned down at him.

"I've come to warn you," she said as if through a thick fog. "Gervais has sent for the Runners. His wife has accused you of murdering Simon Tremarton."

"Is that so?" he said mildly. "Do you know, I have aged a twelvemonth in the space of an hour. Strange… I don't feel it in my bones but just knowing—"

"Alec! You don't seem to understand," Selina demanded and took a step closer. "Gervais means to arrest you for *murder*."

"Yes. So you said, darling," he replied. "I wondered when he'd make his move."

Selina was startled. "Gervais? You have suspicions about that pompous judge?"

"I do, and on several fronts. Accusing me of murder robs me of the same opportunity. I cannot now turn round and point the finger at him, without people thinking I acted out of malicious revenge."

Selina watched Alec get to his feet, a crease between her brows.

"You think he murdered his brother-in-law and by accusing you has deflected suspicion away from himself?" she asked. "But why murder Simon Tremarton?"

Alec flicked her under the chin. "Oh, I could think of one very good reason why a pompous upstanding member of the judiciary would want to do away with the embarrassment of a homosexual brother-in-law who was attempting to blackmail a member of the aristocracy. But no, I wasn't about to accuse our officious judge of murder, though he must remain a suspect surely, but of attempted rape."

"Emily?"

"Yes. The night Emily was attacked, he made the mistake of going to Sybilla's rooms to complain about the boys playing pranks in the servant passageway," he explained. "Obviously he'd panicked

—perhaps he thought he'd been seen fleeing down the backstairs, and hoped to deflect suspicion away from himself by seeking out Sybilla before the boys got to her first with their version of events. Yet all it did was bring himself under scrutiny. What was he doing in that part of the house, in the servant passageway, no less? And in speaking to Sybilla about the judge's most uncharacteristic late-night visit, I recalled a conversation Gervais and I had earlier that night Emily was attacked.

"He spoke and acted like a man three-parts drunk. But I wonder now if he was drunk at all. He waxed sentimental about how sweet and innocent his wife had been at the time of their marriage. And the way he was regarding Emily as he spoke, like prey... Sweet, innocent Emily was about to share Delvin's bed, just as Gervais's wife was doing, and I suspect it was enough to send the judge over the edge. It was an opportunity to have his revenge on a man who had made him a cuckold but whom he couldn't publicly condemn for fear of losing face..."

He shrugged and with a smile kissed Selina's gloved hand.

"Of course it is all speculation on my part..." He seemed to see her for the first time and smiled. "That cloak is very fetching," he said pleasantly. "Sets off your lovely hair." He lifted a corner of the cloak. "Doesn't mourning require widows to wear more somber hues? And if I am not very much mistaken, that riding habit is Florentine green."

"My dear Mr. Halsey," she said with a laugh. "You talk of would-be rapists and acts of revenge and question the lack of proper mourning attire of a hypocritical widow all in the one breath! If I didn't know you better, I'd say it was you who are drunk, but—"

"But you do know me better," he murmured and gently kissed her mouth.

Their second kiss, like the night before on the balcony under the stars, was different. It was full of hungry urgency, passion and need. And here, in the quiet and privacy of the grove, there was nothing to stop them fulfilling that need. Yet, Alec came to his senses and pulled away, blue eyes troubled. When Selina put a hand to his cheek, he kissed it abruptly, then walked a little way off, leaving her by the oak feeling foolish for thinking last night had brought them full circle to where they had begun before her marriage to J-L. He must have had second thoughts. Why had she thought they could begin again? Why had she kissed him as if her future happiness were vested solely in him? Because it was true and she must be a fool.

But she couldn't have been more wrong. Alec wanted to kiss her, and wanted to take the expectation in that kiss to its rightful conclusion. Yet when it came to the one woman who truly mattered in his life he hesitated like a damned schoolboy on his first encounter. So much for the experienced lover, he who had been involved in more than his fair share of bedroom politics! But if he were brutally honest with himself, over the past six years on occasions too numerous to count, he had given and received pleasure from his lovers imagining it was Selina who moved and moaned under him. And now she was a widow. It was obvious she loved him as much as he loved her. He should have been overjoyed that providence had handed them a second chance. But it was overshadowed by a need to win her trust, for her to know that he loved and respected her above all others; that it had only ever been her with whom he wanted to share his life. How was he to explain this to her without appearing condescending, and when he had come within a hair's breadth of asking Emily to marry him?

He came back to pace in front of her. He felt unequal to the task of expressing his feelings—he who was known at many a foreign court for murmuring pretty nothings to steeple-haired beauties only too willing to share his bed—and so he was blunt and unflattering, and at the end of this awkward speech he wondered if any man had ever sounded less romantic.

"Selina! I admit I hated you for marrying Jamison-Lewis, but that doesn't mean I stopped loving you. I convinced myself that there was no point to feeling anything for you when you were married to another. I even went as far as foolishly believing I could replace you. I'm not talking about the casual liaisons I've had. Those women were part of the forgetting process. God knows it's easy enough to satisfy a physical need, but I wasn't any more fulfilled. And then, when we unexpectedly bumped into each other on the stair that day and I felt you against me again, and smelled the fragrance in your hair..." He laughed self-consciously, a hand through his tussled hair. "Damn it, I'm not doing this at all well!"

"Go on," she said gently, stripping off her gloves, a hesitant smile hovering about her lovely mouth. "You're doing splendidly."

He stopped in front of her, dark blue eyes unblinking.

"I went to a Turkish Bath that same night," he confessed. "I was determined to expunge the feeling of you in my arms with the first whore I came across. And do you know, the thought of touching—of *making love*—to another woman so repulsed me that I believe you've made me impotent. So I drank myself to stupefaction instead. And the worst of it is, through it all, since that fateful moment on the stair, I never again gave thought to marrying Emily."

"I've never given any other man a thought."

At that he pulled her into an embrace.

"Then promise me, you little wretch, that this time you will marry me."

She snuggled into his embrace, her cheek against his chest, reveling in the feel of his hard body; such a welcome change from the soft fleshy excesses of a cruel and disinterested husband.

"Can we begin again?" she asked. "Here. Now. As it was six years ago."

At that, he chuckled in his throat. "No. You must marry me first."

"Must I?" she asked, looking up at him as if contemplating his offer. She lifted the hood of her cloak back off her hair, untied the cord that held it at her throat, and let if fall at her feet. "But I lack the moral fortitude to wait out the rest of my mourning," she confessed, and stepped back to untie the bows down the front of her green velvet bodice. "And, I hope, so do you…"

"Darling," he said gently, gaze firmly on her face, and not on her bare breasts through the thin cotton chemise as she let the bodice fall to the carpet of leaves, "I want you to be my wife, not my whore."

She continued on with undressing, untying the tabs that held her petticoats in place, and let the yards of lace and velvet slide down her shapely thighs to her ankles. She stood before him in a transparent cotton chemise that barely covered her thighs, white stockings tied with ribbons up over her knees, and in half boots. She smiled when his gaze finally dropped from her face to openly admire her. And for the first time in six years, she saw lust spark in a man's eyes and was not ashamed of her body—no longer thought of as nothing more than a repellent, necessary means to an end. She felt desired as a woman should be, and by the man she loved above all others.

She wriggled free of the chemise and stood before him, smiling.

"Ah, my love," she said on a sigh, "and I'd hoped to be both."

It needed only that to evaporate the last of his resolve. He gathered her up in his arms and they descended as one to the discarded clothes on the soft deep bed of leaf litter.

MUCH LATER, AS THEY LAY STILL AND QUIET IN ONE another's arms, Alec finally reached for his crumpled shirt, but Selina stopped him. She drew him back down beside her, an arm about his neck, the long sweep of her tangled curls falling caressingly across her breasts.

"Again."

They made love a second time, blissfully unaware that the home wood now crawled with heavy booted trespassers. Two of their number finally stomped into the grove brandishing clubs, and loomed large over them.

THIRTEEN

ALEC AND SELINA SCRAMBLED TO DRESS TO THE HOWLING jeers of four unshaven brutes carrying batons. Alec only had time to pull on his breeches before pushing Selina out of the way as he was struck across the shoulders with a heavy club. He turned on his attackers and fended off another blow by grabbing the lout's wrist and forcing the raised arm out of the air, his other hand planting a direct hit to the man's stubbled chin. The man staggered back, stunned, the sight of his own blood on his fingertips enough to make him fall backwards into a bed of leaves. As Alec shook the sting out of his smarting hand, he was hit again from behind, this time at the base of his skull. The blow knocked him to his knees.

Two more thugs appeared from the thicket and joined in the fray. Selina screamed for help. Dressed only in her chemise, she rushed to Alec's defense, hitting out wildly and indiscriminately at the three men. She was grabbed about the waist and hauled out of the way, kicking back wildly at her captor's legs with all her strength, but her efforts were in vain. A sharp painful tug on her long curls forced her head back against her captor's chest so that she was compelled to watch in horrified disbelief as the Earl of Delvin strode forward, pushed the three thugs aside, and with his whip hand high above his head, struck his defenseless brother with a force fueled by absolute hate.

Alec tried to stand but was forced to his knees again by a series of sharp stinging blows across his bare back. He heard his brother's shouts and then Selina's pleading demands that he stop. But the whipping continued and, in one last act of defiance, Alec dragged himself up again, only to have a boot heel come down heavily in the small of his back. He was in pain, but what drained the fight from him was the realization that it was his own brother who was inflicting such torment.

Delvin lifted his whip hand again, his rage by no means burned out. He had not meant to join in the fray, merely to be an interested spectator to ensure his brother was taken into custody. Seeing Selina naked in his brother's arms changed that. Her look of serene fulfillment told him she had already given herself to his brother. She should have been his; she was *always* meant to be *his*. He wanted to hear his brother beg him to stop, but Alec's silence goaded him on and the whip came down time and time again.

"Damned mulatto bastard! Beg me to stop!" the Earl finally burst out. "Come on! *Beg me*! Lower that sniveling, stinking misplaced pride! Do it! Aye, *freak*—"

"Delvin! Stop it! *Stop it*!" Selina screamed, and made one last effort to break free by kicking the thug in the shin with her boot heel. She stumbled forward and tried to wrest the whip from Delvin, but he merely pushed her away and she fell to the ground, grazing her arm from elbow to wrist. "Cosmo? Oh, thank God!" she gasped, dragging herself to sit up as a large figure thrust his way to the Earl's side and demanded to know what was going on.

For a stunned moment, all Sir Cosmo could do was stare at Delvin's handiwork. But he was not about to stand idly by. He lunged for the Earl's whip hand and easily took the weapon from the surprised Earl, who had let down his guard in his bid to get a response from his brother. Sir Cosmo flung the whip as far from him as he could.

"You're damned-well mad!" Sir Cosmo thundered. *"For God's*

sake, Ned! You're a damned lunatic!" He dropped to the ground beside Alec. "Alec? Alec, dear fellow, are you all right? Speak to me!"

"You interfering dolt!" the Earl snarled. "Can't you see he deserved a beating? The filthy, poxy *bastard!*"

Sir Cosmo stared up at him incredulously. "Have you *no* feeling? This man is your *brother*."

The Earl stared back at him, unmoved. A heavy trickle of perspiration ran down his flushed cheek. "What? This half-breed bastard a Halsey? *Never*," he said flatly, turned his back and walked away.

Sir Cosmo helped Alec to sit up. "Dear God, what a bloody mess," he murmured, surveying his friend's lacerated back. "Selina? Selina, are you hurt?" When she shook her head he said softly, "Put on your clothes, my dear. Then give me a hand. I can't manage him on my own."

Through a haze of pain Alec lifted his head. "Frock coat."

"Don't speak," Sir Cosmo advised. When Alec grabbed his arm and pulled him forward, he had to lean closer to hear him. "What is it, dear fellow?"

"Frock coat… Get it… Keep it safe…"

Selina and Sir Cosmo looked at one another. They thought Alec's mind wandering. Sir Cosmo squeezed his hand.

"Anything to oblige, dear fellow."

"Get it—*now*."

"Of course," Sir Cosmo said soothingly.

Alec shook his head, slumping sideways onto Sir Cosmo's arm as he did so, face contorted with the throbbing pain in his lower neck. He was close to passing out, but first he had to make Cosmo understand. The last thing he wanted was for Delvin to get his hands on their mother's letters. What names had Delvin called him? *Mulatto*? *Half-breed*? *Bastard*? He pushed himself up and felt a hand on his forehead, gently brushing the hair back off his hot face. It was Selina. And there were voices all around him, and people. He closed his eyes and made one last attempt to speak.

"Cosmo. I want... I want... Don't let him—"

"Hush," Selina soothed, mopping his face with a corner of her purple cloak.

"*No! It's important! Important. My frock coat. Keep it safe. Don't let him find the letters.*"

But Selina and Sir Cosmo were not listening and continued to attend to his hurts. He had no idea that they couldn't hear him; that all this he had said in his head. If they were not about to help him, then he would have to do it himself. He tried to look up and felt curiously light-headed. There was a buzzing in his ears. He heard the familiar barks of Cromwell and Marziran. What were they barking at? One of Olivia's deer? He smiled. Far off, people were shouting at one another. He winced. It was all so distracting. He needed to get to the big oak, to get his frock coat, to keep the letters safe. Didn't Cosmo understand how important it was? More important than dressing his cuts and bruises. It didn't even hurt that much; just the ringing in his ears and the pain in his head, which was almost unbearable. But he had to ignore the pain. He had to get to the big oak before the others. If those letters fell into the wrong hands... If Delvin discovered... Why was it so difficult to move his legs? Why couldn't he stand up? It was such a simple thing to be able to do. Why couldn't he...

THE DUCHESS OF ROMNEY-ST. NEOTS WAS FURIOUS. Normally a placid woman who thought it beneath her to indulge in fits of rage, nevertheless, when provoked, she was capable of a white-hot temper that did not easily burn itself out. She was in one now as she stormed through Alec's rooms without announcing herself, scattering the Runners placed by Lord Gervais to keep an eye on the accused.

"Get out!" she screeched at two surly ruffians who lounged on her furniture, and cast a smoldering gaze about the room. It came to rest on Alec who was stripped to the waist and having his wounds dressed by his valet. "How could you?" she demanded. "How—how *dare you*?"

Not caring to dismiss the valet, she proceeded to strip Alec's character of all credibility and human decency, her language so scathing that despite his preoccupation, Tam's ears burned brightly. She paced to and fro in front of the ribbonback chair Alec straddled, her bosom heaving, her voice becoming hoarse, until she finally took a great shattering breath and said,

"You only have yourself to blame for this predicament! As if this absurd accusation isn't enough to ruin your career you get yourself caught out playing at Adam and Eve with Selina in the grove! Her husband's been cold little more than a month, *damn you*! How could you do this to her—to-to *yourself*?"

Slowly and with great effort, Alec lifted his head off his arm that was lying across the top of the chair. There was still a drumming in his ears and such a throbbing at the base of his neck that he was certain his skull must be cracked. He had refused Tam's offer of an opiate. It would have considerably dulled the pain and he didn't want that. He needed to be alert, to think, to tell them what he knew.

He flinched. He wished Tam would hurry and dress up his wounds. What was the boy doing back there? "Careful!" he growled.

"Sorry, sir. Only one more cut to clean and dress and then we'll be done."

"Haven't you anything to say for yourself?" the Duchess asked bitterly.

Alec winced as an astringent-soaked cloth was applied to his back. "No," he answered placidly. "Where is Selina?"

"Getting dressed."

"But is she all right? They didn't hurt her?"

"No. Merely wounded her pride, wicked girl!" the Duchess answered with annoyance. "That buffoon Gervais has two thugs posted at her door, too. It seems he is determined to turn my house into Newgate! Dolt!" She stared at Alec's bent head, with its mane of blue-black curls pulled forward over one shoulder, and said tersely, "You didn't even have the decency to defend yourself!"

There was a moment's silence.

"I was not in a position to do so," he muttered.

Her lip curled. "No, you weren't, were you?"

He lifted his head enough to look at her. "Olivia, I make no excuse for our behavior. Why should I? Convention dictates that we must wait out Selina's mourning before we can marry, and I will abide by that, but why should we deny ourselves earthly pleasures in the interim?" When the Duchess looked away in embarrassment, he said with asperity, "God knows, Selina deserves her Heaven on earth after what that monster was permitted to put her through!"

"Permitted to put her through...?" The Duchess bit her lip. "Yes, we let him be a monster, didn't we?"

When Alec dropped his head back onto his arm the Duchess peered over his shoulder, caught sight of the bloody welts that crisscrossed his back and had to turn away, a hand to her mouth to stop a sob. An arm encircled her shoulders and pulled her into a comforting embrace.

"I—I *never* cry!" she said, sniffing back tears. "I'm—I'm acting a-a *fool!*"

"There ain't nothin' wrong with havin' a good cry once in awhile," Plantagenet Halsey said cheerfully, and made her sit in a wingchair by the bed. "I'll fetch you a glass of claret, and mind you drink it all."

The Duchess was too taken aback to reply. She had had no idea the old man was present. It wasn't until he disappeared that she realized he must have been in the dressing room the entire time of her tirade of abuse. The old man returned with a bottle of claret and handed her a glass with a smile.

"If you don't mind, we'll be gettin' back to patchin' the boy up before he passes out on us again," he said in the same cheerful voice. "I've been brewin' a nasty concoction of Tam's making. Stinks of rotted vegetables and garlic—*garlic!* He assures me it will do the trick. If you ask me, we'll all be passin' out on the stink alone!" He slid in beside the valet and set a dish between them, wrinkling his nose. "You certain this ain't a recipe you swiped from the kitchens?"

"I'm to be marinated, is that it?" Alec quipped. "It smells putrid."

"Oh, it is!" his uncle assured him with a crack of laughter and a wink at the Duchess. He handed Tam a wad of clean cloth. "Now you be quiet and let us get on with it or I'll force-feed you an opiate!"

The Duchess shuddered, a handkerchief to her mouth.

"It's not as bad as it looks," the old man assured her, keeping on with his task. "He's lucky he's got a good head of woman's hair. It saved him from losing his skin altogether."

"Hasn't he been given something for the pain?" When no one answered her she said, "But he must... How can he..."

Plantagenet Halsey put a finger to his lips, and when his task was complete led the Duchess through to the sitting room while Tam set about cleaning up his medicinals and soiled cloths.

"WHAT'S GERVAIS UP TO?" THE OLD MAN DEMANDED without preamble as he closed the door.

"He's downstairs with the rest of his thugs," the Duchess replied. "He's determined to drag Alec from his bed and clap him up in Newgate."

"Over my dead body!"

"It may very well be over your dead body, because nothing I've said has made him waver," the Duchess argued. "He merely spews back inanities about his duty, and due process of law, and poppycock of that nature. I've threatened to bring the whole Privy Council down upon him, and he had the audacity to inform *me* that *I* would be obstructing the course of justice. The man is certifiable!"

"Alec will come out of it all right, you'll see," the old man said unconvincingly. "The accusation won't stand. It's absolute rot. Everyone will see that."

"Of course it's rot! But Alec's foolhardy behavior hasn't made it any easier for him. A man known to him in the Foreign Department was murdered in my gardens and next morning Alec is nowhere to be found until a search of my home wood discovers him and Selina playing at Adam and Eve! You may smirk, but this is serious. Gervais wants to add the charge of rape—"

"*What?*" thundered Plantagenet Halsey.

"Of course it's all nonsense! But you don't seem to understand the seriousness of Alec's predicament. Gervais can and will bring that further accusation, whatever my objections, merely because he can. That Alec seduced Selina when she was barely eighteen will make it worse for him. As for Delvin's appalling behavior—beating his brother as if he were an animal in need of taming…" She shuddered. "To own a truth, Delvin scares me. I'm only too pleased Emily has decided to postpone the wedding."

"He's the very devil, ain't he?" the old man answered dryly. "Father was the same. My father. No heart. Not enough brain to be a decent human being, but just enough to keep him out of Bedlam."

Despite everything the Duchess couldn't help a giggle. "This is no time for levity!"

"No, it ain't," agreed the old man. "As I said, don't you worry. This trumped-up charge of murder won't stick. It won't because Alec is innocent. And because it's our word, and the word of those who were at the ball, against Gervais. He hasn't a hope!"

The Duchess blinked at him. "Oh, but don't you see?" she said in exasperation. "What does it matter if the charge is finally dropped? It's the very fact Alec was charged at all that will be his downfall. I'm not fearful of Alec getting as far as a courtroom, least of all the gallows. Dear God, I'll have every member of Cabinet— of the Lords—petitioning the King if it ever came to that; but it won't. One word from me in the right ear and Gervais will be forced to withdraw his accusation." When the old man scoffed she said, "You can look mule-faced, but that's what I will do! It's all very well to have high ideals. Proclaiming your innocence and smugly waiting for the world to finally vindicate you is all very noble, but it ultimately doesn't work in practice, when it is society who will condemn—"

"Society? Madam—"

"No! Allow me to finish! I know what you think of that, and you can go on at me all you want about the parasitic Four Hundred or whatever you call us, but what society dictates *does* matter. It matters a great deal if one wants to do well in one's profession, as Alec does. No amount of hard work will see him advance in diplomatic circles; he'll never be an ambassador, he'll never even make minister, if he is publicly charged with murder. He'll be shunned. Backs will be turned on him. No one will want his company, here or on the Continent. He might as well retire to the country tomorrow!"

Plantagenet Halsey opened his mouth, then closed it. He wanted to launch into a lecture against his class, against the toad-eating lot of 'em with their insufferable, conceited pomposity. But there was too much truth in what the Duchess said. When all was said and done, he knew only too well what society demanded and what it could do for a man socially. After all, hadn't he been born one of them? And if he were honest with himself, he was more than willing to swallow his pride and sacrifice his principles if it meant saving Alec's character and career from society's censure. No one, *nothing*, meant more to him than Alec.

"Thing is," he said thoughtfully, "why is Gervais so determined to see this through? The man's a toad-eatin' buffoon. If anythin', you'd think your threat about the Privy Council would be enough to have him snivellin' at your fingertips. Don't tell me he's a stickler for the law; not if it means bringin' social ruin on himself. And that's what will happen once you've whispered in the right ear. And he must know that. So, what's he got to gain by stickin' his neck out, eh? Tell me that!"

The Duchess stared at him as if he had said something profound. "I have no idea."

"But I do," said Alec. He leaned in the doorway, a colorful silk banyan hanging loose about his shoulders and he supported at the elbow by Tam, who helped him to a chair.

"Now what's this foolishness?" the old man demanded.

"You should be in bed!" added the Duchess

"I'm not as bad as all that," Alec said quietly. "It's just this infernal headache." He looked at them both. "But it's a little better knowing you haven't disowned me."

"Oh, be quiet!" demanded the Duchess gruffly. "When all's said and done, no one is more pleased that you and Selina have the opportunity to begin anew."

Alec swallowed. "Olivia, about Emily... You have every right to think me a fickle cad."

"Nonsense!" she said stridently, and would have said more except Tam came back into the room, carrying a tray holding a bottle of wine and three glasses. One glass was already poured, and this he handed to Alec before offering wine to the old man and the Duchess.

"Mr. Neave says there's a Mr. Yarrborough downstairs who wishes to speak with Mr. Halsey," Tam told them. "Mr. Neave wants to know if he should send him away until—"

"No. Send him up," said Alec, settling gingerly against the upholstery. He drank deeply from the glass of wine, for his throat was tinder dry and his head was beginning to throb unbearably.

With Tam gone, Plantagenet Halsey turned to his nephew with a frown.

"If you're determined to be foolish and see this Yarrborough fellow, mayhap you can tell us why Gallows Gervais wants you prosecuted."

"I do believe he hopes to deflect suspicion away from himself. But why he thinks accusing me of Tremarton's murder will make a difference to his guilt, I know not!" He opened his eyes to look at his uncle and then his godmother. It was obvious both were no wiser. "I sent for Yarrborough because I suspect Gervais was the judge who had Dobbs hanged."

The old man rubbed his chin. "Not a coincidence that. Am I right?"

"No. If my suspicions prove correct then I should think Gervais was only too willing to close down the brothel and hang Dobbs, if only to extract his brother-in-law from certain scandal." He closed his eyes again. "And before this throbbing forces me to give in to Tam's demands that I take an opiate, I must tell you both that my mother did indeed write letters of confession to Lady Margaret Belsay. I found them—or I should say—selected pages of two letters from Lady Delvin to Lady Margaret, on Tremarton's body. It seems Cosmo was right all along."

Plantagenet Halsey gave an impatient grunt of disbelief. "Who's to say Tremarton didn't fabricate—"

"For your information, Mr. Halsey," the Duchess began, "I, for one, don't believe Margaret Belsay a liar. So if she says Helen Delvin wrote her—"

"Please, Olivia," interrupted Alec, and slowly turned his throbbing head to look at his uncle. "The pages were in my mother's fist. Perhaps it is time you stopped protecting me from the truth, however terrible. In his rage, Delvin called me a half-breed bastard."

"Idiotic rot!" blustered the old man. "Delvin would call you a Chinaman if he thought it would stick!"

"But the Countess of Delvin didn't have an affair with a Chinaman, did she, Uncle?"

Plantagenet Halsey shook his head. "No. Not a Chinaman... Did her letters give you a name, my boy?"

"She confesses to the fact I am her firstborn and to being an adulteress, but as to the name of my father, no," said Alec, a glance at the Duchess who was looking at her hands in her lap. "Perhaps in the pages that are missing she goes further. I was hoping you could save me the search...?"

"I would dearly love to tell you I am your father," Plantagenet

Halsey said. "But I was never your mother's lover. There was a time when I wished I had owned up to it, if only to save you a lifetime of uncertainty. You were indeed your mother's firstborn son and you were born in wedlock; legally you were the Earl of Delvin's heir but, in good conscience, Helen and I—in whom she confided her predicament—could not present you to my brother as his."

"Conscience? *Damn* your conscience, sir!" the Duchess burst out. "It is *your* conscience that has robbed Alec of his birthright!"

"Olivia—"

"Had Helen kept her tongue between her teeth no one would've been the wiser," she continued, ignoring Alec's quiet interjection. "Who's to say Alec isn't the Earl's son? Did Helen tell you otherwise? Did she tell you her lover's name? Did she have any idea to whom she conceived, her husband or her lover? No! And because of your-your *conscience* and Helen's *guilt*, a brute and a fiend, who in all probability is mad, is parading around as Lord Delvin! How can you reconcile *that* with your conscience?"

"Olivia, it has never bothered me that Edward was raised as heir to the earldom," Alec said on a tired sigh. "He is my brother. That he was born after me is neither here nor there. You don't seem to understand—"

"Yes I do!" she said as she resumed her seat and patted tears from her eyes. "You are much too kind-hearted to want to hurt your uncle's feelings. He raised you in the mistaken belief that it is your abilities, and how you use those abilities, that makes you who you are; not fate, not luck of birth. But that's absolute rot! Society doesn't work that way. As the Earl of Delvin you could accomplish much more than you ever will as a junior minister, crawling your way up the diplomatic ladder on your merit!" She threw the old man a sullen look. "And no one knows that better than your uncle."

"And had the situation been reversed?" Alec asked quietly. "Had I been in Delvin's place and he in mine, would you still be of the same mind?" When the Duchess looked away, Alec smiled and closed his eyes. "I at least can sleep easy at night knowing all that I have, all that I am, is rightfully mine."

The old man lightly touched Alec's shoulder. "I did what I thought was right, my boy," he said, but with none of his usual bombastic self-confidence. "Truth told: You could very well be the Earl of Delvin's firstborn."

Alec touched his uncle's hand. "I know you too well, Uncle. If you truly believed I was heir to the earldom, you'd have fought until your last breath to have me acknowledged, but as you did not—"

"Alec!"

"—who I am remains blanketed in fog. Come in, Tam. Where's Yarrborough?"

"He didn't stay, sir," Tam replied. "Lord Gervais spoke with him and took the packet—"

"Damn him!" Alec interrupted. "Then it is as I suspected. Tam, the frock coat I had at the grove, in the outerpocket there are my spectacles and with them is an envelope. Fetch it." He closed his eyes, for a curious sensation had come over him. He felt it wash through him, warm and comforting. And the pain—the thud at his temples and at the base of his neck, the burning feeling down his back—began to melt away to some nether region in the recesses of his mind. He felt as if he was floating in cool water. "Tam put something in my drink…" he muttered.

Plantagenet Halsey wasn't quick enough to catch the glass before it fell and splashed the last of the burgundy over the carpet at Alec's feet. "You'll feel better for a good rest, my boy."

"Too much—to tell. Can't rest now. Must confront Gervais… That letter. Don't let Tam…"

"All in good time," soothed his uncle and called to Tam. "Whatever did you give him?"

"A measured dose of laudanum mixed with wine, sir," answered the valet as he helped the old man manage Alec to the bedroom.

"Well, it's done the trick! Now let's get him into bed."

Tam glanced at the Duchess, who had followed them into the bedchamber and was standing beside the four-poster bed frowning at Alec's limp form.

"Please, Your Grace, we need to put Mr. Halsey to bed."

"I know that!" she snapped, little realizing that what the valet meant was that his master needed to be undressed before he was put between the sheets. When she continued to stand there, it was left to the old man to tell her, and tell her bluntly. "Oh!" She made to leave hastily, then stopped and put out her hand to Tam. "The letter. Give it to me."

Tam blinked and held out his master's gold rimmed spectacles. "I found only these in a pocket of Mr. Halsey's frock coat, Your Grace. The letter—it's missing."

SIR COSMO FOUND SELINA ON THE STAIRS LEADING TO THAT part of the house where the unmarried male guests had their rooms. He had no need to guess where she was headed and wasn't surprised when she was annoyed to be waylaid. Still, he had momentous news to share with her and it couldn't wait.

"Have you seen him?" Selina asked before he had a chance to speak. "Has a physician been sent for? Are those thugs still outside his rooms? What is the Duchess doing about Gervais?"

"My dear, he's in good hands. His valet was an apothecary. I'm sure he's getting excellent care and—"

"But you don't know! You've not seen him," she said and turned to leave.

"Listen to me, Selina!" Sir Cosmo demanded, and pulled her into a wood-paneled alcove. "Alec isn't about to be dragged off to Newgate. The Runners, they're being packed back to London as we speak; reason you were able to leave your rooms. The accusation against Alec has been withdrawn and Gervais can't do a tester about it! That leaves me to deal with Delvin and I intend justice be served. You have my word on it."

Selina viewed her friend with surprise that deepened into

suspicion when Sir Cosmo's assurance was accompanied by a smug grin of triumph.

"What's happened, Cosmo?" she demanded.

He held out a yellowed sheaf of folded paper. "This, my dear girl, is the Countess of Delvin's letter to Lady Margaret Belsay," he declared, and couldn't help a bark of laughter when she snatched it and bent her fair head to the page. "Found it at the grove in Alec's frock coat pocket. I think you'll find it confirms everything your aunt's been saying about Alec and his brother. Certainly made Gervais dance to a different tune!"

Selina handed back the letter. "Where's the rest of it?"

Sir Cosmo deflated. "My guess is Alec has it elsewhere. He don't need more than what's written there to convince anyone he's the rightful earl and his brother's a fraud! Gervais certainly didn't quibble. Just turned bright pink and then a deathly gray. Expect he realizes what an ass he's made of himself."

Selina's frown remained. "But even if what you say is true, Cosmo, how would that convince Gervais to withdraw a charge of murder against Alec?"

"He didn't withdraw it. His wife did. She made the accusation in the first place, and my guess is, under duress. No doubt as soon as she realized Ned ain't the rightful earl, she felt less inclined to his way of thinking. And as the rightful Earl of Delvin, Alec can only be tried by his peers. The Lords, my dear. Not by the common law courts. Not Gervais's jurisdiction. He had to see that if he persisted with this nonsensical accusation, he'd only get himself in hotter water. Still not pleased with my efforts, my dear?"

"Of course!" she said, forcing a smile. Yet she still looked troubled. "Have you shown this letter to Delvin?"

"Haven't had the opportunity. He had the nerve to show himself at nuncheon as if all was right with the world. Of course, those of us in the know put a brave face on the meal for the sake of the Duchess and her unsuspecting guests. But no one had an appetite, knowing Ned had attacked his own brother. For what it's worth, Ned scares me, Selina. I wouldn't be at all surprised if he murdered—"

The sentence went unfinished and Selina watched in horrified silence as Sir Cosmo's eyes rolled back in his head and he crumpled with a heavy thud, lifeless, to the floorboards. Standing over him was the Earl of Delvin. He pointed a pistol at Selina.

"You're coming with me, *Gypsy*," he ordered, and before she could run had her by the wrist. He pulled her hard against his side. "You're going to get me the Ganymede ledger, and then you have some explaining to do!"

It wasn't the greyhounds curled up by the bedchamber fireplace who woke Alec from a deep, dreamless sleep, but the loud hiss of a voice in his left ear commanding him to wake up. It took Alec a few moments to realize he was not dreaming, and then even longer to force himself awake from the depths of a drug-induced sleep that left his limbs weak and his thoughts clouded and confused. There was the unmistakable smell of stale cheroots as he was helped up by a strong arm. He was let go once he was steady on his feet. Alec was grateful for one thing; the agonizing pain in his neck and head had subsided, leaving him with only the dull sting from the lacerations to his bruised back.

Something brushed his legs. It was his greyhounds, come to stand protectively between him and the intruder who leveled a pistol at their master. Alec called them to heel and reluctantly they obeyed, though they continued to growl.

"Going to shoot me?" he asked sluggishly.

Lord Andrew Macara chuckled, showing large tobacco stained teeth, and placed the pistol on the bureau. "At the moment it don't do to wander about this place unarmed." He watched Alec brush the hair back off his face. "Lord, man, you'll never advance in the Foreign Department with hair like a savage! Not quite the thing, is it, what?"

"I don't pretend to be quite the thing," Alec answered thickly and moved into the light. "What is it you wish to tell me?"

"Ah! Figured it out have you? Thought you would. Clever. Too clever. Still, not clever to let Delvin whip you within an inch of your life. Makes you look guilty to take punishment like a dog. Why didn't you fight back?"

Alec looked at him without blinking. "Because I'd have killed him."

Lord Andrew Macara saw that he was in earnest and let out a reckless laugh. "I believe you would have, what! Why didn't you? Would've saved everyone a lot of unnecessary bother."

Alec yawned. "You mean, saved you from explaining matters to your unforgiving, vengeful wife and from condemning yourself in the eyes of your mother-in-law, the only woman whose opinion matters to you."

Macara took a still smoldering cheroot from a gold case, put it between his lips with stained fingers and inhaled a deep satisfying breath, all the time regarding Alec through narrowed eyes.

"Want to tell you what I know. Wasn't going to get involved, not my affair really, and best if unpleasantness sorts itself out but... Can't stand by and watch that nobody judge lord it over Her Grace. Doesn't know his place. Woman's a duchess. Her family's on the Roll of Norman nobles. I can't keep silent, not even for Delvin; not now he ain't marrying Emily. Not when he threatens pretty females into doing his dirty work. Had poor Cindy half crazed with fear. Can't force your mistress to wrongly accuse your own brother of murder and expect to get away with it! Bad Form."

Alec couldn't help a smile. "How did you persuade Lady Gervais to come to her senses?"

Lord Andrew grinned and drew deeply on the cheroot. "Finally got her to agree to leave Gervais, give up Delvin and let me look after her. She knows she'll be well cared for, provided I'm the only bird in that nest."

"Lucky woman."

"Luck? Lord, Halsey, the woman's the most accomplished whore I've ever come across! You should know that, what!"

"I'll have to take your word on it. What about your other—er —family?"

"What of 'em? Sally's a sensible woman, she understands these matters. Won't make a fuss; don't need to. I'll always provide for her and our brats. Everyone's content. Except Charlotte, but she can't afford to bleat about it, not if she wants to keep the high moral ground and a husband to trot out for public occasions. Thank God, the Duchess don't expect me to live with the viper!"

Alec shook his groggy head in humorous disbelief. "You're a better manager than I'll ever be."

"So it's all settled then?" said his lordship. "Gervais don't have a case now Cindy has withdrawn the accusation against you," he added with satisfaction. "She's free of that pompous dullard and you're free to go about your business."

"Not quite," said Alec, an eye to the doorway where Tam hovered in uncertainty. "It's all right, Tam. Be good enough to bring me a glass of lemon water and set out a suit of clothes." When Tam bowed and reluctantly withdrew he added, "Tell me what you know about the night Emily's maid was killed and what you saw in the gardens during the fireworks."

Macara glanced down at the burning cheroot between his stained fingers. "Not much to tell...."

"Then perhaps you will correct my presumptions: The night Emily's maid was killed and she attacked, Cynthia Gervais caught Delvin in the bushes with Emily's chambermaid. You consoled the outraged mistress in the billiard room where you were caught by Gervais, probably—um—*in flagrante delicto*? Reason Cynthia came to my room, to teach you all a lesson and because she'd been left most unsatisfied. Her shoes were muddy and she smelled of stale smoke, as did the billiard room the next day when Cosmo and I went there and found the room unaired and undisturbed from the night before, with wine bottles and glasses and a frock coat in a corner—"

"Ah! That belonged to me," offered his lordship and made no attempt to refute Alec's claims.

"Yes, I thought it did. When I saw Delvin that same evening he was wearing his. But in his eagerness to deflect suspicion from his master, Delvin's valet thought he was doing the right thing by taking ownership of the coat. What I am still to decide is: When Gervais attempted to rape Emily in retribution for his wife's rampant unfaithfulness, did he kill the maid in the process or did Jenny stumble upon Delvin soliciting the chambermaid in the servant corridor, a circumstance she was sure to report back to her mistress, and when my brother's attempt to reason with her failed, he had to kill her or risk his engagement being broken off?"

Lord Andrew Macara stubbed out the cheroot on the sole of his buckled shoe.

"To my way of thinking, Delvin wouldn't give a fig had a maid caught him mounting a kitchen wench. Not reason enough to wring the girl's silly neck, what! No one takes the word of a servant over one of us, and that's how it should be. But Gervais, well, he's not one of us, is he? Don't know his place. My guess is he panicked and broke the maid's neck out of pure cowardice. But what's it matter? Nothing will bring the maid back."

"You hold servant life cheap, my lord," Alec enunciated, taking the glass of lemon water Tam offered him; Macara waving away the second glass without a look at the valet. "And the attempted rape of your niece? How do you view that?"

Macara gave a non-committal shrug. "Charlotte's had a physician to Emily; assured her the gal's a virgin. Marriage prospects not damaged then, are they? That's what matters when all's said and done."

"Is it? What about justice for your niece and fit punishment for the perpetrator of such a cowardly and disgusting act?"

His lordship viewed Alec as if this had never occurred to him. He shrugged. "Well, if it's justice you're after then I'd say his wife openly living as my mistress will just about kill the pompous fool.

As for punishment? One word from Delvin or me and the fellow will hang by his own rope."

"How's that?"

Lord Andrew Macara smiled broadly. "Reason I woke you. Want you to know I'm on your side. Willing to speak out about it if you want me to. Think that's what the Duchess would want me to do, whatever the embarrassment to Charlotte. Can't have her favorite godson carted off to Newgate! You asked about the gardens, when Cindy's brother had that bullet put in him," his lordship added in explanation. "Couldn't be Delvin and it wasn't me. Cindy was pleasuring us both." The quick lift of Alec's eyebrows made him give a shout of laughter and he patted Alec's arm. "Told you she was accomplished! Wager you're sorry you didn't take up her generous offer. So there you are. Delvin has an alibi in me and I have an alibi in him and we both have an alibi in delectable Cindy. And to add icing to the cake, I saw Gervais in heated discussion with Tremarton. Wasn't in a position to think much about it at the time—you get my meaning. But later, with a cool head, I realized exactly what was going on. What! Gervais is your man. He shot Simon Tremarton."

FOURTEEN

ALEC ENTERED THE CHINESE DRAWING ROOM AND ALL conversation between the assembled company came to an abrupt halt. It was not many hours since furtive whispers had circulated the nuncheon table about Alec Halsey's arrest for the murder of Simon Tremarton, and with the Earl of Delvin's blessing. But no sooner was the arrest made, after a struggle with the Runners, so it was said, than the accusation was miraculously dropped by the personal intervention of the Duchess of Romney-St. Neots. No one knew what or whom to believe, but everyone knew that during the fireworks a man was found shot in the shrubbery and that Lord Delvin believed his brother responsible. That the Duchess was able to have her godson set free was the least surprising fact of all. But her intervention did not absolve his guilt.

The ladies stared at Alec from behind fluttering fans, then reluctantly looked away, while the gentlemen quickly repaired broken conversations, many resorting to their snuffboxes for occupation. The Duchess beckoned him and poured him out a dish of coffee, displeased he had not remained in bed nursing his wounds but glad to see him up and about nonetheless. Lady Sybilla went to hand him the dish, but Lady Charlotte, who was momentarily stunned at the gall of the man, grabbed her sister's wrist. Sybilla would not heed her, broke free, spilling coffee into the saucer, and shyly handed the dish to Alec, who accepted it with a smile.

"Do you—Do you feel better for your rest?" she asked shyly.

"Much better, thank you."

Lady Charlotte stood up with a flounce and snapped shut her fan. One smoldering glance cast at Alec and she turned to her mother seated beside the tea trolley. "You will forgive me if I retire early, Mamma. I cannot—*I will not*—drink tea in the company of a-a—one who has dared bring shame and-and disgrace on our family!"

Lady Sybilla gasped.

"Go away, Charlotte!" complained the Duchess. "I suggest it be as far away as Gloucestershire, for I have no use for you here."

Lady Charlotte stared at her. "You are sending *me* away when it is that man who is accused of—"

"Don't waste your indignant breath!" demanded the Duchess. "I'm past patience with you. You know nothing of the matter!"

"Do I not? *Do I not?*" Lady Charlotte said in a shrill whisper. "We shall see who is right, dear ma'am, when society turns its back on us because of your support for this—this—" She waved her ivory fan at Alec. "—*murdering philanderer.*"

Alec bowed to her. "As ever, madam, your public display of sanctimony never ceases to disappoint."

At that Lady Charlotte glared at him, bosom heaving. "I sincerely pity your brother!" she breathed.

"As do I, madam," he said, and returned his empty coffee dish to the tea trolley, back to the woman's affected display of leave-taking. His gaze swept the assembled company. "Selina still in her rooms, Your Grace?"

"Be good enough to move aside, sir!" Lady Charlotte demanded loudly.

"You do us the same courtesy, Madam, and we'll gladly oblige," Plantagenet Halsey growled.

He was supporting Sir Cosmo by the elbow, the large gentleman with a hand to the back of his neck and a squint of pain on his round face. Seeing them, the Duchess was on her feet and Alec went forward to assist his uncle, Lady Charlotte ignored and forced to retreat against the patterned Chinese wallpaper.

"What happened?" Alec asked his uncle.

"Don't know, my boy. Found Mahon sprawled out on the floorboards of an alcove. Would've walked straight passed him if it hadn't been for his loud moaning."

"Moaning?" Sir Cosmo complained. "You get hit on the back of the head and have a lump the size of a chicken's egg—"

"Who did this to you, Cosmo?" asked Alec, and stood aside to allow Lady Sybilla to press a brandy glass on Sir Cosmo.

Sir Cosmo downed the brandy, leaning against the door frame and returned the glass to Lady Sybilla with a smile that was more grimace.

"No idea. From behind, as I said. But Selina—Selina would know. Ask her. I was talking with her when everything went black." His eyes focused on Alec and suddenly, as if he'd remembered something vitally important, he thrust a hand in a pocket of his frock coat, and sighed with relief when his fingers clutched paper. He took out the envelope and handed it to Alec. "Thank God it's safe! Thought the letter might've been stolen; reason for knocking me out. That letter did the trick. Once Gervais read your mother's letter to Lady Margaret, he had no option but to send his pack of thugs back to London with their tails between their legs. Besides which, I pointed out that once the letter became public, the accusation of murder would be taken out of his control and put in the hands of the Lords, as befitting Alec's position as—"

"*No!*" Alec growled. He passed a hand over his mouth in an attempt to calm himself. "No, Cosmo," he said very quietly, "you have gone far enough. Nor do you have any idea of the damage you have done!"

"But, my boy," said the Duchess, "what Cosmo did, he did in

your best interests. And it seems to me that showing Gervais that letter would make the fool see sense."

"Thank you, Aunt Olivia," said Sir Cosmo with a slight bow.

Lady Charlotte, who had not moved from her position against the wallpaper, stared blankly at her mother, then at Sir Cosmo and declared that everyone was talking in riddles.

Alec stared down at the letter. "It's not your fault," he conceded to an abashed Sir Cosmo. "How were you to know that this was one of two letters I found on Simon Tremarton's body, and that this, the second and most recent of the two, is not about me at all—"

"*What?*" said three voices in unison.

Alec glanced at his uncle and then at the Duchess before addressing Sir Cosmo in a low voice. "This letter was written just weeks before my mother's death. She was concerned for a young boy's welfare, a motherless boy who had spent the first twelve years of his life at Delvin. She was worried lest his natural father cast him adrift in the world. So she made arrangements for Lord Delvin's illegitimate son to be apprenticed to an uncle, a London apothecary."

In his astonishment Sir Cosmo forgot all about the lump to the back of his head. "Good God—that boy who's your valet is Delvin's—is *Delvin's* natural son?"

"I believe that's what this letter proves. Yes," said Alec and slipped the paper into a pocket. "It is my belief that Jack risked, and then lost his life, because of these two letters. He was smart enough to have only the first pages of both, the other pages secreted somewhere for safekeeping. Jack threatened to expose Delvin, not about his questionable birthright, but because of his neglect of an illegitimate son, working as a poor apprentice one floor below a notorious male brothel."

When those in earshot had recovered from their surprise and shock, Sir Cosmo said loudly, "And the other letter? What does it prove, Alec?"

"The first, much older letter, proves very little."

"Only that there has been a serious miscarriage of justice," said the Duchess, "and that you are indeed your mother's—"

"No, Olivia!" Alec pleaded. "Say no more!"

"Pray continue, Mamma!" demanded Lady Charlotte, and had the satisfaction of seeing every powdered and plumed head in the room nod in agreement.

But the Duchess demurred under Alec's steady gaze. It was left to Sir Cosmo to be resolute, and he stepped into the center of the Chinese drawing room so that all who had been straining to catch snatches of the conversation taking place at the doorway could hear, and before Alec could stop him he declared, "Alec Halsey is the Countess of Delvin's firstborn and as such is the rightful earl. No doubt you were expecting a wholly different outcome, my lady?"

Lady Charlotte stared wildly about the room at the shocked expressions on most of the faces, daring someone to contradict Sir Cosmo, but no one said a word. An hysterical laugh that was half sob broke from her as she faced the doorway. "Well, my dear," she said bitterly, "that should make you vastly pleased! Did you know? No wonder you tried to scorn one brother to prostitute yourself to the other! I'd not have given you the credit for so much brain. But you ultimately failed in your quest, for this brother has given you up in preference for the riper charms of a widow."

This venomous outburst was directed at Emily, who stood just inside the room in her slippered feet. But if Emily had heard her aunt's outburst she did not acknowledge it for she looked at Alec with a glazed expression.

"Something horrid has happened," she managed to say with a dry swallow. "Something so shocking…Will you go and see?"

"Of course," Alec agreed, and prompted her when she fell silent. "Just tell me where it is you wish me to go."

She nodded as if he understood exactly what she was talking about. "The billiard room. It happened in the billiard room. I heard voices—shouting. I thought it was those rascal boys playing truant and carelessly knocking the balls about. But then there was a loud noise, like something heavy being dropped on the floorboards. And then Mrs. Jam—and then Selina rushed out into the passageway and screamed at me to get help. So here I am, and I haven't the slightest idea what's going on, except that it's all very upsetting!" She heaved a shuddering breath and covered her face with her hands. "I wish I hadn't seen the blood! Blood all over the front of her lovely dove gray gown…" She stared at Alec and then looked at her grandmother through tears. "It's Edward. He's dead. She-she *shot* him."

THE BODY OF THE FIFTH EARL OF DELVIN LAY SPRAWLED face-up across the billiard table. The head was thrown back and one eye stared vacantly at the ornate plaster ceiling. The powdered wig that had framed the pale handsome face in life was oddly askew, revealing a head of very close-cropped blond hair and a shattered skull that exposed what was left of the badly-damaged brain within. The left side of the face was completely gone. What remained of familiar facial features had disappeared under a thick blanket of glistening blood. Cravat, waistcoat and frock, all were blood-splattered. So too was the green baize felt of the table, the spreading pool of blood from under the damaged head creeping towards a leather-bound ledger that lay open near the middle pocket.

Alec took it all in with one look and quickly turned about to demand a footman's frock coat. He hastily threw this over his brother's shoulders and head as Plantagenet Halsey and Sir Cosmo came across the room toward the billiard table. Nothing, however, could hide the violence of the scene presented to them.

Sir Cosmo took one look at the partially-covered body and the great pool of blood with its flecks of brain and bone, and he stumbled out of the room as quickly as his shaking legs would carry him, a handkerchief pressed tightly to his mouth. The old man looked unblinkingly at the billiard table, but his consciousness did not register what his eyes were telling him to see. In a daze he

watched Sir Cosmo flee the room and then turned to Alec as if
requiring some sort of explanation from him. His nephew quietly
and very firmly ushered him from the room and closed the door.
The butler came towards them with a look of polite inquiry, an
under-footman behind him.

"Neave, there's been an unpleasant accident," said Alec.

"An unpleasant accident," repeated the butler, hooded gaze
flickering to the door.

"See that this door is kept locked. I suggest you put two
footmen in attendance. And Neave, no one is to go in there under
any circumstances."

"Yes, sir. Shall I send for Oakes?'

Alec sighed. His hands were shaking. "Yes, I suppose we must.
Thank you, Neave."

The butler cleared his throat. "Sir. Henry said he heard a shot
but—"

"That's right," said Alec curtly, suppressing the butler's curiosity. "I'm looking for Mrs. Jamison-Lewis," he continued, trying to
keep the panic from his voice. "Have you seen her recently?"

"I believe Mrs. Jamison-Lewis was last seen in the company of
Lord Gervais, sir."

"And do you know where they were headed?"

The butler glanced at the old man and then back at Alec and
cleared his throat, "The servant stairs behind the billiard room go
all the way to the roof, sir."

"Thank you. Give Mr. Halsey a good brandy!" Alec called out
as he dashed back into the billiard room and slammed the door.

The butler bowed to the closed door. Never did Neave want to
relive such a bloody weekend as this. He went to fetch the
Duchess's best French brandy.

BY THE TIME HE HAD CLIMBED ALL THE STAIRS TO THE
rooftop, Alec was out of breath and feeling every bruise and cut to
his body. He doubled over with stomach cramp and tried to draw

breath into his lungs as he forced himself to remain calm and in control. It wouldn't do to go to pieces now; not with Selina in mortal danger. Vivid pictures of horror inflicted by the monster who now had Selina in his power flashed through Alec's tired mind: His brother's body limp on the billiard table with his head blown off; Jenny with her neck broken; Simon, a great gaping hole in his side; sweet innocent Emily, near raped in her own home. Selina and he were so close to achieving the perfect beginning to a wretched six years spent apart that it didn't do to dwell on the pain and suffering the respectable judge had caused others. Why had Selina taken matters into her own hands? She should have waited. She should have waited for him. Damn her interference!

There was no need to wrench open the heavy door that kept out the winds that swept across the rooftop. The door was banging wide on its hinges. The cold blast of air carrying a touch of icy rain hit Alec in the face and almost sent him backwards down the dark stairwell. He pressed on and emerged on a narrow walkway with its stone parapet that ran the length of this side of the house and was stopped from turning a corner by the lead flashing of the roof meeting up against a stack of four chimneys. So there was nowhere to run, for either of them.

Knowing this did not stop him from running along the rampart as fast as he could without slipping on the smooth lead-covered boards, made slick from the constant drizzle. He kept himself upright with one hand pressed up against the wall and the other on the stone parapet. Half way along he saw them, Gervais with a hand hard gripped around Selina's arm and tugging her along as if they had somewhere to go. Alec pulled himself up short to crouch undetected, close enough to overhear their conversation and hopefully make a grab for Selina when the time was right. The only heartening news was that Selina was on his side of the walk. Everything else spelled disaster.

. . .

"THIS IS A MISTAKE!" SELINA SHOUTED THROUGH THE drizzle.

"Your mistake, Madam, was getting yourself involved!" Lord Gervais growled as he continued to drag her along the rampart.

Selina tried to pull free. "Do you think this is wise? Coming up here where there is no place to run? Wouldn't it be best to make for the coast? To take a chance on getting across to France?"

Lord Gervais stopped at that. "I? A well-respected judge, *run*? Do you take me for a coward, Madam?"

Selina stared up into his large watery eyes and the rivulets of rain that ran either side of his large pointed nose and shivered. The cold rain had nothing to do with it. "No. I take you for a heartless murderer, sir!"

He laughed as if she had told him a good joke. "Yes. Yes I am."

"What did that poor maid do to deserve—"

Gervais shook his head emphatically. "No! No! I'm no killer of females, Madam! Wouldn't hurt a hair on a pretty girl's head."

Selina dared to huff her disbelief. "No? Do you regard rape as mere sport, sir?"

At that Gervais laughed in her face. "Delvin didn't deserve a virgin bride! He turned Cindy into a whore! A judge's wife—my dearest Cynthia—on her knees for a penniless *fraud*! *Outrageous*!"

Despite her predicament, curiosity overcame Selina's fear. "Penniless? Delvin? But…"

"Delvin lived off handouts from your husband, Madam. Now come along! It's time you and I were leaving this place!"

"To where?"

He took a tentative look over the parapet. "Down there. You and me."

"Down?" And then Selina knew, and all the fear returned and threatened to overwhelm her. She wanted to scream. But she told herself to be calm. "What purpose will that serve, taking me with you?"

"We'll die as lovers do. That's what they'll think. That's what will be written up."

"Lovers!?" Selina was sickened and it sounded in her voice.

"Yes. It's all arranged. I've left a letter. Here in my frock coat pocket. It explains everything. Your husband's disgusting perversions, the male brothel, his beatings, the blackmail. How I turned a blind eye to his tastes and his club until it was all too much for me and I closed the place down on your pleading. How I was racked with guilt but felt compelled through my love for you to do as Delvin bid me until—"

"You're a repulsive hypocrite! You condemn Delvin, but you also took a monthly payment from J-L! You, a respected judge, an upholder of laws, turned a blind eye to what was going on at that male brothel, and would've remained as one blind were it not for others to condemn it!"

"Enough! I've heard enough, Madam! It is time you were joining me in Hell!"

"The Ganymede ledger!" Selina blurted out. "The Ganymede ledger will prove you wrong!"

With one foot upon the parapet Lord Gervais paused, frowning. "Ledger? Delvin stole your ledgers, Madam, but it was I who burned them in the grate."

"He stole my household ledgers and you burned them, you fool! There was a third, one my husband kept specifically for the Ganymede Club. It has your name written up in the columns for all the world to see."

The judge was incredulous. "Then Delvin... That slim volume he held up in the billiard room... He wasn't bluffing?"

"No. For once in his life, Delvin was telling the truth."

Gervais was so taken aback that for a single moment his grip on Selina's arm slackened. It was enough. Selina broke free, turned tail and fled back along the rampart with her heavy damask petticoats pulled above her ankles.

"You're bluffing!" Gervais yelled through the rain as he went after her. "Delvin too! There's no such ledger! Your husband wouldn't have dared put ink to paper. Too damning. Come back here!" he bellowed, and lunged for her petticoats, but what he felt was a hard knock under his chin which sent him staggering backwards.

Alec had shot up as Selina reached him just a few feet from where she had been held captive, and in one swift maneuver, he pushed her behind him and stepped forward with fists clenched, ready to do battle with the judge. Selina fell forward onto her knees and scrambled up in time to witness Gervais's retaliatory strike at Alec's head. But Alec was the quicker and he ducked, sending his opponent's strike wildly through the air past his left ear so that Gervais spun about almost full circle and was totally disorientated in the rain. He groped for the parapet and righted himself, an arm outstretched to the wall and unsure who or what had hit out at him.

"It's over! Give up and come quietly!" Alec yelled, wiping rain from his eyes. "For the sake of your soul, don't go through with this cowardly act!"

Selina stood behind Alec, arms about his waist, feeling the warmth of him and knowing then that she was truly safe. She blinked rain from her long lashes and peered through the drizzle at the shadowy figure of the judge, just feet away and swaying from foot to foot as if in indecision. She wondered what he meant to do and subconsciously held her breath.

Alec took a small step forward, hand outstretched to the judge, coaxing him indoors. And then it was over. In one quick effortless movement Lord Gervais hoisted himself up over the stone parapet and was gone, into the rain and to his death on the graveled drive below.

⁂

St. Neots House was shut up. The furniture was put in covers. Only a small staff of servants remained to see to its upkeep. The rest were sent to the Duchess's country estate in Bedfordshire. The stables were empty of horses and equipage. Two huge travel coaches stood in the circular drive, loaded down with portmanteaux, trunks, and pieces of furniture the Duchess declared she could not live without. The drivers awaited their occupants to be off.

The travelers were standing in the hall seeing to last minute details. Alec found them there, with the Duchess issuing instructions to her gardener for the upkeep of her precious flowers and shrubs while she was absent. He had not been back to the house since his return to St. James's Place three weeks earlier. Legal matters to do with his brother's death, the estates and financial affairs had kept him so busy that each day merged into the next, leaving him little time to himself. When he had received the Duchess's note informing him she was quitting St. Neots House, he had given it little attention, thinking she meant to go into Bedfordshire for a few months of well-earned and necessary seclusion. It was Selina's letter, hand-delivered only the day before, which brought him out of his preoccupation and sent him galloping across country to see her.

She was sitting on a sofa waiting for the Duchess and Emily, Evans beside her, fussing over the fall of her mistress's unruly curls. The older woman saw Alec first and decided she needed a breath of fresh air before being shut up in a coach for hours on end. Before Alec could go to Selina, the Duchess appeared from the back of the hallway and intercepted him, giving him her cheek to kiss.

"You look worn out," she said with concern.

"It comes from many hours closeted with lawyers I have no desire to see."

"How are—things?"

Alec sighed. "In a mess. It will take months to sort it all out. I just hope I don't die of boredom in the meantime. I expect my visit to Delvin to be no better."

"As bad as all that?"

"Yes. I am informed the weeds are only five feet tall on the south lawn, and that with extensive repair work three of the chimneys can be saved from demolition. As to the state of the tenant farms… I'll have to do the rounds before I know the worst."

"You poor boy! You'll have your hands full for months." She glanced at Selina. "Perhaps that is just as well," she murmured and smiled brightly at Alec. "Emily's taking one last look at the garden. I'll just fetch her." And left Alec alone with Selina in the vastness of the marbled hall.

"Olivia's right," Selina said finally, breaking the silence and bravely meeting Alec's steady gaze. "You'll be so preoccupied sorting out Delvin's mess that you won't have time to—the time to—"

"That doesn't make your going away any easier," he said quietly, taking her hand when she stood. "Must you go?"

"The time apart will do us good. You have so much to do as the new earl, and my mourning must run its course if we are to be married, as Olivia keeps insisting, above reproach and with society's blessing." She forced herself to smile. "I've never been to Paris. Talgarth is meeting us there. Won't that be a treat for me?"

"If it were only Paris…"

She looked up into his blue eyes then, and wished she hadn't. "I can't be with you—yet. So I can't stay in London. And we agreed not to announce our betrothal until my return. You don't mind, do you?"

"I want to say *yes* because I'm selfish. I don't want to be left here without you. But I understand why we must wait."

Selina bit her lip and controlled the urge to throw herself into his arms. She must be strong for both their sakes.

"I won't be gone above nine months. Nine months will go so quickly. You'll be far too busy to think about me! Which is as it should be."

He smiled and raised her hand to his lips. "You have a very poor opinion of my constancy, my darling."

Selina turned her head away. "I didn't mean…"

"Forgive me," he said gently, knowing she was on the verge of tears. "I'm being a selfish bore. Nine months will pass soon enough."

Selina nodded, feeling suddenly depressed. She wanted him to stop her from going. She wanted him to be angry with her for leaving him. Somehow that would make their parting so much easier. But he wouldn't get angry; he wasn't like that. And she loved him too well to remain in London and be his mistress. That's what would happen if she stayed. And that wouldn't be good for him or her, not if society found out. Not with the suspicious death of his brother still on everyone's lips. She tried to smile.

"I'll write."

He pinched her chin then lightly brushed her flushed cheek.

"I should hope so. I'll send news about your home for orphans."

"Yes. I'd like to know how it goes on. I'm sure your uncle will keep me abreast of developments."

"Yes, he's very pleased with himself to be a member of the Board of Trustees. He tells me the endowment is well over eight thousand pounds. That was very generous of you; as was your gesture to name the orphanage after Jack."

"Generosity had nothing to do with it," Selina answered truthfully. "I couldn't touch a penny from J-L's sordid dealings in good conscience. Best that it be put to good purpose."

"Jack would have been pleased."

"Yes, yes, he would," she answered and changed the topic. "Did I tell you Cosmo is taking Emily and me to Venice to meet Emily's mamma?"

"Cosmo?"

"You didn't expect us to go all the way to Venice without a male chaperone?"

Alec's shoulders shook with silent laughter. "But—*Cosmo*?"

"And what do you find so amusing?" she asked indignantly.

"Cosmo is such a poor traveler; you and he both! I pity Emily sitting between the grumblings of the two of you. Besides, he has no sense of direction." He touched her cheek again. "I think I'd best come with you to Venice."

"No!" she said before she could stop herself and blushed. "I didn't mean..."

He smiled crookedly and let his hand drop to his side. "It's perfectly all right, my love," he said dryly. "I understand better than you know. After such shocking events, we both need not only time but distance. And then we can start afresh."

"Yes," she whispered. "I hoped... I knew you would understand."

Their moment of intimacy came to an abrupt end when Emily, a large plumed hat over her blonde curls, and Sir Cosmo, fiddling with the shiny big buttons of his traveling cloak, came through from the gardens with the Duchess a step behind giving hurried last minute instructions to the housekeeper.

"Alec! Come to see us off?" Sir Cosmo said cheerfully. "You're just in time. We'll miss the Dover packet if we don't bustle along." He stuck out his hand in response to Alec and they shook hands. "I hate farewells," he grumbled. "I'll write from Paris, and Venice. And wherever else we end up!" He glanced at Emily. "Got to keep an eye on the ladies. Don't you worry, dear fellow."

Alec bowed over Emily's outstretched hand and smiled. "You will keep an eye on him for me, won't you, Emily? He gets terribly lost in foreign abodes and can't speak a word of decent French."

Sir Cosmo was too flustered to refute this, but a tug on his sleeve and his attention was claimed by the Duchess. Emily giggled and nodded and was pulled into the discussion with her grand-mother and Sir Cosmo; all three soon in deep conversation about their upcoming journey. Alec watched them, pleased and relieved to see them all much recovered from Emily's disastrous engage-ment and the awful events of that weekend.

Selina did not join in the conversation. She just wanted to be on her way, dreading the hours of monotonous travel yet eager to be anywhere but in England. She turned to the looking glass, put her bonnet over her apricot curls and tied its silk riband under her chin, aware that Alec watched her as he stretched on his riding gloves.

So much had been left unsaid between them. Yet they both knew it was best not to say too much. Nine months. It was not such a long time to wait. Nine months. Apart it would seem an eternity. But then she would come back to him and they would be married. Yes, the time would pass soon enough.

Alec turned on a heel and walked away, out into the bright sunshine of a perfect spring day.

Alec Halsey's adventure continues in...

Deadly Affair

ALEC HALSEY MYSTERIES, BOOK 2

AUTUMN 1763. Career diplomat Alec Halsey has been elevated to a marquessate he doesn't want and Polite Society believes he doesn't deserve. And with the suspicion he murdered his brother still lingering in London drawing rooms, returning to London after seven months in seclusion might well be a mistake. So when a nobody vicar drops dead beside him at a party-political dinner, and his rabble-rousing uncle Plantagenet is bashed and left for dead in a laneway, Alec's foreboding deepens. Uncovering the vicar's true identity, Alec suspects the man was poisoned. But who would want a seemingly harmless man of God murdered, and why?

LONDON

ALEC HALSEY had accepted Sir Charles Weir's dinner invitation on the assumption he was the only guest. Now, standing in the politician's drawing room surrounded by a dozen unfamiliar faces, he found himself in the midst of a party political dinner. The other guests were all in some way connected to the government, come together to celebrate the fifth anniversary of Sir Charles's election to Parliament, not career diplomats in the Foreign Department like Alec. The guest of honor, the Duke of Cleveley, twice First Lord of the Treasury and the present Foreign Secretary, had yet to descend among them, and Alec supposed this was why the double doors to the dining room remained closed.

Wine glass in hand, Alec sidled to the sash window that over-looked Arlington Street, and turned his back on the crowded and noisy room. He disliked gatherings of this sort. Too intimate. In a faceless crowd, one could remain anonymous and still enjoy the evening's entertainment. Here everyone knew his family's history, had devoured every scandalous detail in the London newssheets about the macabre circumstances surrounding the murder of his estranged brother. Despite the coroner's open verdict, it was Alec whom society blamed for his brother's death, thus condemning the newly-elevated Marquess Halsey to a lifetime of suspicion.

Why had he returned to the city? He should have remained in Kent, where he had spent the seven months since his brother's death resurrecting the family estate. He should be visiting his tenants and seeing to their needs, not wasting time rubbing shoulders with overfed, opinionated politicians, and their parasitic hangers-on, all of whom avoided his eye. There was so much for him to do and learn about his unwanted inheritance that he hardly knew where to begin.

He sipped at the wine and stared down at a sedan chair come to rest on the steps of Horace Walpole's townhouse, and rumi-nated on fate. He had spent most of his adult life on the periphery of Polite Society, a diplomat on the Continent speaking in foreign tongues. His estranged brother's untimely death changed his well-ordered life forever. Did he want to run an estate and take his seat in the Lords? He knew so little about either that a winter posting to St. Petersburg held more appeal. What was he supposed to do with a Marquessate he did not in the least want and one his peers considered he did not deserve? Yet he had been compelled to accept with good grace the newly-created title. As if his elevation from the family earldom of Delvin to the Marquessate Halsey would somehow miraculously expunge from the collective memory of Polite Society his connection to a murdered brother who had hated him with a passion bordering on mania. To Alec's way of thinking, thrusting a Marquessate on him considerably complicated his life, and merely heightened suspicion.

Perhaps he would request a second posting to Constantinople?

He was roused from these musings at the mention of his name in loud whispered conversation over his left shoulder. Overhearing the rest was unavoidable.

"I don't know why Weir in*vit*ed him," whined a weak male voice. "He's not one of us. And when one considers what he did to poor Ned—well!"

"Sir Charles has a motive for everything," mused his female companion. "I wonder…"

"Obviously Charlie fails to see the matter as we do, my lady."

"He's rather handsome in an angular sort of way. Big bony nose and *large*—"

"What? No powder and a scrap of *lace* makes him handsome?"

"—blue eyes," Lady Cobham finished with a crooked smile, appraising Alec from well-muscled calf to coal black curls.

"You're blind! He could very well be mist*aken for an Ame*rican savage."

"Yes. That old ru*mor a*bout—"

"Rumor?"

"—his real papa being a black lackey who took my lady Delvin's fancy has stuck, hasn't it?"

"It's stuck, Caro, because the swar*thy devil*'s a-a half-breed. One only has to look at him to see that!"

The woman sighed deeply. "Yes, just look at him. Common report says he's as virile as a savage…"

There was a snort of contempt. "You're *for* Bedlam, Caro! Egad! The man's unco*uth*, uncivilized, and disrespectful. The Duke won't like him being here tonight, not one bit!"

"I dare say your father won't like it, George, but given the Duke's continued mourning for the Duchess I doubt Cleveley will care who Sir Charles has invited to dine. Can savages have blue eyes?"

"Be reasonable, Caro." Lord George Stanton tucked his chins in his stock and said gravely, "Father is thinking of stepping down from the leadership."

The lady gasped. "You can't be serious? He said so in jest!"

"The Duke, my dear *Lady* Cobham, does not jest. Neither do I. And don't think Father's grief has made him blind to the world. He will certainly have a word with Weir for his lack of moral decency for inviting a man everyone knows but cannot prove murdered his own bro—"

"Oh, look! He's finally here!" burst out Lady Cobham. She gave a nervous titter behind her fluttering fan when Alec stared straight at her. But when Lord George faced the doorway she lowered the fan of carved ivory to underscore her thrust-up breasts before turning to admire the full-length portrait dividing the windows. "I wonder if that's a Reynolds…?" she mused to no one in particular, a sly sidelong glance of open invitation at Alec.

A commotion in the doorway had everybody looking that way. The Duke of Cleveley had arrived. It said much about the man's formidable political and social influence that his mere entrance caused the room to hush. He was soon surrounded by the party faithful, all wanting to be noticed, and Alec had the *satisfaction* of seeing the great man snub his stepson, Lord George Stanton, in favor of a clergyman in tattered collar and cuffs. At least the Duke was not about to allow an arrogant nature to dictate to sense, he thought with a wry smile.

The meal itself was not the ordeal Alec had anticipated. In amongst the twelve courses there was much political discussion and many an impromptu speech praising Sir Charles's five years as Member of Parliament for the rotten borough seat of Bratton Dene. And as Alec was seated between the scruffy clergyman, who ignored him in favor of conversation with the gentleman to his right, and Sir Charles, who sat at the head of the table, he began to feel more at ease. And with the comings and goings of the two footmen with the various courses on offer, he took the time to glance about at the other guests.

The Duke of Cleveley sat directly opposite, looking supremely bored. His Grace said little throughout the discussions, ate sparsely from the many dishes put before him, and continued to drink steadily, although this fact did not affect in any way his political acumen. Alec observed that whenever the Duke tired of the conversation he fiddled with his snuffbox, and that his fellows took this as a sign that they could lower their guard, but no *sooner did they* do so than the great man would offer up some scathing criticism guaranteed to send the diners into a spin of counter-arguments. Alec would never agree with the Duke's politics, but this did not stop him admiring the great politician at work. Now he knew why his uncle Plantagenet found the Duke such a worthy and infuriating opponent, and it made him smile, contemplating what that old gentleman would have to say at breakfast the next morning when he learned just who had been at Sir Charles Weir's dinner party.

Sir Charles leaned in to Alec.

"It's all rather a bore for you, I'm afraid. Don't worry, with the ladies gone to the drawing room, we fellows can have a good port and a rest." He patted Alec's upturned velvet cuff. "I'm glad you came up to town."

"I should've remembered. At school you had a way of getting what you wanted by fair means or foul."

Sir Charles raised his glass. "That's what makes me such an effective politician, my lord Halsey."

Alec flinched. Seven months was not time enough to be comfortable being addressed as "my lord". Annoyed with himself for letting such a social trifle get the better of him, he downed the rest of his wine in one swig. Looking up, he encountered the Duke's penetrating gaze. He stared back at him and the heat in his face said it all, because the Duke set down his glass, took up his snuffbox, and offered it across the table.

Alec shook his head. "Thank you, Your Grace, but I don't dip."

The Duke inclined his powdered head and put the little gold box back on the table. "One of your uncle's many eccentricities is a hatred of tobacco. I read his pamphlet on the subject with great interest. You were raised by him, were you not?"

"Yes, Your Grace. Raised by him to form my own opinions," Alec replied, surprised the Duke had bothered to read anything his uncle had written. "I simply don't find snuff to my liking."

"Ah," said the Duke, dismissing the topic with a long sniff, as if suddenly bored by it. Alec found the mannerism annoying. "Tell me your opinion of the Midanich question."

"Is there a question, Your Grace?" asked Alec. He knew the rest of the diners had broken off their conversations and were listening intently. "I presumed that little corner of northern Europe now put to rest. England ended French occupation of the principality and invasion of Hanover was avoided, which was your government's prime objective. Thus a successful campaign for you, Your Grace…"

The Duke tapped the lid of his snuffbox and flicked open the filigree lid with one finger. His gaze remained on Alec, weighing up his remark, deciding if it contained any hostile insinuation. After all, his government's decision to drive out the French and occupy Midanich had been met with hostility on both sides of Parliament. Alec Halsey's uncle Plantagenet was its most vocal critic. But Midanich shared a border with Hanover, English sovereign territory, and thus keeping the French out was imperative. The strategic move proved successful and helped England win the Seven Years' War.

"I will allow that remark to stand, Halsey."

"As was intended, Your Grace," Alec answered politely.

There was a long silence broken only by the sound of the Duke taking snuff. It was left to Sir Charles to interpret the mood, and he pushed back his chair and gave the nod to his butler, a sign for the ladies to take their leave to the drawing room. The rest of the gentlemen stood, still silent, waiting a cue from the Duke who was oblivious to the tension hanging about him.

With the door firmly closed on the ladies' backs, Lord George Stanton made his way to the sideboard at the far end of the long room where Sir Charles was refilling his snuffbox, and those belonging to guests who required replenishment, from one of a number of ornamental jars kept on the top shelf of an ornate mahogany cabinet. The rest of the gentlemen had undone the last button of their waistcoats and were settling down to the good drop of port the butler had placed on the table in large crystal decanters.

Alec stretched his long legs by the windows opposite the sideboard, escaping the intense gaze of several gentlemen who were diverted when the scruffy clergyman invited himself to sit beside the Duke. The cleric's familiar behavior annoyed these men who had awaited this opportunity to make themselves better known to the great man. Alec noted that it also annoyed the Duke's stepson, who could not hide his contempt for the old cleric. And two bottles of claret had loosened his tongue.

"Listen, Charlie," Lord George hissed loudly and hiccupped. "I thought you were going to do something about him."

"What do you suggest I do with a cleric, my lord?" Sir Charles answered with heavy sarcasm.

"What's he doing here?" came the arrogant demand.

"It wasn't my idea to invite him. I thought that obvious, even to you," Sir Charles answered cuttingly, replacing the stopper to the porcelain snuff jar. He returned this and its companion to the cabinet shelves. "And do, please, lower your voice."

"I'm not drunk, y'know," said Lord George, taking a pinch of snuff from the box offered him. "Thanks. The old badger's come to stay. Can you believe it? Father allowing that dirty piece of filth to stay at St. James's Square? He's got his own room, for God's sake!"

"Perhaps his grief—"

"Oh, come on, Charlie!" scoffed Lord George and hiccupped again. "I miss Mamma just as much but it hasn't unhinged me. It's been a twelvemonth and I call that long enough to grieve. After all, it's not as if mamma was a well woman. She'd been confined to her rooms for the better part of a year before her death. So don't give me that rot about blind grief."

"My lord, I—"

Lord George leaned a large arm on the sideboard, his round face close up to Sir Charles. "Know what I think, Charlie."

"No, I don't th—"

"He's got something over him."

"What?"

"Blackmail."

"That's absurd," Sir Charles replied with a hollow laugh. "What could that old vicar possibly *have over*—"

"You think because you were secretary to the great man for ten years you know everything there is to know about him? Then tell me why Father gives that caterpillar the time of day. Only yest*erday they* were closeted in the library for three hours. Three hours, Charlie."

Sir Charles took Lord George by the elbow and pulled him about so that his back was to the room. "Have you thought that His Grace may merely be carrying out your mother's dying wish?"

Lord George belched. "Eh?"

Sir Charles smiled thinly. "If you recall, my lord, it was the Duchess who requested to see Mr. Blackwell. Just before she went into her final decline she summonsed the cleric t*o he*r bedside. It was he who administered the last rites."

"What? That threadbare nobody presided over Mamma's deathbed?" It was news to Lord George, and he turned and looked down the room at the clergyman who was very much at home with the noblemen about him, joining in the laughter at their bon mots. "Why did she do that, I wonder?"

Sir Charles sighed. "We shall never know now, and I suggest you not bother the Duke with it." He pocketed his snuffbox, closed the sideboard door, and turned the little silver ke*y in the lock.* "If His Grace sees fit to rub shoulders with a threadbare nobody it's not for us to question."

Lord George Stanton gave a snort and slapped Weir's back. "Ever the faithful secretary, Charlie!"

He sauntered off to join the others. Sir Charles grimaced his displeasure and came up to Alec with a smile full of resignation. "You mustn't mind Lord George," he apologized. "He's young, and lamentably, he can't hold his liquor like the rest of us. Makes him say things he doesn't mean. Blackwell's not so bad."

Alec's non-committal reply and the fact he immediately went over to introduce himself to the clergyman had Sir Charles wondering. If he'd not been claimed to settle a dispute on a point of law, he would have followed to hear what his old school friend had to say to a threadbare nobody.

"Mr. Blackwell," said Alec. "I owe you an apology."

The Reverend Blackwell smiled and offered Alec the vacant chair beside him. "Do you, my lord?"

"Yes. I feel rather foolish for not knowing you at dinner, but we have met before, some months back, when on my uncle's invitation the board of governors of the Belsay Orphanage convened at my house."

"Yes, that's right. Forgive me for smiling, but I do know who you are and I am well aware of our previous meeting. I thought it best to allow you the opportunity to acknowledge me or not, as you saw fit."

Alec was surprised. "How could you think I wouldn't want to know you? I admit I've got out of the way of socializing since... I don't come to town often, preferring to spend my time in Kent, yet I enjoyed that nuncheon immensely—all the more because talk centered on the Belsay Orphanage."

"My fellow board members and I are honored to have been appointed, but it is your uncle who is grease to the axle, my lord." The clergyman caught Alec's frown and spread his fat hands in a gesture of sympathy. "The past seven months have not been easy for you. I am sorry for it. A lesser man couldn't have carried it off. Yet, I have every faith in you making the most of a circumstance that was not of your making."

Alec looked up from the heavy gold signet ring on the pinkie of his left hand, harsh lines either side of his mouth. "Thank you for your support, Blackwell."

The vicar nodded and leaned across the table to grab the nearest snuffbox. It was gold and identical in design to the box carried by the Duke. "Pretty, isn't it?" he said, changing the subject. "A gift. I'd never truly enjoyed snuff until given a good blend." He snorted a generous half-pinch up one nostril. "Always smoked a pipe. But this is more agreeable in company." He then snorted the rest up the other nostril and dusted off his fingers on the sleeve of his frock coat.

Alec politely waited, although he had so much he wanted to ask the clergyman. Not least, how he came to be taking snuff from a gold box in an elegant drawing room full of high-ranking politicians, when less than a year ago he had been ministering to the wretched poor in the parish of St. Jude's. He glanced at the Duke surrounded by the party faithful, intrigued by the possible connection between a nobleman of the highest rank and a poor, ill-dressed cleric of no family. The Duke could not be called benevolent. His disdain for those socially beneath him was well known. He was the epitome of what Alec most despised about his own order. Blackwell was a mild-mannered, honest man without pretense and ambition; a person of little worth to a consummate politician such as the Duke. Strange bedfellows indeed.

"My lord, oblige me by refilling my glass," the clergyman said in a thin hoarse whisper, tugging at his frayed neckcloth as if for air.

Alec did as he was requested but one look at Blackwell told him the man had taken ill. His face had changed color and he looked suddenly uncomfortably hot. Sweat had begun to bead on his forehead. Alec felt for the man's pulse and was surprised by the rapid, pulsating beat in his wrist. He loosened the clergyman's cravat, sitting him back in his chair as he did so. This only seemed to aggravate the old man. Blackwell let his head drop back as he sucked in air through a slackened mouth. Alec had the neckcloth unraveled and the man's waistcoat undone, but still Blackwell gasped, his wheezing so loud that the other guests were alerted to his condition, and conversation and laughter ceased.

Sir Charles rushed to Alec's side, calling for his butler to bring a pitcher of water. He turned to his old school friend for guidance, not knowing what to do with the gasping bulk now convulsing in his chair. "What's to do?"

"Fetch a physician!" Alec commanded, his arm feeling as if it was about to break under the cleric's writhing weight.

Just as he said this, Blackwell pitched forward and vomited. A great stinking mass of undigested food splashed Alec's stockinged leg and fell in lumps to the carpet. It was enough to send the onlookers staggering backwards. One gentleman heaved, stuck his head in the chamber pot beneath the table, and followed the cleric's example. Alec held back his own nausea and maneuvered the cleric to his knees where he vomited once more. The great guttural shudders were the last straw for even the most hardened stomach, and the circle of gentlemen surrounding him broke and scattered. Lord George Stanton made the mistake of peering over Sir Charles's shoulder. The stench hit him before the sight, and he reeled back, almost losing his balance had not the Duke caught his stepson by the elbow and thrust him onto the nearest chair.

Alec was at a loss to know how to alleviate the man's suffering. Until a physician could be found, there was not much anyone could do but shuffle about, helpless and uncomfortable. Sir Charles tried to put a tumbler of water to the vicar's parched lips, but it was to no avail. Blackwell, his once sallow complexion now bright pink, continued to gasp, unaware of his surroundings and unable to ask for help.

Then all at once, the convulsions ceased as suddenly as they had begun. There came a collective sigh from around the room. Blackwell was perfectly still, his bald head now minus its brown-haired bob wig, bent forward as if in prayer. He gave one last great shuddering breath and promptly collapsed, face down, into the mess he had created.

He was dead.

"WHAT A WRETCHED end to the evening," complained Lord George Stanton, refilling his port glass.

BEHIND-THE-SCENES

Explore the places, objects, and history in
Deadly Engagement on Pinterest.

www. pinterest.com/lucindabrant

CPSIA information can be obtained
at www.ICGtesting.com
Printed in the USA
LVHW042120190620
658547LV00005B/1195

9 780987 243058